PRAISE

JOSEPH SC

"An auspicious and engaging debut. Mr. Schneider conjures up an original protagonist in LAPD Homicide Detective Tully Jarsdel—and prestidigitates a thoroughly thrilling narrative ride through the mean streets and glittering boulevards of Los Angeles. The reader looks forward to many more Jarsdel mysteries in the coming years."

—Eric Overmyer, executive producer of *Bosch*

"A brilliant first novel. Joseph Schneider's contemporary writing evokes some of Hollywood's most classic crime stories, from *Chinatown* to *L.A. Confidential*."

—Dick Wolf, creator of *Law & Order*

"*One Day You'll Burn* is much more than just an intriguing Hollywood mystery, it's a captivating character study of a unique academic/historian-turned-police-detective who can't keep his deep intelligence from bubbling out—often to his own embarrassment and the reader's delight. Joseph Schneider has created a very appealing character whom readers will definitely want to see more of."

—Kenneth Johnson, bestselling author of *The Man of Legends*

"Schneider redefines the detective genre while giving us a history lesson of Hollywood, the town of dreams it was, and the nightmare it has become."

—Jim Hayman, executive producing director of *NCIS: New Orleans*

"Tully Jarsdel joins the gumshoe greats in this whipsmart riff on sunbaked LA noir."

—David Stenn, author of *Clara Bow: Runnin' Wild* and *Bombshell: The Life and Death of Jean Harlow*

"*One Day You'll Burn* knocked me out. It's a riveting, richly layered detective novel that satisfies and surprises on every single page. Joseph Schneider is a major new talent in the world of crime fiction."

—Lou Berney, Edgar Award–winning author of *The Long and Faraway Gone*

"Schneider's debut enlivens the police procedural with offbeat characters and an appealingly complex hero."

—*Kirkus Reviews*

"The solid debut police procedural is an homage to Hollywood and its history, with descriptive details of corners of Hollywood, classic films, and even traffic jams. The atmospheric mystery introduces a fascinating new detective who will appeal to fans of Michael Connelly's Harry Bosch."

—*Library Journal*

"There's a lot of good detective work and excellent characterization in this debut procedural that features one of the most original heroes to come out of the genre in a long while."

—*Criminal Element*

"*One Day You'll Burn*...stars a memorable character who you will want to see more of very soon."

—*Booklist*

"*What Waits for You* is irresistible. I read it in a blur, and it stuck to me like a shadow when I was finished. Joseph Schneider should be on everyone's radar."

—Jonathan Moore, Edgar Award and Hammett Prize finalist

"Schneider's riveting prose, incredibly original protagonist Tully Jarsdel, and brilliant evocation of a LA add up to a novel you won't be able to put down. A read that will get under your skin and stay there for a while. I can't wait for the next book!"

—Luca Veste, author of *The Bone Keeper*

"LA native Joseph Schneider shows off his roots once again, leading the reader and quirky detective Tully Jarsdel on a richly detailed, highly nuanced mystery through the City of Angels."

—Joseph Reid, author of the Amazon Charts bestselling Seth Walker series

What Waits for You

A NOVEL

JOSEPH SCHNEIDER

Poisoned Pen Press

Cover design by The Book Designers
Cover images © Evgeniya Porechenskaya/Shutterstock, logoboom/Shutterstock
Internal design by Holli Roach/Sourcebooks

Published by Poisoned Pen Press, an imprint of Sourcebooks
P.O. Box 4410, Naperville, Illinois 60567-4410
(630) 961-3900
sourcebooks.com

Library of Congress Cataloging in Publication Data is on file with the publisher.

Printed and bound in the United States of America.
SB 10 9 8 7 6 5 4 3 2 1

For Anna, my best friend
and partner in all things.

PROLOGUE: JANUARY

The nightmare descended on a Tuesday.

Dispatch was fully staffed, since Tuesdays were always busy. Tuesdays and full moons. The full moons made a kind of sense, since they brought with them enough ambient light to allow for more outdoor activity, and more outdoor activity meant more crime. But no one had a theory for Tuesdays; they were just heavy, always heavy.

On the night of the fifth, as the hours ground by, dispatch crackled with armed robberies, smash-and-grabs, assaults, disorderlies, and the regular, mantra-like calls of "deuce"—for the DUI scanner code *23152*. And then, amid the noise, came an almost apologetic request for a welfare check.

Welfare checks were usually called in for seniors living alone, often by a relative who hadn't been able to make contact, and generally ended with the discovery of a body, a call to EMS, and an hour of routine paperwork. The pair of responding officers expected much the same. Then they learned that it wasn't just Bill Lauterbach who couldn't be reached, but his wife, Joanne, as well. The couple had a landline and a shared cell phone, and their daughter had been trying to get hold of them for two days. She was about to buy a plane ticket and fly down from San Jose to see what was going on.

At the wheel of the radio car was Evan Porter, his badge still foreign against his chest in the month since graduation. Riding shotgun was Melissa Banning, his training officer and a rising star in patrol. She'd already been promoted to sergeant, and wasn't even out of her twenties. Porter was older, but he was an ex-marine, and command expected him to be a major asset to the force. He was a big man, six-two and two-twenty, with alert, searching eyes, thin lips, and a sharp, beak-like nose. He was, Banning had thought, the perfect trainee—respectful, calm, and already an expert with the radio codes. But then a week earlier she'd been halfway out of the restroom when Porter, not seeing her, passed by in low conversation with another rookie.

"I'd fuck her, bite her, choke her out, whatever."

His friend chuckled, and the two drifted out of earshot.

Banning hadn't known whom or what Porter was talking about, but the words haunted her. Mostly it was the easy way he'd said them, like describing the best way to cook a steak, like it was something he'd done a thousand times. Thinking of it always conjured a chill, and her revulsion toward Porter only grew when she realized that maybe they'd been talking about *her*. And now that the idea had twisted its way in, she could hardly meet his eyes—not out of fear, but because she was sure he'd see how much he disgusted her.

Their deployments were stiff and formal, the small talk they'd enjoyed those first couple weeks long gone. Each night they drove along, wanly lit by the instrument panel and dashboard computer, Porter restlessly scanning the view through the windshield. Every so often he'd spot something—an expired tag or an illegal left or a failure to signal—and murmur "So what's *this*." For her part, Banning only spoke to give an instruction or a correction, and Porter's responses rarely extended beyond "Yes, ma'am." What was more unsettling than the long silences, however, was how little Porter seemed to mind them. Sometimes she wondered if he even noticed the change in their relationship.

"Request for a welfare check at 1320 Hollyridge Loop. Any units available?" The voice on the other end of dispatch was androgynous and flat. It would've maintained the same disinterested tone if it were announcing a virgin sacrifice atop the Bradbury Building.

Porter responded immediately. "6-Adam-9, go ahead."

"Caller advises hasn't been able to reach parents in forty-eight hours. Parents are elderly."

"Roger, on our way."

"Copy. Proceed Code 2."

Banning checked the time. Nearly eleven, the night just getting warmed up. At least a welfare check would get her out of the car for a while. All the same, it annoyed her that Porter had taken the call without consulting her.

"Next time, weigh in with me first," she said.

"Yes, ma'am." He didn't spare her a glance.

It had rained all week, and the gentle hills above Franklin were sodden. Puddles stood every few feet along the old, pocked road, and trees groaned under their own engorged weight. When Banning and Porter stepped out at the Lauterbach residence, the world around them was alive with water. It rushed past their feet into storm drains, dripped from the leaves of overhanging palms, and filled the air itself in the January chill.

Banning felt a dampness on her skin and glanced up at a streetlamp, where she saw a light mist dancing in the beam. There was something else there, too, tucked in the elbow bend where the lamp arched away from the pole. She squinted, and was able to make out a fat spider's egg. It might've been her imagination, or the work of a mild breeze, but it seemed to tremble as it hung there in its ragged web.

"Ma'am?"

Banning started. She turned and saw that Porter had snuck up close behind her. Had he done that on purpose? She studied him for any hint of mischief, but his face was unreadable. Just that same assured calm he always wore.

"What?"

"Should I call in our location?"

"Why're you asking me?"

Porter blinked. "You asked me to check in with you from now on."

"Not about every little thing."

Porter touched the shoulder mic of his ROVER. "6-Adam-9. Show us Code 6 at the Hollyridge Loop address."

"6-Adam-9, 10-4," the radio crackled back.

The house was a Tudor Revival cottage—timber-framed, with a faux-thatched roof and a wide redbrick chimney sweeping up the left gable wall. Two dormer windows protruded from above and to either side of the front door, so that the house seemed to bear an expression of surprise, but the diamond-shaped panes that stared out from their lead casings were dark. No light glimmered within.

Banning stepped through the wrought-iron arbor that marked the boundary between the sidewalk and the Lauterbach property, passing the beam of her Maglite across the yard and over the ground-floor windows. No doors ajar, no broken glass, no foot-sized depressions in the spongy mulch. The two officers followed the curving flagstone path to the covered entryway, where a note taped to the doorbell advised "Out of order—please knock firmly." The cursive handwriting was done with the studied elegance of a schoolteacher.

It would be difficult *not* to knock firmly, Banning saw. The brass griffin and the knocker hanging from its beak were oversized, absurd, a conspicuous misstep in design. She gripped the ring, which felt much colder than she'd expected, and brought it down three times on the striking plate.

She winced. The sound was terrific, sharp and penetrating. Banning listened, holding her breath, but the gurgling of the wet night made it impossible to tell if anyone stirred within. She counted to thirty, then knocked again.

"LAPD," she called. "Everyone okay in there?"

Thirty more seconds.

Nothing.

Porter was a head taller, so Banning had to look up at him. "Go check out the windows 'round the house. Shine your light in there and see what you can see."

"Yes, ma'am."

He turned to go, and Banning heard him murmur, "Yes, ma'am," again. That smacked of insubordination, but of the kind that was almost impossible to prove. The kind that made you seem paranoid and overly sensitive for reporting it. Well, she wasn't going to let him get away with it. She'd figure out a way to tease out his true colors, show himself for the toxic, misogynistic asshole he was.

She reached again for the knocker, then paused, fingertips brushing the icy metal. A thought had broken the surface of her consciousness, shone its pale belly, then vanished again. What was it? She tried summoning it back, but couldn't. It had been a disturbing thought—yes, even terrifying, and perhaps also an important one. Maybe if she let go of the knocker, then reached for it again...

When her hand seized the griffin's ring, the thought returned, whole and immense—a fanged, venomous leviathan caught full in a lantern's glare.

The thought was this: *Don't knock, or you might wake it up.*

With effort, she pushed it away. It was silly, childish. She was a trained law-enforcement professional, and if there was anything behind that door besides two dead senior citizens, it certainly wouldn't be any match for her Glock 36.

She slammed the knocker against the plate five times in quick succession.

Now you've done it. It's on its way.

"LAPD," she said. "Mr. and Mrs. Lauterbach? Hello?"

"Sergeant Banning."

She spun, hand on her sidearm, and saw Porter had managed to creep up on her again. *I'm gonna make him wear a bell*, she thought.

"What is it, Porter?"

"I think..." He let his voice trail off, then cleared his throat. "I don't know. Something. 'Round back."

He turned, stepping out of sight, and Banning followed. She looked toward the street, where the spinning red and blue lights of their squad car had attracted a few curious neighbors. A hulking man in a brown silk bathrobe stepped through the arbor.

Banning skewered him with the beam of her Maglite. "S'cuse me, sir—I'm gonna need you to stay off the property right now."

"Jeez, wow. Shit." He retreated, lifting his arm to shield his eyes from the piercing light—an oversized Dracula fending off a crucifix.

Along the side of the house grew a forest of blackberry bushes, and the officers had to pick their way along, backs against the flimsy wooden fence separating the Lauterbach lot from the neighbor's yard. The plants were wet, and their thorns sought out Banning's sleeves and pant legs. She emerged damp and covered in scratches; one, on the back of her right hand, felt like a streak of fire.

She looked around for Porter, but couldn't see him at first. The backyard was big, and for some reason he'd turned off his Maglite.

"Here." His voice was low, almost a whisper. She splashed her beam toward his voice and found him standing at one of the windows. He squinted, and she pointed the light at the ground as she approached.

"What is it?"

"In there." He pointed. The window ledge began at his shoulders, so it was easy for him to see inside. Banning would need to stand on something.

Porter seemed to understand the problem. "If you want, I can—"

"No. Thank you."

She searched the area, and found a large, yellow watering can tucked amid some rosebushes. She picked it up, hefted it. It was metal, not plastic, so that was good. She put it in position, held the Maglite between her teeth and, gripping the ledge above her, carefully stepped up onto the can.

The two hundred lumens reflecting back at her made it impossible to see through the glass, so she steadied herself as much as she could with her left hand and took the flashlight with her right. The can rocked under her weight, then steadied. Directing the beam at an angle, she could now make out the living room. A fireplace, liquor cabinet, two heavy sofas on either side of a coffee table. Past that, a pair of double doors opened onto the foyer, where a flight of stairs marched steeply upward. Nothing unusual at all, not that she could see.

"What is it? I don't—"

"There."

Porter's finger insinuated itself into view. "Right there, up toward the top of the stairs."

Banning began moving the light up the staircase one riser at a time.

"Toward the top, I said."

"I heard you—can you shut up please?"

Halfway up was a small landing, and from there the stairs cut rightward at a sharp angle. It was inky black at the top, and Banning's flashlight beam barely seemed to penetrate, illuminating only small pockets before the darkness surged in again.

"I don't..." But then she did.

Someone was looking right back at her. A pair of eyes, still and unblinking. Banning fixed the light on them directly, making sure it wasn't her imagination.

Yes, two eyes, wide open. She waited, waited for some movement, but nothing. God, they were wide—so impossibly wide.

That's because it's on its way. Because you woke it up.

Banning ignored the thought and studied the face more closely. It lay on its side, with only the top half visible—everything below the nose obscured by a baluster. The rest of the man—it did seem to be a man—was far out of view.

"Is it real?" asked Porter.

Banning continued watching the eyes, urging them to blink. She rapped on the window with her Maglite. The eyes remained still.

"Is it real?" Porter repeated.

"Call for backup."

"What is it? An EDP?"

An EDP was an "emotionally disturbed person," a handy designation for anyone butting heads with reality, from the average street-corner babbler to a catatonic schizophrenic. The blessing with EDPs was that they quickly became someone else's problem, hauled off to join the rest of the window-lickers at the mental health facility on Temple Street—a place the cops called "Fantasy Island."

But this wasn't an EDP. The eyes that glinted from the darkness did so dully, more like marbles than glistening, living sclera.

"Call for fucking backup, Porter."

He backed stiffly away, and a moment later Banning heard him speak the request into the shoulder mic of his ROVER. "6-Adam-9, requesting backup. Got a 10-54 here."

Banning noticed that while her trainee had used the correct 10-code for a possible dead body, his voice had lost its clipped, military professionalism. He sounded scared. She was scared, too—couldn't shake the feeling that they'd disturbed something in the big, dark house. Banning thought of spiders, and the way they crouched out of sight, waiting for that telltale quiver in a strand of web. She thought how patient a spider must be, its cluster of inscrutable black eyes trained on its prey from aloft until, its malefic little brain satisfied, it decided to pounce.

She shuddered at that—actually shuddered, and checked to make sure Porter hadn't noticed. He was there, only a few feet away, a hand still draped over his shoulder mic, but his attention was fixed on a spot somewhere high above her head. Banning followed his gaze, saw nothing, then looked back at her partner. "What? What now?"

"The house is bleeding." Porter's voice was low and raspy, as if he couldn't muster enough air.

"What..." Banning scanned the house's exterior, the beam of her Maglite flitting across the stucco. Her eye caught something, and she raised the light again, this time in slow, deliberate seesaws.

On the second floor, beneath one of the dormer windows, a long crack had formed—probably damage from last week's quake. It wouldn't have been noticeable, but now there was some kind of dark substance seeping out. It mingled with the heavily misted air and beaded into drops, which eventually swelled until they grew heavy enough to break free, streaming down the wall like tears.

And it was true—whatever it was, it did look like blood.

"We need to go in," said Banning.

"Don't you think we should wait for backup?"

"No, I do not. Could be a citizen in there needs our help."

Porter didn't have anything to say to that, and the two of them hurried to the back door. It didn't look as stout as the one in front, and there was a little window centered at eye level. This, however, was barred with wrought-iron curlicues, so smashing the glass wouldn't do any good. They'd have to kick in the door.

"Ever had to breach?" Banning's voice was low, quiet, and fierce. She was ready.

"In Afghanistan," Porter whispered. "GREMs off my M4."

"With your foot, Porter."

He considered, then shook his head. Banning herself had no desire to wager her knee against the door's integrity. On a recent drug raid, a friend of hers in SWAT had come up against what appeared to be a flimsy slab of hollow-core composite, only to find—after driving his heel into the panel above the knob—that he'd challenged a fire door armed with three Schlage dead bolts. It would be months before he'd be able to walk without a limp.

"Now's your chance." Banning drew her firearm. Porter, following her lead, did the same. He looked to his supervisor, got a final nod of approval, and positioned himself in a fighting stance—a boxer about to deliver a knockout punch. He took a breath. Then, his gun hand trained at a downward angle, he hurled his weight at the door, concentrating the whole force into a single tactical boot.

The door didn't so much open as explode inward, shearing off an arm's-length chunk of jamb as it went. The wood spun off into darkness, joined by a glinting chunk of metal—probably the dead bolt—along with a spray of glass from the inset window.

"LAPD!" Porter charged in blindly, his Glock gripped far in front like a talisman. Banning followed him, brushing the wall with the back of a hand to find the light switch. The room filled with the mellow glow of a single shaded bulb, revealing a stacked washer and dryer, an ironing board piled with folded clothes, and a red Craftsman tool chest.

Porter blinked, swept the barrel of his weapon from side to side, and shouted "Clear!" before stumbling through the doorway and into the hall beyond.

"Porter!" Banning might not have liked him, but she didn't need to see him get killed. "Porter, wait your ass up!"

"Clear!" he called again, and Banning heard his footfalls hammering their way up the main staircase. She sprinted to catch up with him and knocked something with her hip. There was a tremendous crash but she ignored it, cutting through the unfamiliar hallway until she emerged into a wide, drafty foyer.

She stopped, listening. Her pulse roared in her ears, making it impossible to work out any other sounds. The beam of her Maglite skipped over a sofa, a low coffee table, a baby grand piano. Sensing movement behind her, she spun, lining up her gunsight with a slowly rocking shard of pottery. If the homeowners were still alive, they certainly wouldn't be cheered by the knowledge that one of the responding officers had demolished what appeared to be the world's largest decorative vase.

She then realized the house had fallen totally silent, no Porter blundering through, yelling that everything was "clear."

"Porter!" She pointed the Maglite to her left, and a staircase emerged from the black. The banisters were mahogany, the newel posts anchoring them topped with carved finials of sleepy-eyed cherubs. There was a smell now, too—foul, penetrating high into her sinuses. The smell of old shit.

"Porter!" Banning took the stairs two at a time, wrists crossed so both the Glock and the Maglite moved in sync. She thought of this configuration as her death ray, like the lethal blast from a Wellsian spacecraft. Anything that landed in the path of her Maglite's beam was as good as dead if she so chose.

Past the first landing, she slowed. Ahead were more stairs, a second small landing, then the last flight before she'd reach the body they'd glimpsed from outside. The one with the wide, unblinking eyes.

Banning crept forward, picking her way carefully along on the balls of her feet. A worn burgundy rug ran down the length of the staircase, fastened in place with brass rods, and she hardly made a sound as she ascended.

She came to the second landing, turned, and aimed her light toward the top step. From so steep a downward angle, she couldn't see the body—just the crown of its head and a tuft of hair the color of dryer lint. The smell, however, was much worse.

Banning went on, eyes scanning left, right, then left again. Only when her chest began to ache did she realize she'd been holding her breath. She let out a long, shaky exhale as quietly as she could, and her next step brought the rest of the body's head—which she presumed belonged to Mr. Lauterbach—into view.

She saw now why the corpse's eyes had looked so large from outside. Someone had cut the eyelids from the man's face. Both the upper and lower lids were excised from the left eye, while a few gray lashes told her that the lower lid remained on the right. The nostrils and mouth bulged with a black, mud-like substance that she quickly realized accounted for the terrific stench.

Banning vomited, doing her best to aim the stream over the railing so as not to contaminate the crime scene. For the most part she succeeded. She spat, wiped her mouth on her sleeve, and continued onward.

As she made her way past Lauterbach, her death ray once again making quick, sure slices through the fetid air, she snuck glances at the man's body. In addition to the outrages she'd already noted, the man had been stripped naked. Dozens of bruises and irregular, dime-sized circles—cigarette burns, probably—mottled the corpse's flesh. The body lay on its belly in a pool of congealed blood, but Banning couldn't see the wound that'd produced it. *Femoral artery, maybe? Or...oh God.*

From between the man's buttocks protruded a pale, pruned thing, like a boneless thumb. The end of it, where it had been cut off, was a chewed purple stump. The amount of blood, Banning knew, indicated he'd been alive when emasculated. Perhaps still alive when his own penis had been forced into his rectum.

"Porter," she said, her voice hardly more than a whisper. No more than thirty seconds had passed since her trainee had kicked in the door, but there was a sense she'd traveled somewhere very far away, farther from home than she'd ever been. This wasn't a house anymore; it was a forgotten outpost on a moon, a moon spinning around a lightless, lifeless planet. Part of her was certain that were she to retrace her steps and find her way outside, it wouldn't be into the chill of Los Angeles in January but into a silent, black desert, with sand like talcum powder and a sky of cold, strange stars above. She'd be able to see for a little while, at least as long as the batteries in her Maglite lasted. After that—

A soft moan pulled her back to herself. She listened, unsure whether or not she'd been the one who'd made the sound. But then it came again, like wind in an attic, low and mournful.

"Police!" called Banning. "Identify yourself!"

Nothing. The moan, or whatever it was, had fallen silent.

"I am armed and backup is on the way. Step out slowly, with your hands raised, and identify yourself." As she spoke, her death ray made its sweeps along the upper floor, prodding at every shadow.

"Porter! You okay, partner?" A few minutes ago it would've been unthinkable to call him that, but whatever uneasy relationship they shared, they were still on the same side. And the person who'd done those things to the old man was definitely not.

The moan rose again, and Banning followed it into a narrow hallway whose floral-print wallpaper sagged and bubbled against the weight of time. An oil painting of a shaggy black dog bounding across a foggy steppe hung crookedly to her left. Of the hallway's three doors, two were shut. The last, which stood ajar at the very end, bore a smeared crimson handprint on its glossy white paint. Only a slice of the room beyond was revealed, but it was as black as a well.

"Porter, you in there?" Banning trained her death ray on the door as she approached. Anything that broke that beam of light, anything that wasn't Porter, would get a pair of jacketed .45s crashing through its skull.

She nudged the door with the toe of her boot, and it swung silently away on oiled hinges. Porter lay at the foot of an unmade bed, but Banning wouldn't have known it was him if not for his uniform. The right side of his face was grotesquely swollen, the skin domed and taut over the trauma beneath. His eye was buried somewhere under the outraged flesh, which the hematoma had stained a bright red. His good eye squinted in the glare of Banning's death ray.

"*Unh*," Porter grunted. A vessel burst somewhere in his nose as he tried to speak, and it was as if someone had turned on a tap. Blood streamed from his puffy nostrils. Some also must have been going down the back of his throat, because he began to gag.

That she was in danger, too, didn't occur to Banning immediately. She saw a badly injured officer, and her training told her the next step was to keep him safe. She lurched forward, then froze, realizing suddenly that she hadn't secured the room. Her death ray flashed left—a teak armoire and a built-in bookshelf—then right.

Banning sucked in her breath and squeezed the Glock even more tightly. Between the bed and the wall lay a heap of...something. She didn't know what it was, couldn't make sense of the mass of fabric and limbs and—what? Teeth? Yes, teeth, and that helped her figure out where the face had been. But it was collapsed, mashed in, and the matted hair framing it was soaked in blood. So too was the silk nightgown, which in rare spots shone powder blue. Banning was reminded of what doves or pigeons looked like after they got run over.

Porter's gagging had resolved into violent wet coughs and the occasional "Unh" as he tried again to speak. But Banning couldn't take her eyes from the body. She noticed that the floor all around was stamped with dozens and dozens of shoe prints. They were small, hardly bigger than a child's. Size sixes, sevens at the most. One, which lay across a broken, misshapen hand, was so well detailed it might have been stenciled on. It was impossible to tell exactly how Mrs. Lauterbach had died, but there was no doubt her murderer liked to kick. The mauled remains of a breast, along with crescent gouges in the woman's neck and along her thighs, told Banning that he also liked to bite.

She heard—faintly, but rising—the most beautiful sound in the world. The keening of approaching sirens.

Thank God. Thank God, thank God, thank God.

"*Unh* huh."

Banning tore her gaze away from Mrs. Lauterbach and turned to her trainee. Porter had managed to prop himself on his knees and elbows, and fixed Banning with his single blue eye. "*Unh* huh," he repeated. "Unh huh *beh.*" He choked, spat a cord of bloody mucus onto the floor, and looked back up at Banning. He gestured at the bed, then at Banning's gun, then at the bed again. His eye rolled in its orbit and he lost his balance, slamming onto his chest with a heavy wheeze.

Banning skipped the death ray over the mattress—sheets bunched, pillows stained with an array of bodily fluids—then to Mrs. Lauterbach, then back to Porter. He shook his head, though she could see it was agony for him.

Unh huh beh.

Then she understood, and her understanding seemed to call it, because now it came, out from under the bed, just as Porter had been trying to tell her. Came the way a shadow might, the way it moved, but when it hooked itself around her legs, she felt its weight and its strength. The room cartwheeled as Banning went down.

Pain rocketed through her head as she slammed to the floor. If the fall had stunned her, if she'd grayed out, it was impossible to tell. It was all so dark, and her Maglite was spinning away, her Glock too skittering out of reach. The death ray, broken.

A shadow materialized from the others, rising until it stood over Banning's supine body. She was enveloped in a stomach-churning funk. It was the smell of rotting things, of yawning dumpsters, of the grave, and she wouldn't have believed a living person capable of producing such a stench.

The shadow held a claw hammer.

"Please," said Banning. "Please, I've got kids. Please don't."

The shape didn't answer, just stood, waiting. There was something strange about the way its body was posed, as if it were a robot going through a systems upload. Banning couldn't see its expression, and was glad. What would the face of such a creature look like? Evidence of its nature, of what stoked its passions, surrounded her. Why should she want to look in the eyes of the thing that'd done this? Even if she were only to live a few more seconds, she didn't want to give any of them over to the shadow staring down at her.

Banning closed her eyes. She couldn't control the last sounds she'd hear—her heartbeat, the shadow's low, husky breathing, Porter's hitching coughs, and the gathering sirens outside—but she could control the last things she'd see. She imagined her children, two and seven, curled asleep on the living-room couch one afternoon last summer.

She had been returning home from a shift. She entered as she always did, calling out their names, aching for them to run up and throw themselves into her arms. But her husband, who sat reading a book in his chair by the door, held up a quieting hand. He smiled and pointed to the children nearby. Banning went over to them. Lily, little Lily, had one of her perfect toddler's hands resting against her brother's cheek. The other lay draped over his chest, which rose and fell in the pure, untroubled sleep of the young.

They'd been so beautiful, so overwhelmingly beautiful, and she'd begun to weep in her love for them. Manny had come up behind her then, holding her around the waist, and they'd just stood there—she couldn't say how long—in total awe of what was surely the greatest thing she would ever create.

There, Banning thought. There was a thought she could die with.

A terrific *crack* sounded, and Banning yelped, shielding her face. She heard footfalls, but these quickly faded, and then there was nothing but the sirens. They were right outside now.

She risked a peek from between her fingers and saw the claw hammer on the floor. The shadow had dropped it before he'd fled, and it'd cracked the parquet.

Porter groaned and got up on his hands and knees again. Banning pushed herself to her feet, fought a wave of dizziness, and went over to her partner.

I can still smell it, she thought, helping Porter balance himself on the bed's heavy wooden frame. *Like poison in the air.*

There was a crash downstairs as their backup came through the front door. Shouts followed, along with the familiar calls of "clear" as the team secured the ground level. Porter had thought things had been pretty clear, too, and now he'd need someone to put his face back together.

"Gone?" he asked.

"It's gone."

"Oh. He..."

Banning waited for Porter to finish, but the man only hung his head.

"There's nothing to be afraid of again." She was surprised to hear herself speaking. She hadn't intended to; the words just tumbled out. "Nothing to be afraid of, because nothing can be worse." She wasn't sure if she was consoling Porter or herself, or if perhaps her brain was simply trying to make sense of what it had felt. No—what her *soul* had felt. She hadn't really believed in God until then, but she did now. Because Banning now knew that revulsion could be so deep it touched your spirit, and you couldn't have a spirit if there wasn't a God to put one in you. Just as a force always produces a counterforce, the presence of the shadow had woken something within her that had pushed back, something that had screamed out—

I don't know what I am, but I know I am not you.

1

Tully Jarsdel hated the arm-wrestling table. Loathed, despised, and detested it. And not just because he'd already barked a shin on one of the 14-gauge steel legs, but because it sat right in the center of the break room, turning what had been a generally peaceful place to eat lunch into an aural hell of shouts, grunts, and whoops.

It was a squat thing, the size of a card table. A custom logo—stressed red typeface against a background of fractured concrete—read "Eat. Sleep. PULL," and in smaller print, "Hollywood Station Patrol." At each end was bolted a vinyl elbow rest and a knurled handle. The combatant would plant his arm on the rest, seize the handle with his free hand, and—making as much noise as possible—try wrenching his opponent's limb to one of the touch pads.

Will Haarmann, a patrol officer with rippling forearms and a flat, blandly handsome face, had brought the table in one day, and no one had objected. On the contrary, Lieutenant Gavin was the first to throw his support behind the idea. Maybe if there was enough interest, he announced at roll, Hollywood Division could put on a local championship and open it up to the public. It was just the sort of thing that could take off, become an annual event, even spread department-wide. Just imagine—the LAPD Arm-Wrestling Open, followed by a community-outreach barbecue. A spirited fund-raiser for the families of fallen officers. Over which he would of course preside.

But more importantly, according to the lieutenant, arm wrestling in the break room would foster a spirit of healthy competition and spur a boost in morale. Even Gavin, who put little stock in recent departmental trends like resilience training, sensitivity seminars, and whatever the chief meant by "organizational climate," recognized the importance of morale.

And morale at Hollywood Station was very low indeed.

After the third murder, Angelenos began repainting their houses. Bill and Joanne Lauterbach, the Rustads, and the Santiagos had all lived in white homes. Practically overnight, every professional painting company in Southern California—along with a robust showing of Craigslist amateurs—were booked two months out. Before long, anyone who could haul a ladder and a can of paint was desperately throwing color onto their walls. That lasted until July, when the killer hit the Verheugens in Eagle Rock. The Verheugens' house was blue. You could almost hear him saying—

Nope, not gonna be that easy to figure out.

Half a year had passed since he'd come to Los Angeles. That was the assumption, anyway—that he'd arrived from somewhere else. The idea that he'd emerged from among the city's own ranks was unpalatable. Even by the rock-bottom standards of Hollywood sensationalism, this guy was bad for business. The crimes were too foul, the victims too sympathetic. No, he must be an outsider. Better yet, a foreigner. Still better, a demon.

But in many ways the murders had only been the beginning. Whether it was a run of bad luck or divine retribution for the city's collective sins, no one knew. The only thing all could agree on was that what once had been home was now somehow alien, as if it were now subject to the logic of dreams. As if anything could happen.

There'd been an earthquake just before the Lauterbach murders—a fearsome shaker that ran for a dozen seconds, darkening the southland from Castaic to Mission Viejo. An aftershock tipped the Richter scale to 6.4; some living near the epicenter in Lancaster said it was like "a shout coming from the earth"—a furious, accusatory blast. Others compared it to the roar of a lion. One woman said it sounded like a word: *YOU*.

Following the discovery of the Lauterbachs, the Santa Ana winds—as if summoned by the fear and misery already beginning to settle on the city like a cowl—came sweeping in from the desert. They didn't come alone. Pathogenic fungi, freed from the soil by the quake, were borne aloft by the hot gusts, and thousands soon came down with valley fever. For most, the infection presented merely as a nuisance—a cough, headache, and rash. Others experienced a sickness more at home in medieval Europe than modern-day SoCal. Joint pain, meningitis, weeping abscesses, and lesions in the skull itself. By the time death came to those so afflicted, it was welcomed.

On the heels of the outbreak came the second murder, the one that would earn the killer his name. Like the Lauterbachs, the Rustads were a couple living alone, albeit two decades younger. Maja Rustad crafted art pieces from found objects and sold them online. Her husband, Steffen, had been in a New Wave band in Norway and found a niche teaching guitar to the kids of his Gen Xer fans out in LA.

The crime scene was in Highland Park, putting it in LAPD's Northeast Area and therefore under the jurisdiction of Central Bureau. Detectives Darla Mailander and Tom Claraty were dispatched from the Sixth Street headquarters. The extent of the carnage and antemortem brutality told them they were probably dealing with the same killer who'd struck in Los Feliz, but it wasn't until they checked the crawl space beneath the house that they knew for certain.

Mailander and Claraty wanted to hold back as much as they could from the press, but conceded to their captain that there was one detail in particular the citizens of Los Angeles needed to know.

A press conference was held the following day, and even the hardest of the hardened crime reporters grew unusually quiet when Captain Cheng outlined the killer's modus operandi. Heather Malins of the *LA Weekly* later said it was during that conference that she devised the nickname, mostly because of the way her skin had popped with gooseflesh as the captain spoke...

The Eastside Creeper.

It was as close to perfect as such things went, and everyone thought so. Even the *Times*, which was usually first in dubbing the city's predators, thought Malins had captured the essence of the shadowy thing lurking among them. Not only did it describe the visceral reaction, the revulsion and terror people experienced when learning of his crimes, but it suggested the slyness of a crawling, climbing vine. By the time you noticed it, it was already coiled tightly in place.

The back row of chairs in the Hollywood Station conference room was empty, and Jarsdel picked the seat closest to the door so he could leave once it was over. A few turned their heads when he came in, regarded him with disinterest, and went back to chatting or checking emails. Just one offered him a smile—Kay Barnhardt, the only other detective in the department who'd been promoted straight from patrol to HH2, the new Hollywood Homicide.

What had originally been conceived as a stop-gap measure to address rising crime stats in West Bureau was now an established—if not wholly respected—investigative branch of the police force. The brainchild of Deputy Chief Cynthia Comsky, HH2 had seen a rocky start. Those who'd labored for years to make detective watched with gut-punched amazement as Jarsdel and Barnhardt swept past them. Virtually all the rank and file at Hollywood Station harbored some degree of resentment toward the rookie whiz kids. Even their own newly assigned partners, homicide veterans Oscar Morales and Abe Rutenberg, made no effort to hide their disgust at command's decision. Earning their respect, grudging as it was, had taken a very long time. Jarsdel nearly had to die at the hands of a murder suspect to convince Morales he wasn't just playing at being a cop.

Barnhardt stood and made her way along her row, excusing herself and pretending not to hear the annoyed sighs from those who had to move their feet. She was perhaps forty, though some long-ago sun damage had given her premature wrinkles and made her look a decade older. She had on wire-rimmed glasses, just as Jarsdel did, and kept her thick brown hair in a regulation ponytail. The sober gray suit she'd dressed in that day did her no favors—baggy in the arms and legs, but pulled taut across her oversized bosom. Jarsdel imagined her figure presented more than a few difficulties in a career like law enforcement. Female cops learned to deal with obscene commentary from criminals, but Barnhardt had had to endure the same from her own colleagues. At least two officers so far had been formally reprimanded for making double entendres in her presence.

"Hey," she said, sitting down.

"Hey."

"You're all by yourself. Mind if I join?"

"Please." Jarsdel liked Barnhardt. She'd been a clinical psychologist before she joined the force, and Jarsdel had tracked down a few of her published articles. One, on the pathology of vexatious litigants, impressed him with its originality and stringent scholarship. She was a good thinker, methodical and more than a little relentless. Suspects entered her interview room with the typically flat, steely affect of the career criminal, and often emerged broken, blubbering, and handcuffed.

"Where's your partner?" Barnhardt asked.

"Flu."

"Didn't he get his shot?"

"Yup. Got sick anyway. Isn't happy. What do you know about this?" Jarsdel gestured toward the front of the room, where a woman he hadn't seen before shuffled through some papers at a lectern. She was petite and attractive, with dark skin and East Indian features, her glossy black hair pulled back in a bun.

"Not a whole lot. But I do know *her*," said Barnhardt. "She's famous."

"Famous?"

"In my field, anyway. She's a behaviorist, teaches all over. President of the Pavlovian Society. Specializes in operant conditioning."

"Ah."

"You know what that is?"

He didn't. "I think so. Refresh my memory."

"You know, application of reward and punishment. There was some controversy a few years back about her methods, though no one could deny they worked. Measurably reduced violence in two prisons, while those in the control group stayed the same."

Jarsdel looked again at their guest speaker. Her most noticeable feature was her lips, which she'd painted a vibrant red. It seemed a strange choice, one that conflicted with her conservative charcoal skirt and blazer, but Jarsdel guessed it was some technique of covert influence. He grunted, wondering what the city had forked over for the benefits of her expertise.

"What's funny?"

"Bit pop psych, isn't it? Just seems like a bunch of woo-woo the department's throwing our way to make themselves feel better. We don't need a behaviorist. We need a thousand new sworn officers."

Barnhardt shrugged. "It's not all just theory. She's pretty brilliant. Designs security systems for missile silos."

Lieutenant Gavin entered and hurried past them to the front of the room. He'd undergone a transformation since Jarsdel's first year in HH2. Then, Gavin had been a surly, myopic blowhard, a candidate for central casting's no-nonsense police commander—if absent the wit and charisma such a role usually required. But at some point he'd gotten hold of Bill Bryson's *A Short History of Nearly Everything*, and now—unbelievably—Gavin seemed to consider himself an intellectual, even something of an amateur scientist. He kept spare copies of the book in his office, doling them out with sage authority to those he favored.

Most surprisingly, he'd taken down a photograph of himself posed with the governor, hanging in its place a framed eight-by-ten glossy of Max Planck. The bald, mustachioed physicist gazed morosely back at Gavin's puzzled visitors, most of whom assumed it was a picture of his great-grandfather. Anyone unfortunate enough to inquire was given a sour, disapproving look. "That's Max *Planck*," Gavin would say, and proceed with an error-riddled précis of energy quanta and blackbody radiation. The routine culminated with Planck's winning the Nobel Prize, an honor the lieutenant pronounced as the "noble" prize.

Whereas before Gavin had been obnoxious but predictable, he'd now entered the realm of insufferable pedantry, and he was growing bolder by the day. Physics textbooks—always conspicuously placed—had begun appearing in his office, along with grade-school science paraphernalia like Newton's cradles and Rubik's cubes. A NASA bumper sticker showed up on the break-room fridge one day:

JUST WHAT PART OF
GxmxM/R=mxVesc2/2
DON'T YOU UNDERSTAND?
IT'S ONLY ROCKET SCIENCE

The whole business infuriated Jarsdel because, for one, the man hadn't earned his pretensions. He was the worst sort of imposter, surrounding himself with the trappings of a culture that wasn't his own, as if those books and the bumper sticker and that ridiculous picture of Planck could compensate for what was plainly an average brain.

And he was getting away with it.

Jarsdel had picked up the first few murmurings, things like, "Gavin's no fool," or "Guy must be pretty smart." The most irritating had come from an attractive patrol officer who, upon leaving Gavin's office after a meeting, remarked, "Wow, did you see what he was reading? I didn't even understand the *title*." It wasn't so much her words but the awed delivery that made it sting.

Gavin shook hands with their guest speaker, then edged her out of the way. He spoke into a mic clamped to the side of the lectern. "Okay, folks—hey." Gavin flicked the mic with his finger, sending a percussive bolt through the speakers. Conversation quieted down. A few officers winced and rubbed their ears.

"Okay," Gavin repeated. "Thanks. Okay. We're gonna get started. As you know, we have a special presenter today, right? But what you may not know is that our presenter is Dr. Alisha Varma, president of the Pavlov Society. These are people who do all kinds of very complex, very deep research on pressing scientific concerns related to behavior. You know who Pavlov was?"

No, thought Jarsdel. *He's not really going to—*

"Ivan Pavlov was a doctor who discovered he could condition his dogs to salivate by ringing a bell. That's because every time he was about to feed them, he rang that bell, so even when he wasn't about to feed them and rang the bell anyway, the dogs still got excited. That's called *conditioning*. And that's what Dr. Varma does." He pointed at her without taking his eyes off the audience, as if challenging anyone to contradict him. A silence followed. Varma endured it with a frozen smile, reminding Jarsdel of a bride weathering a speech by the drunken best man.

"So that's what's going on," Gavin said with a nod. "Your department's provided you with the top, absolute top in her field. I expect your full attention, obviously. And your cooperation with anything Dr. Varma wants to move ahead with. Okay. Let's give her a round of applause."

Gavin backed away, clapping his hands, and waved at Varma to step forward. She adjusted the mic, glanced down at her notes, and looked out over the audience.

"Good morning." Jarsdel realized he'd been expecting the accent of a Maharashtrian Brahmin—the dusky, mellifluous, vaguely erotic offspring of the British raj and Indian aristocracy. Instead, he got the flat, CNN-standard timbre of Grosse Pointe, Michigan.

There were a few mumbled replies from her audience. Varma smiled at the anemic reception. "And that's about what I expected," she said. "I get much the same at every department I speak at. A few months ago I gave a seminar to An Garda Síochána cadets in Dublin, and I'm not embarrassed to say the ones that weren't asleep were playing *Jewel Quest* on their phones. At first, anyway. And I'll tell you something else. You don't need me."

A few heads that'd been bowed toward handheld screens glanced up, mildly curious. Most consultants didn't start off by asserting their own uselessness.

"What's going on in your city right now is painful. And as is the case with any painful experience, you can't conceive the end of it. It's especially upsetting considering last year marked nearly two decades of consecutive annual *drops* in homicide, down to 238—or 4.3 per 100,000. That's a record low. But since January you've already topped 250 homicides, with six months left to go before they hit the reset button on stats. If the trend continues, you're looking at numbers you haven't seen since '81. But I'm telling you right now, it's unlikely my ideas are going to be of any help at all."

Jarsdel scanned the room. Nearly everyone now had their attention on Dr. Varma.

"I say that because, mathematically speaking, Los Angeles has been following in step with the global decline in violent crime. These last few months, then, have been anomalous—a freak drift toward lawlessness spurred on by a cocktail of factors. Now we can speculate on what those factors may be and try to address them piecemeal, but we may never know exactly how it happened and, really, it's not even that important. What's important is recognizing what's happened as an anomaly, meaning that regardless of anything you or I do, odds are your numbers are going to stabilize, then return to an approximation of their previous downward trend. Any system, whether it be simple or complex, tends to regress to its mean level of performance after an extraordinary event.

"Let's say the situation was flipped, and you'd only had—say—*ten* homicides so far this year, and instead of me standing in front of you, it's the chief of police. And he's telling you what a great job you've done. Now would you think it actually had anything to do with you? Probably not. And you'd probably be very skeptical such a pattern would continue. Complex systems generally don't change overnight, not for the better and not for the worse. In other words, things are going to get back to normal with or without my help."

Gavin looked uneasy. This didn't appear to be part of the script. His arm twitched, as if he wanted to raise his hand to ask a question, then stilled.

Varma shrugged. "Then again, history provides us with countless examples of the status quo being upturned—events that would've been considered unlikely or even impossible before they occurred, but which of course happened anyway. We try to assign some inevitability through hindsight, but that's a classic bias. So, yes. It could be as bad as it looks. It could be the city's been plunged into a terrible and unforeseen crisis. The point is, we don't know one way or the other. But what we can't afford is to take the chance that things will get better on their own. We simply can't."

Jarsdel looked at Gavin, who now nodded along with Varma's speech. Apparently it had once again found its moorings. Varma glanced at him, then looked back at her audience—left, center, right, center, left.

"I have the feeling you agree. Good. Let's get started."

The house is bleeding.

Those had been the last words Officer Evan Porter remembered speaking before waking up in Hollywood Presbyterian's ICU. A weapon had been found at the scene, a thirty-two-ounce claw hammer stolen from the Lauterbachs' tool chest. It was consistent with Porter's injuries.

He'd only been struck once, but the blow had been devastating—a bone-pulverizing crack that ruptured an eardrum, shattered six teeth, and collapsed the orbit of his right eye. When it was determined that vitreous fluid was leaking into his bloodstream—which would've caused a catastrophic, ultimately blinding autoimmune attack—a complete enucleation of the damaged eye was performed.

Upon admission, Porter was given a dose of thiopental and put into a coma until doctors could be sure he hadn't suffered brain damage. In this, he'd been lucky—the CT scan showed no evidence of cerebral contusions, edema, or hemorrhage. After five days, and during a brief abatement of the January rains, Jarsdel and Morales had paid him a visit.

He was sitting up when they came in, his remaining blue eye fixed on the TV opposite the bed. The rest of his face was in bandages.

"Officer Porter," Morales said, "I'm Oscar Morales, and this is Tully Jarsdel. We're detectives at Hollywood Station."

Porter raised the remote and turned off the TV. His eye shifted from one man to the other, then he pointed to his mouth.

"I know, your jaw's wired," said Morales. "They said you might be able to get some words out, but it'd hurt. We don't wanna put you through anything, but we need some answers. Can always get you something to write on, so let's just do our best and see what happens."

Porter gave a single nod.

"I guess the first question is obvious. We already talked to Officer Banning, and she didn't see his face. What about you? You see it?"

Porter closed his eye. The detectives exchanged a look, uncertain if he'd fallen asleep.

Jarsdel stepped forward. "Sorry, did you—"

Porter's eye opened again and focused on Jarsdel. "No." Only his lips moved; all the rest was locked in place, making his voice sound angry.

"No? Is it that you don't remember what he looks like, or you never saw his face to begin with?"

"Don't know." Porter grimaced.

"You mean you don't remember at all?"

Another single nod.

"Would you be willing to be hypnotized? See if we can jog anything?"

Porter answered immediately. "No."

"What do you mean?" asked Morales. "Why not?"

The officer was silent. Either the answer was too long to be worth the trouble, or Porter wasn't in the mood to give it.

"Okay," said Jarsdel. "Let's move on to—"

"No, wait, hang on." Morales pointed at Porter. "You run ahead of your partner, get your face caved in, nearly get her killed, too, by not following procedure. Now LA taxpayers gotta carry your ass for the rest of your life. And you're not gonna do everything you can to help us out?"

Porter's single eye blazed back at Morales, but still he gave no answer.

"Wow. What a hero."

Jarsdel held up a hand. "Let's move on. What exactly prompted you to enter the house?"

Porter swallowed, grimaced again. "Bleeding. House was bleeding."

"Officer Banning mentioned that as well. You saw a red substance seeping from a crack near the second story."

"Blood."

"Yes, that's true. It was blood. And you pointed it out to Officer Banning. Then what?" By now Jarsdel had his notebook out and was making shorthand jottings as the conversation went on.

"Told me breach."

"Officer Banning ordered you to breach the door?"

"Yes."

"And did you?"

"Yes."

"And then what? Did you identify yourself as a police officer?"

Porter closed his eye. "Forget."

"You don't remember?"

"Probably said 'police.' Probably. But don't remember. Once inside, don't remember."

"Don't blame you," said Morales. "I wouldn't wanna remember, either. I'll tell you this: I know Melissa Banning, and she'd've *washed* your dumb ass if you hadn't gone and—"

"Oscar." Jarsdel gave his partner a weary look.

"Fuck it," said Morales and turned to leave. "I'll wait outside. No, actually I'm gonna run down to the gift shop and buy this hero some roses."

Once Morales had gone, Porter appeared to relax. "Hates me." He tried a smile. It was ghastly, and he seemed to know it. He let his face go slack.

"I really need you to think hard, hard as you can. Anything you can tell us about what happened to you. A piece of jewelry maybe, or a tattoo, or even a scent—cologne or deodorant or bad breath."

"All hate me."

"What?"

"They. All. Hate. Me."

"I don't know anything about that," said Jarsdel. "But we gotta catch this guy, and you're the only one who can still tell me something."

"I wish it killed me."

"You wish he'd killed you?"

"I'm scared."

"Why?"

Porter didn't answer.

"Why? It's over."

Porter's eye, bright as a shard of glass, shuddered in its socket. It flicked right and left, as if searching the room, making sure the two of them were alone. "I'm scared I'll remember."

"That you'll remember?"

"Yes."

"Remember what?"

"Everything. In the house."

"I don't understand," said Jarsdel. "You're scared you'll remember? Won't it be a big help to everyone if you did?"

"Not to everyone." Porter grunted.

"Yeah? You're done, huh?"

"Oh yeah. I'm done."

Jarsdel glared at him. "You think it was somehow special, what you experienced?" He waited and, when Porter remained silent, continued. "So now you're what—just going to recuse yourself from this investigation?"

"I'm a faithful man."

"What?"

"I'm religious."

"What's that have to do with anything?"

Porter's face tightened, and he groped around for something at his side. Jarsdel saw it was an analgesia pump. Porter clicked the button, dispensing some more painkillers into his bloodstream. He relaxed a little.

"What does religion have to do with anything?" Jarsdel repeated.

"I'm tired. Wanna sleep."

"Tell me and I'll go."

"I'm just... I believe in God, but I've never seen him."

"Great. So?"

Porter closed his eye. His breathing slowed. "Don't believe in Devil, but I've seen *him*."

Jarsdel frowned. "You remember what he looked like, then?"

"No. No. Never want to. But I know I did see him. Because. It's like. My soul. My soul hurts now."

"His soul hurts, huh?" Morales made a right onto Vermont, toward Hollywood Boulevard. A man in a gray suit and red tie paced the corner, shouting into a microphone. A woman hovered nearby, clutching flyers and guarding the man's amp, which spat out a feedback-streaked tirade in Spanish.

"That's how he put it," said Jarsdel.

"What does that even mean?"

"I suppose it's a kind of Zapffian crisis. An unmooring in the 'liquid fray of consciousness.'"

"Jesus, Tully. Forget I asked."

They parked on Russell and walked in silence to Fred 62, a faux-retro diner that'd sprung up during the Los Feliz renaissance of the '90s. It was a time when newly minted hepcats—men with glistening rockabilly pompadours and wallet chains snaking into their pegged trousers—prowled the Derby and the Dresden Room, when the radio was as likely to play Sublime as Big Bad Voodoo Daddy and everyone knew how to jitterbug, if only a little. Twenty years later, the party was definitely over, the hepcats and hepkittens having traded their bowling shirts and polka-dot dresses for the anonymous uniforms of middle age. Music no longer filled the night, and the Derby was now, perfectly, a bank.

Somehow Fred 62, with its wall of Golden Age headshots and green leather booths, had survived. But its self-aware charm wasn't the only reason guys like Jarsdel and Morales stopped by; since the death of Jay's Jayburger, Fred's made the best burger in Los Feliz.

The lunch rush was over, and the detectives picked a table in back, far from the door. Once they put in their order—two Juicy Lucys with sides of onion rings and coleslaw—Jarsdel brought out the Lauterbach murder book. Murder books were royal-blue three-ring binders containing every scrap of evidence related to a particular homicide case and were divided into twenty-six numbered sections—from the crime scene log to the witness list to the ambulance and medical records. And though it might've sounded like one, it wasn't a nickname—the standardized face page and table of contents were titled *Los Angeles Police Department "Murder Book"*—just like that, in quotes.

This one was already thick with documents. Pictures, too, more than a hundred, but Jarsdel was careful not to turn to them before lunch. Brown DYMO tape in the binder's upper left-hand corner indicated the case number, victims, and the assigned detectives. This one read as follows:

```
MURDER        DR 21–0825790
VICTIMS       LAUTERBACH, JOANNE ROSE
              LAUTERBACH, WILLIAM ALAN
              1320 HOLLYRIDGE LOOP
DATE/TIME     1-5-21
DETECTIVES    JARSDEL/MORALES
```

"Okay," Jarsdel said to his partner. "You wanna go first?"

"No." Morales chuckled. "No. Fuck no."

"All right. I'll go." Jarsdel pulled the murder book closer and scanned the first few pages. Statements from the officers who'd found Banning and Porter from the EMTs who'd taken them to Hollywood Pres, from neighbors—none of whom had heard or seen anything strange, a transcript of their interview with Banning, their own notes from the scene, and the Lauterbachs' autopsy reports.

"I'm on pins and needles," said Morales.

"Just gimme a sec."

Morales sighed and began scrolling through emails on his phone. "Whoa, my lucky day. Check it out: 'Would you bang a fifty-year-old? Hot, lonely housewives wanna meet YOU for casual sex.' The only concern is would I be discreet. Hell yes, I'd be discreet. I'm *Mister*—"

"Please, could you stop?" said Jarsdel. "Okay, here. Let's start here. With what Porter says to Banning."

"'The house is bleeding,'" said Morales. "Sounds like one of those concept albums. Featuring the hit single, 'My Soul Hurts.'"

"What interests me is the viciousness of it. Dr. Ipgreve can't even say conclusively how many times Joanne Lauterbach was struck, because in addition to the hammer blows, we've got countless kicks and stomps. Leached an estimated five pints of blood into the floorboards. Looks like she was hit by a truck."

"Worse."

"Yeah," Jarsdel agreed. "Worse."

"So what does that tell us?"

"He's enraged. Either he believes the Lauterbachs deserved to die or he's using them as surrogates for someone he can't get to physically." Jarsdel considered. "Overkill tactics, lack of bindings. Didn't even bring a weapon, far as we know. Hammer was already there. So were the cigarettes he used to torture the husband. Disorganized offender. No planning. Impulsive."

"Disorganized." Morales chewed on the word. "You're back to that FBI shit again."

"I know it annoys you, but it's apt."

"You think so? What about the campsite?"

Jarsdel opened his mouth to speak, then saw Morales's point.

In dusting the house for prints, they'd found a large grouping on and around the basement door. Someone had been handling it a lot, as if trying to open and close it as quietly as possible. The detectives had picked their way down the narrow wooden staircase into a dank cellar, where a sump pump kicked on every few minutes to expel rainwater. There was a hulking water heater with rusted, cobwebbed valves and an assortment of rat traps, several of which had been sprung. Overhead swayed a single caged incandescent bulb. Around them in all directions stretched the crawl space, the dirt-floored underbelly of the house. Most of it was filled with decades of accumulated detritus—sticks of old furniture, countless cardboard boxes labeled in Sharpie, plastic bins loaded with holiday decorations and cold-weather clothing, empty file cabinets, suitcases, and any number of rickety, rotting, dust-caked odds and ends.

But in one spot, it was clear items had been pushed aside. The dirt bore fresh scuff marks, revealing darker soil beneath, and there the detectives could make out patterns left by shoe treads. Morales followed the trail with the beam of his Maglite. His breath caught.

"No fuckin' way."

Jarsdel joined him, peering into the crawl space. About ten feet in lay a blanket and a pillow. On either side were scattered perhaps a dozen empty cans of pantry goods. Jarsdel could identify labels for pork and beans, sweet corn, hearts of palm, peeled Roma tomatoes, and turkey chili. There was also a quart of half-and-half, an empty tin of kippered herring, and several bottles of vanilla-flavored Ensure.

Jarsdel didn't think he'd ever seen his partner truly amazed until then. "How long was he *down* here? I mean, you've got... I don't even know. Tully, you smell that? Is that piss?"

It was. Once the junk had been hauled away and evidence technicians could get to work, fifteen puddles of urine in varying states of dryness were counted. Ipgreve said that could be two or even three days' worth but maybe longer if he'd also been using one of the bathrooms inside the house. That would also account for why he hadn't defecated in the crawl space.

The results had come in that morning, just before they'd gone to see Porter. Crime lab techs had been able to identify the presence of three DNA profiles in both the downstairs bathroom and the one adjacent to the master bedroom. Two of the profiles matched those of Bill and Joanne Lauterbach. The third, from an unknown donor, matched the urine in the cellar along with the fecal matter stuffed into Bill Lauterbach's mouth.

Another puzzle that had recently been solved was exactly how the killer had gained entry. All the house's locks were intact, none of the windows had been broken, and the alarm company hadn't reported any unusual activity—except that no one had armed the system in the last three days.

Morales had been the one to figure it out. He'd been retracing

Officer Banning's steps as she'd investigated the grounds. He found the yellow watering can she'd used as a step stool to peek inside and see Bill Lauterbach's empty eyes staring back at her.

Low on the exterior wall, hidden behind a lush, flowering dogwood, a hole had been carved. It would've been practically invisible the night Banning and Porter arrived, blanketed in darkness and too far below anyone's line of sight to be noticed. It was more or less rectangular in shape, perhaps one by one-and-a-half feet at its widest, maybe big enough to admit a ballerina. Crime scene techs had found hair follicles matching the killer's DNA snagged along the top edge of the opening.

They'd also found a slice of flexible, translucent yellow plastic stuck in mud nearby. It looked like a corner piece cut from a larger square—sharp and triangular on one side, concave and crescent on the other. What it had come from, indeed whether it was something the killer had brought with him at all, no one knew, but it went into evidence along with everything else.

He'd stayed in the Lauterbach house maybe as long as a week while his victims went about their lives unaware. During the day, he listened to them from beneath the floorboards as they talked about their grandkids or Bill's upcoming fifty-year fraternity reunion or Joanne's osteoporosis. At night, he crept up the cellar stairs to use the bathroom, steal food, and watch his prey. Jarsdel and Morales believed that was the killer's biggest thrill—seeing how long he could live among them, how close he could get without them knowing. Near his makeshift bed, they'd found a pillowcase stuffed with items pilfered from the house, things like the TV remote, a hair dryer, Bill Lauterbach's hearing aid and bridgework, a pair of candlesticks. He wanted them off-balance, confused, sensing in some way they'd fallen under his shadow, but not knowing the true nature of the threat or where it came from.

It must have been, Jarsdel decided, like living in a haunted house.

Now, sitting in their booth at Fred's, Jarsdel tried to answer Morales's question. *What about the campsite?* If their offender was disorganized, it would've been impossible for him to lie low for so long. The kind of behavior he exhibited up until the homicides demonstrated control, not a lack of it.

"Point taken," said Jarsdel. "So he's a mixed offender, with both organized and disorganized aspects to his pathology."

Morales wasn't impressed. "Who cares what he is? Gotta let go of that Quantico shit. I been doing this a lot longer than you, and none of those labels ever did me any good. Even with the serials. No, we look at it like any other homicide. Odds are he knew them, so we go through every plumber and electrician, handyman and gardener they've had. Motive, means, and opportunity: it's a classic for a reason."

Jarsdel tried to hide his disappointment. Metrics appealed to him; he ascribed to Lord Kelvin's overall philosophy that if it can't be measured, it isn't science. And Jarsdel believed that anything worthy of study must therefore also be measurable. This included, of course, human behavior. Being able to name and catalog something didn't merely enhance understanding; it gave the observer a certain power. The magic of taxonomy was its ability to strip a thing of its mystique. Identifying the killer by genus and species would contain him, define and limit his shape. Pull him at least a few inches out of the shadows.

Lunch arrived, but the men only picked at their food. Morales took a few perfunctory bites, then asked the waiter to box up the rest. Jarsdel said he didn't want his leftovers, and the table was cleared. Their bill arrived a moment later, weighted down by a couple peppermints. Morales unwrapped one and popped in his mouth, then rubbed the cellophane between his fingers. Jarsdel found the rasping, crackling sound annoying, but said nothing. Finally, Morales spoke.

"He'll do it again."

"Why? How do you know?"

"It's what they always say in movies. After they find the first crime scene, they always go, 'He's just getting started' or 'He's got a taste for it now—look out.'"

"Ah. Right."

"You don't watch movies."

"No."

Jarsdel stood. Morales followed, throwing down a few bills. It was his turn to cover lunch.

"You should, you know. Watch movies. Part of our culture here."

"Send me your top five," said Jarsdel.

"Yeah, you won't watch 'em. I know you. If it wasn't written a thousand years ago, it's not worth your time."

"Two thousand, actually. Other than Byrhtferth and Kushyar ib Labban, the eleventh century was pretty much an intellectual wasteland. Oh, and Li Qingzhao. I like her."

The two headed for the door, and Morales gave a weary sigh. "You know, what's funny is all your lofty, hard-learned bullshit won't do you nearly as much good in this job as watching *Training Day* a few times. Or in this case, *Manhunter*. Because I'm telling you, he's gonna do it again."

And he did do it again. And again, and again. In each instance he hid somewhere in the house prior to the murder. From as few as a dozen hours to—in the case of the Rustads—perhaps as many as five days.

"He creeps," Heather Malins of the *LA Weekly* had told her readers. "He creeps, and he watches, and he waits. I hereby dub him the Eastside Creeper. And while I don't believe the death penalty actually solves anything in the long run, I really don't care. This guy needs to be deleted, like a piece of buggy software. We don't need to study it, we don't need to understand it, and we don't need to reason with it. We just need to get rid of it."

Malins wasn't alone in her thinking. Right around that time, members of local neighborhood watch groups began coalescing into roving bands of vigilantes. They pulled all-night shifts, guarding street corners with walkie-talkies and clubs and cans of pepper spray. And the talk was, if they did find him, he wouldn't be turned over to the police.

On a night in early June, when summer in Los Angeles was still gentle as a warm bath, high school junior Ben Bauman and his girlfriend, Jenna, were necking in her Hancock Park bedroom. Ben wasn't supposed to be there, but Jenna's parents were out for the night and weren't due back until late.

The teens were lost in each other; deliciously, blissfully lost. And while neither expected that that night would be *the* night, there was still the giddy sense that things could slip just a little out of control, that perhaps their kissing—raw and urgent as it was—would no longer be quite enough. Not with the windows open, and the electric summer night spilling in, and the jasmine blooming so high and sweet and strong in the air. And yes, her fingers were finally making the first exploratory tugs at his zipper when they heard the unmistakable sound of the garage door rumbling up.

Jenna's eyes went wide. "Oh my God."

"Who's that? Your parents? What're they doing back already?"

"Shit. You gotta go—go! Get up!"

Ben rolled off the bed and stepped into his flip-flops. Jenna was at the window. "It's them, they're pulling in."

"Shit!"

"Oh my God, I know, I know—*fuck*."

"What do we do?"

"You can't go downstairs, they'll see you."

"So what do we do? Tell me!"

"You have to hide."

"*What?* No, I'm not hiding. If your dad finds me, he'll shoot me. *No*."

Somewhere in the house, a door slammed. Jenna gave Ben a pleading look. "They're gonna come up and check on me. You gotta hide."

Ben grinned. "I'm gonna go for it. It's classic."

"Go for what?"

"I'm gonna go out the window."

"No, you'll—"

"C'mon, it's perfect. So '90s."

"Ben..."

But he was already crossing the room. There was no screen on the window, and when he put his foot on the sill, his toes poked over the edge. He turned a final time to Jenna. She too was smiling by then. There *was* something classic about a lover slipping out the window.

"I'm Skeet Ulrich," said Ben. "And you're Neve Campbell."

"Yeah?" said Jenna. "Then I guess I have to do this before you leave." In one swift motion, she pulled off her T-shirt and bra. Ben's mouth dropped open. He couldn't help it. He'd never seen a girl like that before, not in real life, and hadn't really been sure what to expect, what it would actually be like to see her that way. He knew that men had looked upon women for thousands of years, knew it intellectually, but couldn't imagine anyone had ever before experienced what he was experiencing now. How could they have felt this warm, this fulfilled, this delightfully overwhelmed? If they had, why would they have wanted to do anything else? Anything else but just stare and stare and stare, taking in every exquisite detail.

"Jenna..."

"See you in class," she said.

Ben lowered himself quietly onto a narrow section of the first-floor roof. The red clay shingles were heavy and didn't move when he put his weight on them. He let go of the sill and got down on all fours, moving laterally along until he could get close enough to a nearby jacaranda tree. The roof was dusty, and he'd need to wash his clothes and take a shower when he got home, but who cared? *He'd seen her breasts*. Not even fully naked! Just her breasts, and oh what a total cosmic *rush*...

Across the street, Ted Degraffenreid—the volunteer on Creeper patrol who guarded that block of McCadden Place on Mondays and Wednesdays—looked up at the sound of rustling leaves and creaking branches. At first, he thought he couldn't possibly be seeing what he appeared to be seeing, but what else could it be?

The figure nimbly descended the tree and jumped the last few feet, landing on the grass. It looked around, making sure it hadn't been noticed, and crept across the yard, doing its best to stay in darkness.

Degraffenreid wasn't in law enforcement, but he'd been waiting years—perhaps his entire adult life—for the moment unfolding before him. He was a mechanical engineer by trade, had an appreciation for elegant design, for the transmission of force through a superior structure to an inferior one, and for the ultimate yielding of the latter. He loved the math of it, loved how the want and will of human passion were irrelevant in true matchups of strengths and weaknesses. A hundred newtons of force was a hundred newtons of force, and any opposition that couldn't muster at least as many in return was bound to fail. A deficit of a fraction of a fraction of a percent was enough to guarantee that failure, regardless of any other factors.

Doubt, however, remained. What if there was some alchemy in emotion, some hidden potential afforded by desire, or anger—or even insanity—that could overwhelm the math? Absurd. But still, such ideas persisted. So Degraffenreid wished to test his mastery of the physical world, test it against something both physically and emotionally powerful. Something that required nothing in the way of restraint or mercy. A mugger would've been good, but he hadn't been mugged since he was a teenager. And laws could get so complicated when it came to self-defense. His fantasies had evolved, growing more elaborate in the last few years. Now he believed a rape in progress would be the ideal scenario. The benefits of such an event would be practically incalculable. He'd be able to systematically destroy another human being, drive mass and metal against collagen polymers, striking through to the bone beneath—a remarkable natural composite material whose very objective was *not to break*.

He would be able to savor this experience without the slightest fear of punishment—quite the contrary, he'd be rewarded, lauded by a grateful community. Then of course there was the surviving female. Degraffenreid's arrival would coincide with her purest moment of need, the precise second in which she realized she was helpless to defend herself, but before she experienced substantial psychological trauma. Her exultation felt during and after the rescue would therefore be untarnished by any lingering disorders and translate directly into an unshakable desire to worship Degraffenreid. This worship would naturally include the basest of sexual favors.

But this—*this*, was so much more than he could've hoped for. If he were the one to apprehend the Eastside Creeper, he'd be a true hero—a hero unlike any since the dragon slayers of myth and legend. As he crossed the street on silent wing-walker boots, this thought, more than any other, lay at the forefront of his mind.

Around his neck he wore a whistle—titanium, coated with orange photoluminescent paint—that would send out a hundred-decibel shriek if he wanted it to. He could blow it now, alerting his fellow guardsmen to the danger, but he chose not to. He didn't need their help. The Creeper was one man. More a boy, really, now that he could see him better. Not particularly big and strong, but it didn't take size and strength to bash in helpless old ladies with a claw hammer.

Degraffenreid continued to close the distance between himself and the Creeper, who gave no sign he knew he was being observed. Degraffenreid reached down to his belt and drew his weapon. Marketed as the Whack-A-Do Fish Bat, it was a beautifully conceived instrument. With a housing of 95A Durometer urethane hugging a core of 7/8-inch 2011-T3 aluminum and a pound of lead shot, the fish bat was as deadly as a pernach mace, but with a greater capacity for transforming potential energy into the kinetic variety.

Degraffenreid hefted the bat, marveling at the power it lent his arm. The Creeper slunk along, now on the sidewalk and heading toward Fourth Street. Not too fast to call attention to himself, but it was amazing how guilty he looked. Everything about him screamed *criminal*.

When he was close enough to touch, Degraffenreid spoke.

"Hey. Stop in the name of the law."

2

Morales answered the door wearing an open purple bathrobe, argyle-print boxers, and a black T-shirt featuring a portrait of Pancho Villa next to the words "MEXICAN. NOT Latino. NOT Hispanic. NOT Mestizo." His eyes were glassy, his nose rubbed raw, and he clutched a wad of tissues.

"Come in at your own risk," he said.

Jarsdel went inside, picking his way around a Lego project in progress—a scale model of a Saturn V rocket.

"Ephraim's into space shit now," said Morales, closing the door. He shuffled over to the couch and fell into it, raising a palm to his forehead. "I wanna just *die*, man."

"I won't stay long."

"Not so loud, not so loud."

"I'm talking too loud?"

Morales nodded, keeping his eyes closed. "And your voice resonates in a weird way. In my ear. *Buzz-buzz*."

"Sorry, can't do a whole lot about that."

"Just say what's up and lemme go lay back down."

"*Lie* back down."

"Dude. So help me God, I don't care if I'm sick. I will summon the strength to throw your bony ass out that door."

Jarsdel tried to think of how to begin, then decided on the simplest way. "RHD's taking over all Creeper investigations as of Monday. Task force. We turn over everything to Captain Coryell."

"So we're off, huh?"

"Advisory capacity as needed, but yes, looks like it."

Morales grunted. "Good. Let it be somebody else's problem."

Jarsdel didn't answer, and his partner cracked open a bleary, red-rimmed eye. "Not you, though, huh?"

"I would've liked to have seen it through, yeah."

"Tully Jarsdel. Savin' the world, one shitbag at a time. So's that everything? The task-force stuff? Coulda just called, you know."

"I was hoping to do some triage. Maybe talk about what's next. Got four bodies on ice to choose from."

Morales slumped onto his side. "Uh, no. Haven't you ever been sick before? If I wanted to do that, I'd be at work right now. You're the skinny..." Morales pressed the tissues against his face and sneezed hard. It sounded like someone stepping on a set of bagpipes. He mopped at his nose and mouth, then closed his eyes. "God. Fuck this. I got a flu shot, right? So why's this happening? I don't know. Like a train going through my head."

"What were you going to say?" asked Jarsdel.

"What?"

"You were saying I'm the skinny something."

"Oh. Yeah. Skinny sadist. You look harmless. Mr. Scout Leader. Mr. Dudley Do-Right. But you're the skinny sadist. Ha. I like that." Morales closed his eyes again.

Jarsdel stood. "It's alliterative, but it'll never catch on. Too burdensome." He'd endured enough nicknames from his law-enforcement brethren and hoped to quash this one at the start. "Prof," a dig at his academic background, had faded away when he'd solved his first major case. But a few months later, following Jarsdel's repeated chidings that Morales used too many paper towels after washing his hands, his partner finally shot back. "You remind me of my dad. It was always, 'I ain't made of money, turn off the light,' or 'Don't roll down the windows when I drive—eats up more fuel.' For a guy who doesn't got any kids, you sure got the routine down cold. You're kinda like everybody's dad."

The name caught on stationwide, with Will Haarmann—he of the loathsome arm-wrestling table—being its biggest booster. Now even rookie cops were calling Jarsdel "Dad." They did so innocently, copying their superiors, likely believing it was a title that connoted respect or deference. Jarsdel then had to correct them—an unpleasant, awkward exchange for both parties.

"By the way," he said as he headed toward the door. "The department hired a civilian. Some kind of behaviorist. Guess the city council and police commission are concerned we're making them look bad. She's gonna be meeting with every sworn officer in Hollywood Station. Just letting you know because you'll have to make an appointment."

"What? No, fuck off."

Jarsdel shrugged. "Gavin's gonna lean on you, then. He thinks she walks on water. I'm seeing her Friday to get it over with."

"*Why?* What's the point? I don't wanna go talk to nobody. 'Specially someone Gavin thinks is hot shit."

"She's gonna work with us on implementing some new crime-prevention strategies. It's all very esoteric sounding. But according to Barnhardt, she knows what she's doing."

"I'm not doing any of this trendy, feel-me-hear-me-touch-me stuff. Why does everyone always wanna complicate police work? Fucking Mickey Mouse *bullshit*."

"Had a feeling the news would perk you up." Jarsdel reached for the knob, then paused, frowning at it. "Did you do hand sanitizer or anything? I don't know if I wanna touch that."

"Not contagious anymore. I don't think, anyway. Shit, maybe I got valley fever, and this is the last you're gonna see of me."

"Can you open it?"

"I'm not getting up."

Jarsdel sighed and gave the knob a quick twist, then wiped his hand on his pants. He turned back to Morales. "Get better soon. Work's just not the same without your boundless good cheer."

Morales had his eyes closed again, but he still managed to raise a middle-finger salute. Jarsdel made sure to close the door just a little harder than necessary on his way out.

Over a month had passed since Jarsdel last saw his parents, and it hadn't been pleasant for any of them. His dad, Robert, a retired lit professor who was beginning to look more and more like Orville Redenbacher, had stormed out of his own dining room. Robert's husband, Darius Jahangir, whom Jarsdel called Baba, had departed from his usual Persian stoicism and broken a spatula against the dinner table.

It had begun as a variation on the usual theme—Jarsdel's career in law enforcement—with the same circular arguments, passive-aggressive wheedling, and icy looks from Baba. But Jarsdel hadn't been in the mood that night, and Dad had seemed determined to force a confrontation.

"How do you do it, Tully?" he'd asked.

"Do what?"

"Talk to that partner of yours all day. What's his name again?"

Jarsdel blinked at his father. "Morales."

"Right. He doesn't even have a BA, does he? An associate degree, I think you said it was. Criminal justice or criminal persecution or whatever they call it. I can't imagine what you two discuss. I mean, there are only so many times you can sing 'Wheels on the Bus.'" Dad laughed, sending a blast of hot, wine-soaked breath into his son's face.

Jarsdel put down his knife and fork, steepled his fingers, and spoke with as much calm as he could muster. "Dad. It is very, very important you—"

"Here we go." His father shook his head, smiling sadly. "You've lost your sense of humor. Along with everything else."

"Dad," Jarsdel repeated. "It is absolutely imperative you hear me on this. Are you listening?"

"*A pedibus usque ad caput.*"

"Good. Because this is the last time we're going to have this conversation. For two reasons. One, I find the subject utterly tiresome. That should really be enough, I think, but you may not agree. So I'll add another. When you make remarks as profoundly stupid, as fractally wrong as—"

"You're so boring when you get self-righteous."

"*—as fractally wrong* as the one you just made, you seem to be flirting with sophomania. And that depresses me, because I know you really are brilliant. But when you so pompously blunder into areas you know nothing about, when you squirt out these inanities, you sound like a dumb person pretending to be smart."

The color drained from his father's face. He folded his napkin into a neat little tent and stood. "Pretending to be smart? All right. Why don't you follow me, and we can take a look at some of my pretend degrees."

"Good *God*. Did you hear anything I just said?"

Baba finally spoke up. "He heard you insult him."

Dad adjusted his glasses. "How this job has hardened you. You never would have dreamt of speaking to me that way before. Extraordinary. But I suppose if being a policeman can coarsen as refined a person as you, then it's no wonder the depravities your profession arouses in its lesser lights."

"I'm speechless," said Jarsdel.

"If only you were," said Dad.

"Think I'm gonna leave."

"Seems like a fine idea."

"You've officially abandoned coherent thought."

"Oh, go fuck yourself." Dad swept out, slamming the dining room's French doors. But they didn't catch, swinging lazily open again and giving Jarsdel a final glimpse of his father—a thin, bent man clutching a handkerchief to his face as he ascended the stairs. For the first time in his life, Jarsdel thought his father looked old.

There was a terrific *crack*, and he turned in time to see the head of the spatula used to serve that evening's fish course go spinning into the air. He wasn't sure what had happened, then noticed the remaining handle poking up from his baba's fist.

Jarsdel was astonished. Baba pointed the spatula handle at him like an épée. "Out."

"Are you serious?"

"I'm telling you to go."

"Most assuredly." Jarsdel stood and put on his sport coat. All the while Baba kept the bent metal tip of the spatula handle aimed toward his son's face. "This is extremely strange behavior. Am I supposed to feel threatened by that thing?"

"Why? What if you were? Would you shoot me?"

Jarsdel gave him a look of purest contempt and left without answering.

He hadn't been sure how they'd get past that night. He was absolutely resolved not to be the one to break the silence between them, and he was certain Baba's stubbornness matched his own. If anyone was going to try to make peace, it would be Dad, but Baba might try to talk him out of it.

Jarsdel had been wrong, however. It was Baba's name that showed up on his caller ID as he drove home from work. He did a double take, then accepted the call as he passed through the security gate and into Park La Brea.

"Hey."

There was a sigh on the other end—relief, perhaps, that Jarsdel had answered. "Hey," said Baba. "You have a minute to talk?"

"Sure, I'm just looking for a parking spot."

"You're driving? You shouldn't be on the phone while you drive."

Jarsdel rolled his eyes. "It's on speaker."

"What?"

"I said *it's on speaker*. It's hands-free. Forget about it. Anyway, what's up?"

Another sigh, then, "Your dad and I have been talking."

"Okay. That's fantastic."

"We've done a lot of thinking, and we feel we owe you an apology."

Jarsdel would've been less surprised if Baba had called to tell him he was considering joining the Foreign Legion. He tried not to let it show in his voice. "An apology."

"Yes."

He spotted an open space he could probably fit into, but it would require some concentration. "Hang on a sec," he said. It took him a few tries, but he eventually parked and cut the engine. "You there?"

"I'm here."

"An apology for what, exactly?"

"I need to spell it out?"

"I think so, yes. There are any number of things we could be talking about."

"I didn't have to call, you know."

"And I didn't ask you to. But since you did call, I want to know exactly what's being discussed. I'm not—"

"You're punishing me. You get to punish me now, right?"

Jarsdel wanted to slam his forehead against the steering wheel. "Can you chill out, please? I was going to say that I'm *not* punishing you, actually. I want to talk, and I'm being absolutely genuine. That's not even my *thing*, by the way. I don't do that. That sneaky double language and stuff."

"So by implication, that's my thing? Manipulative?"

"If you're legitimately asking, then yes, I think both you and Dad have a tendency toward a passive-aggressive style of argument. And I think you delight in laying little logic traps for me. But I really don't want to get into a whole new fight right now. If you're honestly calling to apologize for something, I want to... I want to honor that."

There was no response for a while, and Jarsdel thought Baba might have hung up. He was about to hang up himself when the man finally spoke. "This is all very sad for us. We love you on a level you can't conceive. You don't have any children of your own, but maybe one day you will, and you'll see what I mean. And when your son has this explosive talent, this intellect, and you know he could be a legend, and he goes off and... Well, it's—it's heartbreaking."

"Uh-huh. This doesn't really sound like we're breaking any new ground here. So now I feel like you're pulling a bait and switch on me. Saying you're calling to apologize just so you can—"

"No. No. You're right. It's… I have trouble letting go of something. That's me. Always been that way. Hard for me to see things end, you know. Definitively end. I think there's actually a word for that."

"Finifugal."

"What?"

"*Finifugal.*"

"Right, that's it. Well. There you go. That's me." Baba let out a shaky breath. "How about joining us for dinner?"

"When, tonight?"

"Sure, unless you've got plans."

Jarsdel only considered for a moment before shaking his head. "I just got home. Very long day. I'd be in traffic two hours getting over to your end of town."

"Actually we're already over here."

"What do you mean? In my apartment?"

"Across the street. At the Farmers Market. We have reservations in a half hour at Monsieur Marcel. Table for three, in case you could make it. We hope you do. Even if it's just to say hello."

Jarsdel didn't hesitate. "I'll be there."

"You will?"

"Of course."

"That's good, Tully. Thank you."

After he hung up, Jarsdel went inside to change. He lived in one of Park La Brea's garden apartment units—a two-story townhouse of painted brick. Its patio opened onto a sprawling communal lawn, and Jarsdel had put up a sturdy privacy screen so he could enjoy his evening wine without interference from dogs or errant Frisbees.

He put his badge and cuffs on a curio shelf to the left of the door, below a portrait of Lady Mary Wortley Montagu. It wasn't a print; he'd commissioned it from a Cal Arts student in a self-indulgent fugue after his last girlfriend had left him, and at a cost of $2,400. It still stank of oils, but he didn't care. Every time he came home, the eighteenth-century beauty and autodidact was there to greet him. He'd read all of Lady Mary's diaries and letters, and concluded with the firmest of certainties that had they been contemporaries, they would have fallen deeply in love.

Jarsdel put his weapon in his closet's floor safe and changed into a cream-colored aloha shirt, on which tawny mermaids strummed ukuleles beneath coconut palms. After locking up, he left the Park La Brea complex and crossed Third toward the Farmers Market.

Monsieur Marcel was a small outdoor bistro with a good wine list and a jambon-brie sandwich that was worth crossing the city for. His parents were already seated, Dad's hand resting on his husband's, the bottle of Bordeaux between them nearly empty. Baba said something that made him laugh, and he looked up, catching sight of Jarsdel.

Dad waved, and Baba turned to watch his son approach. Both men smiled, but guardedly. Jarsdel gave each a hug before sitting. Dad's arms felt thin, even bony, and something must have shone on his face because Robert asked him if everything was all right.

"Fine. Just a hell of a day." Jarsdel sat at the place setting next to Baba.

"You want to talk about it?" Dad asked.

"No. It's nothing serious. Just a lot of paperwork."

Jarsdel thought his parents looked relieved he didn't want to discuss his job. Baba put a hand on his shoulder. "It means a lot to us that you came."

"Guys..."

"No, we...we've been challenging. Very challenging."

"You're passionate. That's something I understand."

"We know you do," said Dad. "But all the same. We haven't given you any support, none at all, since you started your new job."

That statement annoyed Jarsdel, and he was tempted to say so. His "new job" had been a successful career for more than six years. He'd become a homicide detective in one of the most competitive and prestigious departments in the world. And why couldn't either of his parents for once actually *say* what he did out loud?

But he restrained himself. They'd come to make peace—so they said—and he was going to give them the benefit of the doubt. "Thank you," he said. "Appreciate you saying that. You should also know that it's not as if I'm squandering my intellect. I really feel I'm giving my full self to my work."

A waiter appeared, filled Jarsdel's wineglass, and took their orders. Once he'd gone, Baba spoke up.

"You were saying you're feeling fulfilled. By that I take it you don't miss academia."

"I don't," said Jarsdel. "I don't miss it. Because I'm applying everything I learned to my work."

"In what way?" Dad asked.

Jarsdel studied his father, then decided the man was genuinely curious. "I get to use my brain, the brain I built. You and Baba think there's a divide between all those years of study I put in and my detective work. It's funny because out of everyone, you're the guys I shouldn't have to explain that to. You're the ones who told me, from as early as I can remember, that to be a student of history is the noblest and most intimate pursuit, that nothing else brings you closer to humankind. Remember *qui bono*?"

Baba nodded.

"You told me virtually anything could be framed through that question—who benefits. It's the central theme behind every act our species commits. Motive. And motives can be lofty or they can be absurd and petty, but they beat underneath it all. You taught me that when I was in kindergarten. *Qui bono*. I loved that."

Dad signaled the waiter, pointed at the empty bottle, and mouthed "Another, please." Jarsdel looked from one father to the other, trying to discern how they felt about what he'd said. "Interesting argument," said Baba. "May I ask you something?"

"Sure."

"Are you part of that case? The Creeper?"

A chill passed over Jarsdel at the mention of the name, and the ebullient chatter of nearby conversations, the bustle of the market, seemed at once muted, distant. "A small part. He's hit three other areas besides Hollywood. And actually I found out today it all got turned over to RHD. Sorry—that's Robbery-Homicide Division. So except for occasionally giving my expertise, such as it is, I'm pretty much off it now."

"Are you glad of that?"

"No. I don't want to get into the details because we're about to have dinner, but it's one of those cases that grabs on to you."

"So what happens if you apply that old question—*qui bono*?"

"In regards to the Creeper? Who benefits?"

"Right."

Jarsdel was puzzled. "He does. He benefits. Serial homicide is a purely selfish act."

"Then how does an understanding of motive help draw you any closer to catching him?"

"Well, it's not a panacea. It's a starting point. Creeper's an outlier—not really the sort of case I was referring to. I meant the kind of situations when you don't have a suspect. In this case, we do know who it is. I mean, not his identity, but we know that it's one guy and why he's doing it."

"No need to get defensive, Tully."

"I'm not. It just seems like right away you're trying to chip away at my thesis. But the Creeper's not your typical criminal. Thank God."

Baba held up a hand. "I apologize. He's just been on our minds a lot. That Santiago one was in San Marino. Pretty close."

"I know. Yeah it's...it's rough."

"The papers don't say what he does. Somehow that makes it worse. They'll say beaten to death or stabbed or strangled, but you can tell they're leaving a lot out."

"Please, Dary." Dad grimaced. "Please no more. Let's talk about something nice. We haven't seen our boy in a long time."

From somewhere nearby came a crash, followed by an angry shout and a woman's scream. Jarsdel and his dads turned to see a man wearing a gas mask vault over the railing separating one food stand from another. In one hand he gripped a stack of red flyers, in the other, a plastic spray bottle. He slammed into a middle-aged couple, and all three went to the ground. There were more screams, along with howls of pain and fear.

Dad gasped. Baba reached across the table and gripped Jarsdel's arm.

"Outta the way! Stop!" A West Hollywood sheriff's deputy bolted from around the corner, fists pumping. The gas-mask man had barely made it to his feet when the officer hit him. It was a perfect tackle—shoulders, elbows, and knees working together to drive the opponent flush with the cement.

The flyers scattered, one of them close enough for Jarsdel to see what they said. Across the top in a thick, blocky font were the words, "VALLEY FEVER A LIE! GOVT'S MOJAVE BIO/NUKE LAB MELTDOWN!" Below that was a single long paragraph, crammed margin to margin in tiny print and extending to the bottom of the page.

"Don't move!" the deputy commanded, whipping out his cuffs and snapping a bracelet over the gas-mask man's wrist. But he must've had tunnel vision from the adrenaline, because he hadn't yet noticed the man was still holding onto the spray bottle.

"Hey—look out!" Jarsdel shot to his feet, jerking his arm free of Baba's grip and running to assist the deputy. He wasn't fast enough. The gas-mask man pointed the nozzle of the spray bottle over his shoulder and began squeezing the trigger. The deputy flinched, then knocked the bottle away and slammed the man's face against the ground. Something in the housing cracked, and he let out a groan.

Jarsdel arrived just as the deputy let go of the suspect and began rubbing his eyes.

"LAPD," said Jarsdel. He wrenched the suspect's right arm back and finished cuffing him.

"Ach, fuck! What he hit me with?"

The gas-mask man began bucking. Jarsdel pinned him with his body weight and held him still. He turned to the deputy. "I'm off duty. You call for backup?"

"Yeah...*shit*. Sprayed me with something."

"Hey!" Jarsdel called out to anyone who'd listen. "I need some water over here. Lots of fresh water. Help us out."

"Shit *burns*."

"C'mon, people, water!"

A few mostly empty bottles of water rolled their way. No one wanted to get close.

Jarsdel grabbed one of the bottles, uncapped it, and thrust it toward the deputy. "Here, you got it? Rinse out your eyes. Pour it all over."

From the parking lot came the whoop of a siren and the squeal of brakes. While the cop shook the water onto his face, Jarsdel bent low toward the suspect's ear. "What'd you spray him with?" The man didn't answer. "You just assaulted a police officer. That's already a year in jail. Any real damage and it's aggravated battery. Four years. What's in the bottle?"

The man murmured something. A shriek sounded from a few yards away. It was the woman who'd been knocked down. "Ooh, Jesus—my hip! I think it's broken! Peter!"

Jarsdel bent closer to Gas Mask. "What? Say again."

"The fuck *off* me."

"What's in the bottle?"

The woman screamed once again. "Peter, no! Don't touch it! Don't *touch* it!"

If the suspect had replied, Jarsdel hadn't heard. "What's in the bottle?"

"Acetone! Fucking acetone."

Jarsdel turned to the deputy, who'd finished dousing himself with water and was now blinking rapidly. "Feels a little better," he said.

"It's acetone," said Jarsdel.

"It burns like shit. I'm gonna..." He paused, noticing the dozens of phone cameras recording them. "I'm gonna need medical. *Man*." He seized the handcuff chain binding the prisoner. "I got it from here, thanks."

Jarsdel gave him a nod and stood. Other officers were approaching fast. Nothing else made that sound, not all at once—the urgent footfalls of big men, the rattle and jangle of equipment, the bursts of radio chatter.

He looked back toward the restaurant. His dads were still at the table, watching him. He waved to show he was okay.

Four deputies charged in, breaking off from each other with choreographed precision. One went to check on the injured, another helped with the gas-mask man, and the last two secured witnesses before they could scatter. Some applauded, as if this were the final act in an eclectic piece of street theater.

Jarsdel made his way back to Monsieur Marcel through the gathering crowd. As soon as he sat, the waiter appeared.

"Excuse me, but we just wanted to let you know that your dinner is on the house tonight."

"Oh. Thank you, but that's not necessary."

"We'd really appreciate treating you and your friends."

"That's a very kind offer, but I'm not allowed to receive gifts."

The waiter looked uncertain. "Okay. Well. Thank you, though, for your service. Please let us know if there's anything we can do."

When he'd gone, Jarsdel finished the wine in his glass and poured himself some more. His parents watched him in silence.

"What is it?"

Dad and Baba glanced at each other. "That was"—Baba considered—"very hard to watch."

"Yeah, well, it wasn't a lot of fun to do."

"Does that sort of thing happen often? You just run into a situation?"

"Not as much anymore. Haven't been in a real fight since patrol."

"A *fight*?"

Jarsdel put down his glass. "Hey. Guys. Let's just hang on a sec. I was really happy with the way the evening was going. I think we were making some actual progress in understanding each other. Let's not undo that now."

"Excuse me—sir?" One of the deputies had approached their table. "Blake said you helped him out with the suspect. Appreciate that."

"Sure, of course," said Jarsdel.

"And you're LAPD?"

"Yeah. Homicide, out of Hollywood Station."

"HH2?"

Jarsdel blinked, both surprised and a little flattered. "Yes."

"Well, we hate to mess up your dinner and everything, but we'll need you to talk to us about what happened and what you saw."

Jarsdel wanted to protest, but he knew it was useless. He'd be lucky if this was the extent of his involvement with the gas-mask man. More likely, there'd be a subpoena and a court date in his future. He got to his feet. "I won't be long," he told his parents.

They exchanged another look. "We're probably gonna take off. Long drive back to Pasadena."

Jarsdel hesitated. "I really wish you'd stay."

Neither man answered. As Jarsdel went with the deputy, he saw the waiter come out with their food, and Baba signaling for the check.

After he was done meeting with the deputy, Jarsdel went back to Monsieur Marcel on the off chance he'd been wrong about his dads. He wasn't—they were gone. The waiter handed him his dinner, boxed and still a little warm.

"You can have it here, if you like. Your friends wanted to take theirs with them, so I wasn't sure."

Jarsdel thanked him and took the food back across the street to his apartment. As he was about to cross Third, he noticed one of the gas-mask man's flyers taped to the base of a streetlight. After reading a few lines he tore it free and tossed it in a trash can. The city was sick, and the last thing it needed was more poison. He considered wandering the neighborhood, looking for more flyers to tear down, but he was tired and hungry and wanted the evening to be over.

Once inside, he turned on a new Jeff Peterson album he'd bought, *Ka Nani O Ki Ho'alu*, and prodded at his food. He didn't have enough enthusiasm to eat, and after a few minutes tossed his leftovers in the fridge. Jarsdel poured himself a glass of Meiomi pinot noir, tucked himself into the corner of his sofa, and picked up Dr. Alisha Varma's textbook. It was called *Matter over Mind: Security Concerns from a Psychosocial Perspective*. He'd purchased a copy after attending her talk. The prose was stiff and clinical, even for a textbook.

"A structure designed to welcome visitors," she wrote, "consists of a harmonious marriage of affordances and visual transparency. A business indicates its accessibility by offering clear modes of entry, and these are designed to provide as little resistance as possible. Automatic doors pose the least impediment, requiring nothing of the customers other than their presence. These doors also allow for large purchases to be easily transferred from the store. An abundance of glass windows and an illuminated interior signify openness, trustworthiness, freshness, and cleanliness.

"Obstacles, if present, are scaled to assist and encourage proper physical interaction with the space. Barriers, for example, are only built high enough to signify a path or a boundary, not to obstruct the view or frustrate a determined infiltrator."

Jarsdel skimmed ahead. He was due to meet with her the next morning, and he wanted deeper insights into her thinking than why shopping at big-box stores was such a breeze. The following section, "Anti-Affordances," looked more relevant.

"According to Gibson, an affordance is any characteristic of the environment offered to the animal—whether for good or ill. A flower is an affordance to a bee, but so is a pitcher plant to a fly. For our purposes, however, we'll follow Dr. Norman's narrower definition. An affordance is therefore an environmental cue or signal intended for a prospective actor upon that same environment. In other words, the inclusion of an affordance affects a causal relationship with usability, or human-centered design. The reverse is also true: the lack or purposeful omission of an affordance restricts usability.

"But what of the anti-affordance? Here we finally encounter the proactive deterrent, and I include in this definition..."

Jarsdel put the book down and rubbed his eyes. It was getting late, and he'd had too much wine. He wasn't in the mood to hack his way through Varma's text.

Outside, someone screamed.

It was no mere shriek of revulsion or fear—a spider dropping onto your shoulder, perhaps, or a pan of hot oil catching fire. This was the high, sustained scream of absolute, mortal terror.

Jarsdel froze, listening. The night seemed to listen and wait, too. When no other sounds came, he opened the floor safe in his closet and took out his service weapon. Holding the Glock 40 at his side, he crossed quickly through the apartment, opened the front door, and stepped outside.

He'd been expecting other doors to be open, concerned citizens peering out. He'd tell them he was with the police and ask them to point him in the direction of the commotion. But the street—in fact every street in view—was empty.

Jarsdel reached back inside and traded his weapon for the Maglite he kept in a caddy near the door. He flicked it on and cut left, sweeping the beam over parked cars and hedges and—was that a man, crouching low in the dark? No. One of those old-fashioned wire-mesh trash cans. Jarsdel had mistaken the refuse bag as some kind of rain slicker. Now that he looked more closely, he saw there was no resemblance at all. Strange how the eye and the brain conspired against their host.

"Hello?" Jarsdel called. "Everyone okay?"

Nothing. Park La Brea was a large, multibuilding apartment complex—really its own gated village—with the Farmers Market to the north and the La Brea Tar Pits to the south. Jarsdel lived on Maryland Drive, not far from the Third and Burnside vehicle entrance gate, and he thought he'd check with security to see what was going on.

The guard, probably a UCLA student, was writing a screenplay on his laptop. A tag on his uniform read "Bachelor," and it took Jarsdel a moment to realize that was the man's name, rather than a decree of his marital status.

Jarsdel knocked on the jamb, and Bachelor looked up.

"Hey, I'm a resident here but I'm also LAPD." Jarsdel showed his identification.

"Oh," said the guard, staring with amazement at the badge. "What's—what's going on? I've only been on shift for like a half hour, so if something happened..."

"I heard a scream. Three or four minutes ago. You hear anything?"

"A scream? I don't think so."

"No one called anything in to you?"

"No. Where was it? Inside the complex?"

Jarsdel frowned. "I don't know. It was loud. I guess it might've come from off the property."

Bachelor took a clipboard off his desk and made some notes. "This is an incident report. You guys probably use the same kinda thing."

"I'm familiar."

"And you say you heard this scream when?"

Jarsdel shook his head. "Forget it."

On his way back to the apartment, he became aware of a growing chorus of sirens. Turning the corner onto Maryland, he saw the lurid red and blue lights of emergency vehicles. They splashed the sidewalk and danced on the buildings beyond the small pedestrian gate on the La Brea side. He debated going out there, but whatever it was, there were already plenty of officers on scene. If they wanted to know what little he had to tell them, they'd canvass his block.

Before he went back in, he noticed that despite all the police activity, still no one had ventured out to see what was going on. That the arrival of the Creeper had diminished daily niceties had been something Jarsdel was learning to live with, but this was something new entirely. Now his fellow Angelenos didn't even seem to enjoy the relative pleasure of gawking at each other's misfortunes.

3

Another tremor—not as powerful as the last one, but still formidable—jolted the city awake just before sunrise. This time, some claimed the sound of the quake closely resembled the word *over*. Or perhaps it was *older*. What did it mean? It was perfectly vague, and invited dedicated speculation. Whatever it was, it certainly couldn't be good.

Appearing that morning on *Good Day LA*, UCLA psychology professor Lorimer Todd tried to rein in such superstitions, assuring the audience that the attribution of speech to the earthquake was the result of a cognitive illusion. "It's audio pareidolia. We tend to seek out patterns in random fields of data. We do it with our eyes when we look at clouds or tree bark, and we do it with our ears when we play Black Sabbath records in reverse."

Jarsdel didn't care if the earthquake recited all five stanzas of "Ode on a Grecian Urn." He guarded his sleep jealously, and to have it snatched away so rudely had soured his morning. He was even less enthusiastic than before—if that were possible—to meet with the LAPD's lauded consultant.

Dr. Alisha Varma had set up her makeshift office in a small, mostly unused conference room. The place smelled like old coffee, and Varma had put out several small beeswax votives to combat the odor, giving the overall impression of a low-rent spa. She'd also had a bookshelf installed, which already bulged with manuals, textbooks, and federal, state, and county legal codes. The walls were bare—no degrees, maps, or calendars—save for one piece hanging to the left of the desk: a print of a bleak Renaissance masterwork.

The painting depicted three men, bloated, their expressions stupefied, who lay sprawled on a patch of barren earth beneath a bent and leafless tree. There was food all around—a wheel of cheese, pastries, savory pies—and stranger offerings as well. A soft-boiled egg ran on squat, fleshy legs, a spoon jutting from its open shell. A roast pig, carving knife already slipped into its flank, meandered near a bush made from loaves of bread. Meanwhile a half-dressed knight squatted under a lean-to, his mouth open wide; in the distance, a figure clutching a wooden spoon crawled out from a mass of what looked like dough or pudding.

Jarsdel thought the piece a little strange to be hanging in the office of a department employee and supposed it was part of some one-size-fits-all strategy Varma used to psychoanalyze her visitors. She hadn't arrived yet, which was suspect in itself, and Jarsdel would be amazed if she didn't lead off by asking what he thought of the painting. "Sorry, I'm late," she'd say. Then, indicating the painting, "Weird, huh? Some people say it reminds them of their dreams. Does it resonate at all?"

On the desk in front of him was a perfectly square, leather-bound volume. It wasn't a book, though. Instead of pages, there were plastic sheets, hundreds of them—each a different color. Out of curiosity, he picked it up and began thumbing through them. They seemed to be samples of some kind, each one having its own name. Equator Dawn, Picasso Blue, Seasick Green. They reminded him of the names for different hues of paint you'd find at the hardware store, though none of those would've been called Seasick Green or Bastard Red.

"Sorry, had to use the restroom." Varma crossed the room briskly on her lean, shapely legs. "Really should've scheduled these in twenty-five minute chunks instead of half hours. Live and learn."

"Not at all," said Jarsdel, beginning to stand.

"Oh, no need to get up." Varma gently touched his shoulder and the two shook hands. Instead of going behind her desk, she rolled her chair around to his side. She pulled up close, their knees almost touching.

"Like those gels?"

"Sorry?"

"What you're holding," said Varma. "Color's a magical thing. It affects our moods, our emotions, even our actions."

Here we go, thought Jarsdel. He set the sample book back on her desk. "Uh-huh."

"Part of my job is in R&D, and I spend a lot of time with color. Work with lighting designers to find out which hues are most offensive to the human eye."

"Why is that good?" asked Jarsdel.

"You'll see. Presentation's next week. Hope you can make it. Anyway, you're Detective Jarsdel. Am I pronouncing that right?"

"Yes."

"What's the derivation of that, if you don't mind my asking?"

"It's English. Almost extinct, actually. I think my dad and I are the only Jarsdels outside the UK. And they've only got a handful over there."

Varma smiled, revealing a slight overbite. "How interesting. An endangered surname. I don't think such a thing ever occurred to me." She cocked her head. "You know, you look familiar."

"I was at your presentation."

"No, from something else. Maybe you look like an actor or something?"

This had happened to Jarsdel before. "I was on a case not too long back. It got some publicity. Possible you came across my picture somewhere."

Varma studied him. "Did someone do a book on that? The murders?"

"Two, far as I know. Might be others by now. Had all the right ingredients. Pathos, torture, insanity, theatrics. And nonsexual serial homicide is rare, so when it comes along, people eat it up."

"Oh." Realization dawned. "*Oh*. Right. I think I know the one you mean." She looked at him with renewed interest. "The, um, that insane Hollywood guy. You were the one who caught him. So you're kind of famous now, right?"

"Not even a little," said Jarsdel.

"Even compared with your peers?"

Jarsdel shrugged. "I guess. Doesn't do me any good at work."

"Still." She leaned forward. "You're probably good publicity for the department. Someone people can get behind. I mean, how many lives did you save in just that one case, I wonder?"

"No way to say."

Varma pursed her lips in thought. The two sat in silence a moment.

"Well," she said eventually. "I want to start off by thanking you for coming in. I assure you my presence here isn't in any way a reflection on the work done by you and your fellow detectives. I also imagine this whole thing probably strikes you as a bit unusual."

"Isn't it?"

Varma's smile broadened. "Not as much as you might think. It's true that folks like me usually work more behind the scenes, and the changes we suggest are implemented with more discretion. But every technology—whether physical or social—requires a design, and virtually every design can be improved. I'm here to make some adjustments, and the kind I'm planning require the participation of everyone in this division." She paused, evaluating him. "You're skeptical."

"No."

"It's okay. You're not gonna hurt my feelings."

Jarsdel considered. "I'm curious, mostly. I know enough about bureaucracies to question their motives. They rarely do anything for the right reasons, and this feels more like a cover-your-ass maneuver in case the city keeps going to hell."

To his surprise, Varma laughed. "I agree completely. It's definitely a case of CYA. But just because they do things for your so-called 'wrong reasons' doesn't mean the goal itself isn't worthy. A whopping fine might be the only reason a power plant doesn't dump its waste in some pristine river, but the result would be the same if the executives were dedicated environmentalists: the river stays clean."

"Fair point. What do you need from me?"

Varma raised her palms in a gesture of magnanimity. "Anything you like. Anything you want to tell me. What you think about the force, for example. How it's commanded, how it can be improved. Totally between us. Or perhaps what could be done proactively on the street. Hollywood Area is, in a very real sense, a laboratory. We're going to try things that haven't been tried, and see how they work. I've been given pretty wide latitude."

Now it was Jarsdel's turn to smile. "How the force is commanded and how it can be improved? I see. And am I protected by doctor-patient privilege?"

"No. I'm not your therapist and you're not my patient, so I'm not legally bound to keep our conversations confidential."

Jarsdel was about to protest, but Varma cut back in. "But c'mon, how long would I be in business if employees of the organizations I consult for didn't trust me? I give you my *word*, if I need to communicate anything you've shared in this or any other meeting, your name absolutely will not be used. I'll also make sure nothing you've told me is traceable back to you. No obvious details that would mark you out in some way."

"That implies," said Jarsdel, "your judgment is refined enough to discern which details would mark me out."

"My judgment is excellent."

"Really?"

"You don't have to take my word for it. For what it's worth, I'm a member of the Prometheus Society."

"Oh." Jarsdel nodded. "I guess that's pretty impressive."

"Haven't heard of us?"

"I..."

"Don't feel bad. We've only got about a hundred members. You know Mensa, I presume? The hi-IQ society?"

"Sure. Actually, my uh..." Jarsdel cleared his throat. "Ex-fiancée was a member. She even put it on her business card."

"Understandable. Lots of folks do. Puts you in the top 2 percent of the human population, intelligence-wise. That's about one out of every fifty people. The Prometheus Society only admits members at the 0.003 percent mark, or about one in thirty thousand."

Jarsdel was glad he hadn't shared how he actually felt about people who advertised their IQs. "Okay," he said. "But can you really equate judgment with intelligence?"

Varma smiled but didn't answer the question. "Let's start off easy. How safe do you feel? While you do your job, I mean. What's your sense of the vibe out there?"

"You should talk to patrol."

"I will. But right now I'm talking to you."

Jarsdel shrugged. "I'm a homicide detective. The vibe is generally not good."

"How do you mean?"

"Well, I guess I mean by the time my partner and I show up, the damage is done. I don't get to do a whole lot of conflict resolution."

"Okay. So you—"

"Not much schmoozing in general with the living public. We don't visit grade schools, hand out police badge stickers to the kids." Jarsdel didn't know why, but he felt himself growing angry.

"Is that what you think might be missing? More community outreach?"

"That's..." Jarsdel sighed and shook his head. "That's not even my point. Forget it."

"I don't want to forget it. Please, go back and see if you can develop that idea some more."

Jarsdel looked at Dr. Varma, matching her curious, clinical gaze with as much dead-eyed disinterest as he could muster. "What exactly is your role here? Are you my superior now? If I decide not to cooperate, what's the consequence?"

"You don't wish to cooperate?"

"Don't do that. If you want anything from the people at this station, you're going to have to answer questions directly. You don't have to be in the Prometheus Society to spot Psych 101 from a mile away."

Again, Varma laughed. "Touché. Then I'll do my best to be direct. No, I'm not your superior, and I'm not sure what the consequences are. I've been asked to inform command who met with me and who didn't, but what they do with that is up to them. Fair?"

"Fair as can be, I suppose."

"Good. Then see if you really can try to answer my question. How safe do you feel?"

Jarsdel thought of the bodies, broken, savaged. He thought of the funerals. He'd been at each of them, heard the most desperate, soul-rending cries a human being could produce, seen enough shock and misery and hopeless, bottomless grief to last a hundred lifetimes. The names too. He'd read them so often they might as well have been seared onto his brain. Sometimes he recited them before he fell asleep: Lauterbach, Rustad, Santiago, Verheugen.

There were others, too, those he'd come to think of as the Creeper's secondhand victims. The first, only sixteen years old, was spotted sneaking out of his girlfriend's house after her parents had come home unexpectedly. A vigilante, thinking he was witnessing the Creeper fleeing his latest crime scene, beat the boy into a coma. In another case, a middle-aged man with fragile X syndrome had wandered from his group home and into the wrong backyard. His trespass earned him a hollow-point round to the chest. A third, not so innocent, had been trying to steal a flat-screen from an apartment. He'd been chased by a mob of tenants and thrown down a flight of concrete stairs. And those were obvious cases. In a city this size, there were sure to be more.

But above all, Jarsdel thought of the mundane moments he'd

exchanged with his fellow Angelenos over the last year, and how telling they'd been. All the things that hadn't been there before—dark half-moons under the eyes of cashiers and baristas and parking-lot attendants, how a hand trembled from exhaustion as it poured a drink, the suspicious flick of a stranger's eyes if he passed too close on the sidewalk. Smiles, once freely given, were thinner, stiffer, or absent altogether. Park in an unfamiliar neighborhood and you could guarantee someone would copy down your license plate.

"It's under strain," said Jarsdel.

"Strain?"

"Like everyone's waiting for something to happen. So to answer your question, no, it doesn't feel safe. It's like...it's like a coiled spring."

"Say more about that," said Varma, scribbling on a legal pad.

"Psych 101 again."

"Sorry."

"I guess, you know, the best way to put it is we're tired, we're all tired. It's been going on too long."

"What's been going on too long?"

"The Creeper."

"Okay."

"It's like we're all kids again, and there's a boogeyman in the closet."

Varma nodded, her pen flicking across the page.

"Terror," said Jarsdel, "is exhausting. It's a war of attrition, and what's being attrited is an overall feeling of relatedness, of connectedness. We're all alone now, in a way. The boogeyman separates us."

"Separates you how?"

"Saps our trust, our compassion."

Varma looked up from her notes. "Is that something you can really quantify?"

"Crimes against persons has more than doubled in the past year. Little things—fighting over a parking spot, noise complaints, a dog shitting on someone's lawn—that extra ingredient you need to push it over into something physical, it's already there. Everything's got some nitro on it these days."

Varma put down her pen and legal pad. "If you could make a single change, what would it be?"

"What do you mean? Change what?"

"Change anything. Within reason, of course. Something you could implement given adequate resources."

Jarsdel considered the question carefully. It was pie in the sky, of course, but no one had ever asked him that before. What—if given the power—would he change?

"My parents had this book when I was a kid," he said. "It was bound in black velvet. Title was silvery white—just jumped out at you when you picked it up, and maybe that's why it's the first thing I ever remember reading. It was called *We Who Bump in the Night*. And below that it said, 'No matter where you lay your head, there's always something under the bed!' Each two-page layout was a profile of a boogeyman from a different culture, accompanied by a piece of original art.

"I'm not sure if this book was, you know, deliberately, thoughtfully engineered to terrify children, but that's the effect it had on me. Each profile was written in first-person, from the point of view of the monster. Even the title—*We Who Bump in the Night*... I don't even know how to describe it to you, but from my perspective as a little boy, a young kid, I thought that somehow this book was actually written by these creatures. That made it so much more frightening to me, for some reason."

He paused, collecting his thoughts. Varma let him take his time. Jarsdel was glad she didn't ask him to get to the point. He wasn't even sure yet what that point was going to be.

"Funny thing was," he continued, "as scared as this book made me, I'd read it over and over again. Sometimes between little gaps in my fingers, just letting bits of images and words in at a time. Anyway, they'd tell you their names, where they lived—what country, I mean—and what they'd do to you if they got hold of you. They seemed to take such delight in all the suffering they caused, and all the fear they'd work up inside you while they were doing it. Mètminwi was the worst, for me anyway. The Haitian boogeyman. It doesn't sound like a scary name, but then he tells you what it translates to in English: the 'Master of Midnight.' He's tall as a house, with glowing yellow eyes, and he lurks the streets and slips between houses, snatching anyone who's out late."

"What's he do with them?" said Varma.

"Sometimes he eats you, other times he takes you away someplace and you're never seen again. I used to tape my blinds to the walls at night so not even the tiniest bit of window glass would be left uncovered. He was tall, and he'd be able to see me in there while I slept, right through my second-story window. I couldn't take a chance he'd change his routine—or as I'd say now, his MO, right? Because maybe a night would come when he hadn't caught anyone outside, and he'd be frustrated, and hungry, and thought he'd bend his rules a little. All he'd have to do is break my window, reach in with one of those long, spidery arms of his, and that'd be it."

Jarsdel noticed his heart was beating faster, and marveled at a fear so powerful it could stalk the adult the child had become. Then he noticed Varma sneak a glance at her watch, and that shook him from his reverie.

"I don't know what I'm getting at," he said.

Varma offered a reassuring smile. "You don't have to."

"Right. I know you've got someone else coming in a couple minutes."

"I do, but I think this has been helpful."

Jarsdel stood, barely able to resist giving the kind of disdainful grunt his partner was so fond of. "All right. Good meeting you." He was almost out the door when Varma spoke.

"You didn't answer my question."

Jarsdel turned to face her. "Which?"

"If you could do anything, make any realistic change, what would it be?"

This time Jarsdel didn't need to think. The answer came quickly and easily. "I'd make it harder for him to hide during the day."

4

Less than an hour after Ben Bauman was declared brain dead, detectives were on their way to arrest Ted Degraffenreid for second-degree murder. He was out on half-a-million-dollars' bail for the initial assault, but the toxic publicity had gotten him fired and he now spent his days tinkering in the garage of his Hancock Park home.

He'd been expecting the knock on his door for a week, ever since Bauman's parents had announced they were planning on taking their son off life support. Now that it had finally come, Degraffenreid was ready.

"Door's open—c'mon in."

Two detectives and two officers entered Degraffenreid's house to find him in the kitchen, pouring something from a two-gallon plastic container into a large stockpot. "Just doing a little cooking," he said, as a pale gas began rising from the pot. Degraffenreid suddenly collapsed, striking his head on the kitchen counter as he fell. The container he'd been cradling slammed onto the tile next to him, spraying liquid everywhere.

"Ah shit, what'd he do?" one of the cops asked. He hurried forward and knelt by the man's side, checking the pulse on his carotid. "It's weak, I think..." The cop shot to his feet, clawing at his right pant leg, which was now soaked through with whatever Degraffenreid had been pouring. "Whoa! Whoa—shit! My leg!" His eyes bulged in pain, then, without warning, rolled back to the whites as he too collapsed to the floor.

"Mike!" His partner, Emilia Torres, made a move toward him but one of the detectives held her back.

"Out! Everybody out! It's gas!"

The three stumbled outside, Torres yelling into her shoulder mic. "Officer down! Need backup and hazmat now! It's gas. Oh God." Questions came shooting back through her radio from dispatch, but Torres didn't answer. She braced herself against the door jamb as a thick rope of drool came spilling from her mouth. She clutched her stomach. "I'm not well. Not very well." The crotch of her uniform darkened with urine.

The detectives, as if responding to a prearranged cue, dropped in unison and began to convulse, their heels tapping a frantic tattoo on the flagstone path.

"What?" Torres raised her head, brow furrowed in confusion. "Oh. Yeah. Not too well. Not too well at all."

The entire block had to be evacuated, and it took hazmat until sundown before residents were allowed back into their homes. Degraffenreid had filled the stockpot with nearly two pounds of potassium cyanide crystals—more than three thousand times the lethal dose, but harmless unless ingested or, as Degraffenreid had done, mixed with sulfuric acid. The result was a cloud of hydrogen cyanide gas, the same stuff the state had once used to carry out executions in its death chamber. The engineer and erstwhile vigilante had even made sure the temperature inside his house was above eighty degrees, so the gas wouldn't condense. Cleanup teams had to fumigate the site with anhydrous ammonia to neutralize the poison. Even a stray pocket of gas hiding in a closet or between the slats of a bookshelf was enough to maim someone for life.

Torres and the two detectives were all expected to make partial recoveries, but their careers were over. All had suffered brain damage and were expected to develop seizure disorders. Torres was the worst off of the survivors, requiring a tracheostomy and gastric feeding tube.

Mike Bradford, the patrol officer who'd rushed to save Degraffenreid, was pronounced dead on arrival at Cedars-Sinai. Both the chief of police and the mayor spoke at his funeral, praising the fallen officer's selfless bravery and urging the city to unite in peace and brotherhood. After the service, dispatch issued Bradford's end-of-watch call.

"7-Adam-5." Every police radio in the city fell silent a moment, as if waiting for the dead man to respond. Then dispatch spoke again. "No answer 7-Adam-5. 7-Adam-5 out of service. Officer Michael Bradford, you are end of watch. Gone but not forgotten."

That night, the Creeper struck for the fifth time.

5

There'd been four in the Galka family. Benjamin and Margot, in their late forties, and their two sons—Bowie, nineteen, and Zephyr, seventeen. Together they'd made up the Galka Players, a bluegrass band that had performed at the LA County Fair only a week before.

Their house was in Topanga Canyon, a sparsely inhabited range of the Santa Monica Mountains, with Malibu on one side and the San Fernando Valley on the other. Those who made the canyon their home liked the solitude, liked the clear, cool nights in a place you could actually see the stars.

The Galka house was far back from the twisting boulevard, high up in the woods. The trees and dense brush separating their property from their closest neighbors on Nuez Way gave the impression they lived in some remote corner of Old California. You could easily imagine running into a gold prospector or a band of Tongva Indians. It was a perfect place for musicians, who could play as often and as loudly as they wanted without getting any noise complaints. It was also why no one had heard their screams.

The Creeper hadn't had any trouble getting in—didn't even need to carve one of his signature holes into the roof or crawl space. His method of entry was likely the doggie door belonging to Banjo, the Galkas' husky. Most adults wouldn't have been able to squeeze through; even otherwise skinny men would've been blocked by their own shoulders and hips. But for the Creeper, the front door may as well have been wide open.

Jarsdel struggled to get to work that morning. He'd had trouble falling asleep the night before, which in turn made him anxious he wasn't getting enough rest, which naturally made it even harder to doze. The cycle continued until his body succumbed to pure exhaustion, casting him into a troubled corner of his subconscious, where his dreams were strange and full of dread, and he always sensed the presence of something just out of sight, watching, pursuing him.

When Jarsdel arrived at Hollywood Station and found himself confronted with the news of another Creeper slaying, he simply didn't have enough strength left to remain professionally aloof. A profound helplessness pressed in on him. He'd joined the police just to avoid that sort of feeling. No longer would he be a spectator, a passive academic who did little but complain. No, he'd be a vigorous participant in the evolution of human consciousness.

If ever there were a case to prove his worth, it was the Creeper. Appalling sadism, unimaginable suffering. And it had been within his reach—his to solve, and now it was gone.

After three hours of unproductive desk work, he decided on an early lunch. He might be hungry again by the afternoon, but if he ate now he'd probably have the break room to himself. That decided him. He retrieved his food from beneath his desk and made his way down the station's main hallway.

His lunch was uninspired—a few disks of cold falafel—but he had one of his Arnold Palmers to look forward to. He'd gotten into them recently, making his own black tea and lemonade at home, then mixing them in a thermos with plenty of ice. Not too sweet—just a kiss on top of the tea. He found the potion calmed him.

Once inside the break room, he brought out his copy of *Matter over Mind.* The chapter he was currently slogging through was titled

"Contemporary Themes in Security Ethics." But at least he was alone, and at least it was quiet.

It lasted perhaps ten minutes.

Haarmann arrived first, but he was quickly joined by three other officers—all patrol, all rock-jawed and buzz-cut. As they entered, they each gave Jarsdel the classic "SWAT nod," a single jut of the chin that managed at once to both acknowledge and dismiss. Jarsdel didn't return the greeting. He went back to his book, found the spot where he'd left off, and continued reading.

Ours is really the first generation to concern itself with the rights of the trespasser. It has long been an accepted truth—worldwide and across every civilized culture—that an interloper gambles his life when he breaches a restricted area.

"Hey, check it," someone said.

Reflexively, Jarsdel looked up. Haarmann had his phone out, holding it so his buddies could see. The screen wasn't visible to Jarsdel, but as Haarmann swiped through the images, the men hooted in approval.

"What's her name?"

"She's—"

"That's an *ass*."

"Madison. My new badge bunny."

"Trampolicious."

Jarsdel tried tuning them out. He'd almost succeeded when two of the men took their spots at the arm-wrestling table, clamped their hands together, and began.

"Pull! Pull!"

"Go, go, go!"

"You tired already? Oh man, don't quit on me, baby. Whoo! That's it...*that's* it!"

Jarsdel glanced up, enraged, then tried to find his place again in his reading.

...rights of the trespasser. It's long been an accepted truth—But he'd read that already, hadn't he? He skimmed ahead.

While the decision in Hynes v. New York Central Railroad *(1921) did not expressly mandate duty of care for trespassers, it did set precedent in expanding the responsibilities of landowners beyond immediate property lines.*

"Check it out, he's got long arms. Look at him go. Long arms generate more torque."

There was a terrific groan. It was answered by another, equally passionate. These were both followed by a volcanic grunt as the match ended.

"Whoo! Holy shit, Will—you see that?"

"It's grip strength, that's what I'm telling you guys. Spend as much time's you want on your vanity muscles, but in the end it's all about grip strength."

"You use the Gripmaster?"

"—Captains of Crush, he uses—"

"Oh yeah, for real? How you know you're makin' progress?"

"Got a dynamometer. Rated for two hundred pounds, and I got the fucker maxed out. Figures that puts me ahead of just about anybody."

"Shit, that's—"

"Excuse me." Jarsdel spoke with his teacher voice, the same one he'd used with college freshman, the same one he used while testifying. It got their attention; all four looked over at him. "Yes, thanks. That's actually extremely loud, and it makes it difficult to enjoy my break time. Would you gentlemen consider maybe finding another place to put that thing?"

Haarmann stared at him in confusion. "Wait, what?"

"I'm asking if you guys wouldn't mind taking the table somewhere else. It'd be nice having the break room back."

Haarmann's expression became one of curious amusement, as if he were watching a child playacting at being an adult, but ultimately missing the mark. "Look, Dad, the LT said it was cool, so—"

"Detective Jarsdel."

"Huh?"

"My name. It isn't Dad. It's Detective Jarsdel, *officer*."

"Oh, right. Detective. I'm sorry, tell me again how many years you been LAPD?"

"Okay," said Jarsdel. "All you had to say was no, if that's the way it's gonna be. I was only trying to be polite and see if we could work something out."

"Tell you what—why don't we wrestle for it?"

"Pardon?"

"Have a seat. You beat me and we'll find another room. You lose and we stay. Seems fair."

Jarsdel regarded him as coolly as he could manage. It wasn't easy. Everything about Haarmann—the small, deep-set eyes; his upturned, vaguely porcine nose; the twisted little mouth; even the way he stood, with his elbows turned out to maximize the outline of his biceps—it all rankled Jarsdel, at once smothered and repulsed him.

Eventually he found his voice. "Sorry, but you're suggesting we engage in a physical contest to determine primacy of the break room—is that accurate?"

"Easiest way to work it out."

"Wow. You're not *even* wrong."

"What's the—"

"Not even wrong. Your premise—that there's anything to work out—is false. This is a shared break room, and *this*"—Jarsdel stabbed a finger at the arm-wrestling table—"effectively turns it into your personal clubhouse. And your answer to this non-premise, that we resolve the matter through what's essentially a trial by combat, is at best a fallacy of relevance—ignoratio elenchi, if we're being precise. So you're guilty of compounding idiocy with further idiocy."

"Careful, Dad. You—"

"*Which*—are you listening?—is actually pretty impressive."

Haarmann's buddies, who'd been watching the exchange with undisguised glee, now looked toward their chieftain to see how he'd respond. Haarmann took a step toward Jarsdel, paused, then took two more steps. He was now close enough for Jarsdel to feel his breath. Jarsdel didn't flinch. He returned the patrolman's beady stare with plenty of his own venom.

Haarmann cocked his head. "You're in the wrong world. You know that, right?"

"No. You're in the wrong room."

"There was a guy like you back when I worked Valley Bureau. Threw his weight around, got in my face." Haarmann turned to his friends. "I ever tell you about this guy?"

The men shook their heads, grinning.

"Weirdest thing. Someone beats the shit out of him one night, just fuckin' pops him. Duracell shampoo, full deal. It's like he's waiting for him, too. No cameras, no witnesses. S'fucked up. And the guy's not much of a cop—you know—mostly talk, and that's the night he finally gets it. He understands now. No street degree. You can't fake that, can't fake a street degree. You might have sunshine tumbling out your asshole far as those pointy heads at PAB are concerned, but you gotta ask yourself—how's that working out for you in the real world, right?"

Jarsdel reached up to touch the scar above his ear. Enough hair had grown over it to keep it covered, but he could easily feel it just beneath—a thick worm of tormented flesh stretching from the base of his skull all the way to his temple. It throbbed when his heart rate sped up—seeing a beautiful woman could be enough to set it off—and sometimes it laid him up in bed with eye-popping headaches.

Not long ago, Jarsdel would've been rattled enough by Haarmann's performance to begin issuing preemptive apologies, but since the night of the scar he'd gained new insights on fear. The man who'd given it to him had intended on killing him, and there was nothing quite like fighting for your life to put things in perspective. He thought of that night, of the battle, and of his own willingness—perhaps raw instinct was a better word—to kill if it meant he might live. At the memory, the man now before him seemed less important.

Jarsdel smiled. There was no artifice in it, no intent to throw Haarmann off-balance or engage in any further playground brinkmanship. He felt a surge of the purest gratitude at being alive, gratitude that the greatest threat in his life was this smirking patrol officer. But something in his expression must have given the other man pause.

Jarsdel stood, chewing the last of his falafel, and tossed the carton into the trash. "Sorry to hear about your colleague," he said, unscrewing the top of his thermos. "Policing's a dangerous job. They ever catch the guy who did it?"

Haarmann's swagger returned. "Gosh no, they never did. And you know it wasn't long after that he decided to cash in his chips. Ten years too early though, so forget about the pension. Bummer-ooni."

"Bummer-ooni," Jarsdel agreed, and upended his thermos over the arm-wrestling table.

The two officers who'd been seated sprang up from their chairs, cursing. Haarmann and the others watched as the amber liquid and ice cascaded down. Jarsdel poured the Arnold Palmer over one vinyl pin pad, then the other, then dumped the remainder on the custom logo centered between them. He let the thermos continue to drip, then gave it a little shake to splash a few more drops onto the table. Once the dripping slowed, Jarsdel replaced the cap on his thermos. He took his time, locking eyes with Haarmann. The muscles along the cop's jaw tightened and loosened, tightened and loosened. But he made no move toward him.

Jarsdel nodded at the patrolmen and ambled out of the break room.

6

We all had chores growing up," said Dr. Varma. "But my older brothers always thought they had it tougher than me. They were the ones who had to muck out the gutters or haul heavy boxes down from the attic. But I would've happily traded with them, because one of my duties was cleaning out the garden shed.

"I dreaded this job. Every time, no matter what, I'd always run into spiders. They were just part of the work, always there, always scattering when I'd lift a pot or move a box of trash bags. I didn't know if they were venomous, but that's not what really mattered. What bothered me was how they always came back and set up their little colonies in there."

The detective squad room was filled to capacity, which usually only happened during mandatory meetings called by Captain Sturdivant or the chief himself. Jarsdel noticed that several patrol officers who usually didn't work Wednesdays were also attending, in uniform, their faces stern and eager as they watched Varma's presentation. The Galka homicides, it seemed, had put everyone in the mood for answers.

"It occurred to me, eventually, why I kept running into those spiders. It wasn't because I moved stuff around that was the problem. It was because I didn't move stuff around nearly often *enough*.

There's only one word that matters when it comes to crime—to all kinds of crime, whether impulsive or premeditated—and that's *stagnation*." She let the word settle in a moment, then repeated it. "Stagnation. It's that simple.

"This isn't a new idea, not by any means. I'm sure you've heard those old sayings. 'Idle hands are the devil's playthings,' or 'He that is busy is tempted by but one devil; he that is idle, by a legion.' It's long been noted that humans are restless creatures and crave excitement. This excitement, the excitement that's borne of stagnation, is usually destructive. The purposelessness, the lack of drama and vigor, these all impel us toward overcompensating, grasping at bigger thrills."

Varma crossed to an easel. It bore a huge blowup of the underside of a human forearm. Thick blue veins pushed out against the pale flesh. A caged work light, currently turned off, was clamped to the top of the easel.

"I wonder," said Varma, "how much of the narcotics pumped into human bodies every year is done simply to stave off restlessness. Some species of sharks drown, you know, if they stop moving. This makes physical sense—they depend on ram ventilation, on the steady supply of oxygen moving over their gills—but is there more to it? Idleness is a kind of uselessness. And if the creature were experiencing total idleness, if there were truly nothing for it do, might it on some deep level perceive its own futility? Happy, fulfilled people don't, as a rule, commit crimes."

She reached behind the easel and flicked a switch. The light mounted above the photograph snapped on, bathing the photograph in a strange glow. There was something unpleasant about it, a kind of shimmer that irritated the eye.

Varma laughed. "I can see by some of your expressions that my light is already doing its job. And I'm guessing you're probably not too eager to rush out and buy one for your bathroom." She passed her hand in and out of the beam. As the light struck it, it appeared to move in alternating slow and jerky motions. Jarsdel looked down at his lap and rubbed his eyes.

"The human eye requires a very high rate of oscillation in order to perceive a constant flow of light. Anything less than a frequency of about 50 Hz—that's fifty cycles, or flickers per second—can induce headaches, eye strain, even nausea. A faint strobe effect is also noticeable, as you've probably discovered. But!"

Varma held up a finger, using it as a focal point for her audience's attention, then swept it in a slow, graceful arc toward the photograph of the forearm. "Notice anything?"

Jarsdel examined the picture. When he wasn't looking directly at the light, it was easier to do. Still, he didn't see anything of particular interest. A genderless forearm, a few ripples of sinew...

"No?" Varma searched the room, but no one offered an opinion. "Well, I suppose in a way that's the point. You don't see anything different because you don't know what to look for. But an intravenous drug user certainly would. Please look closely. Ready?" She turned off the light, and then it was obvious.

The veins, the network of sky-blue vessels beneath the skin, seemed to jump out from the picture. Hadn't they been there all along? Jarsdel remembered them when Varma had first presented the photograph, but something about the light must have washed out their color.

There was a murmur of excited conversation. Others had seen it, too.

"How about now?" Varma asked. Then, to drive her point home, she turned on the light again. The veins seemed to vanish. This time there were a few grunts of surprise, and the murmuring of the crowd grew louder. Smiling, Varma held up a hand, and the room quieted down.

"What you're witnessing is the power of a compound ultra-narrow spectrum organic light-emitting diode bulb. It's called PuraLux and represents a tremendous leap in area-denial technology. And because I still want us all to be friends, I'll go ahead and turn it off."

There was some scattered laughter, and Varma cut the power. The veins on the forearm popped out once again.

"Security need not be barbed-wire fences, snarling Dobermans, or an increased police presence. Rather, security can and should be integrated into all facets of civil engineering. The shape, texture, and visibility of the physical environment itself should address safety concerns and play an active role in discouraging crime. You probably heard of CPTED, or crime prevention through environmental design. This is the next step—a deterrence that's practically invisible. People won't know why, but they just won't much enjoy hanging out in areas covered by these lights. IV drug users won't be able to find their veins, so they'll go elsewhere. We also examined findings from European studies concerning the unique properties of pink wavelengths, so we've blended those in as well. Imagine the least flattering fluorescent lighting in an airport bathroom, and multiply that by ten. That's the effect pink lighting has, and it's been demonstrated to disperse teenagers before they decide to congregate."

A hand poked up a few rows ahead of Jarsdel. Varma nodded at the questioner.

"Uh, yes. What about the effects of this light on the drivers of passing cars?"

"That's an excellent question," said Varma. "Tests have indicated there's no measurable effect whatsoever on the performance of a driver who might glimpse the light. Besides, we're not recommending the deployment of PuraLux for street lamps or anything that would potentially interfere with the operation of heavy equipment. Instead, I'd like you to think about public parks at night. I'd like you to think about the service entrances of hotels, apartment buildings, restaurants. I'd like you to think about the kind of good a light like this could do in conjunction with a broader area-denial strategy. You see it's not simply about preventing crime. It's about preventing the opportunity to commit the crime. Even deeper, really—it's about stopping crime even before the potential criminal considers the unlawful act."

Varma put her hands together as if in prayer and regarded her audience with renewed gravity.

"This is the potential we have here. By judiciously employing research-based techniques of socio-civic engineering, we can actually change thought. The impulse toward crime is dampened, even in the habitual criminal, if the opportunity to commit the act is absent. And I'll take it further. *Neuroplasticity*. The proven concept that the physical shape of the brain changes in response to the formation of neural pathways—and likewise to the disuse or dormancy of existing new neural pathways. In other words, you change the thought—and you change it often enough—and you change the brain. Change the brain... Well, you've just changed the world."

7

In the gunmetal gray of morning, as Los Angeles struggled from its torpor, employees of the Bureau of Street Lighting—a branch of the Department of Public Works—fanned out across the Southland. They gave particular attention to public parks—MacArthur, Griffith, Elysian, Lake Hollywood. They changed out the bulbs inside all restrooms maintained by the city and, because PuraLux was rated for outdoor as well as indoor use, replaced exterior lights as well.

That done, they turned their attention to freeway underpasses. These areas were poorly lit—if they were lit at all—and provided shelter for the homeless. Some became accustomed to the lull of cars humming across the concrete overhead, to the thrum of the earth beneath them. They snored as the Public Works personnel stepped between their sleeping bags and army surplus blankets and piles of castaway T-shirts, and began changing out the bulbs. A couple turns, and the PuraLux glow washed across the slumbering bodies. A few winced and turned over. Others woke, irritated, and watched in confusion as the workers finished screwing on the protective housing over the new bulbs.

Once this was done—and with the aid of computerized maps—the workers began replacing all exterior lighting on downtown city property. The process would likely take weeks, but Dr. Varma had triaged the locations in order of importance. The Stanley Mosk Courthouse, the Men's Central Jail, and Skid Row were first.

Though the operation was carried out in the wan light of early morning, both the *Los Angeles Times* and the *LA Weekly* got wind of the proceedings. Reporters from both papers intercepted city workers as they traded burned-out old fluorescents for the certified ten-year PuraLux bulbs. None gave comment, but that didn't dissuade reporters. If anything, the cold reception piqued their curiosity, and it wasn't long before television news outlets like KCAL 9 and KTLA joined their peers. Cameras zeroed in on the Public Works personnel. The men were at turns shy and annoyed. They were just replacing old bulbs, and weren't interested in becoming part of any controversy.

Roberto Contreras was no different than any other city employee at the supervisory level. He did his job, ground away at the years with dogged resolution, and looked forward to a pension that drew closer by the hour. But he got caught, on camera, gesturing to a grimy, darkened fixture outside the LA Public Library Something about that gesture, and the bland, thin-lipped expression on his face, inspired outrage. What was he up to? Whom did he really represent? And what was this sudden impulse to repair derelict lighting in Los Angeles? Surely anyone who could manage such a business-as-usual affect didn't have the public good on his mind.

Contreras became the face of the city's dark scheme, whatever it might be, and his picture soon appeared beside bold headlines and outraged opinion pieces. His identity was leaked, and he had to change his phone number. But that only made him more attractive game. Late one night someone threw a brick through the living room window of his Alhambra home, and the following day his twenty-year-old son was run off the road. The infamous picture of Contreras with his hand raised toward the light fixture was photoshopped—an SS uniform pasted over his coveralls—and distributed throughout his neighborhood.

The Bureau of Street Lighting offered Contreras an early retirement package. He accepted.

Still, during all of this, old bulbs were taken down, new ones put in their place. The light spilling out from the PuraLux bulbs was terrifically bright and harsh. It also made a large percentage of those who stood in its beam feel headachy, nauseous, or just generally uneasy. Those who worked in buildings near PuraLux fixtures complained of an increase in both the frequency and intensity of nightmares.

8

From *Matter over Mind,* Chapter 7: Consequences of Poor Enforcement

The most widely overlooked characteristic of crime, of wrongdoing, is its seductiveness. When an illegal act is committed, two powerful ideas are communicated. The first is that such an act is possible. This may seem an obvious point, one so obvious it isn't worth mentioning; upon closer scrutiny, however, we see that without the successful commission of a crime, it remains abstract—in the realm of theory. It isn't until a crime is carried out in the physical world that it is given life, that it is translated from conception to execution.

Here it may be helpful to draw a parallel to the work of Oxford scholar J. L. Austin, specifically in regard to his groundbreaking speech act theory. Austin posits that speech can broadly be categorized as performative and nonperformative. In other words, does the speech change the world in some meaningful way, or is it simply air? (True, phatic communication—what we might call small talk—serves a social purpose, but it doesn't transform one established fact into another.)

Professor Michael Drout gives a simplified explanation of the difference between performative and nonperformative speech. If, during a baseball game, a fan in the stands shouts that a player is out, that speech is nonperformative. The fan may proclaim his opinion as forcefully as he likes, but he lacks the required authority for his words to have an effect. On the other hand, the exact same words may be spoken by the umpire, and the world is then changed. The scoreboard immediately reflects this change, and a set of benefits and consequences are set into motion. This type of speech is indisputably performative.

I reference Austin's idea of performative speech because a similar conceptual model is effective in mapping the impact and transmission of criminal behavior. Once a new crime is committed, not only is a heretofore untested means of profiting from lawlessness revealed to be effective, but even the most average of criminals are able to devise dozens of fresh variations. A crime is an effective, if perverse, performative act. It indeed changes one established fact into another, but it's also seemingly capable of self-perpetuation, spreading from community to community, even country to country—an infection of ideas. The true magnitude of a crime's repercussions is therefore impossible to determine, since its influence is expended temporally and has no definite end.

It could be said that there's no upper limit to the damage a single crime may cause. If we may borrow the parable of Cain and Abel for the purposes of a thought experiment, we can argue that Cain pioneered the concept of murder—that but for him it would not have existed. Murder, then, was in a sense "invented" and passed along as a viable method of resolving conflict. We can extrapolate that there must also have been a first theft, a first embezzlement, a first sexual assault, a first mugging, a first confidence game, and so on.

The second message communicated through the commission of a crime is subtler, and more difficult—if not impossible—to properly quantify. It can probably best be equated with the bandwagon heuristic, which is easily summed up in the rhetorical question, "Everyone else is doing it, so why can't we?" In other words, a successful criminal act reveals a flaw or deficit in human processes that invites exploitation and, depending on the ease with which it's perpetrated, may entice otherwise ambivalent and even upstanding citizens into breaking the law.

Let's say, for example, a city imposes a toll on a roadway, but to save costs decides against installing a collection booth or employing a toll agent. Instead, motorists are asked to deposit twenty-five cents in a pail every time they use the road. Signs are posted advising that avoidance of the toll is a criminal offense. Lacking effective enforcement, however, this new statute is obviously doomed to failure. But what's truly insidious is the effect this ineffectual law is going to have on the populace.

From a social standpoint, an easily broken or unenforceable law is far, far worse than no law at all. Regular violation of a law diminishes the value of the entire legal system and encourages disregard and disrespect of society's moral fabric. Those who consider their law-abiding lifestyle a point of pride begin to feel foolish. Why, they reason, should they go through the trouble of obeying codes and ordinances if so many others do not? Why should they pay the twenty-five cent charge if there's no consequence for not doing so? Why should they have to carry the burden of public responsibility? Indeed, when you think of all those quarters stacking up, what's the purpose of being virtuous if those who transgress are "rewarded" with extra pocket change?

The seduction I spoke of before becomes almost irresistible. Soon the once proudly law-abiding citizen forgets her quarter, but promises to pay it the next time she comes through. She neglects to do so, then begins a cycle of justification. She minimizes the importance of a single quarter to the city, then two quarters, then three, and so on. When this strategy is exhausted, she changes to a sturdier one. She questions the true value of a law if the city doesn't bother enforcing it. The natural next step is to wonder what other laws might be circumvented or ignored. The final step is concluding that the following of *any* statute whatsoever is at the discretion of the individual. The rule of law is thus subverted, replaced with the ever-shifting standards of one's "personal code" or, worse, mobocracy.

Jarsdel had grown to like the way Varma presented her ideas. They were plain but unassailable—obelisks of intellectual rigor. In a way, the absence of any writerly filigree made the work all the more impressive. Her logic and hard factual data spoke for themselves.

He set the book down and took a bite of his lunch. He'd walked the few blocks from the station to I Panini di Ambra, a small café on Hollywood Boulevard that served good, simple cuisine. Morales had taken him there first, and he usually ran into someone he knew from work, but he never had to worry about Gavin. Word was the lieutenant hated Italian food, which made him a barbarian as well as a buffoon, but at least Jarsdel could count on the place as a sanctuary.

He was almost done with a toasted Valtellina sandwich—bresaola, arugula, olive oil, and a thick slice of Grana Padano cheese on rustic bread—when he caught a familiar silhouette in his peripheral vision.

It was Alisha Varma, waiting to pick up an order. Jarsdel felt a small thrill. A moment ago he'd been carried along on her ordered streams of rhetoric, and now here she was. Hard to miss, too, in a cream-colored business suit and matching shoulder bag, dark-brown high-heeled shoes, and painted lips. That cherry-red hue she'd worn previously. Jarsdel realized, amused, that she was clad in the precise colors, head to toe, of a Neapolitan dessert.

He saw she was fiddling with something in her purse, and he waited for her to look up and notice him. The expression on her face was serious, focused. Jarsdel finished the last of the panini and rose from his chair. "Dr. Varma?"

She glanced around, then spotted Jarsdel just as he approached. Her expression seemed startled, perhaps even worried, even though he thought he was giving her his most winning smile.

"Are you okay?" she asked.

It was an odd question. Maybe she'd forgotten who he was. "It's me, Detective Jarsdel, from Hollywood Station."

"Of course," said Varma. "I mean, what can I do for you?"

"One sec." Jarsdel went over to his table and returned with *Matter over Mind*. He tapped the cover. "I wanted to tell you, I really admire this. And this is going to sound odd perhaps, since I'm talking about a textbook on security—but I find it kind of beautiful."

Varma blinked. "Beautiful?"

"The purpose behind it, and the meticulous formulae you've devised for reducing human suffering."

"You've actually read it?" she asked, surprised.

"I did. Reviewing some of my favorite sections, in fact. I suppose I see it as a kind of blueprint for peaceful coexistence. Neutralizing crime by denying it nutrients, by denying it a place to take root."

"I'm glad you think so. Hope the city agrees."

"There's just one thing I had a question about, if you've got a sec."

"Sure. I mean, when my order comes up, I'll have to—"

"Real quick." Jarsdel sidled close to her and thumbed through the pages. She smelled good, but it wasn't cloying. A tropical smell. You had to get near to smell it—a lotion, maybe a shampoo.

"Here," said Jarsdel. "This section where you talk about Elk River Penitentiary. And how after implementing your suggestions about rearranging the common-room furniture and then adding several large, unbreakable mirrors, violent assaults dropped by an average of twenty-five percent."

"That's right," said Varma, with some pride.

"I don't get it, though. It's such a simple, easy thing to do. Inexpensive. You'd think other prisons would be interested in making those adjustments."

"You'd think, but as you can probably guess, bureaucracies aren't in much of a hurry to embrace change. Besides, what's the incentive to reduce violence in prisons? Some people might see that as going easy on crime, right?"

"But what about the guards? Keeps them safer, too."

Varma nodded. "Preaching to the choir."

"Twenty-five percent is huge," said Jarsdel. "Was that a monthly average? Or..."

"Yearly. The study looked at the previous year's numbers and compared them to after we put in my anti-affordances. It had to do, actually, with a reduction in the chances of being involved in a violent incident, and that did in fact come out to twenty-five percent. I know, it's not really clear from the text. I'm gonna have a look at that with my next edition."

"Right," said Jarsdel, closing the book. "Well, anyway. Very impressive work."

Varma's order came up. Two glistening, steaming slices of margherita pizza. She hardly gave them a glance. "You know, I've been wanting to tell you, something you said the other day really stuck with me."

"It did?"

"You were the one who came in and told me that story about that book you read, right? The one that scared you when you were younger?"

"*We Who Bump in the Night*."

"Yeah, that's the one. And on your way out you said that one way to fight evil is not to give it a place to hide during the day. That really spoke to me as a metaphor. Because it's easy for it to hide at night, in its own environment, but where does it go during the day? Where's it vulnerable? I started thinking about that, and about vampires in their crypts. Because they're not indestructible. They're powerful and frightening when they're in control, but there's also a situation where *they're* the ones who should be afraid. And their main weakness is that, like everything else, they have to rest. So you definitely reaffirmed some of my philosophies. And if—no, forget that defeatism. I'll say *when* my next project is revealed, you'll understand even more."

Jarsdel's attention kept wandering to her lips—so red—and how when they moved, they flashed glimpses of the most dazzlingly white teeth. "You got something else brewing?"

"Sure, but I'd really appreciate it if you didn't say anything to anyone. It's supposed to be under wraps until the big reveal next week."

"Bigger than PuraLux?"

"Different. But again, please don't—"

"Would you..." Jarsdel began, then cleared his throat. "I don't want your food to get cold. You're welcome to join me, and we can keep this conversation going. And if you have some free time afterward, maybe we could walk and talk."

The smile playing at the corners of her mouth sharpened, bringing a dimple to her cheek. "I'd like that. It's nice to finally talk to someone around here who gets what I'm trying to do. Kinda slammed today, though." She patted her purse. "Gotta go over my interview notes. Some other time maybe?"

"Sure," said Jarsdel. "Should I call you?"

"I'll get in touch."

"Cool. Well, it was good running into you."

He went back to his table and gathered up his trash, crumpling the wax paper into a tight little ball. Varma took a spot outside, and Jarsdel watched as she brought out a thick folder and began turning the pages. Everything she did had a refined elegance about it. Even the way she took a bite of her pizza, holding the slice far from her spotless lapels. She made some margin notes and brushed an errant lock of hair behind her ear.

As Jarsdel left the restaurant, Varma glanced up from her work and met his eyes. The look was brief, but it was enough to suggest that perhaps she would get in touch after all. He headed back to the station feeling better, lighter than he had since the Creeper had come to his city.

Jarsdel knocked on the lieutenant's door. The blinds were down—normally a signal he was in a meeting or on the phone, but he'd just poked his head out a few moments earlier and called across the squad room.

"Hey! Jarsdel! Come!" Then he'd swung the door shut.

No one liked being summoned to Bruce Gavin's office, where he could torment his subordinates privately and at leisure. His unique bouquet of hectoring, backhanded compliments, finger-pointing tirades, and ponderous philosophizing—made worse by his recent dabbling in the sciences—had come to acquire its own modifier. When one suffered under the lieutenant, one was "Bruce-alized," and Jarsdel's impending Bruce-alization earned him a roomful of sympathetic glances as he approached the office.

At Jarsdel's knock, Gavin's strident voice spoke up again. "Yup! Open!"

Jarsdel entered and, following a gesture from the lieutenant, sat in one of the chairs facing the desk. "Good to see you, sir."

"It is?" said Gavin. "You don't even know why asked you in here. Could be I'm giving you freeway therapy."

"What for?" Jarsdel tried not to give any sign of distress—that'd be blood in the water to Gavin. Freeway therapy was a tried and tested method for getting undesirables to quit the department. They'd be assigned to stations as far as possible from their listed home addresses, subjecting them to what could easily amount to a four-hour round-trip commute.

"I didn't say I *was*," said Gavin. There was a textbook on his desk—*Fundamentals of Organic Chemistry*. He appeared to notice a blemish on its cover, and rubbed at it with his thumbnail. "Got something to tell you, and it's one of those things you're either going to love or you're going to hate. Or you may not even care, I don't know."

Jarsdel nodded. Gavin had pretty much covered every possibility.

"How's your partner? Still got the flu?"

"Yes, sir," said Jarsdel. "Says he's a little better. Hopes to be back by Monday."

"Is he actually sick, or is this just so he can use up some personal days?"

"I was at his house a couple days ago. Looked pretty awful. He joked about it, but I think he really might have a touch of valley fever."

The lieutenant scoffed. "Whatever. Okay. Reason you're here—you know that team down at Homicide Special?"

"Team, sir?"

"The Creeper Task Force."

"I do, yes."

"It's run by a Detective III, Goodwin Rall. He in turn reports to Lieutenant Sponholz, who in turn reports to Captain Coryell of RHD."

"Okay," said Jarsdel. "Yes."

"Well. They've asked me to put either you or Morales on loan to work the case full time. I decided you should go."

The Creeper. You'll get a shot at him after all.

Jarsdel tried to conceal his excitement, lest Gavin change his mind. "Why me? Morales knows the Creeper just as well as I do, and he's got a lot more experience."

"We need him here. There're certain skills you just can't learn out of a book. Even a way of moving, moving physically I mean, that... that just *galvanizes* a suspect."

"Galvanizes. Right."

"He's an experienced detective—what do you want?"

"Are you sure we can't both go? He and I work pretty well together."

Gavin gave a squawk of laughter. "That so? News to me. Thought you'd both be grateful for some time apart. No, just you. Actually a pretty great opportunity, so I guess in a way I'm doing you a favor."

"When's the transfer go through?"

"It's not a transfer. You're on loan. And you're coming back when they kick your ass out or you bust the Creeper."

"Okay. When am I going?"

Gavin leaned back and regarded the portrait of Max Planck. Then he plucked one of several copies of *A Short History of Nearly*

Everything from a nearby shelf, glanced at Jarsdel, and put the book back. "Immediately," he said.

"Today?"

"Immediately. Well, technically tomorrow."

"And Morales knows about this?"

"He'll be told."

Jarsdel considered. "What about HH2?"

"It's not going anywhere. Not as long as I'm in charge."

This, Jarsdel knew, was as brazen a lie as could be. Not only had Gavin openly derided HH2 since its inception, but he'd tried to have it shut down at least once before.

"But the caseload. Morales and I are backed up as it is. Gonna be hard for him to make a lot of progress by himself."

Gavin gave a satisfied, humorless smile. "No one said he'd be by himself."

"I'm not sure what you mean."

"Got a pinch hitter for you."

"He's getting a new partner?"

"Uh-huh. Will Haarmann."

Jarsdel thought of the arm-wrestling table. Of the terrible grunts and groans, backslaps and whoops. "Haarmann's in patrol."

"Not anymore. Passed his detective's exam." Gavin waited, studying him, probably hoping for a reaction. Jarsdel was careful not to give him one. He picked his words carefully.

"I'm not complaining or questioning a command decision or anything, but doesn't that go against the established format of HH2? I mean, as outlined by Chief Comsky."

"Huh," said Gavin. "What do you mean exactly—*as outlined*?"

"Sorry?"

"You said, 'As outlined by Chief Comsky.' What does that mean?"

Jarsdel shifted in his seat. "I'm just referring to the format as I understand it. Experienced homicide detectives paired with, uh, qualified candidates."

"You say 'qualified.' That's an interesting word to use, don't you think? Do you know that Will Haarmann has been serving the Los Angeles Police Department three times as long as you? What does that say to you, qualifications-wise? Or did you think you were the only one smart enough around here to deserve a promotion?"

Jarsdel saw the conversation wasn't going anywhere good. "Sorry, sir. Guess I'd be lying if I said I didn't care if my job's waiting for me once this detail's over."

"Don't you understand *physics*?" Gavin's expression was of the kind of disgust reserved for the willfully stupid.

"Physics, Lieutenant?"

"Yeah. Goddamned physics. You know, that tiny force that runs the whole *universe*. Don't you understand it?"

"I'm not sure I do. Not in conjunction with this issue."

"This isn't just physics," said Gavin, "it's chemistry. So it's all related. Do you know what entropy is?"

"I'm not... I understand it's a tendency toward chaos."

"Ha—*no*. That's a huge misconception. Entropy is very simple. Very simple but also very misunderstood. It has to do with the distribution of energy. The universe prefers high entropy, did you know that?"

"No, I didn't."

"Well, it does. Greatest possible dispersion of energy. So basically if I have a light bulb hooked up to a power source—you follow me?—if I have this *light bulb*, then the power from that source goes to that bulb, right?"

"I—"

"But if I have, say, three bulbs hooked up to that same power source, what's gonna happen? Is the electricity gonna go to just one bulb and not the other two? No. No, it isn't gonna do that, right? It's gonna go to all three equally, but dispersed, de-energized. Each bulb will be lit, yes, but dimmer than just one would be. *That's* entropy."

Jarsdel's gaze wandered up to the photo of Planck. Their eyes met. In context, the scientist's hangdog expression seemed an attempt at commiseration. *Insufferable, isn't he? And you've only been here a couple minutes. Imagine what it's like for me. I have to listen to him all day.*

"You wondering who that is?" demanded Gavin.

Jarsdel's attention snapped back to the lieutenant. "No, sir."

Gavin was disappointed, Jarsdel could tell. One fewer lecture to inflict upon a captive audience. "Entropy," Gavin said, circling back around. "That's what Dr. Varma was talking about, you know. I was probably the only person in the room that got that. Your concerns about your job, your job waiting for you, that's ego—okay? And you're not thinking about entropy, because you don't understand physics. Hate to break it to you, but this is bigger than just *you*. We can't afford to hold a spot open here while you're on the task force. Because it's our job to contain and funnel that destructive energy that otherwise would be spread out all over the city. Due to entropy."

Jarsdel nodded. "That makes sense." He wanted out, and was willing to say anything if it meant Gavin would set him free.

"And as far as that comment goes, the one where you said 'as outlined by Chief Comsky,' you're in error there, too."

"Okay."

"You're in error because this situation goes way beyond any of Chief Comsky's pet projects. You're being loaned out on request of RHD's captain, who got the go-ahead from the chief himself. That's the chief of *police*, of the entire department, not just of West Bureau. You follow me?"

Jarsdel tried to look thoughtful. "I certainly do. And I'll keep entropy in mind, moving forward."

Gavin smiled. "I'm glad you said that. Because your responsibilities with Dr. Varma's survey don't end with this RHD gig. I still expect your cooperation with whatever she wants to pursue. You do your initial appointment with her yet?" Gavin asked.

Jarsdel nodded. His scar had begun to throb, sending out waves of sickening pain.

"Good, that's a start." He raised his hands, clapped them together once. "Thus concludes the meeting."

Back at his desk, Jarsdel gathered his planner and phone and tossed them in his briefcase.

"Got everything?"

He looked up to see Haarmann, arms crossed, his close-set eyes lit with naked delight.

Jarsdel picked up his copy of *Matter over Mind*, threw it into the case, and faced Haarmann squarely.

"Excuse me."

Haarmann waited a beat, then stepped out of the way. He made a grand, sweeping gesture in the direction of the station doors. "Take it easy, Dad. Make sure to stay regular."

Jarsdel strode past him and through the intake area, where he had to step over the extended legs of a sleeping arrestee. He pushed through the doors into the parking lot, squinting in the harsh sunlight, and double-clicked the unlock button on his key fob.

He opened the passenger door, set his suitcase on the seat, then walked around the back of the car to the driver's side. He grabbed the handle and swung the door open.

Heat, bright and sudden, across his fingers.

Jarsdel looked down, more confused than hurt. Then he saw the blood—great blooms of it, welling up fast. He flexed the joints and saw three little mouths open in his flesh. His index, middle, and ring finger. With grim fascination, he cupped them together. Blood began pooling in the crevices. When he had enough to fill a teaspoon, he spread his fingers apart, and could hear the fat drops hitting the ground.

He dropped to one knee and examined the handle. A sliver of metal blinked in the sun. With his right hand, he pulled a pen from his pants pocket and prodded at it, but it didn't move. Jarsdel bent lower and angled his head.

Someone had stuck a razor blade to the back of the handle. Thick green goop, some kind of epoxy, held it in place. Perhaps a quarter centimeter of steel jutted from the underside of the molded plastic—not enough to be noticed, but certainly more than enough to do damage.

Haarmann.

Revenge for desecrating the arm-wrestling table.

Jarsdel stood and examined his hand, tilting it back and forth in the saturated afternoon light. The cuts were deep.

He looked around, expecting to see Haarmann and his goons leering at him from the station-house doorway, but no one was there. They were playing it smart. What about cameras? Surely there must be some surveillance on the parking lot.

Yes, three cameras, each capturing a different angle of view. Anyone messing around his car would've been center stage, unmissable.

He popped the trunk with his good hand and swatted the contents around. He found what he was looking for wedged behind the gas can: "Bag o' Rags," it said on the plastic sleeve. Inside were strips of cotton T-shirt cloth. They came in handy for wiping off dipsticks or cleaning up spills. He plucked several free and wrapped them around the weeping gashes, gripping them tightly, just to make sure he could. No severed tendons. And he still had sensation in the tips of his fingers, which was also good. At least the nerves were intact.

He considered going back inside the station and asking to see that day's surveillance footage, but he didn't want to run into Haarmann while he was obviously injured. Instead, he slid into the driver's seat and pulled away, making a left on Sunset before cutting across Highland, Western, and Vermont. Finally he arrived at Hollywood Presbyterian.

The ED was packed. A nurse glanced at his hand and put him behind a constipated baby, a boy with an eraser up his nose, and a gardener who'd swung a machete into his own shin. Blood had soaked the man's pant leg and the battered sneaker beneath, and he now left vivid red shoe prints across the vinyl flooring whenever he went to peruse the waiting room's meager stack of magazines. He didn't like being fussed over—assured the staff he was fine and only there because his boss had forced him to come. He protested more loudly when the staff insisted he put a plastic bag around his shoe. In a modern retelling of Cinderella, an ED nurse knelt at his side, hazmat bag at the ready, trying to ensnare the dripping foot as the gardener insisted he wasn't going to pay for this procedure, and that it was being done without his consent.

Jarsdel got out his phone to check his email and pressed the home button. The screen stayed dark. He pressed it again, and when nothing happened he held down the power button. Five seconds, ten. Nothing.

"Piece of shit," he murmured. He held down both buttons at the same time.

Still nothing.

Jarsdel sighed, putting the phone back on his hip.

He took eleven stitches in total and a bottle of Vicodin and paid for them out of pocket. His LAPD insurance would've covered everything, but he didn't want there to be a record—didn't want to have to explain what happened, which would've launched an investigation, which in turn would've given Haarmann even greater satisfaction. Besides, Jarsdel wanted his response—once he decided on it—to be a surprise.

By the time he made it back to Hollywood Station, it was nearly six o'clock, the sun low and fat in the sky. Keeping his left hand in his pocket, he pushed through one of the old, swinging glass doors and approached the desk sergeant, Curran.

"Hey, I'm wondering if you could help me. Looks like somebody keyed my car out there in the lot. You by any chance tell me how I can get the security footage going back to this morning?"

Curran was puzzled. "What, out there? Where cops park?"

"Yeah, if you can believe it. Guy must've just come right up and done it. Pretty stupid, with the cameras everywhere."

"Or pretty lucky. Those cameras went down this morning."

"What do you mean?"

"We haven't had a feed for eight hours at least."

Jarsdel shook his head. He hoped he hadn't heard correctly, that the real answer had been lost somehow. "I'm sorry, you're saying we don't have security cameras trained on our own parking lot? At the police station?"

Curran's eyes narrowed. "Now look. It's not my fault they're not working, so why're you giving me shit?"

"I'm just amazed we don't have functional cameras to protect our own officers. Why're they down?"

"I don't know. Started getting funky this morning. Some problem with the hardware. Embarrassing too, with that doctor—that security consultant or whatever—looking around the place."

"You don't think it's astonishing? Truly astonishing?"

"What? What do you mean?"

"Did someone do something to them?"

"*I don't know*, Dad—like I said I got nothing to do with any of that."

"Okay," said Jarsdel. "Don't say that, please. That 'Dad' thing."

"Wasn't it your partner who started it?"

"Ex-partner."

Jarsdel marched back out to the parking lot and nearly sliced the fingers of his right hand before remembering to enter through the passenger side. He'd deal with the razor once he got home. A thought occurred to him then—what if Haarmann had put something on the blade? Feces or something, like they used to do with punji sticks? He got out of the car and bent down next to the driver's side door, sniffing the handle.

Nothing he could detect, but that didn't mean it wasn't there. He cupped his hands around the door handle and took a deep breath. A pungent smell, but more likely whatever chemicals made up the epoxy. Probably no feces, then, and they'd disinfected the wound pretty well at the hospital. Gave him a tetanus booster, too, because he couldn't remember the last time he'd had one.

Haarmann. Goddamned Haarmann. How would Jarsdel answer this?

His hand ached terribly, and he thumbed the cap off the bottle of Vicodin and dry-swallowed two of them.

If he retaliated, he ran the risk of Haarmann catching him in the act and reporting him to Internal Affairs. Even if he got away with it, at least as far as the higher-ups were concerned, he might inspire an even more serious counterattack. Obviously Haarmann was already comfortable inflicting permanent physical injury. What would he do if Jarsdel gave him good reason to be angry?

A squadron of geese passed overhead, honking as they went. To Jarsdel the sound had a kind of gloating, mocking tone about it. He reached for the door handle again, caught himself just in time, and went around to the passenger's side. He scooted across to the driver's seat, banging his knee on the gearshift as he went, and started the engine. As he backed out, he threw one last disgusted look up at the impotent security cameras.

9

The last time Jarsdel was at the Police Administration Building—or PAB—was during his promotional exams for the new Hollywood Homicide. The full details of the program hadn't yet been disclosed, and Jarsdel believed he was simply submitting himself for detective. Six weeks later he'd been called back for interviews with Deputy Chief Cynthia Comsky, a polygraph examination, and finally a meeting with the police commission.

Upon reentering the sleek concrete-and-glass facility, he remembered the surging anxiety and self-doubt he felt at those previous visits, and reminded himself he was now there on official business. More than that—he was on his way to Homicide Special, perhaps the most renowned department of murder police in the country.

Robbery-Homicide Division—RHD—was located on the fifth floor. When he pressed the button, the elevator gave a faint purr, and he was there. Everything in PAB was like that—powerful and efficient, a monument toward the ideal of justice as a disinterested but immutable force.

The halls were cool, hushed. When Jarsdel encountered other officers, he always found them moving quickly and speaking in low voices. He checked his email again for the room number, and found it a few doors down from the Robbery Homicide office. He was unhappy to see the shades were drawn. Was he late? He opened the door, knocking as he did so.

Inside was an ovoid conference table, but only one of the seats was taken. A woman of perhaps fifty, wearing jeans and a plain white T-shirt, thumbed absently at her phone. She wore her detective's shield on a beaded chain around her neck, and the gun on her hip was a .38-caliber Colt six-shooter. She offered Jarsdel the barest glance before going back to whatever she'd been looking at.

Jarsdel sat on the opposite side of the table and was about open to where he'd left off in *Matter over Mind*, but in came another new arrival. He was wiry and skittish and looked too young to be a detective, but he too wore a gold shield around his neck. He gaze flitted around the room as if he expected there to be more to see than just Jarsdel and the woman. Eventually he seemed satisfied and gave Jarsdel a nod before taking his seat.

A man wearing a heavily starched white shirt came in, head down, scanning a few sheets of paperwork spilling out from a manila folder. He was dark skinned, his head a massive, gloriously smooth orb. He wore a thick but ordered mustache and a brown paisley tie.

He pulled back a chair and sat. "LT'll be here in a minute," he said, without looking up from his work.

No one answered, and the man didn't seem to mind. He shuffled through his papers, took a sip from a giant red thermos, and checked something on his phone.

The door to the conference room swung open once more. A tall, thin man stood there, looking concerned, either as if he wasn't sure he was in the right place, or if he thought he might have just interrupted something. In one hand he carried an old-fashioned black doctor's bag. His face was lined but handsome, and he had large, soulful eyes. He tried a hopeful smile.

"Hey," he said. "Don't want to interrupt anything, but I thought I'd come by and say a few words."

The man who'd entered a minute or so before, with the bald head and the mustache, turned around in his seat. "LT. Yeah, of course. We're all here."

"I see that. All on time, of course. And I'm the late one." The newest arrival picked a seat and dropped into it with a sigh. Jarsdel saw he wore a novelty tie—some kind of futuristic cityscape from the pages of an old comic. Saucer-shaped buildings and zipping spacecraft and crowds of jumpsuited astronauts wearing fishbowl helmets. It definitely wasn't regulation, but Jarsdel supposed from a distance its sepia tones made it look sober enough.

"First I'm gonna apologize. A few high-profile cases just came down the pike. The Creeper of course, yes, and thank God we've got you all on that. But there's also a UCLA kid who got shot, and naturally she's here on a student visa. Ecuadorean national. Jesus. It's just, well—it's everything you'd expect with something like that, with the State Department and consulates involved. And we got other stuff, too, of course. Not like your everyday homicides go on hold just 'cause we got a serial, right?"

The woman who'd already been in the room when Jarsdel arrived raised her hand. "Excuse me. Are you the lieutenant? In charge of Homicide Special?"

The man shrugged. "As much as such a thing can be a, you know, an in-charge kind of thing. I manage it, you could say. And I do so under the command of a far more capable and experienced colleague. And if you haven't met Captain Tricia Coryell yet, you should all go introduce yourselves. Anyway," he waved a hand, "yes, I'm Lieutenant Sponholz. But I would actually be really just fine with all of you calling me Ed. Plain old Ed." He laughed, and clapped the dark-skinned man on the shoulder.

"I can see this guy sitting here looking uncomfortable while I'm talking to you, so I kinda have to out him here. This is Detective Goodwin Rall. He's a Detective III, so he's senior in Homicide Special. And he is a man who cares very deeply for protocol. So I constantly have to tell him not to defend me, because he'll actually tell people they're not to listen to my requests to call me Ed, and that they have to stick with 'Lieutenant' or 'LT.' With all due respect to my super cop, you really can call me Ed." He turned to Rall. "You picked up this do-or-die pecking-order stuff from Uncle Sam, right? Marines?"

Rall frowned. "Army."

"Army. Apologies. This is the guy," he told the group, "like in those action movies where they say, 'Oh, he's the best of the best, Green Beret, two tours in wherever but after that his file goes dark and we don't pick him up for fifteen years and it's all very classified.' Well. Detective Rall is that guy. He's the John Rambo of Homicide Special."

Rall didn't answer, but wore enough of a smile to let Sponholz know he didn't mind the attention.

Sponholz pointed at Jarsdel. "You're Marcus Jarsdel, right?"

Jarsdel nodded. "Uh, Tully, please. Yes, sir."

"Tully—you got it. Okay, so this is interesting, because I don't know if anyone else at this table knows about HH2 or what you've achieved, but I think it's really something." He touched Rall on the shoulder. "You know HH2, right?"

"I know Gavin," Rall said. "All I need to know."

"Ah. Now then, now then. It's my fault for bringing it up. I forgot about the two of you, But let's, uh..."

"We're good, sir. No further comment."

"Appreciate it," said Sponholz. "So we've got Detective Jarsdel from Hollywood Homicide 2. We've also got Ibrahim Al-Amuli—I'm good with my pronunciation there?"

"Yeah. Yes, sir," said the youngish cop at the end of the table.

"Detective Al-Amuli is from Topanga Area, where the Creeper struck last. The Galkas. Now, Topanga Area—and please correct me if I'm wrong—that was at one point one of the great pot-growing strongholds in the state. Now that it's legal, what do you guys do all day? I mean, when you're not dealing with serials."

"Got plenty of problems up there," said Al-Amuli. "Plenty. Gangs, tagging, assaults. Lots of assaults. Biker bars. Got a case last week with a guy who killed another guy by throwing his drink at him. It was a shot of Everclear, and the guy he threw it at was lighting a cigar with this hand-torch thing, and whoosh. Everclear ignites and sets the guy's head on fire. His *head*, man. Whoosh."

"Wow."

"Yeah I think he had hair spray or something that acted as like an accelerant or something, because when we got him—and his head was still smoking by the way, even though they'd already put out the fire—when we got to him it was like this giant raisiny thing. This black charred thing on top of a body. Wild."

"I see," said Sponholz. "And on that note, I'll introduce Detective Darla Mailander. Detective Mailander was one of the responders to the Creeper's second known scene. The, uh, the Rustads. And I know everyone at this table's seen some—well, seen some shit, right? From what I gather, the Rustad scene was pretty much as bad as they come."

Mailander, the woman who'd already been waiting in the room when Jarsdel arrived, didn't comment, didn't even offer a nod of courtesy. Sponholz gave no sign he took offense.

"So this is it," he said. "Our team. Three detectives with personal experience in Creeper homicides, and my senior guy in the unit, Detective Rall. It's a very simple structure. Detective Rall will work with you directly on day-to-day aspects of the investigation. Larger command decisions'll be kicked up to me, and if they're above my paygrade, they'll go to Captain Coryell. But again, like I said, the everyday stuff, the nuts and bolts of it all, go through Detective Rall. He's managed serial task forces in the past, including the Bell Gardens Butcher. Also, despite his rather, uh, *stern* demeanor, he's actually a pretty nice guy once you get to know him." He turned to Rall. "I leave anything out?"

"No, sir, not that I can think of."

Sponholz stood. "In that case, I'm gonna be off. I hate to run like this, but I've got an Ecuadorian diplomat, of all things, breathing down my neck, along with some extremely upset parents flying in from Quito or some such place and—miracle of miracles—all our Spanish translators are busy. So it's that kind of day."

Sponholz paused on his way out the door. "Just so you know, I'm tremendously grateful you're all here. Believe me, I sympathize with how not-fun it is to be yanked off whatever cases you're on and kicked over to RHD. But if it's any consolation, no one in this task force, least of all me, is going to take you folks for granted. You're here to do noble, necessary work. So thank you."

Offering a final smile, Sponholz disappeared into the hallway. Rall was about to speak up, but Sponholz leaned back into the doorway. "Oh. Sorry. It just occurred to me that I was planning on doing a kind of one-on-one thing with each of you new folks. Just get my sense of you a little bit better. When you all get a chance, do me a favor and drop by my office, cool? Thanks." He was gone again.

This time Rall waited a good ten seconds before speaking. "Yeah, so the LT's a good man. He's nice, too, which doesn't always work for me. And I ain't talkin' behind his back or nothin'. He knows I'd be fine sayin' this to him if he were right here. So what I'm tellin' you is don't take advantage of the vibe 'round this office. You're gonna work hard, and the minute you might be thinkin', 'Oh, I can slack off 'cause maybe the LT's soft,' just remember me. Because I get a say on your next set of fitness reports, and if you treat this detail like a vacation, it will be noted. And I will make sure this is the last time you set foot in RHD. Any questions about that?"

No one had any.

"Okay. First set of assignments. Al-Amuli, you're on victim selection, how he's pickin' 'em. I want you to cross-reference the hell out of these targets. They live far apart, so anything you find in common oughta throw up a red flag. COMPSTAT's got nothin' so far, so you're gonna have to get creative. High school yearbooks, relatives who've done time. Long shots are encouraged."

With his index finger, Al-Amuli chicken-pecked Rall's suggestions onto his phone's memo pad. "Got it," he said.

He turned his attention to Jarsdel. "You're Morales's partner, right?"

"Yes, sir."

"We worked Bell Gardens together. He couldn't make it here or what?"

"The lieutenant wanted him to stay in Hollywood."

"Who? Gavin?"

"Yeah."

Rall blew out an annoyed gust and shook his head. "Whatever. You're gonna be lookin' at any unusual activity in the vicinity of the Creeper attacks. Start with arrests and field interview cards. He could've been stopped for anything. Loitering, squatting, indecent exposure, Peepin' Tom shit, pissing on the sidewalk. Check it out. Then I want ticketed or towed vehicles on our victims' streets or within a reasonable radius. Finally, I want you to look at anything unsolved. Thefts, break-ins, trespassers, vandals, carjackings. Could be we get this guy pawning someone's jewelry or driving a hot car. Questions?"

"No, sir. Sounds like a good start."

Rall gestured at Mailander. "You're out of Eagle Rock, right?"

Mailander sighed. "Yup."

"You don't like it?"

Mailander gave a perfunctory shrug.

"Okay, since you're a real people person, I'm puttin' you on canvassing. And this ain't gonna be some namby-pamby deal. You gonna run the granddaddy of all canvasses. I don't care if we talked to these citizens a dozen times, you talk to 'em again. You nail down every moment of their lives while the Creeper was doin' his thing with their neighbors. I do not accept 'no witnesses,' so don't bother bringin' me back 'no witnesses'—just expand your perimeter."

Mailander glowered, but said nothing.

Rall addressed the whole group. "Meanwhile I got a mountain of physical evidence to process and compare: tool marks, sneaker treads, blood spatter, hair, clothing fiber, fingerprints, DNA, and every fuckin' substance come out of a body. Only thing that guy didn't bother leavin' at the scene was himself. And let's be clear—this ain't just a full-time job. It's more than that, bigger. LT needs you, I need you, you come in. And you can forget overtime. We put the safety of the citizens of this city before our comforts and conveniences."

When no one complained or raised a question, Rall continued. "Okay, so we're gonna meet here right back in this room tomorrow after lunch. We'll say 1:00 p.m. At that meeting each of you is gonna bring me somethin' good. You never know where your investigations are gonna intersect, so those meetings are crucial. We all good? Okay."

Rall stood and left the room. He did it so suddenly and without ceremony that it took a moment for the remaining detectives to realize the meeting had ended. They began gathering their things, but before anyone could leave, Al-Amuli spoke up.

"So hey, I think we should probably exchange numbers and stuff. 'Case we come across anything and wanna compare notes, you know, or just get to know each other over a couple beers. Could be workin' together a while."

But Mailander was out the door before he'd finished.

Al-Amuli looked startled. "Yikes. This team's kinda cringy. Awkward moment centrale. No offense if you're friends with any of them."

"No," said Jarsdel.

"In Topanga they'd kick you out if you were wound up this tight. You gotta get along with people. Shit's different over here. I don't know—don't think I like the vibe. Anyway, you gonna go over and talk to the LT? What's his name again?"

"Sponholz." Without thinking, Jarsdel grabbed the phone on his belt to check the time. His stitches yanked on the suddenly extended flesh, and it felt as if he'd grabbed a high-voltage wire. He hissed and dropped the phone.

"You okay?"

"Fine." Jarsdel picked up the phone with his right hand and hooked it back onto his belt.

"My assignment's big, don't you think? I mean, all those things Rall wants me to check? I'm just thinking it's gonna take some time, and I don't know if he's like expecting miracles or anything, but I hope he's realistic."

Jarsdel didn't know what to say to that, and Al-Amuli went on. "You, what he gave you, that seems more doable, 'cause you're workin' with facts. I gotta get creative, linkin' things together. Maybe he doesn't like me or something. You think you could give me some help on my end?"

Jarsdel couldn't hide his surprise. "Help?"

"You know, whenever you finish up your own stuff."

So this is the Creeper Task force, thought Jarsdel. *Not exactly Elliot Ness and his Untouchables.* "I better get going," he said. "Good meeting you."

"For sure." Jarsdel left Al-Amuli in the conference room and wended his way through the corridors back to Homicide Special. Sponholz's door was open, and he waved Jarsdel into his office.

"Thanks for coming."

Jarsdel shook his hand and took a seat.

The lieutenant smiled without showing his teeth, an expression that might've been mistaken for a grimace if it wasn't for the way his eyes lit up with warmth and overall joie de vivre. "So this is just an informal 'Hi, how are ya.' You'll of course be reporting mostly to Detective Rall, so we won't be spending too much time with each other, but I wanted to thank you for coming on board."

"Great to be here, sir."

"*Oh.*"

"Sorry?"

"Oh, you don't... It's not necessary, with the 'sirs' and so forth. I still feel a bit like an impostor as it is, and when people call me 'sir,' it just drives it home even more. You know, I understand you and I have quite a bit in common. Well, I mean, everyone in command knows about HH2 and all the great work you folks are doing down there, but I confess I've followed your situation with particular interest."

"My situation?" said Jarsdel.

"You being a detective. I was all for it from the beginning, not that I had any say one way or the other, but I thought HH2 was a terrific idea. And then I found out more about you and your background, and I suppose you could say I've been rooting for you."

"Oh. I appreciate that."

Sponholz made a gesture of dismissal. "No need to *appreciate* it. Not like I actually did anything for you. All I mean to say is I suppose I felt like we were cut from the same cloth, and that if you succeeded, it would impart some magical, retroactive affirmation on my own status. I'm not even sure I'm phrasing that cogently. You know what I did before I joined the force?"

"I don't think so, no."

"Really? I'm surprised Lieutenant Gavin didn't mention it." Something about the way he said Gavin's name made Jarsdel suspect he wasn't a fan.

"Well, I was a lot like you," he went on. "Not history per se, but not too far removed either. Theater."

The surprise must have shown on Jarsdel's face, because Sponholz laughed. "I know," he said. "Probably the worst thing I could have on my résumé to become a policeman."

"Director? Playwright?" asked Jarsdel.

"Actor," Sponholz mouthed the word, then held a finger to his lips. "But back in those days we did everything. It's your world, and you take care of it. Set building, costumes, makeup, lighting. Show's always gotta go on, right? Someone was sick or evicted or stoned, you'd have to fill in for them. No one gets to be irreplaceable. You learn that quick in theater. Helps prepare you for the real world. But with all that insurance stuff these days, actors are spoiled rotten. God forbid they sprain a wrist hammering together some scenery." He grimaced. "But let's keep all this between you and me. Goodwin knows, but I'll get endless hell from the rest of these guys. And if anyone around here digs up my publicity photo from *The Bacchae*, I might as well retire on the spot."

"You were in *The Bacchae*?"

"Royce Hall, 1983. You know it? Right, 'course you do. Former classics professor, I'm told."

Jarsdel felt a twinge, as he always did when the subject arose. "Not a full professor. I was in a PhD program."

"Ah."

"Are you still active in theater at all?"

"You kidding? No. No, sir. Beyond making sure I grab whatever show's in town, absolutely no. And I don't even think that's gonna happen this year with the earthquake. You been by the Pantages since January?"

The Pantages Theater was Old Hollywood royalty, right on the Boulevard just east of Vine.

"No," said Jarsdel. "Not doing well?"

"Heartbreaking." Sponholz grabbed something from under a paperweight and held it out. A small, glossy rectangle. Jarsdel immediately recognized the iconic white half-mask, though he'd never seen the show himself.

"*Phantom of the Opera*," said Sponholz. "Third row, center. I was gonna get a refund, but then they keep telling me they'll reopen soon. And they might've, but now I'm extremely skeptical, especially after that last quake a week ago. *LA Times* says big foundation problems, et cetera."

"But *The Bacchae*," said Jarsdel, still impressed. "That's—well, I don't want to go off on a tangent, but that's easily my favorite by Euripides—maybe my favorite play of all time."

"Well, there you go," said Sponholz. "Knew we'd get along."

"You were Dionysus?"

"Pentheus. When I wasn't swinging around like Quasimodo, hanging lights off the grid."

Jarsdel felt an old and powerful enthusiasm well within him. "'Your name points to calamity. It fits you well.'"

"Ha! Haven't heard that line in nearly forty years." Sponholz seemed to enjoy the memory a moment longer, then his expression wilted. It fell so quickly and completely into a tragedian mask that Jarsdel was caught off guard, thinking Sponholz was about to recite some more dialogue from the play. But the lieutenant didn't speak, not at first. His eyes, wide and earnest, moistened a little, and he leaned forward on his elbows.

"Detective, we're in a hell of a fix. I was still just a teenager in '81, but I remember the headlines, and I remember the sirens. Seemed constant, just like now. Peak year in violent crime. And I remember the Night Stalker in '84. I don't know if you were even born yet, but if you want to know what it was like, just look around. You understand what I mean, don't you?"

"Yes."

"The people are scared. And when people are scared, they do stupid things—reckless, impulsive, dangerous things. So it's not just that we have to catch this monster to protect whoever's next on his list; we gotta protect the next Ben Bauman, the next poor kid who's gonna get beaten to death because somebody thinks he's our guy. And I tell you, it's..." Sponholz made a flowing, almost encouraging gesture with his right hand, as if urging his own thoughts along. "I... *God*...it's hard. You know? The ugliness, the sheer ugliness."

He held out his hand, flat, a few inches above the desk. "I have been *empowered*"—he struck the desk for emphasis—"by the state of California"—*whack*—"by the Los Angeles Police Department"—*whack*—"and by the goddamned chief of police and the captain of RHD"—*whack, whack*—"to drag this foul, putrescent, slithering thing into the full light of justice. That is my task. That is *our* task."

Now Jarsdel was certain Sponholz had become misty-eyed. He'd never seen a commander get emotional before, and it made him a little uneasy. But at the same time he couldn't help admire the lieutenant's uncensored compassion for the victims and his righteous anger at their killer.

Sponholz exhaled loudly, giving his head a sad little shake. "I get worked up. Ask anyone. Guess I just have a hard time believing we still do things like this to each other. As those in my parents' generation used to say, 'We can put a man on the moon, *but*...' And fill in whatever after that. Can't cure cancer, can't put an end to poverty, et cetera. But for me, it was always murder. We can put a man on the moon, but we can't stop fucking *killing* each other. Astonishing."

"It's why I joined." Jarsdel blurted it out. He didn't know why, but he felt if anyone could understand his motives, it would be someone like Sponholz.

A ghost of the lieutenant's smile returned. "Did you? Then good. We need that. And we'll continue to need that as this case moves forward. Because for much of it, we're going to suffer. Our social lives, our personal lives—these will suffer—but so will our dreams, our psyches, every corner of our subconscious minds. There won't be any place to hide from it. In a way it'll be like having him in there, just like he was in those houses. Until we catch him."

"I'm ready for that," said Jarsdel.

"No," said Sponholz. "No one's ever ready for that. It's not the kind of fight you can prepare for. But you're willing, and that's what matters most." He stood, extending his hand, and the men shook. "Come by my birthday party, will you? It's this Saturday at the Tiki-Ti. If you don't have plans, of course."

"Sounds great—thanks for the invite."

"Pleasure to have you with us. Now let's go and shut this fucking guy down."

Jarsdel didn't bother dusting the razor for prints. If there'd been any, he would've smudged them completely when he'd tried opening the door. And even if he hadn't, Haarmann would've known to wear gloves.

The epoxy held it fast. He tried tearing it free with a pair of needle-nose pliers, and stopped when he felt the handle itself give an ominous little snap.

After leaving PAB, he drove the car the few blocks to Motor Transportation Division on Judge John Aiso Street, the LAPD's fleet operations headquarters. The mechanic who examined the handle didn't seem surprised. "Seen worse," he said.

Jarsdel didn't ask for elaboration. "When can I get it back?"

"That razor's on there good. Have to get you a new handle." The mechanic straightened up, running a hand through his mane of silver hair, and noticed Jarsdel's bandaged hand. "Dinged you up, huh?"

"How long for the handle?"

"Oughta get here by Monday. Tuesday at the outside."

Jarsdel tried not to look as annoyed as he felt. "Why so long?"

"Too late to put in the order today, tomorrow's Friday, then you got the weekend. Your model's already four years old. Thought of putting in a request for a newer one? Parts'll come quicker."

"So what do I do? What am I gonna drive?"

"Got a cruiser you can take."

"Wait—you don't have any unmarked cars? What if I have to do a stakeout or follow a suspect?"

"Not sure what to tell you. You want to drive this one out of here, you're more than welcome."

"*Shit.*"

The mechanic waited for him to make up his mind. Jarsdel glared at the few millimeters of steel protruding below the handle. His hand ached in sympathy. "Fine," he said.

"There's some paperwork."

"Of course there is."

An hour later, a patrol car pulled up to where Jarsdel was waiting. The silver-haired mechanic stepped out. "Probably been a few years since you been in one of these. Pretty much the same. Gas's still on the right."

"Wonderful."

"You familiar with SkyTrace?"

Jarsdel shook his head. He could feel his pulse beating in the slashed fingers of his left hand.

"Then I'd stay away from that little console there." The mechanic pointed at something to the right of the driver's seat. "Just equipped them this year. Wanted to see how Contra Costa Sheriff's liked it, then we sprung for 'em."

Jarsdel bent close so he could see. A simple black box with two switches, both in the down position. One was protected by a hinged, plastic cube, presumably to prevent it being toggled accidentally. A small LED burned yellow. "What's it do?"

"Pursuit abatement system. That switch there means it's off, and the light means it's unarmed. Otherwise it'll be green. Activate the second switch and..." The mechanic led Jarsdel to the front of the cruiser, where a trapezoidal hatch had been fitted into the grille. "Lid pops open, out fires a GPS tracker. Compressed air cannon. Tracker's fitted with this very sticky putty. Magnet too, 'case the putty doesn't stick. Got an eight-hour battery on it. Then you just kinda hang back and follow the suspect vehicle on your computer. Lot safer for everyone. Get pretty good accuracy, too—laser paints the bumper of the suspect vehicle. Just gotta account for drop if it's more'n about fifty yards ahead."

He held out the keys. There were two fobs. The first, built into the car key, was the standard array of lock and unlock buttons. The second, sleek and egg-shaped, bore only a single gray button. "You can activate it remotely. Writing a citation, guy starts to take off. Nope, gotcha. Independent system, too. Works even if the engine's not running. Gotta press it twice to avoid accidental discharge."

Jarsdel took the keys without comment. All he could think about was how much the patrol car would slow him down. Black-and-white fever, every car in front of him hitting the brakes once they spotted him in the rearview. Citizens flagging him from the sidewalk, eager to file a complaint or get him to resolve a dispute.

Haarmann. Fucking Haarmann.

Jarsdel's hand began to ache as his pulse kicked up. As if in answer, the scar above his ear sent out a bolt of pain. He grimaced, headed back toward the driver's seat.

"Not even a little impressed?" asked the mechanic. "Most guys can't wait to try it out."

Someone had taken out a hydrant on the corner of Oakwood and Sycamore, and now a twenty-foot geyser baptized the crawling southbound traffic. Jarsdel was stuck beneath it for close to a minute—a limbo in which the world shimmered ghostly beyond the deluged windshield, and the only sound was the roar of water against metal.

He turned right at the next intersection, passing the New Beverly Cinema. Quentin Tarantino had bought the building in 2007, saving it from destruction, and programmed each month's showings. And since all the 35mm prints came from his personal collection, watching films at the New Bev was kind of like hanging out in the director's own screening room. According to the marquee, July was dedicated to LA crime stories. On offer that night was a double feature: *The Limey* with Terence Stamp, followed by Boris Karloff in *Targets*.

When he got back to his apartment, the first thing Jarsdel did was pause to admire the portrait of Lady Mary. It really was a beautiful piece, and it softened the daily return to his silent, empty home. A bargain at $2,400.

His phone hummed, and he snatched it from his belt. Morales. He took the call and brought the phone to his ear.

"Yeah."

"*Yeah?* That's it? I come to work this afternoon, drag my ass in there, still sick as shit, and find out you been transferred to PAB? And on top of that I'm workin' with Haarmann? You plan on telling me any of this?"

"Oh."

"Uh-huh. Now I get Gavin not calling and telling me—he's a dickhead first class. But you I don't figure."

Jarsdel fell into his wingback chair, using his free hand to massage his brow. He did it without thinking, and his stitches pulled. Searing, electric pain. "Ow—*shit*."

"What happened?"

"Nothing. No—actually, you should definitely know. You hear about that thing a couple weeks back between me and Haarmann? The arm-wrestling table?"

"Everyone knows. Said you lost your shit."

"Lost my shit? Well, that's interesting. Especially considering that in retaliation, our resident Cro-Mag glued a razor blade to my door handle. A *razor blade*. Cut the hell out of my hand. Lucky I didn't sever the nerves."

"Holy shit."

"So that's why calling you about the PAB thing might've slipped my mind. This happened just yesterday." Jarsdel thought for a moment. "But don't tell anyone. Don't want it getting back to him that I know who did it."

A pause on the other end. "Okay. So you got proof?"

"He threatened me. In front of witnesses. But no, that's it."

"You sure? 'Cause this is enough to get him kicked out the department, easy. Throw a charge on top, too."

Jarsdel felt anger surge inside him. "The station cameras were out."

"Out? What d'you mean—like—"

"Yes. Malfunctioned. Convenient, huh? Anyway, the important thing here is that your new partner's an extremely dangerous, disturbed individual. Get you killed under the right circumstances."

Morales considered that for a while. "What about when it's all over? They hookin' us back up, or am I stuck with Haarmann now?"

"Gavin was deliberately vague. It's a golden opportunity for him to fuck with me. And with HH2. I get the sense since it's less a priority for Comsky since there's no mayoral race on the horizon."

"But hey, least you're on the Creeper Task Force now. Congrats."

"Yeah."

"You don't sound so thrilled."

"It's not that. Just...complicated." Jarsdel thought of Mailander and Al-Amuli. He'd always assumed task forces were made up of the most elite investigators in the department. It was obvious to him now that they were more like storage units for undesirables, a way for commanders to dump their least favored investigators without formally transferring them.

"I get it," said Morales. "Performance anxiety. Now you gotta put your money where your mouth is. RHD's big leagues."

"Yeah, maybe that's it."

"You'll be fine, partner. Hey, you wanna come by the house? Got a present for you. Something in case you actually catch the motherfucker."

Jarsdel was distracted. His wounds had begun singing again. "Thanks, but I'm beat, and my hand's killing me. I need to take a rest."

"Yeah, okay. Take it easy."

"Hey, be on your guard around Cro-Mag, okay? That dumb-ass jock routine's just that—a routine. There's something else going on there."

Morales didn't answer. Jarsdel could hear the bright, chirping voice of a child somewhere in the background—unintelligible—and his partner's own baritone response, assuring the boy he was almost done with his call and to start the movie without him.

"Gotta run." Morales was back on the line. "Promised him we'd watch *NeverEnding Story* together."

"Sounds long."

"It's an hour-and-a-half, asshole. You didn't watch that when you were a kid?"

"No, only PBS, and only for an hour on Saturdays."

After Morales hung up, Jarsdel held the phone in his hand, trying to think of someone to call. His apartment seemed somehow quieter than it ever had before, and the silence bothered him. His dads were out of the question, and he didn't know anyone on the task force nearly well enough to call just to talk.

He turned on the TV so at least there'd be some conversation going while he got ready for bed.

10

As the commander of the Media Relations Division approached the bank of microphones, Jarsdel noted how exhausted he looked. His gray mustache was neatly trimmed, his sideburns cut sharp above the ear, but his skin was waxy with sweat and fatigue. His uniform no longer fit, straining and puckering, evidence of what guys like Haarmann would've called donut tumors.

"Good morning. I'm Captain Sam Schirru, S-A-M, S-C-H-I-R-R-U, department spokesperson. I want to start by introducing our first speaker—we have two speakers here today—and once they're done, we'll go ahead and open it up for questions and answers. Our first speaker is Captain Tricia Coryell, Commanding Officer of Robbery-Homicide Division, which is our elite team of investigators here in the Police Administration Building. She oversees all aspects of the division, which includes, uh, in addition to Robbery Special and Homicide Special, the Special Assault Section, Cold Case Homicide Special Section, Gang Homicide Unit, and the, uh, Special Investigation Section."

Schirru mumbled his way through the last few words of that sentence. The Special Investigation Section was chartered as the LAPD's tactical surveillance unit; among its duties were tracking some of the city's most violent habitual offenders. This meant the

SIS often had to intervene during a criminal act, and such confrontations frequently ended with a dead bad guy. This had earned the unit a reputation as a kind of death squad, and Schirru didn't want the dozens of assembled journalists to become distracted by its mention.

"So, uh, ladies and gentlemen, please welcome Captain Coryell." He backed away and crossed his arms. He looked like he was asleep standing up.

A tall, dark-haired woman stepped out from the assembled crowd of officers, detectives, and administrators. She had the build of a professional athlete—imposing and broad shouldered. She spoke without notes, eyes scanning the room as she spoke.

"Thank you, Captain Schirru. And good morning to all of you and thank you for coming. We all know why we're here today. Our city is being terrorized by a very evil individual we know as the Eastside Creeper. It's not necessary at this point to get into the details, and I think we're all familiar with them by now anyway, but we can say with certainty these are some of the most vile and depraved crimes in the history of Los Angeles. Our purpose here today is to introduce to the media and the people of this city the dedicated investigators whose job it is to end the Creeper's reign of terror and bring him to justice.

"This case covers a wide area of our county, and at one time would have been vulnerable to communications issues between different branches of our police force. What I'd like to emphasize is that this is a one-hundred-percent unified investigation, bringing together detectives from each jurisdiction where the Creeper committed his crimes. There is going to be absolutely no intradepartmental lag time on this, no delay in communication and sharing of evidence between those jurisdictions. The same detectives who originally handled those cases are the same ones who are going to be on this task force."

Coryell gestured at where Jarsdel was standing. "These experienced investigators are going to work around the clock in pursuit of the Creeper, and will not stop until he is in custody, or in the ground."

There was some murmuring among the journalists at the ferocity of the captain's statement, but she ignored it.

"I'm now going to introduce my colleague, Lieutenant Sponholz of Homicide Special." She stepped away, joining Captain Schirru. Sponholz approached the lectern and adjusted the mic.

"Thank you, Captain Coryell. And good morning, everyone. My name is Lieutenant Edwin Darrel Sponholz, uh, that's S-P-O-N-H-O-L-Z, and I oversee Homicide Special and therefore I'll also be overseeing the Creeper Task Force. As Captain Coryell indicated, the team is comprised of experienced detectives, and these have been sourced—uh, *drawn*, rather, from each affected area. In direct day-to-day command of the team is Detective III Goodwin Rall—Detective Rall, could you raise your hand please?"

Rall did so, and the news cameras swung briefly in his direction.

"Detective Rall is senior in Homicide Special. Under him we have—and if these detectives could also raise their hands as I call their names—Darla Mailander of Northeast Area, Marcus Jarsdel of Hollywood Area, and Ibrahim Al-Amuli of Topanga Area. Together, these men and women are going to show the Eastside Creeper the meaning of swift justice."

Sponholz cleared his throat. "Excuse me." He coughed, paused, then regarded his audience with the same sudden gravity he'd displayed to Jarsdel in his office. His eyes once again became dewy with emotion.

"On a personal note, I would just like to say the following: that we now find ourselves in a, uh, unique—a *very* unique situation."

Jarsdel flinched at the hoary redundancy, then covered by rubbing at his neck. Hopefully it only looked as if he'd had a muscle twinge.

"And that is, I think," Sponholz continued, "that we have an opportunity to demonstrate to both the citizens of Los Angeles and to, uh, well to the entire *earth*, really, the virtues of the American justice system. We have here a man who is utterly without remorse, without mercy, without pity, and therefore not at all deserving of those qualities from the rest of us, from civilized society. And *yet*—and this is what's truly remarkable—he will nonetheless be granted every right and protection provided under the law. It is our ability to rise above our revulsion for this man and adhere to our principles that sets us apart as a nation. And so I wanted you all to know that despite the hateful, utterly despicable nature of these crimes, we remain strong, we remain united. If this most foul excuse for a human, one whose offenses defy imagination, is guaranteed due process, then so are we all."

Jarsdel was struggling with Sponholz's speech. The "very unique" line bothered him of course, but so did the syntax in that bit about the "citizens of Los Angeles" and of the "entire earth." So essentially Sponholz had just said "citizens of earth," which sounded like something out of an Atomic Age serial. Beyond Jarsdel's syntactic concerns, however, he thought the speech exceeded the limits of the lieutenant's job description. Why was he editorializing? The police enforced the law, they didn't comment on it.

But when Jarsdel glanced at Captain Coryell, she seemed enthralled, offering quick little nods of support as Sponholz went on.

"And in case he's watching, there's something I'd like him to know." Sponholz pointed an accusing finger, as if the Creeper were standing right in front of him. "*You will not* get away with this. *You will* be caught. There is no place you can go where we won't follow you, no cave deep enough or dark enough. *You will* answer for your crimes."

He gave a long, dramatic pause. No one ever applauded at press conferences; they weren't supposed to be political rallies. All the same, Sponholz's speechifying earned him a few scattered claps. These were echoed around the room until even the most grudging brought their palms together at least once, just to show they were on the side of truth and justice.

He's still an actor, thought Jarsdel with some admiration. *Still loves to be onstage.*

"Thank you," said Sponholz. "And now I'll take questions."

Los Angeles isn't always easy to love.

Maybe that's because there are really two cities, like sisters. The first comes on strong, doesn't care what you think of her. She's a pro, fast and ruthless, and she'll roll you for all she can. After a day or two, you're back on the plane with your Universal Studios T-shirt and a flimsy, personalized clapper board—you know, that wooden thing they whack together just before they say "action"—and until then you didn't realize just how empty and cheated you could feel.

That was it? *That's* LA?

The real Los Angeles makes you work for her. She hangs back awhile, maybe even for years, while you beat your way with gritted teeth and guidebook through jungles of decaying monuments and souvenir shops and coughing tour buses and a breed of gridlocked traffic that *surely can't be a daily thing*—can it, really?

Sunset Boulevard is one way to meet her. You might not think so—such a hackneyed, obvious pop culture trope—but it's true. It cuts across the city for twenty miles, from the beaches of Pacific Palisades to the cafés and *pupuserias* of East Hollywood. Drive it from one end to the other, and then at least you'll know if you and Los Angeles have a future together.

Right around La Brea Avenue, Sunset and Hollywood Boulevard begin running parallel with each other, separated only by a couple blocks, vying for their share of our love. On Hollywood you've got the Chinese Theatre, the Walk of Fame. On Sunset you've got the Cinerama Dome and Amoeba Records.

The rivalry doesn't last long. Like the crazed, mercurial souls summoned by its name, Hollywood careens suddenly off course, veering southward and smashing into Sunset in one of the most baffling and dangerous intersections anywhere in the state. And that's the end of Hollywood Boulevard. Sunset, no worse for the wear, continues its stately march toward Downtown.

It's at that schizophrenic six-way intersection, at 4427 Sunset Boulevard, that sits the Tiki-Ti.

Jarsdel had only been there once. The day he'd turned twenty-one, his dad, Robert, had been driving the two of them to meet Baba for dinner at Musso's in Hollywood, and he'd suddenly spun the wheel hard to the right and stomped the brake.

"Whoa, Dad! What're—"

But Robert was already out of the car and pulling open the passenger door. "Good lord, you're twenty-one! Have to pop in for a drink. Just one, I promise, but you've got to see this place."

That day, Robert Jarsdel had ordered a Singapore Sling for himself and a Zombie for his son. Robert was heftier back then, by at least fifty pounds and most of it muscle, and could really put away his drinks. When they'd jumped back in the car, Jarsdel was giggling. Robert shook his head in dismay. "You're a cheap date, Tully. You and Baba both."

Tiki culture was born in Los Angeles after the death of Prohibition. Of all the liquors suddenly available to a desperately thirsty Southland, rum was cheapest, but few knew how to capitalize on such an unknown, exotic spirit. Then along came Donn Beach. Born Earnest Raymond Beaumont Gantt, Beach had a talent for satisfying white America's craving for far-flung locales, dark island rituals, and the promise of forbidden pleasures under a swollen tropical moon. He opened his first restaurant, Don the Beachcomber, and in so doing fathered the Tiki zeitgeist.

Tiki was a celebration of the generic, nonexistent tribes filling out orientalist pulps and Hollywood adventure films, the sort that might welcome a wise Caucasian ruler and award him a hundred willing wives. Beach's motto summed it up best: *If you can't get to paradise, I'll bring it to you!* It was claptrap, but it would somehow make the extraordinary leap from overtly racist kitsch to a beloved and enduring part of American folk culture.

Images of bone-nosed natives dancing around cauldrons of boiling missionaries gave way to grim-faced idols, Yma Sumac recordings, and coconut bras. Before long, Tiki art became depopulated of its noble savages altogether, and from then on it was never made quite clear exactly who carved the masks and totems, and assembled the quaint bamboo huts. They were just *there*, somehow, and now we could enjoy them, too—just pull up a stool and grab a mai tai. By subtracting the race from the racism, Tiki accomplished what Mammy cookie jars and Yellow Peril dime novels never could.

Buoyed by the postwar surf craze, beach party movies, and Cold War escapism, Tiki managed to hold on until the '70s—being considered, ironically, a bit square for that particular decade. But Tiki managed to ride the coattails of the Los Feliz renaissance—as long as everyone pretended they loved it in a postmodern way—and thence passed into the grasping, culture-hungry hands of millennials. It was officially here to stay.

The interior of the Tiki-Ti was about what you'd expect if you could step inside a Martin Denny album cover. Blue, red, and green light seeped from between Fu Manchu mugs and liquor bottles and midcentury mementos—souvenir football helmets and lava lamps and battered vanity plates—the colors meeting in garish but alluring puddles around the bar. The whole thing was a capsized treasure ship of bygone knickknacks, the city's last great original Tiki bar. A shrine to a culture spun from whole cloth, as authentic a treatment of Polynesian civilization as Sleeping Beauty Castle was to medieval Europe.

Jarsdel wasn't much for romanticizing about the past, as a rule found things like Ren Fairs and theme restaurants disconcerting. A waiter dressed as a pirate was less likely to arouse his amusement than thoughts of the sugar trade or of actual pirates like L'Ollonais, who liked to roast his prisoners on a spit. Those throwback all-American diners, with their mini jukeboxes and rounded bar tops, would've had Whites Only sections during the actual 1950s. But even Jarsdel couldn't resist the nostalgic charm of the Tiki-Ti. Like everyone else, he found it simply too much fun to dislike.

"Hey, hey, you made it." Sponholz took him by the arm and

guided him to a lean woman wearing a bob haircut. "This is Amy, my wife. Amy, I'd like to introduce you to one of my superstars on the task force. Detective Jarsdel."

"Call me Tully." Jarsdel shook the woman's hand. He tried meeting her gaze as he did so, but her face was dominated by a true showpiece of a nose—an arched, imperious appendage that continually poked itself into view. She took a sip from a fluted glass, three fingers extended daintily. Her nails were long and glossy, with French tips.

"Ed's been going on and on about his team," said Amy. "Said if you can't catch him, no one'll be able to."

It was probably meant as a compliment, but it soured the mood all the same. The Creeper had shown up, in his own little way, right there in the Tiki-Ti. Jarsdel decided to change the subject.

"You work at PAB as well?" It wasn't an unusual question. Many who chose law enforcement as a career found spouses in the same field. Some of the demands of the profession were easier to bear if both parties suffered together.

Amy Sponholz obviously thought otherwise, sending a derisive hiss through her remarkable nose. "Uh, *no*, no thank you whatsoever. I'm in real estate."

"Oh," said Jarsdel. "Yeah, I understand. Definitely not for everybody."

Amy nodded, but she was already looking around the room for someone else to talk to. She spotted someone and waved. "Excuse me," she said, moving off.

Sponholz took Jarsdel's arm and guided him to a quiet corner of the bar.

"Hey, means a lot to me that you came."

"Not at all, sir. It's my—"

"Bah. Please, enough."

"Sorry."

"Yeah, c'mon. We're all in this together. Rank. Ugh. You know I was never into any of that. I'm an actor, right? I mean at *heart*, you know, I'm a liberal arts guy. All this rank stuff actually kinda gives me the willies. What's the point of it, other than to create boundaries, right? I mean, that's its purpose."

Jarsdel nodded. "I guess, yeah."

"Did you know," Sponholz said, taking on a conspiratorial tone, "I once was in a play with Cybill Shepherd? We even had a kissing scene. Definitely the good old days, back when we were both young and beautiful. Well, she's still beautiful, actually." He chuckled. When Jarsdel didn't respond with the requisite awe, Sponholz was disappointed. "Hey. Think you'll be able to relax around me?"

"It's not so much that. Just thinking about work. About *him*."

The lieutenant's expression became grim. "I know how it is. We all want him bad."

"Even your wife brought it up—which is understandable, of course. I just see every day how essential it is for us to catch him. For the city. Not only his victims, but for the whole city."

Sponholz rubbed Jarsdel's shoulder. "Look, you're a hell of a guy and I'm honored to have you on my team. Tonight, though—huh?—tonight we're gonna put all that ugly crap aside and have some tropical drinks. Not drivin', are ya?"

Jarsdel smiled. "No. I'm doing Lyft."

"Good. Because this..." Sponholz extended a finger and tapped the wall three times, hard. "This is one of maybe five places in the city worth getting completely blotto."

The next hour passed in a saturated color wheel. Jarsdel poured chilled, expertly crafted secret recipes down his throat at a pace that quickly made them all taste the same. He wandered away from the bar top with his latest find—a Ray's Mistake, tall and deeply, forbiddingly pink. There's always a single drink that's the first of too many, the one you shouldn't have picked up, and that was the one.

Some time passed. He glanced around to see where he'd landed and found himself at a low four-top with Rall, Mailander, and

Al-Amuli. They each were battling their own sixteen-ouncer of Ray's Mistake. He looked at his own glass. Half of it was already gone.

"Hard to sit," said Rall. "Just sit and have a good time. At all anymore. You know?"

None of the detectives answered. Jarsdel plucked the wedge of pineapple clinging to the rim of his glass and ate as much of the meat as he could. It was bland and out of season, but at least it was food.

Al-Amuli looked around the table and downed the rest of his drink. "I still think of that scene. Up in the canyon. They should have nightmare insurance on this job. Like maybe one...I don't know...like maybe one "blowjob" guaranteed for every nightmare. Just to make up for it."

Mailander scowled at him. "Thanks. You know we don't have to hear every dumb-ass idea that shows up in your head."

"Just sayin'—"

"Yeah and what you're saying is disgusting. I hate that word. I just hate it. "Blowjob." Horrible word."

Rall held up a hand. "Hey, hey. C'mon, *chill*, people. We ain't on duty right now. Ain't on the clock. Let's just take a breath."

The detectives sat in silence for a while. Jarsdel wasn't surprised that it was Al-Amuli who broke it.

"My partner—you know, my normal partner back at Topanga—he said yesterday someone crucified a cat."

"What, you mean literally *crucified*?" asked Rall.

"Yeah. Be surprised some of the shit goes on up there in the canyon. It's real, like, frontier territory, like, wilderness. Misfit land."

Jarsdel found himself annoyed by Al-Amuli. He didn't like the way the man spoke, casting about with words, approaching but never quite reaching his point.

"Lots of nature," Al-Amuli went on. "Animals. Trees. So lot of that stuff just ends up kinda incorporated into everyday life. You got the city right there, you know, if you follow the boulevard down out of the canyon, city problems and such, but then you go up into the canyon, into the hills there, and it's pretty rustic. Police gotta be, like, you know, *savvy*, 'bout both the urban and the rural."

Mailander glared at him. "What are you talking about? What does any of this mean?"

"What? What'd I say?"

"I'm just not following—"

"But why're you getting all upset?"

"I'm not *upset*."

"Did I offend you?"

"What—"

"No, I mean, like, did I *offend* you or something? Have I done or said something that has *offended* you? Because since day one, you been like this with me, and as far as I know, I've been nothing but a gentleman."

Mailander flushed. "Um, what does being a *gentleman* have to do with anything? We're *colleagues*. I don't see how *gender* makes—"

Rall rapped his hand on the table, making the glasses rattle. "Hey. Hey, c'mon."

"*No*." Al-Amuli stood, leveling his index finger at Mailander. "This person has been cutting at me since day one. And I do not like it, but I have been civil and I have been professional. But in moving forward I will not accept this, uh, this *toxicity*. This is an issue of morale, and this person here, this person right here does not contribute to the morale of the team."

Mailander's voice shook with rage. She spoke slowly. "Get your finger out of my face."

Rall rapped on the table again. "Enough."

Crack team, thought Jarsdel. *Creeper's days are numbered.*

Sponholz appeared at the tableside, hair stringy and damp with sweat. He brushed away a dangling forelock. "Hey, everything okay? People are looking around."

"Sorry, LT," said Rall. "I think they just need to cool off. Stress and liquor don't mix."

"Right." He noticed Al-Amuli's still-extended finger. "Sounds like a good idea, right? Everyone cools off?"

There was no reply, and the lieutenant touched his arm. "Detective. Hey, this is my birthday party, you know." He gently pushed Al-Amuli's hand so he'd stop pointing at Mailander. Al-Amuli allowed his hand to be moved, but as soon as Sponholz let go, he swung the finger back into position. To Jarsdel it looked like a compass needle finding magnetic north.

A change came over Sponholz, though Jarsdel couldn't say exactly what. It was a combination of things—a narrowing of the eyes and a hard set to the jaw were part of it, but there was a deeper shift, far below the surface.

Jarsdel watched as Sponholz seized Al-Amuli's bicep. The fabric of his shirt stretched taught as the lieutenant's fingers dug in. He spoke in low, almost seductive tones. "Now you're going to leave, and we can be friends again on Monday. Because this is my party, and you're pissing on it, and I don't care if you're younger or stronger or faster, but if you don't haul your cookies right out the goddamned door, I will *shut you down*."

He released Al-Amuli's arm. The detective stumbled and braced himself on the table.

"I'm out," he said, his voice thick with alcohol. "Man, I feel… I'm sorry, LT."

Sponholz smiled. "Apology gladly accepted. Get yourself home. Clean slate Monday morning."

"Yeah? Shit. I'm such a…" Al-Amuli waved to Rall, Mailander, and Jarsdel. "I apologize."

Jarsdel closed his eyes and felt the world spinning. He'd gotten drunk, truly drunk, and knew he'd now be a prisoner of his own poisoned body. When he opened his eyes, Al-Amuli had his hand extended toward Mailander again, but this time in friendship.

"To you I especially want to apologize. I'm not saying it's an excuse—but I can tell you…and again this isn't an *excuse*… I've been really worn down by this whole case, and it's just very new to me. This kind of pressure."

Mailander sighed and gave his hand a single limp shake.

"Ever since that earthquake," said Al-Amuli, dropping his arm. "Remember? That earthquake, way back in January. All from there. Lost a sculpture. Living rock, a tree growing into living rock. Bodhidharma, you know, dude brought kung fu to China. Expensive. This import-export place in Chi-town. Earthquake totaled it, dropped it onto the hearth? The heart. Heart of the fireplace. Dropped it there and broke. I'm... *Fuck*. All right. I'll see you guys. Super cringe."

Sponholz watched him go, his expression thoughtful. He took the now-empty seat at the table. "He's right. About the earthquake. Like the Creeper came right out of the ground along with valley fever. Those spores don't just attack people, you know. Lost two trees to some fungus recently. Two random trees in a whole stand of them. Like soldiers who drew the wrong straws in their platoon."

"Heard that can happen," said Rall.

"Damn earthquake. Source of all my troubles," Sponholz said to the group. "Probably gonna cost me my ticket to *Phantom*, too. My beloved Pantages." He looked over at his wife, who was bent over her phone, lazily thumbing the screen. "She never gives a shit about theater. Good thing we met after my divorce from Thespis, or I don't know what we'd have had in common."

He swung his attention back to the group. "Anyway, hope that didn't come off as too harsh. With Detective Al-Amuli. Some people, you gotta penetrate through layers of defenses before they actually hear you."

There were murmurs of agreement.

"I don't want you to think any less of him. Because this might be a little embarrassing for him next week to think about. He's a good detective. Wouldn't be here if he weren't. So I'd appreciate it if you have some compassion moving forward. Our team's more important than any little squabble. It really is. We're here to save lives." He laughed and shook his head. "This is the last thing I wanted to talk about tonight, but here we are. I guess it's right that we can't get away from *him*, from our guy. Maybe we don't get nights off. Maybe we don't get breaks. He doesn't take any breaks, does he? And his victims, they don't get breaks either."

Sponholz slapped the table and stood. "You all take care. Amy and I are gonna head out in a few minutes anyway. Long drive back to Northridge. You know she actually booked a town car for me tonight? Amazing lady."

"G'night, LT," said Rall.

"Yeah, good night, sir," said Mailander.

"Thank you," Jarsdel mumbled. He looked at his drink again, at the last inch or so of Ray's Mistake in the bottom of the glass. It would be cool on his throat, yes, but it wasn't worth it. "I need a water," he said aloud.

Mailander glanced at him, then slid her glass of ice water over. "Here. I don't have cooties."

Jarsdel drained the contents, letting some of the ice spill into his mouth and sucking greedily on the cubes. "Thanks," he managed. "I'll get you another."

"I'm fine."

From somewhere not far away, and growing ever closer, a police siren howled. As it faded, another took up the call, passing right outside the Tiki-Ti before rocketing off to whatever new tragedy awaited.

Jarsdel's fingers began throbbing. This surprised him. He probably had enough alcohol in his system to sit through an amputation. But his fingers burned where Haarmann had cut them. He could feel the skin growing around the stitches, and the stitches pulling back at the skin, fighting it as it healed.

Heads lowered, the detectives allowed the sirens to fade completely, then got up one by one and left the bar.

11

ReliaBench was a beast—an eight-foot-long reinforced concrete tube, two feet in diameter, supported by thick steel beams set into the sidewalk beneath. You could sit on ReliaBench, sort of—as long as you did so without leaning backward or to either side—but you wouldn't want to do it for long. Five minutes at most, and you'd be grateful when your bus arrived.

Varma had declared war on the city's bus stops, identifying them as breeding grounds for crimes of opportunity. According to Varma's philosophy, time bred mischief. The less time a person could spend at a location, the less likely he was to break the law. By targeting bus stops, Varma was removing places to stop and think and, ostensibly, contemplate bad behavior. And if the city's vagrants, of which there were a record number, had fewer places to rest their weary limbs, then that was good, too.

LA didn't have the budget to replace all of its nearly fourteen-hundred bus stops with ReliaBench, so it fell back on statistical data to lay out its implementation strategy. Not surprisingly, the city's COMPSTAT system found comparatively few incidents of criminal mischief at bus stops in Los Feliz, West Hollywood, Sherman Oaks, Studio City, Toluca Lake, and Laurel Canyon. Those could stay, for the time being. But East Hollywood, Panorama City, Santa Monica,

Venice, Culver City, and most of the rest were on the high priority list.

Reinforced concrete isn't expensive—limestone, clay, gravel, sand, and water, all packed around a rebar skeleton. Casting the ReliaBench tubes was therefore relatively cheap—less than ninety dollars per unit in materials. Compare that to the amount of money and manpower the city expended annually on emergency responses to incidents at bus stops, and you had an obvious win.

If that had been the only incentive, however, ReliaBench still might not have been deployed. But Varma had packaged her product with two emerging and dazzlingly attractive technologies. The first was a self-healing capability. Even quality reinforced concrete may crack, and when it does, water slips in and causes the rebar to rust and swell—eventually compromising structural integrity. But Varma's concrete had been impregnated with the bacterium *B. pasteurii*. It could lie dormant for decades, but snap awake if released from its calcium silicate hydrate bonds by an invasive trickle of water. All it needed was food, but that too had been provided in the form of a simple starch added in with the concrete matrix. The bacteria would feed and multiply, all the while excreting waste in the form of calcite. Calcite, being a chemical ingredient in concrete, fills the crack and the wound is closed.

Sure, that was all interesting stuff, but what really got the approval for Varma's project, along with the ten million to fabricate and install ReliaBench, was the self-cleaning feature. Each bench was treated with a coating of titanium dioxide, a colorless substance which, when struck with the sun's UV rays, generated free radical ions that would attack dirt particles on an atomic level. But the benefits went beyond mere appearances; self-cleaning concrete also breaks down airborne car pollution, making the city a cleaner, healthier place. The idea of giant, self-healing, crime-deterring air filters was simply too attractive to pass by.

So in they came, flown into position by cranes and harnesses and shouting men, then lowered and fitted onto their posts. No one would much want to sit on the new ReliaBenches, let alone lie on them. The concrete wasn't polished—the sand and pebbles comprising the aggregate plainly felt to anyone interested lying down. Just to make sure, however, the city removed a select number of bus stop canopies; in case anyone got too comfortable, maybe the weather would persuade them to leave. People tried anyway. One man suffered a broken arm after tumbling off in his sleep.

There wasn't much pushback, at least at first. The most notable incident involved an angry Boyle Heights man who attempted to lever a ReliaBench from its supports with a tire jack and roll it down Whittier Boulevard. The scheme was doomed to failure from the start. ReliaBench weighed in at nearly two tons. The citizen succumbed to a hernia and, upon waking in the hospital, found himself cited for disorderly conduct.

That same week, Varma unveiled her third crime-dampening strategy, Sonic Fence. It was a sturdy plastic device, weatherproof and shock resistant, about the size of a deck of cards. To protect Sonic Fence from destruction, it was always mounted high up and housed behind a steel cage.

If PuraLux assaulted the sense of sight, and ReliaBench the sense of touch, Sonic Fence declared war on the human ear, emitting a high-frequency whine. In an *LA Weekly* article, Heather Malins wrote, "It's not that it's loud. It doesn't need to be loud. It's penetrating. How best to describe it? Imagine a radial saw. Flip it on and listen to that screech. Good; now touch that spinning blade to a cast-iron frying pan next to an idling jet engine while a goat gets attacked by a pack of hyenas, and you've got the dulcet tones of Sonic Fence."

The technology acted upon the stereocilia—tiny, sensitive hairs of the inner ear. And since people lose their stereocilia at predictable intervals throughout their lives, Sonic Fence could be calibrated, with a turn of a dial, to affect ever narrower age groups. The broadest setting could be heard by everyone, and was probably the most unpleasant. Malins commented that "[it] should be tested in earnest on coma patients, as even the most vegetative specimen would surely work out a way to get up and leave if confronted with such auditory rape."

But a hard twist to the left made it so only listeners under twenty-four could hear it. This gave Sonic Fence almost messianic status at places like the David Farragut Transitional Care and Rehab Center, whose frail, elderly patients—along with anyone visiting—frequently found themselves targets of muggings by local MS-13 bangers. The hoodlums woke in the late afternoon, and by evening circled the facility like flocks of carrion birds. Sonic Fence kept them at a distance, flushing them from their usual ambush points.

Its most noticeable victory, one that earned grudging praise even from the solidly anti-Varma *LA Weekly*, was in reclaiming a neighborhood playground in San Pedro. Dedicated in 1933 as the George E. Waring, Jr. Community Park, it had for the last decade been annexed as a hangout for the area's larval criminals. Patrol officers referred to them collectively as the FFA—Future Felons of America. The life-sized bronze statue of Waring—"The Father of Metropolitan Sanitation"—was probably the single most vandalized object in the city, an irony appreciated by no one.

And while the delinquents usually started showing up after dark, families stayed away regardless of the hour. Ignoring the profanities, gang placas, and crudely scratched cocks and pussies decorating the play structure, a trip down the twisty slide was likely to end atop a pile of cigarette butts and spent glass pipes. Digging in the sandbox was an even riskier proposition, guaranteed to include the discovery of several lumps of cat shit and, occasionally, a greasy condom with a nicely filled reservoir tip.

Then one morning at sunrise the folks at the Bureau of Street Lighting arrived. A two-man team strapped a single, solar-powered Sonic Fence unit to the trunk of a nearby palm. They turned the dial to the right, the arrow pointing at the word ALL AGES, and set the activation time from 9:00 p.m. to 6:00 a.m. To discourage any would-be Tarzans from climbing up to disable the device, the men wrapped a square yard of slick sheet metal around the tree a few feet up from the bottom. As a bonus, it would also keep out palm rats.

That's all it took. The cigarette butts and glass pipes began to disappear. Tentatively at first, then in a flood, the neighborhood's children retook Waring Park. Their parents repainted the play structure and raised money for a new water fountain. They dug out the fetid, probably hazardous sandbox and brought in a hundred bags of fresh, silky white sand. They even installed a cover to keep the cats out at night. And though no one had heard of the man in whose honor the park had been named, the statue of George E. Waring, Jr. was lovingly restored, its brass polished to a high sheen.

12

There wasn't a cafeteria inside PAB, so every day Jarsdel worked on the task force he had to eat out. To save time, he waited until the lunch rush was over, then took the short walk over to Señor Fish. It was the closest place to get food, just off PAB's main entrance, and it was probably the world's safest restaurant. LA might continue to devolve along its jittery, paranoid course, but a meal at that particular Señor Fish was guaranteed to be peaceful. Misbehave in there, and you'd quickly find yourself kissing the floor, courtesy of the dozen or so officers dining there at any given time. The chief himself, who stopped in at least once a week for an order of chilaquiles, might even be the one to clap on the cuffs.

That day Jarsdel was enjoying a fried shrimp burrito, knocking it back with a large agua de jamaica, a daily treat he now allowed himself. The iced hibiscus tea was as sweet and red as hummingbird nectar, and he supposed even his sturdy metabolism wouldn't be able to keep up with the stuff forever.

He'd snagged a large table and laid his work out before him. Statements from patrol officers, private security companies, firefighters, paramedics, even garbage men. All had worked in their official capacities near a Creeper crime scene. Each had been given the simple instruction to describe any unusual activity in the neighborhoods in question.

In reading the statements, Jarsdel began to feel there was a whole other world that existed outside his awareness. He'd assumed that as a homicide detective he was already in tune with every bizarre, cruel, or otherwise repugnant thing that went on in his city. Not on a case-by-case basis of course—Los Angeles was vast—but at least in a broader, thematic sense. That assumption, he now saw, was incorrect.

Location: 5100 Block, Mount Royal Drive, Eagle Rock

A postal worker recounted emptying a public mailbox a quarter mile from the Verheugen crime scene. Inside, along with the letters, the man discovered a pile of long blond hair. The shortest strand was two feet, the longest nearly twice that. His first conclusion, that the hair was a misguided donation to a cancer relief organization, perhaps Locks of Love, was quickly dismissed. Instead of being cut, the hair had been ripped out by the roots. The worker reported the find to police as well as to postal inspectors, but so far nothing had come of it. Jarsdel certainly agreed that it fit under the broad category of "unusual activity" he'd laid out in his questionnaire, but if it was related to the Creeper, he couldn't see how.

Location: 2000 Block, Hyperion Avenue, Silver Lake

Next up was a duo of paramedics who'd been contacted because, according to their dispatcher—who was herself relaying information provided by the caller—"a man in business attire appears to be in physical distress." Arriving on scene, the paramedics agreed that the man did certainly appear to be in distress, but weren't at all certain what the caller had meant by "business attire."

What they found was a Caucasian male—later identified as Dylan Roswurm, thirty-three—clad head to toe in full samurai battle dress, crawling down Hyperion toward Lyric. Behind him was a trail of blood extending several blocks. When emergency personnel intercepted him, the man admitted he'd tried to die honorably by means of seppuku—ritual suicide by disembowelment—after losing his job at Line of Fire shooting range. The procedure had been much more painful than he'd expected, and the wounds he'd inflicted were ultimately superficial.

When he was informed he was going to be put on a forty-eight-hour hold over at Fantasy Island, however, the man's story changed. Now it was the Creeper who'd attacked him, stabbing him with his own katana before fleeing into the haze of an August afternoon. As far as Jarsdel could make out, that patently idiotic statement was the only reason the report had been kicked over to him.

Obviously not relevant, Jarsdel wrote at the top of the page, underlining the word *not* with three firm strokes. His phone buzzed. He didn't recognize the number, but it was local. He touched *accept* and brought the phone to his ear.

"Jarsdel."

"Hi, this is Jonas calling from Motor Transportation Division."

Jarsdel brightened. "Terrific, when can I pick up the car?"

"Actually we're calling because it's gonna take a little longer than we thought. The door handle's on back order."

Jarsdel exhaled. "Okay. How much longer?"

"Could be up to two weeks."

"Wait, seriously? For a door handle?"

"It's an older model, and—"

"Yeah, I know, never mind." He pinched the bridge of his nose. "What am I supposed to drive until then?"

"You still have the patrol car?"

"Yes, but it's really not ideal for what I do."

"Don't know what to tell you. Sorry, sir."

"Okay. You're sure that...okay. Thank you." Jarsdel hung up. He put Roswurm the would-be samurai to the back of the pile and read on.

Location: 5900–6000 Block, Foothill Drive, Los Angeles

A mere two blocks from the Lauterbach house, patrol officers responded to several complaints of a fiftysomething white male going from house to house selling "Creeper Insurance," which would remit huge payouts if a policyholder was killed in a certified Creeper homicide. Officers were unable to locate the salesman. Jarsdel turned the page.

Location: 8013 N. Stoker Drive, Highland Park

Across the street from the Rustad house. Wanda Heitkamp, a widow of eighty-two, reported a figure outside her bedroom window. Her bedroom was located on the second floor, and the culprit had allegedly been peering in from the top of an avocado tree. She thought it was probably a man, but it was hard to tell for sure from the build, which was very petite. No, she didn't get a look at his face. Yes, she had an idea whom it might be.

"An agent of the Israelite Defense Forces," she'd said. "My father was in the German army, you know, during the war, and now these people just won't leave me alone. Even though I had nothing to do with any of that." She also indicated they were tapping her phone and slipping unspecified "toxins" into her water supply.

Jarsdel turned the page.

Location: 6874 Joston Avenue, San Marino

Three houses down from the Santiago homicides. A mysterious package delivered to the home of Zack Brandsted, a single father. The item consisted of a large cardboard box wrapped in brown paper, and contained nothing but packing peanuts. No return address given. Package turned over to postal inspectors.

Location: 9452 Atkins Place, San Marino

Half a mile from the Santiago homicides. A very large, unidentified insect, possibly a centipede but "a heck of a lot meaner," crawled from the wedding album of Frank and Sheila Kubly. They considered the event suspicious because the album had previously been secured inside a fireproof safe which neither had recently opened. Their conclusion was that they were being targeted by the Creeper, and that he'd planted the insect as a sign they'd been marked. They were however unable to provide an explanation for how he'd gained access to the safe.

Location: 7034 Nuez Way, Topanga Canyon

One block from the Galka house. Sam Judkins, a widower, reported a prowler casing his property two weeks prior to the homicides. Someone had apparently ascended his oak tree and was watching him getting ready for bed. Judkins wouldn't have seen the man, except the rising moon had silhouetted his head and torso. By the time Judkins made it outside with his shotgun, the figure in the trees was gone.

Jarsdel flipped back through the pages until he located the report from Wanda Heitkamp. He put the two side by side, reading a little of one, then the other.

"So," he said. "You like to climb trees."

Mailander, Al-Amuli, and Rall sat at the conference table. Jarsdel stood before them, arranging his paperwork. "Just a quick second," he said.

"What's the tea?" asked Al-Amuli.

Jarsdel glanced up. "Almost done."

"Spill the tea."

Mailander shot him a look. "What are you, in middle school?"

"*Ta-da*," Al-Amuli sang. "Knew it wouldn't be long before you were at me again."

"Shut up, people," said Rall. "Tully, you ready?"

"Okay," said Jarsdel. "Sorry, wanted to make sure I had everything right. So..." He handed each detective a copy of three separate reports. "I think we've got something pretty definite. He, uh, well—he likes to climb."

Rall scanned first one document, then the next. The other detectives were slower, but Jarsdel could see their eyes flicker with interest as they too caught up with his own revelation.

"I dismissed the first one because it sounded nutty. Wanda Heitkamp. But based on the other reports, I think there really was someone outside her window. Just not the 'Israelite Defense Forces.'"

"*Israel* Defense Forces," corrected Rall, still reading.

"I'm quoting her directly."

The door to the conference room opened and Sponholz stepped in, wearing another of his space-themed ties, this one a print of the Hubble Deep Field. Thousands of galaxies spiraled and blinked against the dark.

He set down the black doctor's bag he used as a valise. "Sorry I'm late. Stuck on the phone." He sagged into a chair. "It's official. LA run of *Phantom*'s canceled. Pantages is a wreck, apparently. Needs a new roof... Don't know when I'm gonna get my refund. And I can't help but think of all those poor actors out of a job." He looked around, cheeks reddening. "Sorry. You were all in what looked like a pretty intense meeting before I came blundering in here. Anything that'll cheer me up?"

Rall crooked a thumb in Jarsdel's direction. "Tully got somethin'."

Sponholz's eyes blazed with interest. "Tell me."

"Well," said Jarsdel, "I've got three reports here from neighbors peripheral to the Creeper slayings. Couple houses, maybe a block over in one direction or another. Pretty consistent in their similarities. The complainants glance out an upper-story window and see someone looking back in on them. A kind of Peeping Tom, but he's agile, climbs trees. Also described as having a very slight physique."

"We get a description? Please tell me we got a description."

"No, sorry."

"Shit."

"Yeah. But I think this could be one of his victim selection routines. He starts the observation process outside the home, sees how much the victims get his juices flowing. I looked at photos of places he actually did strike, and sure enough, there's something available to climb either on or very close to the property. Mostly trees, but with the Rustads it was a telephone pole, and with the Santiagos it was probably the neighbor's roof. Someone looking down from there could easily see into the Santiagos' bedroom."

"Hey," said Al-Amuli. "We ought let the press know. Frustrate his routine a little. Least get people to keep their shades closed."

Rall's ever-present frown deepened. "Do more harm than good. You don't want a bunch of citizens plugging away at tree trimmers or telephone linemen. And it's a solid thing to keep to ourselves, root out false confessions."

Sponholz looked at Mailander. "Anything else?"

Mailander shrugged. "Not much. I spoke to a neighbor who'd been out of town during the original canvass."

"Which scene?"

"Sorry. Rustad."

"Okay."

"And she said she thought she heard shouting one of the nights we think the Creeper was in the house."

"Was she able to make out any words?"

"Not sure. Maybe the word 'stop' a couple times, but that's all."

Sponholz sagged. "That's it? That's everything?"

"Well, it's been months," Mailander protested. "People's memories fade, and false memories start to grow. I mean, there's other stuff, but I don't think it's worth reporting."

Sponholz flapped his hand in a reassuring gesture. "Hey, hey. Of course."

"I mean I can go through it all if you *want*. Just so you don't think I'm out there wasting taxpayer dollars, dicking around the city."

"Hey. It's understandable. I'm not upset with you. Everyone knows you're doing your best."

Mailander settled back in her chair, scowling.

Sponholz turned his attention to Al-Amuli. "And you?"

Al-Amuli was nodding. "Absolutely."

"Okay, let's do it."

"Well, my assignment was to work deep background, look for commonalities between the victims. See if maybe there's a chance they're connected in some way."

"Yes, I know all that, of course. So what's new?"

"There's actually a lot of stuff."

"Such as?"

Al-Amuli produced an iPad and flicked on the screen. "So Esperanza Santiago and Sam Verheugen both went to the same high school—John Marshall."

Sponholz grunted. "I went to Marshall. Two years ahead of Heidi Fleiss, actually. Almost asked her to prom, but then I found out she was a sophomore."

"Who's Heidi Fleiss?"

"Never mind. Keep going."

Al-Amuli looked back at the screen. "So yeah, they went to Marshall, but way apart. Santiago graduated in '88, and Verheugen in '79, so I don't know if that's much of a connection. Another related potential puzzle piece is that Joanne Lauterbach used to be a teacher. Not at Marshall, but at Franklin Elementary. Might be something, might not. Uh, let's see, what else? Ah, here we go. Sam's wife, Beth, owned a fabric store: You Sew & Sew. Guess who shopped there?"

He paused, looking up, an eyebrow arched dramatically. "Maja... Rustad."

When there wasn't a reaction, Al-Amuli clarified, "Killed at the hands of the Creeper along with her husband, Steffen."

"Yes, we know," said Sponholz. "Any reason to believe that connection's important?"

Al-Amuli held up his palms. "I'm just doing what Detective Rall told me, which is deep background on these victims. I figured we could feed this new info into COMPSTAT."

"What else?"

"Well that one was pretty much my biggie, but there's all kinds of little things. Like the Galkas and Steffen Rustad played some of the same venues. And both recorded albums at the same studio on Melrose. Uh...oh, this is a good one—Bill Lauterbach's dad was an architect, and he actually designed the house the Verheugens lived in. Crazy, right? That one was *not* easy to find out."

Sponholz looked grim. “I think we’re kind of missing the point. The idea isn’t to see how many coincidences we can spot between these people. The idea is to find a common thread that links them together in some meaningful way. Some way that might help us identify how he’s picking them.”

Al-Amuli wasn’t cowed. If anything, he looked vindicated. “Good. I’m glad I’m not the only one then who thinks this is a shit detail. Face it—whole thing’s random. There’s nothing linking these guys together. Creeper’s an opportunist. Just floats around the city and lands when he feels like it. Boom, here. Boom, there. He’s a tornado, touching down according to who-knows-why. This house gets spared, that one doesn’t.”

He moved aside his notes, revealing the Galka murder book. He tapped the cover. “We still call him the Eastside Creeper. That’s crazy. You can’t get more Westside than Topanga Area and still be in LA. One end of the city to the absolute other, snatchin’ birthdays the whole way across. There’s no sense to it.”

Sponholz drummed his fingers slowly on the table. “I’m not frustrated. Well, that’s not true—I *am* frustrated, but it’s more a matter of how this just seems to keep circling the drain. I’ve never had this kind of experience where every inch of headway is so damn hard-won. I know you’re all working your asses off, so there’s really not much else Detective Rall and I can ask of you. But, I gotta tell you, if I *do* figure out a way to ask more of you, I’m gonna have to do that. Because we’ve got a frightened city and a mad dog running wild out there, and we’re the ones who’re supposed to button this mess up. And—goddamnit—it’s just *not coming together*.”

He stood and began kneading the muscles at the back of his neck. The group watched him with apprehension. “I think we need to start over. Revisit our strategy. My feeling is that in all this digging, if there was something to find we would’ve found it by now. Goodwin, thoughts please.”

“I’m with you, LT,” said Rall. “But I don’t see a whole lot we’re leaving out. Pickin’ this city apart, man. Got ’em chasing everything—the good, the bad, and the goofy-as-shit—but they ain't come across nothin' worth pursuing. Detective Mailander here spent two days just interviewing dog walkers. If you got something we haven't tried, tell us and we'll do it. Nobody likes to lose, and we're losing."

Sponholz had wandered over to the thermostat. "Boiling in here." He tapped the screen until he hit a temperature he liked, then went to stand under one of the vents.

"Could look at parolees again," said Al-Amuli, turning pages in the Galka murder book.

"Kinda already did," said Mailander.

"Yeah, thank you, I know that. But that was mostly California, right? I'm saying we cast a wider net."

"And what good's that gonna do? No prints in IAFIS or Interpol, and his DNA didn't match anything in CODIS."

"Let's pretend for a second I'm not the one who came up with the idea, so just listen without judging, okay? What if there was some kind of mistake or glitch or something, and his info never made it into the system?"

Rall sighed, but Al-Amuli went on. "You know that's the problem with us today—too reliant on technology, when we need to be more common sense. Just think it through: what's more likely—that this guy's never served time, or his prints got deleted somewhere along the way? Or..." his expression brightened. "What if it's no accident? What if someone deleted his file on purpose?"

Mailander squinted at him. "Who?"

"Remains to be seen. I agree that it remains to be seen. Remember Jack the Ripper, though? One of the theories as to why he got away with it is because he was an aristocrat or something. Had connections."

Jarsdel would have been amused if the suggestion hadn't come from a member of the Creeper task force. Mailander groaned aloud.

Al-Amuli went on. "Seriously, what if that's kinda what's going on here? Maybe the Creeper's some celebrity's kid? An actor or a studio exec, maybe. Protected."

Sponholz looked up at the vent that should have by now been sending down jets of cooling air. "Can't be broken. This is PAB. System's only a decade old."

"Probably a placebo button," said Jarsdel.

The rest of the team turned to him. "The thermostat," he clarified. "It's probably a placebo button. Temperature's set by the building engineer, and the thermostat's just there to give you the illusion of control. Most people report feeling more comfortable after adjusting a thermostat, regardless of whether it actually works or not."

"You making this up?" asked Sponholz.

"No, sir. It's in this book I was reading on environmental influences. Same person who designed PuraLux."

"Makes sense," said Al-Amuli. "Always thought those 'door close' buttons on elevators were bullshit." He'd reached the crime-scene photos in the Galka murder book. He stared at them, hypnotized by their horror.

Sponholz approached the thermostat with renewed interest. He tapped the screen a few times. "Huh," he said. "Assholes."

"LT." It was Rall. The detective's expression was anxious.

"Huh?"

"What's the move?"

"Oh." He shrugged. "I don't know. I really don't. Just keep on keepin' on, I suppose."

On his way back to the conference table he happened to glance down at the open murder book. He stopped, fixated on something in one of the pictures. Al-Amuli was about to turn the page but Sponholz anchored it in place with his pointer finger.

Al-Amuli looked up, confused and irritated. "What is it?"

Sponholz didn't answer, but his eyes were alive, keen with interest.

"Everything okay, LT?" Rall asked.

"Bastard..." Sponholz murmured. Jarsdel waited, sensing more coming, but nothing did.

A long silence passed. Finally Sponholz looked up. "It's just so heartbreaking. Whole family like that. Just wiped off the map."

No one said anything. After another moment's study of the photographs, he grunted and gave a sad shake of the head. He made it back over to the table and began rummaging through his doctor's bag. "Yes indeed. Another week of this, and I'll be ready to take Detective Al-Amuli's advice and start looking at gossip rags for leads." His voice dropped into the resonant baritone of an old-time radio announcer. "Another exclusive scoop from *Checkout Stand Loser Impulse Buy*. Son of studio head at Movies By Committee—MBC—revealed to be the long-sought Eastside Creeper." He brought out a tube of lip balm, applied it daintily over his lips, and dropped it back in the bag.

Jarsdel studied him. The lieutenant was in performance mode again, but why? It seemed odd, coming on the heels of whatever he saw in the murder book.

Surveying the group, Sponholz smiled slyly. He continued in his announcer voice, "Family and friends, emboldened by the young man's arrest, finally come forward. Juvenile forays into coprophagia, necrophilia, cannibalism, pyromania might have been early warning signs, they say. Did dear old dad's connections keep his boy's prints out of IAFIS?"

He picked up his doctor's bag. "Sometimes I forget I have the rest of Homicide Special to run. I'll be in my office if you need me." On his way out the door, he stopped, touching his forehead. It was a bad pantomime of an absent-minded man trying to remember something.

"Oh, right. Say—um, Tully. Detective Jarsdel, rather, so long as we're on the clock."

Jarsdel blinked in surprise. "Sir?"

"Funny little hunch, probably a waste of time. But do you have the Lauterbach murder book handy?"

"Sure. It's on my desk."

"I'll snag it if it's okay with you."

"Of course."

"Something I want to check out."

Rall's interest was piqued. "Want to let us in on the big discovery, LT?"

"I don't want to say, in case I'm wrong. Which I probably am. Ciao." Then he was gone. The detectives looked at each other, perplexed.

"Lemme see that." Rall reached out his hand for the Galka murder book, and Al-Amuli handed it over. "What page was he on?"

Al-Amuli got up and stood behind Rall. "Keep going. In the photos. There—no, go back one. There. That page right there."

Jarsdel and Mailander crowded in as well, searching the pictures for anything that might have interested Sponholz.

"You see anything?" asked Al-Amuli.

"I see all kinds of things," said Rall.

"I mean—"

"Quiet, man. Let me think in peace a goddamned second."

Jarsdel was glad none of the pictures showed the Galka boys. He wasn't in the mood just then for the Creeper's particular brand of mayhem. There were six pictures laid out across two pages. Three of them were of the exterior of the Galka house. A shot of the garage, the mailbox, and the front door, which stood ajar. A smear of dried blood in the vague shape of a hand was visible on the wall nearest the doorbell. It looked like the killer had stumbled upon exiting and caught himself there.

The next three pictures were interior shots. The entryway, upon which a small table held a basket of dusty pinecones and, Jarsdel noted queasily, a coil of human feces. A close-up of a framed family photograph, with more blood smears on the glass. Another close-up, this time of a piece of dark-red plastic lying against a background of shaggy brown carpet. An SID tech had set a ruler next to it for comparison. Just over an inch at its widest, and obviously trimmed from a larger piece. A neat, ninety-degree corner, with the opposite side arcing gently inward but not neat enough to have been factory cut. Something about it, particularly its shape, seemed strangely familiar, but he couldn't place it.

"Got me," said Rall. "No idea."

"Think he's just messing with us?" said Al-Amuli.

"He wouldn't joke about this kinda thing." Rall shut the murder book and handed it back to Al-Amuli. "He'll let us know if he got anything."

Jarsdel and the others dispersed, filing out of the conference room and back to their desks.

There wasn't much else Jarsdel could get done that day—at least nothing that necessitated him hanging around PAB. He had another stack of reports to cull through, and that was a job that could just as easily be done at home in the company of Sonny Chillingworth's honeyed voice and slack-key guitar.

"Hey, Tully." It was a woman, but she spoke in tones too pleasant to be Mailander's. Jarsdel turned around in his swivel chair and saw Alisha Varma. She wore one of her business suits—dark green this time—and of course her trademark red lipstick. A large visitor's badge was pasted over the slope of her chest.

Jarsdel couldn't hide his pleasure in seeing her. "Hey."

"This is where you work," she said, looking around. "Not really what I expected. 'Homicide Special.' I was thinking big wooden desks, slowly revolving ceiling fans, wanted posters with darts sticking out of them, or—"

"Yeah, I know," said Jarsdel. "Looks more like an insurance firm. Same thing I thought. You're not here for me, are you?"

"No. I mean, I am now, but my appointment was with the chief."

Jarsdel tried not to look impressed. "So what can I do for you?"

Varma pulled up a chair and sat next to him. "Nothing really. I was in the building so I thought I'd stop by and say hello. I was also giving some more thought to what we were talking about the other day. About vampires. Vampires hiding out, taking refuge so the Van Helsings of the world can't get to them while they're most vulnerable. So I took it further, tried to see how an idea like that might apply to the case you're working. The Creeper."

"How so?"

"Well, have you considered searching for him with that in mind? Thinking of him basically as a vampire? Where's his crypt, right? Where does he go between attacks? Does he blend in, or is he obviously bonkers?"

It was a good question, and Jarsdel considered it thoughtfully. "LA's a big city. He gets around a lot, which suggests he's not so crazy that he can't drive or take public transportation. But there's also some suggestion that he's delusional—I'm not saying he doesn't know the difference between right and wrong, but that he may not care, or he may believe he has a condition that exempts him from moral law. Ever heard of Richard Trenton Chase?"

"No, who's he?"

"The 'Vampire of Sacramento,' so he kind of ties in to what you're saying. Suffered from a kaleidoscope of schizophrenic delusions and believed he had to kill people to stay alive."

"Like what?"

Jarsdel shrugged. "Incomprehensible stew. UFOs, Nazis, all the usual suspects. And he's similar to our guy in that he left heaps of physical evidence. But unlike our guy, he got caught fairly quickly. The Creeper's more organized. And he invariably picks houses he knows he can hide in for a while."

"How does he know that before he goes in? Does he look at blueprints at the public records office or something?"

"I asked myself the same question, but no, that would leave a trail. My theory's that he's a burglar. And he cases old houses, those likely to have basements and attics and crawl spaces, and makes the decision whether to stay after he breaks in—scopes it out from the inside, basically. If it doesn't conform to his needs, he just steals what he wants and leaves."

"Ah," said Varma, "so by that reasoning, many of his crimes are reported as simple burglaries, and not as Creeper attacks."

"Correct."

Varma shuddered. "And all those people, they have no idea how close they came to the full experience."

"Correct also."

"Doesn't it bother you? Being a garbage man?"

"I'm sorry—what?"

"Coming along after the fact to deal with the bodies. Cataloging the mess and managing all the emotional fallout. It's more like garbage cleanup than law enforcement. Doesn't that bother you? That you're not really there to enforce the laws as your job description suggests, but—I don't know—more...*maintain* the laws? Keep them relatively functional, but only after the fact?"

"You're not the first person who's made that comparison."

"I know, but still...it's like having a drafty old mansion, and there's always something leaking, but the only reason you know it's leaking is there's a big puddle on the ground. Only then do you know to clean it up. I mean, when's the last time you actually got to put a firm stop to something bad, to save a life or stop someone from getting hurt or robbed? Put a stop to something bad before it could finish its course?"

Jarsdel considered Varma's question. He answered honestly. "Never."

"Never," she repeated, looking both disappointed and unsurprised.

"That big case you were impressed by, the one you asked me about. I only saved myself. There was nothing satisfying or noble about it. I just didn't want to die. And I didn't stop anything big, anything beyond myself. Damage had already been done."

"So you were on the cleanup crew on that one, too."

"No. I was part of the mess."

Varma bowed her head. "That's a huge thing to share with me," she said. "I'm grateful, and I admire your candor." She lifted her gaze and looked at him closely. "I hope you have the opportunity someday. To stop someone truly evil, to save someone. I think that would be the most incredible, fulfilling thing."

Jarsdel didn't comment, and Varma's gaze wandered to the bandages on his left hand. "What happened?"

"Oh. It's fine." Jarsdel made a lame gesture to show the fingers were in good working order, but the stitches pinched. He must have made a face, because Varma's expression grew concerned.

"Looks painful."

"Nah, not really." Then, before he could stop himself, he added, "Someone glued a razor blade to the door handle on my car."

Varma's eyes widened. "Wait, really?"

"Yup. Hazards of the job, I guess."

"Oh my God. Where'd it happen?"

"Right there in the parking lot at Hollywood Station."

"But there's cameras!"

"Ah." Jarsdel gave his head a rueful shake. "Out of order."

"Unbelievable. Do you know who did it?"

"I've got a pretty good idea, yeah."

Varma leaned closer. "Who?"

"Can't prove it, so it doesn't really matter."

Varma thought for a moment. "*Oh*. Does this have anything to do with that thing a little while back? With the arm-wrestling table? What's his name..."

Jarsdel shrugged. "Possible."

"I'm so sorry. What a horrible, stupid, juvenile thing." Suddenly, Varma brightened. "Hey. What are you doing right now?"

"Just work."

"I mean do you have any plans?"

"Korean barbecue, wine, slack-key guitar, sleep. Nothing too exciting. Why?"

"How'd you feel about going on a little field trip with me? There's something I'd like to show you."

"Where?"

"It's a surprise."

Jarsdel wanted to go. He looked back at his desk, where the Lauterbach book had been before Sponholz borrowed it. In its place was his bulging folder of reports.

"I really think you'll like it," said Varma.

"Is it far?"

"You know where Watts Towers is?"

"Sure. I've seen them, though. My dads took me when I was a kid."

"Not so much the towers exactly," said Varma. "But what they accomplished. Because that's the next phase."

He looked his phone. Half past three. That time of day, it would take them an hour to get there. He glanced again at the reports.

"I guess if we caravan," he said. "I gotta wrap all this up by tomorrow morning."

"Excellent." Varma stood. "Hopefully you see now that I hadn't forgotten."

"Forgotten what?"

"I said I was gonna get in touch, remember? That day we ran into each other at the restaurant."

"You did?" said Jarsdel. "Forgot that part."

Varma flashed him a look—part amusement and part something else. Jarsdel couldn't say for sure what it was, and it was gone quickly, but in the moment it had been there he'd found it intoxicating.

"No, you didn't," she said.

Where does the water flow?

You can tell a lot about a city by asking that question, Jarsdel thought.

Los Angeles is a desert, with most of the water feeding its lawns, gardens, and swimming pools the legacy of shady dealings and outright theft. Owens Valley—once the "American Switzerland"—was bled dry, its lake emptied, its farmers left destitute. It was vampirism at a civic scale; Los Angeles slurped at the aqueducts, swelling, growing fat, while Owens Valley shriveled into a barely hospitable wasteland, becoming the very desert LA was pretending not to be. The larceny didn't go entirely unpunished, however. The now-dry lake bed—an ancient volcanic deposit of selenium and arsenic—became airborne, dusting the entire Southland with toxic particulate matter for the better part of a century. Efforts to restore the valley saw some success, and it had only recently lost its dubious position as the single worst source of dust pollution in the entire country.

Flush with its victory in the water wars, Los Angeles celebrated the life-giving bounty with a management decision of shocking, even aggressive stupidity. Instead of conserving the resource and using only what was needed, planners went out of their way to spend the water as irresponsibly as possible. What was even stranger, their hubris paid off, creating a cultural icon as inseparable from the city as red carpets, searchlights, and the Hollywood sign. Whether it had been a kind of mad genius or simply stopped-clock syndrome, the scheme worked—at least from a publicity perspective.

Palm trees.

Tens of thousands of them. Now a ubiquitous sight anywhere in LA, before 1930 there were hardly any of the towering Mexican fan palms lining modern Wilshire Boulevard. The whole thing was a way of selling the city to the tourist trade, pitching it as an exotic Mediterranean paradise. Never mind that palm trees aren't really trees at all, more like stalks of hard grass, and that they don't clean the air or provide any fruit or shade. And never mind that in return for their lack of utility, palms demand more water than most actual trees. Style wasn't bound by the constraints of propriety or logic. The city would have its useless, giant alien sticks, each a proud middle finger to the ruined Owens Valley. It was fitting that they grew higher in Los Angeles than they ever had in the wild.

So where does the water flow?

You won't find brown lawns in Beverly Hills or Hancock Park or Benedict Canyon. What you will find are lots and lots of hundred-foot palms. You'll find fountains, too. The Mulholland Memorial Fountain at the corner of Los Feliz Boulevard and Riverside has been appearing as a backdrop in wedding photographs since 1940. It's a five-tiered art-deco gem and, with a 50,000-gallon capacity, celebrates the greatest American water thief with fitting brazenness.

But Watts is different. Watts is in South LA, a flat, arid slice of the basin crammed with postwar tract homes, fast-food restaurants, and liquor stores. At their peak, there'd been more than seven hundred liquor stores in South LA, or about ten per square mile, and it took neighborhood activist groups like Community Coalition to reduce their number to a tolerable level. It was hard enough growing up in the ghetto without the environment itself setting you up to fail. It's not just that there weren't a lot of pretty water fountains; there also weren't a whole lot of libraries, coffee shops, or safe public parks.

If you get off the Harbor Freeway at Wilmington and follow it from there to 112th, crossing the train tracks, then onto Willowbrook, and finally onto 107th, you'd never guess you were about to see one of the most unusual works of art anywhere in the world. Cobbled together from concrete and rebar, castoff squares of tile, shards of pottery, glass, mirrors, and seashells, Watts Towers emerges above the skyline like an alien castle. Seventeen conical, Gaudiesque spires shooting up from a grotto of archways and sculptures and reef-like alcoves. In the sunlight, the scavenged ornaments embedded in its bands and loops glitter like jewels.

The story of the towers was one of Tully's favorites. They'd been built by one man, Simon Rodia, an illiterate Italian cement finisher. He'd begun the project in middle-age and worked on it for more than thirty years. And he'd done it without blueprints, without power tools or scaffolds, without a single bolt or welded joint or even a nail.

Unfortunately, he'd also done it without permits or an inspection from the Los Angeles Building and Safety Department. This became a problem when Rodia mysteriously abandoned the property, handing the deed to a neighbor and boarding a northbound bus, never to return. The city wanted the towers torn down, but fierce community resistance forced a compromise. If the towers could pass a load test, they could stay. The chief of Building and Safety attached a winch to the tallest tower and yanked on it with 10,000 pounds of force. Rodia's creation didn't so much as tremble.

Since then, the towers had survived mostly unmolested, weathering six big earthquakes and two major incidents of civil unrest. And despite being located in one of the city's most disadvantaged neighborhoods, not a single carved initial or zigzag of spray paint mars their otherworldly beauty.

As miserable as the traffic was, Jarsdel was pleased he'd only been two minutes shy of correctly estimating the travel time. He liked being good at that sort of thing. And he also had an audiobook of *Diogenes the Cynic—Sayings and Anecdotes* to keep him company.

Varma was already out of her car and pressed against the perimeter fence by the time Jarsdel found a parking spot. She didn't look away from the towers even as he approached. Still, she knew he was there and spoke to him when he took his place beside her.

"Probably seen them a hundred times. And each time there's something new." Varma turned to him then, her expression shy, cautious. "What do you notice?"

"About the towers? I told you, my dads brought me here when I was a kid. And back then this neighborhood was a lot more dangerous."

"Were you frightened?"

"Of what?"

"Gangs. I don't know. Anyone who might not appreciate a white boy from the suburbs treating Watts like a tourist attraction?"

Jarsdel thought that over. "Not frightened, I guess. Just a little on edge, because I could tell this was kind of a different world. And there was a guy right over there, shouting." Jarsdel pointed to the plot of grass and trees adjacent to the towers. "Just shouting as loud as he could at everything."

"What year was it?"

"I don't know for sure. 1992, maybe '93."

"Rough time for South-Central."

Jarsdel didn't correct her, but no one called it that anymore. The words "South-Central" had earned such a stigma that the city discontinued the use of the term in the early 2000s.

Varma gestured at the area around them. "So even though this was—back then, at least—one of the most dangerous places you could go around here, your parents took you?"

"They love art. And on some level, I think, they thought it was impossible—or at least unlikely—that we'd come to any harm here. In the vicinity of the towers."

"They were right," Varma said immediately. "They were absolutely right, and I'm proposing to take that idea and expand it. See how far it can go."

"How do you mean?"

"You see the beauty in front of you. This extraordinary thing, brought into being by the love of a single person. New Zealand's ambassador a while back, when he toured the country, he had one day to spend in Los Angeles. He could've done anything he wanted, but he came here. Not to Universal Studios or the Beverly Hills Hotel, but here."

"Okay," said Jarsdel. "Still don't think I get it."

"Turn around and you'll see."

Jarsdel did. He saw tidy, single-story homes, their windows laced with bars.

Varma pointed at them. "Look at those houses. Orange, baby blue, green. That one there's got flowers painted on it—see? Big mural of roses and—I'm not sure what those are, daffodils or something, but look at the way it spills over onto the garage. And there, see that hummingbird painted on the eave? And if you look more closely, you'll see even the walls in front of the houses are covered with mosaic artwork. And that bench—a public bench, but did you ever see anything like it? And it's all put together, it all tells a story. Palm tree, a wading duck, some kind of elemental creature or angel or something, lotus blossoms. It's a unified work of art. The whole block took on this mantle. They saw what Simon Rodia had done and decided that in their own way they'd keep it going."

Jarsdel looked at her. Her smile was distant, as if she were envisioning a possible future.

"If the last few months have shown us anything," she said, "it's that ugliness is catching. But see? Right here, you can see it. So is beauty." Varma turned to meet his gaze. "I had to slow down the crime first, give us some room to breathe. But only so we could move forward with what's next. All of my work is based on this street right here. It's what got me going, and it's what keeps me going during the rough patches."

"You're interested in the healing, transformative power of beauty?"

"Exactly."

"And how does that fit in with designing security systems for missile silos?"

Varma's lip twitched. "I think that's a cheap shot. I have to pay bills like everyone else. And wouldn't you rather have those kinds of places secure?"

Jarsdel considered. "Maybe a little cheap. Apologies."

Varma took his hand. Her skin was warm, her palm moist with sweat. He caught that tropical scent again—plumeria, he decided. It made you think of fronded beach bars and cool hotel rooms. "I want you on my side," she said.

"I am on your side."

"I've been getting threats, you know."

Jarsdel frowned. "No, I didn't know. From whom?"

"They're anonymous, of course. Two postcards from Death Valley saying 'Wish you were here.' Other things, too. Little notes and stuff."

"Bring 'em over to the station."

"I threw them away. Didn't want them in my apartment."

"Oh. Next time please don't. Save all that kind of stuff. I'm happy to hold on to it for you if you don't want it."

Varma squeezed his hand and he turned to her, leaning close. She matched the movement, standing on her toes, wrapping her free hand around the back of his neck. Their lips met, and she curled her fingers in his hair, pressing her body against his as they kissed. Her boldness excited Jardel, but she soon broke away, her cheeks flushed.

"My goodness," she said, wiping the corner of her mouth with a finger. "Got me all smudged up."

"Sorry," said Jarsdel, leaning in again.

Varma took a small step back and held up her hand. She smiled, but her eyes were serious. "We're getting ahead of ourselves."

"How do you mean? Gavin's not watching. Although I'm sure he'd love to have me drummed up on some obscure officer conduct charge."

Varma held his gaze a moment longer, then looked down at her feet. "We have to wait a little. Before we can do anything serious. It's a really crucial time for me, and I can't have any distractions. Oh *God*, I realize how awful that sounds, but that's not what I mean. Just for a few weeks."

Jarsdel could smell that scent on himself now—heady and tropical. He tasted mint, too. She must have had one in the car on the way over. He wanted more of her, and tried not to show his disappointment.

"Okay," he said. "I understand."

"You do?"

"Sure."

"Because the thing is, I also need your help, and I don't want you to feel like this...this thing that seems to be happening between us, that it has strings or anything. That would be weird. I want it to be real, you know?"

Jarsdel wasn't sure what she meant. "Need my help? With what?"

"I have a city council thing coming up on the fifteenth. You wouldn't have to go out on a limb for me or anything, maybe just talk about the state of the department's cameras and how it affected you."

"Oh. I suppose I could. But I don't know why anyone would bother listening to me. I'm not a tech guy or anything."

"Are you kidding—what about your hand? A decorated homicide detective gets assaulted—"

"I'm not decorated."

"Still, a homicide detective gets assaulted on city property, at a *police station* of all places? You could talk about how with an upgrade to my system, it never would have happened."

"Not technically *assault*," said Jarsdel. "Criminal mischief. Mayhem, maybe. Not quite as impressive."

"I think you're handling it amazingly well. You could've brought a lawsuit against the department for failing to maintain its cameras."

"I guess. Wouldn't solve anything. But sure, I'll be in your corner." He thought of Haarmann and his plastic, game-show-host smile, and knotted his good hand into a fist.

"My system, the one I'm proposing," said Varma, "would have all law enforcement camera feeds routed to a secure, dedicated installation. One that's responsible for monitoring and preserving all the footage for easy recovery. I'm talking flawless, uninterrupted service, with built-in redundancies. Power outages, civil unrest, human error—no longer a problem. Malfunctions or equipment breakdowns could be spotted and dealt with right away."

"You're very passionate about this."

"Oh, I'm *very* passionate. People behave better when they're being observed. Well, more specifically, when they *know* they're being observed."

"Sometimes, I guess."

"Sometimes? You do realize I've put more than a little thought into this."

"Mob mentality—"

"I'm not talking about mob mentality. That's a very specific situation. I'm talking about you: the individual, reasonable person. You're walking down the street, eating a sandwich. A giant slice of tomato falls out and splats on the ground. It's biodegradable, no big deal, right? You leave it there and keep going."

Jarsdel shrugged. "Not necessarily."

"It's hypothetical. Please bear with me. Now repeat that scenario, only you notice a PTZ mounted above you."

"PTZ?"

"Pan-tilt-zoom camera. Only it's encased in a darkened, semitransparent globe, so you have no idea if it's looking at you or not. The eye-in-the-sky cameras in casinos—you've seen them. Now what do you think you're going to do? I bet you'll pick up that tomato."

"That's a bet you'd win," said Jarsdel. "Never liked the whole biodegradable excuse. *Spit* is biodegradable, and I have a powerful aversion to spitting. You'll have to come up with a different hypothetical."

Varma squinted at him. "You're being difficult."

"Maybe."

"Why?"

"I don't know." It was an honest answer, so he gave it more thought. "Sorry. I think I like finally being able to really talk to you. And if that means messing with you a little, or getting challenging, it's only because I'm feeling comfortable."

"So you're basically the awkward kid in third grade who'd show a girl he liked her by pulling her pigtails?"

"Pigtails," Jarsdel agreed. "Also throwing little bits of paper at the back of her neck. Telling her she had big teeth."

"What a Casanova."

"Yeah. So at least you know it comes from a good place. Hopefully that makes it a little less annoying."

"Unlikely. But we'll see."

Jarsdel smiled. It felt good to smile like that, in the fullness of the moment. She was wonderful, and she was brilliant, and she had kissed him. Something about his expression must have appealed to her, because she returned the smile.

"Hey," she said. "What're you thinking?"

"I'm thinking I admire you."

"Admire me?" Varma looked surprised.

"Have you ever heard of Lady Mary? She was the wife of the British ambassador to Turkey, early eighteenth century."

Varma laughed. "That sounds like an extremely obscure person. Why on earth would I know who that is?"

"She wrote these terrific letters about the time she spent over there, helped expose the West to the culture of the Muslim Orient. She was also a celebrated beauty, and—well—she's one of my heroes, kind of my big historical crush. She took a big chance and got her kids inoculated to smallpox, which wasn't being done in

England. Western medicine had mostly dismissed inoculation as crazy, but she saw the science in it. Because of her, experiments in Europe got kicked off, and when the next epidemic struck, London lost only a fraction of the people it would have. Compare it to Boston, which lost a quarter of its population that year."

"Okay," said Varma. "And why are you asking me about her?"

Jarsdel hesitated. "If I explain it, it'll sound stupid."

"Now I'm definitely curious."

"I guess you remind me of her in some ways."

"Even the part about being a celebrated beauty?"

"Very much so."

"Really?" She bit her bottom lip. It was a coquettish gesture, not the sort of thing he would have expected from her, and that made it even sexier. "Okay. I like this conversation. What else?"

"She was brave, the way you are. Tough, uncompromising. Used her brain. Even when people told her she was wrong, she didn't let it throw her off."

Varma drew a featherlight finger down his chest. "I'm lucky to know you. In more ways than one." Their lips met once again. When they'd finished, she gave him a little push. "You're gonna have to stop doing that. Or you're gonna get me to do something I don't think I should do yet."

"Could bend the rules a little."

"Now if I did that, I wouldn't be the woman you claim to be attracted to." She put an arm around his waist. "Couple more weeks, okay? Just let me get past this city council thing."

Jarsdel tasted the mint again. Savored the scent rolling off her.

"And after that..." Varma shrugged. "Then we can have some fun."

A flower is an affordance to a bee, Jarsdel recalled from Varma's book. *But so is a pitcher plant to a fly.*

He pushed the thought away.

"Sounds good," he told her.

13

Jarsdel was the first to see the lieutenant's face, and his shock must have been apparent.

"Yeah, I know," said Sponholz, shuffling over to the conference table. "But before you say anything—no, I wasn't mugged, and no, it's not serious."

Rall looked up at his boss. "Shit, LT, what happened?"

At that, Mailander and Al-Amuli turned in their seats to see what was going on.

Sponholz was a wreck. His lip was split, and the skin around his left eye was puffy and dark with bruising. Three parallel scrapes, already scabbed over, marred his other cheek.

"It's too embarrassing," he said. "I'd love to tell you all I foiled a bank robbery and these are my nobly earned war wounds. But I think a quick check of the local news will prove me a liar. So not only is it embarrassing, but I'm going to have to tell the goddamn truth to everyone who asks."

"What, you and the woman get into a fight?" Al-Amuli asked the question with a knowing grin.

"Such a *dick*," Mailander sighed.

"Uh, no, actually," said Sponholz. "That's kind of an inappropriate thing to say, Detective, even in jest."

Al-Amuli nodded. "Yeah, I'm just..." He shrugged.

"Please be mindful of stuff like that. Especially in today's climate."

"Yeah. 'Course." Al-Amuli looked down at his hands.

"Anyway, no. I was fixing a part of our eaves where birds had been nesting in this tiny hole they'd found. This is out at Amy's ranch in Shadow Hills, and you know, when you don't go out to a place often enough, it begins to fall down around your ears. I mean, she goes there all the time, but she never notices things like that. Little things—you know, like *animals* living inside the structure of our property. Oy."

He slumped into a chair. "Idiocy. You know, you forget sometimes, when you get to be my age, that you should really be hiring professionals. But when you're stubborn the way I am, you still try to do everything yourself. So I'm up there trying to put in this little screen to keep the birds out, and I thought they were all gone, but one of them flies out right toward my face."

"A bird did that?" said Rall.

"No. A tree. I fell off the ladder and right into an oak. Grabbed at the branches, as you can see, trying not to plummet to my death. So here I am clutching at these things, getting cut up, taking all kinds of damage, working my way down the rest of the way to the ground. Naturally I fall about five feet, sprain my ankle, my wrist." He lifted his hand and rotated it in its joint, wincing. "There goes my tennis game. Absolutely humiliating. And of course I definitely am not getting back up there to put up the wire. So now I look like I got jumped, and I have to call someone anyway. Fantastic."

He stroked his tie. That morning's selection was a showstopper—a photograph of H. G. Wells surrounded by renderings of scenes from his books. There were Morlocks, time machines, Martian tripods. All these were set against a quote, which emerged in bold strokes, presumably a copy of the author's own handwriting: "...slain, after all man's devices had failed, by the humblest things that God, in his wisdom, has put upon this earth."

"Sorry to change the subject," said Rall, "but we were curious about yesterday."

"Curious?" Sponholz's eyes twinkled.

"C'mon, LT, what you got?"

"Are you asking if I've made progress on the case?"

Rall crossed his arms.

"If that were true," continued Sponholz, "it would mean I spotted something in the murder book that you missed. Explicitly, it would mean this old man here got wise to an angle of investigation that had eluded Detective III Goodwin Rall. Career badass, outdone by a failed actor turned brasshole."

Rall's expression remained stern, though Jarsdel could see the corner of his mouth twitch.

Sponholz raised his hands in a placating gesture. "It would be cruel of me to ask you to acknowledge that. Particularly in front of your subordinates." He stood and crossed to the whiteboard mounted on the east wall. Picking up a dry-erase marker, he shot a smile to the group and began writing. It didn't take long for him to finish, and when he stood aside he gave a stiff bow.

Jarsdel stared at the board. He glanced around to see if it meant anything to the others, but they looked as puzzled as he was.

In a cheery, lime-green scrawl, Sponholz had written the number: *1000000000000066600000000000001.*

The team's bafflement only seemed to excite the lieutenant more. "No math whizzes in here, huh? Well, this is properly spoken as one nonillion, sixty-six quadrillion, six hundred trillion, and one. It's an interesting number. For one, it's palindromic—same backwards as it is forwards. But you'll also notice smack dab in the middle is that creepy, old 666. The Number of the Beast, for all you Iron Maiden fans out there. And on either side of the 666 are thirteen zeroes. *And*, the whole thing is exactly thirty-one digits long. Thirteen reversed! This, my friends, is known as Belphegor's prime. Divisible only by itself and the number one."

"Whoa," said Rall. "Hang on. What's this—"

"Almost finished. You see, there's another way to express it, and that's like this." Next to the original number, he wrote an equals sign, then $10^{30} + 666 \times 10^{14} + 1$. He capped the marker and turned back to face the group.

Rall shook his head. "Sorry, LT. You're gonna have to slow down for us mere mortals. What's this got to do with the murder book?"

"Don't feel bad." Sponholz tossed the marker back onto the pen tray. "If I'm being absolutely honest with you, I didn't know half this stuff until last night. But here, I'll show you what got me going." He gestured at the Galka murder book in front of Al-Amuli, and the detective handed it over to him. Sponholz flipped the pages, his expression clouding when he reached the crime-scene photos. Eventually he found what he was looking for, and turned the book around so the rest could see.

It was the six photos from the day before. The garage, the mailbox, the bloody handprint near the front door. On the opposite page, the bowl of pinecones garnished with shit, the blood-smeared family photo, and the little piece of dark red plastic.

Sponholz swept the book slowly back and forth. "Anyone see it?"

No one did. Grinning, Sponholz tapped the picture of the handprint on the outside wall. "Right there."

Everyone leaned forward. Jarsdel was growing frustrated. The only number he could see was the placard giving the street address—10306. That didn't match what Sponholz had put on the board. Well, not unless you...

"Ah—think we got a winner." Sponholz was pointing at him. "Go ahead, say what you see."

"I guess," Jarsdel ventured, "if you were to read the exponents as whole numbers, you'd get *one zero three zero six six six one zero one four*. But if you stopped after only five digits, you'd get *one zero three zero six*, which I suppose matches the Galka's address."

Sponholz made his finger into a pistol and pointed at Jarsdel. "*Psht*. You got it."

Rall looked as perplexed as Jarsdel felt. "Yeah? Huh. Definitely woulda missed it. What's it mean?"

"It means," said Sponholz, "that we're dealing with witches.

Forgive me—no, I'm not referring to people with actual supernatural powers. But whoever the Creeper is, and keep in mind it may be several different people, he's turned on by the occult."

"What about the other addresses?" asked Jarsdel.

"See, I knew you and I were on the same wavelength." Sponholz brought a sheet of paper out of his pocket. "I confess, not all of these were easy to figure out. Anyway, here we go. Verheugen. 2549 Thelma. Add the two and five, and you get seven. Add the four and nine, and you get thirteen. Lucky and unlucky numbers, right there. And the street, Thelma. That's only missing one letter; add an *e* and you get *Thelema*, which is an occult spiritual group. Moving on to Rustad. There we've got 8010 Stoker. I'm not sure what the numbers mean yet, but Stoker is obviously a reference to the author of *Dracula*. That's supported by the Santiago address, which is 6880 Joston. And 6880—get this—is known as a 'vampire number,' which is a little complicated to explain why but has to do with the way it's factored." He put the paper back in his pocket.

Mailander raised her hand. Sponholz nodded at her. "Yes?"

"What about the Lauterbachs?"

"1320 Hollyridge Loop. Yeah, still trying to work that one out. But you've got thirteen right at the front, so I don't think that's a coincidence." He reached up and carefully touched his scratched cheek. "Really nailed myself with that stupid branch."

They detectives sat in silence, contemplating Sponholz's revelation. Jarsdel scanned their faces, seeing if any of them were actually buying this. The leaps the lieutenant was making bordered on the absurd. Besides, they'd already considered and rejected the witchcraft angle. Nothing at the crime scenes backed it up. No inverted crosses or pentacles drawn in blood. Sponholz was so adamant, though, so certain this was the key, that Jarsdel thought maybe he was missing something.

"This is going to be our focus," said the lieutenant. "I want you to toss Fantasy Island again, top to bottom, but this time let's narrow our search. Look for anyone in and out of there with any of that

Devil bullshit going on. Tattoos of goats' heads and what-not. Pay attention to self-harm, too. Dick piercings and nipple bolts, all that stuff's typical of that crowd. Some people even get prosthetic horns—what're they called?—subdermal implants. And if you don't get lucky there, fan outward. State hospitals. Metropolitan, Coalinga, Atascadero. The neuropsych ward at UCLA. Still dry, then look national. Get a list of every 5150 recently relocated to the Golden State, emphasis on the pasty-faced, black lipstick variety."

"But we've done all that already." It was Al-Amuli. He spoke in a soft, murmuring tone of the sort used by children who want to complain without getting in trouble.

Sponholz was unfazed. He even offered a smile. "Then do it again, this time with real direction. Now you know what you're looking for."

"But he would've come up in prints."

Sponholz's smile broadened. "As I recall, you were the one who made the suggestion that his prints may have been deleted. Perhaps purposefully."

Al-Amuli sagged. "Yeah, I guess. Just a ton of work we already did."

The lieutenant ignored him. "We're close, people. I can feel it. If he isn't scared of us yet, he should be."

Overall, Jarsdel thought, Oscar Morales was right about very little. Well, very little in a quantifiable sense. He'd often been right about procedure, interrogation strategy, motive, suspect behavior. Things that were difficult to measure, that depended on experience instead of stringent academic analysis. The stuff he was right about was—to use a cooking analogy—the flavor, as opposed to the ingredients.

In other words, Jarsdel quietly admitted to himself, Morales was generally right about the most important stuff.

And so, grudgingly, Jarsdel decided to take his former partner's advice to absorb a little cinematic pop culture. He'd heard Morales rattle off the titles often enough that they were easy to recall. *Zodiac, Manhunter, Frenzy, Peeping Tom, Henry: Portrait of a Serial Killer, M,* and a dozen others. In most cases it'd been cheaper to buy the movies than stream them. In they came, day after day, horror and death cinched in sober, mustard-yellow mailers. Jarsdel would sit in his wingback chair with his dinner and a glass of wine, and suffer through them. No, that wasn't fair—some were very good. On offer that night, however, was *Maniac*, the tale of a suety, lumbering psychopath who went around scalping people and stapling the trophies to the heads of his mannequins. Jarsdel's dinner, a takeout container of capellini, went for the most part uneaten.

Jarsdel had never been a movie lover, hadn't seen the point in surrendering the entirety of the creative process to someone else. With books, it was just him and the words, and he could determine—to some extent—where they'd end up taking him. His own mind was the movie screen, and he prided himself on its richness, its subtleties, its perfection. No film could touch the excellence of the images he'd already crafted inside his head.

On screen, the titular character stalked a woman through a subway station. Jarsdel had to be up early if he wanted to beat the morning traffic, and decided his filmic education would simply have to make do without this particular masterpiece. He turned off the TV, but as he was setting the remote back on the coffee table, his stitches pulled and he dropped it. The pain was sudden and startling, and he gasped.

Before he knew what he was doing, he had his phone out and was calling Morales. He picked up on the first ring.

"It's eleven o'clock."

"And I've been watching *Maniac*. Misery loves company."

"Hang on," Morales grumbled. "Signal's shit this side of the house."

Jarsdel waited. About a minute later, Morales came back on. "Okay, what is it?"

"*Maniac*. Wanted to extend my gratitude."

"You got the original, right? 1980?"

"Oh, it's as 1980 as you can get. Probably the foulest, grimiest thing I've ever seen. You can practically smell the movie through the TV screen."

Morales laughed. "Yeah, that's the one."

"So how's it going with Haarmann?"

A pause. "Haarmann?"

"Your new partner."

"He's not my *partner*. Just temporary."

"Does he talk about me at all? About what he did to my hand?"

"Nope."

"Wait, really?" Jarsdel was surprised. "Not even an off-hand remark or anything?"

"Yeah, nothin'."

The Cro-Mag was capable of greater restraint than Jarsdel would've thought. Which made him even more dangerous.

"Tully, you there?"

"Yeah, I'm here."

"Got quiet on me there. Okay, man, I ought—"

"What's he like? As a detective?"

A longer pause this time. "Shit, man. I don't know. He's okay, I guess. Nothin' special."

"You make it sound like he's not all that bad."

"He's—don't get me wrong—he's definitely got his annoyances. Real tac whore, gotta have every shiny little toy within department regs. And he's got like two or three badge bunnies. Extra-long lunch breaks, almost every day."

"Huh."

"Comes back smelling like those samples of perfume they put in magazines. They still do that? Have the perfume on that little paper strip inside of magazines? My sister used to save those. Never bought a bottle all through her teens."

Jarsdel grunted. "Well, I hope you're washing your hands a lot."

"Hey, there he is. There's the Dad I know and love."

Despite himself, Jarsdel smiled. "Just don't let your guard down. Around the Cro-Mag."

Morales yawned. "Okay. Gotta get some sleep." He hung up.

Badge bunnies, Jarsdel thought. *Extra-long lunch breaks.*

He looked down at his hand. Most of the dressings were off now. Three large Band-Aids were all that covered the stitches. He tried bending his fingers, and the stitches pulled right away. It felt like he'd just grabbed an oven rack.

Before he could change his mind, he had the LAPD website up on laptop. It didn't take long for him to find what he was looking for, and he began typing.

Jarsdel's phone buzzed on his nightstand, rattling against the varnished wood. The sound pierced straight through to his dream, in which a Valentine's Day picnic with Pliny the Elder was suddenly interrupted by the arrival of a giant bee. The phone buzzed again, and Jarsdel snapped awake, flinging out his hand to catch the damn thing before it could make that noise once more.

The screen told him it was Goodwin Rall. Had they caught the Creeper?

No. More likely another crime scene. He braced himself for the news, and answered.

"Yeah, it's Jarsdel."

"Hey, Tully. We need you, man."

Jarsdel was already out of bed and stepping into a pair of jeans. "Sure, on my way. Where am I going? Where'd he hit?"

"It's bad, man. Gonna change everything. Nothing like this ever..." Rall exhaled shakily.

"What is it? I need to know where to go."

"It's the LT's old lady, man. Sponholz's wife."

14

Jarsdel added his own blue and red lights to the vehicles gathered outside the police barricade, and more cars continued to arrive behind him. Thankfully, the house was tucked down a remote Northridge cul-de-sac, so they didn't have to worry too much about crowd control.

Jarsdel stepped out of his car, felt how muggy and thick the air was already, and tossed his sport coat back onto the passenger seat. After putting on a pair of nitrile gloves, he approached the patrol officer guarding the tape and signed his name on the crime-scene log. The officer lifted the yellow banner, and Jarsdel stepped through.

The sky was streaked with hints of peach and blue, but it still wasn't light enough yet to see much detail, so he got out his Maglite and examined the pavement in front of Sponholz's house. There was no blood, not that he could see. He edged closer, paying careful attention to the mailbox and the area nearby. The best print he'd ever found had been a bloody palm on a mailbox, left by a suspect when he'd tripped during his panicked flight from an assault. He was hoping he'd have similar luck this time, but the box was clean.

"Hey, Tully." The voice was low and husky with emotion. Jarsdel turned to see Rall standing at his side. Before he could think of anything to say, he'd been seized in a crushing hug.

Jarsdel struggled to breathe. "Yeah, I know," he managed.

Rall released him, then clamped a hand on each of his shoulders. "I knew Amy ten years. This mother*fucker*..."

"Where's the lieutenant?"

Rall let him go. He furrowed his brow, then shook his head. "The lieutenant. Oh man, yeah. They got him out of here. He was...as you'd expect."

"He found the, uh... He found his wife? He was the one who discovered her?"

"Don't know. I'm guessing one of the first, yeah. Couldn't get a whole lot out of him. The initial responder was the alarm company. Guy set it off when he broke in."

Jarsdel glanced toward the open front door. "Through there?"

"Nah, in the back. Off the kitchen."

"We're sure it's him? The Creeper?"

"What do *you* think? Who *else*? Jesus, man."

"Right," said Jarsdel. "Of course."

"Place is covered in prints anyway. We got the best fingerprint girl in the Valley on her way. Gonna eyeball 'em, compare with what we already got—just to confirm—but you *know* it's gonna be our guy."

"Very likely. Yeah." Jarsdel hardly knew Rall, but now their boss's wife had been murdered, and that meant they were, in a sense, comrades in arms. At war. "Anything you need, sir, please let me know. We'll get him, you know. We'll get him for sure."

To his surprise, Rall gave a sad smile. "Think so? Fucker's a ghost." Twin tears spilled down his cheeks, and he rubbed them away with his wrist. "Better go in. Want you to see what he did."

Jarsdel nodded and headed up the brick walkway. The plot was typical of the neighborhood: a two-story, single-family detached home of uninspired, early '80s architecture, and a small fenced-in yard. He slipped a pair of booties over his shoes and stepped inside.

The locks on the door looked good. Both the knob and dead bolt were Medeco—pretty much tamper-proof unless you were a pro. There was an alarm-system panel immediately to his right. A rectangular display gave the time, date, temperature, and the day's weather forecast in the form of a grinning yellow sun. A block of text read *System not ready—FRONT DOOR OPEN*. Jarsdel pushed the door shut. The text now read *System ready*. Jarsdel reopened the door for the forensic technicians and began walking the ground floor.

He took his time, moving slowly through the entryway, living room, and kitchen. The Sponholzes had installed a small wet bar off the dining room. Above it hung a custom neon sign, and though its coils were now dark, he could still read the words.

LIFE IS A CABERNET! ED & AMY FOREVER.

An FSD tech slipped past him with a hushed "Excuse me" and mounted the stairs for the second floor. Jarsdel waited a moment, then followed, taking each step as silently as possible. The Sponholz house was a tomb now, a place of the dead, and demanded a certain deference.

At the top of the stairs, he glanced around and caught sight of the tech stepping into a room branching off the main hall.

Jarsdel took a breath. Certain aspects of the job became easier over time, and these differed for every detective. For him, the bodies themselves weren't so bad anymore. At first they'd tormented his dreams, his waking life too. He'd see their split faces and swollen, purple hands every time he closed his eyes. But that had faded. Now, aside from the rare, truly astonishing cruelties, like those visited upon the Lauterbachs, there remained few things that could elicit true visceral revulsion. Sadness, yes—a deep, twisting, grinding sadness—but that was different.

Others weren't as lucky. They had an internal threshold, a limit on the sheer quantity of horror they could tolerate. They'd be on the job twenty, thirty years, and seem to be fine. No meetings with the department shrink, no breakdowns, no crises. Then one day a scene would come along—and not necessarily the grisliest or most depraved—and that would be it. Transfer or retirement or, more often than those law-enforcement recruitment pamphlets cared to admit, suicide.

But not everything grew easier. He was reminded of that fact as he stood outside the room. Because for Jarsdel, the suspense was the hardest part. In that, nothing had changed since his first crime scene. The knowing that he was about to see the body, those endless moments just before he turned that last corner or opened that tent flap or shone his Maglite into that trunk. To finally be forced to see what he'd been called there to see, what it was his job to see, induced the most heart-slamming terror. Sometimes he moved quickly, forcing himself forward so he could put the feeling behind him as soon as possible. Other times he was unable, frozen as he was now. Still other times he let the reveal happen gradually; first a foot or a set of curled fingers, or maybe he'd start with the smallest bloodstains and slowly work his way toward the bigger ones until he finally reached their source.

He knew it didn't make sense, how he could remain crippled by the anticipation of looking upon the bodies while, simultaneously, becoming more or less inured to *actually* seeing them.

The technician poked her head into the hallway and spotted Jarsdel. "Detective? You can come in if you're ready."

Jarsdel, who'd been holding his breath, let it out in a ragged wheeze. He told his legs to move, and they carried him dutifully onward into the master bedroom.

Amy Sponholz lay naked across the bed, left arm tucked somewhere behind her back, her right bent far above her head—palm facing outward—in the manner of someone hailing a taxi. From between her splayed legs jutted a broom.

The FSD tech—gloved, masked, and wearing a hairnet—glanced over from her examination of blood spatter on a lampshade. She seemed to consider saying something, then returned to her work. Jarsdel approached the body, checking the carpet as he did so to make sure he wasn't stepping on any evidence. He made it to the side of the bed opposite the technician and returned Amy Sponholz's vacant, milky stare. Even in death, the nose was a distraction, rising defiantly above the rest of her features—an assertion of selfhood, one final protest against the anonymity of death.

It was Jarsdel who broke the silence. "Anything you can tell me?"

The tech once again looked up from her work. "She fought him, and that helps us out. She's got some blood on her teeth—you can see if you look—but I didn't notice any wounds anywhere in or around her mouth. That's not to say they're not there. Even a small cut in the mouth bleeds a lot, but—"

"She bit him?"

"I think so." She pointed a gloved finger at the spatter she'd been examining. "Here on the shade you've got a directional tail on this blood, like he jerked his hand away. And on the floor by the bed you've got a few more drops, straight down onto the carpet. I don't think any of these came from her. She'd have been fighting, trying to get away, but these are like I said, straight down. Like he's not moving, just holding his injured hand."

"Good for her," Jarsdel said. "Gave us another way to ID him." He bent close and studied Amy Sponholz's neck, which was bruised and swollen. "Strangled?"

"Yes, but I'm not supposed to confirm—"

"I know. Not asking you to sign anything." He looked down at the broom. It had a blue plastic handle and ended in a clump of dirty yellow bristles. He couldn't tell how much of it the killer had shoved inside her, but it was enough to keep it from slipping out on its own.

"If you're wondering about the, uh, the broom," the tech said, "it looks like it was done postmortem. There's no indication she tried to stop anything happening down there. All the perimortem trauma's around the throat. You can see the scratches. I think he broke her hyoid bone."

Jarsdel saw what she meant. There were no defensive wounds whatsoever around her thighs or pelvis, no sign she'd fought off an attacker. Instead, as the tech had said, the attention was focused on the neck area. Deep troughs had been raked across her throat, chin, and sternum. It had been a brutal fight for each breath.

Was the broom a kind of revenge? Because she'd made the killer work so hard to take her life, he'd found it necessary to defile her corpse?

"Any idea how long he was in the house?"

The tech looked up from the bloodstains on the carpet. "Sorry?"

"How long was he here? Anyone know?"

She thought it over. "Far as I know, he broke in while she was asleep."

"Wouldn't the alarm wake her up?"

"I'm not sure about any of that. But listen, I don't think I'm the one you should be asking these things. Have you spoken to Detective Rall? He can tell you more. I'm just here for the physical evidence."

Jarsdel looked down at the broom again. "How long do we have to keep that there like that?"

"Hmm? Oh." The tech faltered. "I'm assuming it stays until we finish photographing the scene. Maybe take a 3-D scan of it, since the, the husband was a, uh, lieutenant. Our unit has a Deltasphere," she said with a hint of pride.

"Okay."

"Yeah, I know. It's upsetting. A little upsetting."

"Yeah. It is."

Silence returned. Jarsdel wasn't sure how much time passed, but eventually Al-Amuli appeared.

"Hey."

Jarsdel glanced at him, nodded, and bent to take a closer look at Amy Sponholz's fingers. Al-Amuli joined him, craning his neck to see over Jarsdel and blocking the light.

"What do you see?"

"Not much, currently. Can you move?"

"Sorry." He stepped back. Jarsdel lifted the corpse's wrist and turned it toward him. The nails that'd been so exquisitely manicured at the LT's party looked like they'd been bent with pliers—a few at ninety-degree angles. She'd fought and clawed him as ferociously as she could.

Mailander arrived. She said nothing, passing Al-Amuli without a glance and going to the foot of the bed. She stared at the body, almost as if waiting for it to speak.

"I'm going outside," said Al-Amuli. "Too many cooks in this kitchen."

"No, I'll go," said Jarsdel. "Give you guys some room to look around." He squeezed by the two of them and paused at the door. There was a simple push-button lock on the bedroom side of the knob. He bent down to examine the latch and strike plate. No tool marks or scratches, and all the hardware was intact. On the exterior knob, a small hole allowed for the insertion of a slim tool to disengage the lock in case of emergency. An eyeglass screwdriver or even something as simple as a straightened paper clip would do the trick.

The alarm had gone off, that they already knew. So did Amy Sponholz lock the bedroom door? True, it wouldn't have slowed the Creeper down much at all, but it would've been an obstacle nevertheless. And how people overcame obstacles said something about who they were, about their state of mind.

The lock was pristine. There was no question—it hadn't been forced. And the Creeper didn't seem like the kind of person who'd take the time during a home invasion—alarm blasting in the background—to procure a small tool to pop a nuisance privacy lock. There was only one explanation that made any sense: Amy Sponholz hadn't locked the door, even after hearing the alarm go off.

Maybe she'd left the bedroom to investigate. Jarsdel covered the few steps from the bedroom to the top of the stairs and looked down. From where he stood, he could easily make out the entirety of the staircase as well as the foyer. The doorway leading to the kitchen was just off the main entrance. If the killer had indeed broken in through the back, he would've had to come out that doorway to get to the stairs. Amy Sponholz would've had plenty of time to see him and run back into the bedroom before he got to her. Unless, Jarsdel considered, he knew exactly where he was going and had already climbed the stairs.

Troubled, he made his way downstairs and back outside.

Rall was leaning against a black and white. With him was Captain Tricia Coryell of RHD. She looked so furious that Jarsdel was reluctant to approach her. But then she noticed him and he didn't have a choice.

"Captain," he said, advancing cautiously.

"Detective Rall says she was strangled," Coryell managed through her anger.

"Yes, looks that way."

"And she was violated? With a broom?"

"Yes." Quickly he added, "But the tech says it looks postmortem."

"I don't give a *shit*," Coryell spat. "That is the wife of a fucking homicide lieutenant."

"I know, absolutely."

"I don't give a shit for *postmortem*. What, like that fucking makes it okay?"

"No, Capt—"

"How would you like it if someone shoved a broom up your dead mother's pussy, Detective? Or *your* wife's?"

"Hey." Rall reached out a hand to touch her shoulder, then thought better of it. "He didn't mean it that way."

Coryell didn't even hear him. All that existed in her world at that moment was Jarsdel. "Oh, *ha*, you'd say—right? Well, at least it was *postmortem*. So we can all laugh about it."

Jarsdel decided silence was the best answer. Anything he said would only make her angrier.

"Captain," said Rall. His voice was quiet but firm. "He's just sayin' she didn't suffer through it."

Coryell walked away a few yards and stopped with her back to them, hands on her hips. She bowed her head and Jarsdel could see the broad shoulders beneath her suit coat rise and fall as she took deep, calming breaths. Rall and Jarsdel waited, but it didn't take long. In less than a minute, she was on her way back. She stopped before them, chin held high.

"Detective. I owe you an apology."

Jarsdel shook his head. "It's fine, Captain."

"If you're interested in issuing a complaint against me about my conduct, I'll understand. There won't be any hard feelings on my end, and I'll ask Detective Rall here to give you his support as a witness."

"No," said Jarsdel. "That's... No. Not at all."

Coryell gave a single nod. "In that case, consider I owe you one." She grimaced and massaged the bridge of her nose. "Jesus, I'm still trying to wrap my head around this."

A trio of new technicians arrived, escorted by one of the uniformed officers, and signed in at the crime-scene tape. One, a slight woman no more than five feet tall, gave directions to the others before splitting off with the officer, who led her into the house.

"Good," said Coryell. "At least we'll know for sure pretty quick."

The time dragged by. Jarsdel glanced at his phone. Almost seven. He wondered where the Creeper was now, and how he'd made it away so cleanly.

"Excuse me, Detective Rall."

"What?"

"Do we know yet if Amy was alone?"

"No."

"No she wasn't alone?"

"No as in I have no idea. LT's a fuckin' wreck. Give the man some space."

"I wasn't suggesting we try for an interview. But it seems very likely she was alone, don't you think?"

Rall sucked some air between his teeth. "Why're you harping on this, you know, at this particular juncture?"

"Because otherwise it would've been suicidal, right? Break into a cop's house while he's home?"

Rall shrugged. "Yeah. Obviously."

"So how'd he know Sponholz's routine? How'd he know when he'd be home and when he wouldn't?"

"Prob'ly staked out his place. Waited for him to be gone."

"Huh."

"What?"

"Seems kind of risky. Stake out the house of the man who's chasing you." Jarsdel looked around. "Pretty empty street, too. Not a lot of activity. You'd probably notice a strange car or someone who wasn't supposed to be here."

Rall surveyed the area and nodded. "True. But maybe it's like..." He didn't finish his thought. The fingerprint technician had come striding out of the house. She moved fast, stripping off her gloves as she approached.

"Which one of you is Captain Coryell?"

Coryell lifted a hand. "What do you have?"

"The prints at this scene match the exemplars I was given. Same as Eastside Creeper."

"You're sure?"

"There's no doubt. Counted twenty points of comparison, which is the gold standard, and I could've kept going."

"Thank you. What was your name?" Coryell had her field notebook out.

"Mendez, first name Xochitl. That's X-O-C-H-I-T-L. The X is an 'sh' sound."

"And you're with Devonshire Area, or...?"

"Sheriff's Department, actually. I have a friend at Northridge Station, and she asked if I could come by as a favor."

"Appreciate it. Thank you. Mind hanging around just in case we need you again before the scene is cleared?"

"I'm here to stay, Captain. If I can contribute in any way, I'd be grateful."

Coryell and Mendez shook hands. "Lucky to have you," said the captain.

Once Mendez had moved off, Coryell turned to Jarsdel and Rall. "You both good here? I'm gonna go check on Ed. Want him to know he has all our support."

"Sure, Captain," said Rall.

"Just so you're aware, I plan on telling him the Creeper's going to be in custody before the end of the summer."

Rall pursed his lips. "That's, uh, like five weeks, uh, Captain."

"It sure is." Coryell moved off toward her car. Rall watched her go, his expression mild, and waited until her taillights disappeared around the corner before speaking.

"I wanna call her a bitch, but that ain't fair. She were a dude we'd all say she had 'command presence,' right?"

"What were you about to say before?" asked Jarsdel.

"Huh?"

"You were about to say something. I said the thing about how you'd notice a strange car or a person, and you said that maybe it was like...and you didn't finish."

"Oh. Yeah. I was gonna say maybe it's like the other cases. Like where he hides out in the house. Maybe that's how he knew she was alone."

"I guess," said Jarsdel, but inwardly, he knew it didn't make any sense. Because if the Creeper had been hiding in the house, he would've attacked both Sponholzes while they were in bed and helpless. And the murder itself was too quick, too clean for his usual style. This felt like a blitz attack, a crime of opportunity he couldn't resist passing by. But that brought Jarsdel back to the same problem: how had the Creeper known Amy was alone? And how had he gotten in? And why hadn't she locked the bedroom door?

"Nah, that don't work," said Rall. "He'd've killed 'em both. And our boy likes to take his time. Choking's too quick." He looked at Jarsdel. "You were thinkin' the same thing, weren't you?"

"I was considering it, yes."

"Speak up, then. Ain't got time to waste tiptoein' 'round everybody's egos."

Jarsdel considered. There'd been something else he'd been wondering about, but hesitated in bringing it up. But now that Rall had invited him to offer his ideas, he thought it would be a good opportunity.

"I'm curious about the broom."

Rall nodded. "Good. Why?"

"Where'd it come from? I mean, yes, it was probably already in the house, but from a cleaning closet or the garage or something. I just have a tough time thinking it was somewhere in the bedroom and the guy just picked it up."

"So the question is," Rall said, "why'd he go hunting for the broom in the first place? Wasn't much of a weapon. Plastic handle and all that. At the Lauterbachs he gets a claw hammer. Rustads he uses that gas shutoff wrench they had out back. But here he picks up that flimsy-ass broom. Was he just looking for anything to—you know—to do that thing he did with it? Maybe."

"Maybe," Jarsdel agreed. "In that case it looks like this: I'm the Creeper and I've developed a fixation on the LT for leading the task force that's hunting me. I track him down, follow him from PAB, or throw his name into a data dump. Either way, I end up at his house. Somehow I realize Amy is alone. I can't resist, so I get inside."

"In some ingenious way," said Rall.

"In some heretofore unexplained manner," Jarsdel agreed. "The alarm goes off—we're presuming—and I don't know how long I've got until the LT comes back, so I attack the wife. Then, to show what an asshole I am, I go scavenging around the house for something to profane the body. I see the broom..." Jarsdel furrowed his brow. "Albert DeSalvo—the Boston Strangler—he did that to one of his victims. Broom handle. Diseased minds think alike."

Rall frowned. "Boston Strangler—what was that, like fifty, sixty years ago?"

"I wasn't suggesting it was a copycat. Just thinking aloud. Anyway, there are a few missing pieces, and it looks like the Creeper got very lucky on a couple points, but I guess it could've happened that way." Jarsdel prepared himself for the reaction his next request was going to earn from Rall. "I want to talk to the LT."

"Hell no."

"I know he's hurting, but it needs to be soon so we can put a timeline on all this. Whatever the unis come up with from their canvassing isn't going to mean anything until we nail down exactly where he was and when."

"I said forget it."

"I'm willing to do it," said Jarsdel. "And I understand. You've known him for years, and disturbing him in the midst of his grief feels like a violation of his privacy. But you know the best chance we have of balancing the scales is slipping away from us by the minute. The earlier we talk to him, the better our info's going to be." He weighed his next words carefully, then said, "Only thing is, I'd leave Mailander and Al-Amuli out of it. Nothing against them on a personal level, but I'm concerned about crowding the guy. And I don't think his rapport with them is all that solid."

Rall stared at him, jaw muscles flexing. Jarsdel couldn't tell what the man was thinking, but he took a small step back just to be safe.

Finally, the detective spoke. "Al-Amuli's a toolbox, and Mailander's got no finesse. If we're gonna talk to the LT, I'm gonna be there, too."

"Good," said Jarsdel. "And if you'd prefer doing it alone, that's fine."

"No. Since you don't know him as well, you might ask questions I wouldn't think of. Can only help. But we got ground rules. LT's a sensitive guy. Too sensitive, maybe. But he's got a brain. Always been gracious, always respectful. Knows how to delegate. He's a good leader, a solid LT. Different strategy, different command style than the guys I was used to, but effective."

"I'm unclear. So what are the ground rules?"

"I don't want him pushed. His wife's murdered. She was his whole world. I know it's the first thing we do—look at the husband. But we already got the prints back, and it's for sure not him. So when we go in there, I don't even want a hint of suspicion in what we say. I'm talking about tone. That sort of shit's injurious to a person. Dealing with loss, then with people insinuating you had something to do with it. So I don't care if his story's jumbled up or whatever, we don't push. Let him come to us."

Jarsdel was surprised. "That's fine, of course. I'm curious as to why you'd assume I'd come at him from that angle."

"You're a walkin' textbook. Everyone knows that. Mr. Procedure. You do what it says in the literature regardless of what the world's telling you. So I'm reminding you what the world's telling you here—the LT ain't our guy, so don't treat him like your typical surviving husband. That clear?"

Jarsdel didn't trust himself to speak right away. Rall was suggesting he had no instincts—that the only reason he operated by the book was because he didn't possess any judgment of his own. He shrugged. "Appreciate your sharing your concerns. I'm happy to let you guide the interview."

Rall began to head off to his car. Jarsdel added, "You know it's starting to feel a little bit like this isn't really a team. Like we're not equals."

"We're not equals," said Rall, without turning around.

There was a cot in Devonshire station, for use by detectives working long shifts, and the desk sergeant said Sponholz had been asleep in there for three hours. Rall let his boss sleep, and it wasn't until ten in the morning when word came to them that Sponholz was awake.

When Rall and Jarsdel entered, the LT was sitting on his cot, sipping a mug of coffee. He looked as if he'd aged ten years. He'd fallen asleep in his clothes, which clung damply to his skin. It was stifling in the little storage room where they kept the cot.

Sponholz glanced up as they entered, but said nothing.

"Good morning, sir," said Rall.

No answer.

"We came by to pay our respects," said Rall.

"You came by to knock out a timeline," said Sponholz. His voice was like the sound of wind through a seashell, hollow and weightless.

Rall and Jarsdel exchanged a look. "That's true," said Rall. "We want to give your wife the best chance of getting some justice."

"Amy was the third of four siblings. Grew up in a Tampa trailer park, lived off food stamps and surplus government cheese. Endured regular sexual abuse at the hands of an uncle. Skip ahead a couple decades and she meets me. Gets the whole cop's wife treatment. Absentee husband. Wanted kids and I didn't. She's never had any justice, so why start now?"

"I'm sorry, sir," said Rall. "But you know—"

"Yeah, I know. Let's get it over with."

"Would you rather talk to me alone?"

"Tully can stay," said Sponholz. "More heads in on this, the better. And the sooner we can put this...*animal*...in the ground." He choked back a sob on the last couple words. He closed his eyes and took a long breath in through his nose, held it, and exhaled. His eyes opened. "Okay. Go."

"Tell us everything you can, from the beginning."

Sponholz thought it over, then shook his head. "I'm all addled. Agitated. I don't know where to start. You'll have to be specific."

"Sure, no prob. Um, I guess...how did you come to know your wife had been..."

"Murdered? It's okay to say it. She was. She was *fucking murdered*." He wiped at his eyes with his sleeve.

Rall held up a calming hand. "All right. How did you come to know she'd been murdered?"

Sponholz collected himself, sighed, shook his head again. "I came home. I'd been out. All the way across town at PAB. Schedule was all screwed up from the case. Must have been two-thirty when I finally finished up. I was wired on coffee. Just wired. I thought I'd get in a workout and then go home and crash. Just sleep until the afternoon and then come on back between lunch and evening rush hour. I do it that way and sometimes can make it in forty-five minutes. This is stupid—don't know why I'm telling you all this. Okay, I'm focusing. I work out. I shower, but I don't bother shaving. Get in the car and make it home, and it must have been sometime around four thirty. Place is a circus. My phone starts going nuts right around the time I'm pulling in. Security company's there, and by then so is Devonshire PD. I knew, right when I saw it, I knew it had to be Amy."

Sponholz held back another sob, then slapped the sides of his face with both hands. Five times, fast. "Jesus, okay. I tried to get inside, and of course the officers were doing their job and they wouldn't let me. I was angry, I think I was angry, and I probably said some pretty terrible things, but they were very calm and professional and didn't let me past the tape. One of the unis told me there'd been an incident, and of course I've given that line myself a few hundred times. So I knew. I knew what'd happened. And that it was him. That he'd been the one who'd done it."

Jarsdel wasn't sure if Rall wanted him to speak or not, but he wanted to clarify something about Sponholz's story.

"Sir, do you have any idea how the killer gained entry?"

Sponholz blinked at him. "Huh? What do you mean?"

"The alarm was set. We know that of course because the signal went to the security company's dispatch. And we know it was the back door that was set off. It's been electronically recorded."

"Okay, yeah," said Sponholz. "What's the question?"

"There's no evidence of forced entry. And you've got pretty good locks on all your doors. Did you have a hide-a-key he could've picked up? Or one under the mat?"

"Gimme a second to think. I don't know. A hide-a-key's possible. Maybe years ago we put out one of those fake rocks. Nothing under the mat, no. I'm thinking, trying to think." Sponholz squinted, as if he could will the memory into focus. "Goddamn it, yes. It was Amy. She's been getting lazy about that stuff, leaving doors unlocked, especially that one because it opens onto our yard and not the street. She doesn't take it seriously, and I remember I said to her, I said, 'Hey, this is no joke. We got a killer prowling the city and God knows what other nutjobs crawling out of the woodwork these days.' But she *forgets*. She forgets to do it. Yes. We just had this conversation, must have been a couple days ago."

Jarsdel nodded "Any thoughts on how the Creeper might've known you weren't home?"

"He must have been watching us, right?"

"Possible. Do you keep a gun in the house?"

"Other than my service weapon? No."

"So your wife wouldn't have had access to a gun while you were out."

Sponholz sighed. "Gentlemen. I am tired. Very tired. Got nothing left. Can we continue this in a few hours? Or tomorrow?"

"Of course, sir," Rall began. "You let us know—"

"Actually," Jarsdel said, "I'd like to go for just a couple more minutes if we can. I'm curious about..." He paused, noticing Rall's frigid stare.

"We are more than happy to continue this conversation later," Rall said to the lieutenant, keeping his gaze knifing into Jarsdel.

Sponholz lay back on his pillow and closed his eyes. "Thank you. I know you guys have to do your job. So I appreciate the reprieve."

"Anything we can do, sir," said Rall. "I don't need to tell you we're gonna get this guy. Just rest up, and you let us know when we can talk again."

Rall turned to go and waved to Jarsdel to follow. Reluctantly, he left the room. Once the two of them were outside, the door closed behind them, Jarsdel spoke up.

"I think we're making a mistake not talking to him."

Rall pointed at the door. "He just had the worst night of his life. Something neither of us can imagine."

"Yes, and the longer we wait, the muddier his recollections are going to be. That's the freshest Creeper scene we've got so far. Even the tiniest details matter, and he's gonna lose them."

"LT's a pro. He knows what to focus on, what to hang onto."

"Still has a fallible human brain. Those're important details. How the Creeper got in, all that minutia with the alarm. How exactly he knew when to strike."

"Nothin' there that can't wait."

"Sir, if a witness is coherent, we interview. I get it. I get your sense of compassion. But it's misplaced. We can help the LT more in the long run by getting through this."

Rall smiled, but it was a mirthless smile. "That man in there has put away some of the city's worst offenders for thirty years. We're gonna give him some professional courtesy. You know, you're the kinda cop who'd ticket his own mother." Shaking his head, he moved off. Jarsdel heard him mutter, "Swear, s'like I fuckin' got stuck with Mr. Spock."

15

Father Ruben Duong was a balding man of sixty, and so thin his parishioners often arrived at Mass pressing bags of food into his arms—homemade coconut sponge cakes and sweet corn pudding and bánh patê sô, a savory puff pastry filled with ground pork. Duong always accepted the gifts graciously, then made the short trek over to Skid Row, where he handed them off to any of the thousands of homeless roaming Downtown LA.

Duong had been a child when Saigon fell, plucked from a Catholic orphanage—and a likely death at the hands of the besieging Viet Cong—by President Ford's Operation Babylift. He almost made it onto the first transport, but gave up his spot to a friend who needed medical care. The plane, a Lockheed C5-A Galaxy, crashed just after takeoff. Most of the orphans aboard were killed. Duong never learned if his friend was among the dead or if he'd survived.

The orphanage had saved him from abandonment, Ford had saved him from the VC, and fate had saved him from the crash. If God was trying to tell him something, He'd gotten Duong's attention.

Father Duong tolerated no frailty. Whenever he felt a desire beyond selfless service to others, even a physical need, he quashed it. His mind and body were important only to the extent that they furthered his work, but neither was going to be his master. Conquering oneself wasn't merely virtuous; it was essential in being an agent of God, Whose voice could not be heard over the constant din of the ego.

On both of his knees, hidden below his long Roman cassock, were tattooed the initials "M.K." These stood for Maximilian Kolbe, the Polish friar who'd volunteered to be starved to death in Auschwitz to spare a fellow prisoner—a total stranger—from the same punishment. Duong had learned of him while studying at the Fuller Theological Seminary, and considered him a perfect servant of the divine. When he saw that Kolbe had died on August 14, the same date records showed he himself had been abandoned at the Saigon orphanage, Duong resolved he must follow Kolbe's example of pure selflessness.

After being assigned to Our Lady of Guadalupe in Downtown, Duong had devoted himself to the problem of human suffering. He ran a soup kitchen in the church's parking lot every Sunday, volunteered as a chaplain in the Men's Central Jail and as a counselor for the California Youth Authority. He allowed runaway teens to sleep in the rectory while he himself lay on a foam mattress in the utility closet. When an ex-con he'd been counseling couldn't afford to pay for his mother's funeral, Duong sold his own car and covered the bill himself.

Duong was also responsible for several gang ceasefires. If a dispute erupted, he was brought in to arbitrate, and his rulings were final. Both the Vatos Locos and Sureños dubbed him "El Santo," while the Crips and their associates called him "Gandhi."

In 2005, when tales of his deeds made their way to the *LA Weekly*, he was asked why he worked so hard for the good of others, most of whom he'd never met and would never see again. His answer, which his parishioners printed onto bumper stickers and T-shirts, was short and to-the-point: "You and I are not *we*, but one."

Rumor had it that he slept perhaps three hours a night. Others insisted he didn't sleep at all, that his consciousness was linked with the shoreless sea of God's loving wisdom, and that such a divine connection exempted him from mundane human needs.

In late 2019, Duong was appointed president of the Los Angeles Interfaith Council. He was awarded the Key to the City a year later. Duong couldn't attend the ceremony because he was giving out jackets and cold-weather preparedness kits to Skid Row families, so Rabbi Michael Kaplan accepted the honor on his behalf. After shaking the mayor's hand, Kaplan told the audience that "Father Duong would never say so himself, and it's possible even he isn't aware of it, but I think—and I'm not alone—that he's one of the Tzadikim Nistarim, the hidden righteous ones. In our faith, these are the thirty-six perfect souls, always thirty-six and always among us, who do God's work here on earth. And we also believe that it is because of these dear ones that God allows us to continue on. That He spares us, chooses not to make of us another Sodom, another Gomorrah, no matter our sins and our crimes and our failure to follow His will, because these sacred thirty-six stand among us."

As the ceremony at City Hall came to a close, a very different meeting was just getting underway across the street at PAB. Seated were Paul Stout, the LAPD's chief of staff, Gloria Williams, director of public affairs, and Commander Brittany Lee of Transit Services Group. After a short lecture, they watched enthralled as Dr. Alisha Varma made the thick blue veins on Councilman Ken Peyser's arm vanish in the flicker of a PuraLux lamp.

Father Duong railed against PuraLux upon its release and organized a protest in partnership with the Los Angeles Mission. Before the march on city hall, thousands gathered in Pershing Square to hear him speak. His small stature belied his voice. It seemed to roll out of him—a thunderous timbre worthy of an Old Testament prophet.

"They call it 'PuraLux.' As a euphemism, it ranks among the best—or worst, depending on your view—standing shoulder to mendacious shoulder with such standbys as 'enhanced interrogation,' 'pacification,' and 'cleansing.' For truly PuraLux is a foul thing, an abominable thing. It is a weapon aimed at the least fortunate, at those who cry out for compassion and succor. Instead of offering our brothers and sisters in poverty the merest gesture of goodwill, our city grinds them underfoot.

"When Juan Crespí encountered what we call the LA River, now a polluted trickle that makes its way alongside our freeways between banks of concrete, he was so struck by its beauty that he named it 'El Río de Nuestra Señora la Reina de los Ángeles de Porciúncula'—'the River of Our Lady Queen of the Angels of the Porciuncula.'" He paused there, letting the significance of the name settle on his audience.

"Dear friends, that saddens me," he continued, "because the Porciuncula was the church in which Francis of Assisi carried out his work. Francis, who traded the silken costumes and bulging larders and bacchic galas of his family estate for coarse brown cloth and cincture. For the company of the destitute, the leprous, and the mad. What would Francis say of PuraLux, I wonder? What would he say of a thing so thoughtfully engineered to attack the dignity of man? To strike him when he is at his weakest? To deny him the simplest of rights—a place to rest?"

But when ReliaBench debuted, Father Duong was conspicuously silent. When asked by a reporter if he was planning another protest, his answer was oblique. "Treat a man like an animal, and he behaves as animals do. Treat a man like a criminal, and he behaves as criminals do." The interviewer waited, microphone extended for the third term of the truism—surely there would be a third, there always was—but the priest had apparently finished. As he walked away, Duong murmured something. The reporter wasn't sure exactly what he'd heard at that moment, but events shortly to come convinced him it was "He who does not take his cross and follow after Me is not worthy of Me."

Then came Sonic Fence. Again, silence from Duong. Then a week later, early on the morning of August 14, his parishioners placed calls to every news station in the city, informing them that their spiritual director was going to make a statement on the corner of 5th and Crocker—the geographical heart of Skid Row—at three o'clock that afternoon.

When reporters arrived, the first thing they noticed was the ReliaBench that had recently been installed at the intersection. Someone had covered the concrete tube with garlands of flowers, so many that only the tiniest swatches of dull-gray rock were visible.

Father Duong, in his forbidding Roman cassock, sat amid the fragrant petals.

"Why's he all wet?" a KTLA reporter asked. "He just get out of the shower?"

"Something smells," said another, this one from FOX 11. "What is that?"

"I love you all," said Duong, producing a cigarette lighter. "All," he repeated. Holding the lighter near his heart, he smiled, closed his eyes, and thumbed the striking wheel.

Father Duong burst into flames.

The fire was hot. Duong had poured enough accelerant around the ReliaBench that no one could get close enough to rescue him.

His parishioners dropped to their knees, clutching rosary beads and murmuring prayers, as reporters shouted at their cameramen and shielded their faces against the tremendous heat.

Duong didn't make a sound as he burned, but eventually lost consciousness and tumbled backward. His bare feet remained in view above the ReliaBench, pedaling the air as his nerves fired. The flowers—purple, red, buttery yellow—curled into black smudges.

16

The summer sun cast its scorching, unblinking eye on Malibu. The water glittered back, sapphire, rolling to white as it struck the sands of Zuma and Point Dume, right up to the beach chairs and slowly cooking bodies of SoCal elite.

It hadn't rained since March, a half-hearted sprinkle that had done little more than moisten the topsoil, and now the soft chaparral and coastal prairie grass had turned the color of hay. The same chaparral and prairie grass stippling the hills and hugging the twenty-million-dollar mansions tucked among the coves.

High up on the stilted pool deck of just such a mansion, two boys gathered a stockpile of leftover Fourth of July sparklers. The goal was to see how many they could light at once. What they were doing was dangerous—the boys understood that, instinctually if nothing else. They sensed the pregnant menace in the heat and in the crisped, sun-beaten land all around them. But they'd thought this through. They were on a pool deck after all, and if things got out of control, they could easily toss the sparklers into the water. Besides, they were nowhere near the parched vegetation. There were only scattered patches of it climbing the rocky slope behind the house; most of it was far below them, carpeting a gentle hillside teeming with rattlesnakes and California alligator lizards.

The day buzzed with life. Insects thrummed. A hot breeze stirred dust and pollen into the air.

The first boy gripped the bundle in a small fist sticky with Popsicle juice, while the second held out the flame of his father's cigar torch. The tips of the sparklers glowed momentarily red, then burst to violent life, showering both boys' hands and feet with stinging bits of molten aluminum.

The first boy yelped and dropped the sparklers. Most scattered harmlessly on the deck, but a few rolled off, dropping fifty feet before vanishing into a patch of shade beneath the house. An ordinary match would've gone out, might have even been cool to the touch as it hit the tangle of brown tinder below. But the sparklers flared even brighter, and landed hot. The insects fell quickly silent, and then there was new, hungrier sound in the still afternoon.

A trio of news helicopters passed overhead as Jarsdel pulled into Hollywood Station. They beat their way westward, and he watched until they dipped out of sight. A twinge of anxiety vibrated through his guts. He couldn't help wondering what they were in such a hurry to cover. Vultures of human misery. He could only hope it wasn't another movement in the Creeper's symphony of horror.

Jarsdel avoided the detectives' squad room. Seeing Morales and Haarmann together would only piss him off. Instead, he cut around back, passing the imbecilic and eminently useless desk sergeant, Curran.

"Thought you were at PAB," the man said, glancing up.

Jarsdel considered answering, but couldn't think of anything nice to say. Sometimes the advice they gave you in preschool wasn't all that bad.

He made it to Varma's office. Her door was open, and she waved when she saw him.

"Hey, glad you came."

"Not at all. Grateful you could make the time to see me. I know things are busy."

"Definitely one way to put it. Come in—what can I do for you?"

Jarsdel sat across from her, just as he had the last time he'd been in her office. It was different now, after the moment they'd shared at Watts Towers. His attention was drawn once more to her lips. He knew what they felt like now, how soft they were, and wanted to feel them again. Wanted them pressing against his own.

Then he saw that day's *Los Angeles Times* poking out of her bag. Above the fold, hundreds of candles burning in the night, illuminating the ghostly hands and faces of their bearers, all clustered around the site of Father Duong's self-immolation. The ReliaBench had been removed, but it didn't matter. The bus stop at the corner of 5th and Crocker was now a shrine.

Jarsdel raised his eyes to meet Varma's. He could only imagine the opposition she now faced, and suddenly he felt selfish coming to her with his problems. "I don't want to lay any more...bummers on you. And as I say, I don't want to impose, but—"

"Yeah, please though," said Varma. "I don't have a ton of time, so if you can tell me how I can help, that'd be phenomenal."

"Of course. I've been struggling with what happened to Lieutenant Sponholz's wife. And it's a tricky situation, because my team isn't really...well, much of a team."

Varma's smile became stiff. "I remember telling you I'm not a therapist, yet it seems like that's the road we're going down."

"No. I'm here for your expertise as a security professional. Well, mostly for your keen sense of logic."

"You're trying to flatter me."

"I'm being honest. I'm counting on your inductive powers to show me a way out of this. My thought was that I was gonna give you a picture—essentially—then ask if you could work backwards, tell me how it came to be."

"Still sounds a little outside my wheelhouse."

"Maybe," Jarsdel agreed. "But would you be willing to give it a crack? No shame if it doesn't come together. I assure you, you'll be in good company."

Varma tapped her pen against the table, considering. "Ten minutes. That's all I have."

"Then I won't waste any time. We got back the DNA results from under Amy Sponholz's fingernails. The nails were totally mangled and bent, so it was obvious she'd fought off her attacker. It follows that she'd have his DNA all over her hands, and lots of it under her nails, maybe even his blood."

"It follows," said Varma.

"But it wasn't there. No human matter at all. Instead, we got traces of leather. That means our guy was wearing gloves."

"Why's that so unusual?"

"Because he *wasn't* wearing gloves. His prints were all over that bedroom. They matched our exemplars perfectly. It was the Creeper, no doubt about it. Something like one in two hundred billion that someone else would have the same prints. That means the Creeper put on gloves to strangle Amy Sponholz, but wasn't wearing them the rest of the time."

Varma chewed on that a moment. "And your question is why would he do that?"

"That's one of my questions, yes."

"Okay. Do we know for sure he brought the gloves with him?"

"No. I don't know. Why's that important?"

"Because he might have found them there, in the bedroom."

"Found the gloves in the bedroom? In the middle of summer?"

Varma's mouth twisted in derision. "In a *drawer*, obviously, or in the closet somewhere. You were the one who came to *me* for help, remember?"

"Yeah, of course. Sorry. I suppose he could have found them, yeah, but why put them on?"

"Because he's role-playing. It makes sense with someone like that. He's seen who knows how many movies where people strangle each other while wearing black leather gloves. Always wanted to try it himself. The opportunity presents itself, and he certainly can't pass it by."

"That could be it," said Jarsdel. "But he was in a hurry. Alarm was blasting. I just can't see him stopping to put on gloves. And how would he have gotten her to just sit still while he did it? Just like, hey, hang on a sec while I get ready to strangle you?"

"Again," said Varma, her expression hardening. "You came to *me* for *my opinion*."

"Sorry."

"Is that everything?"

"He didn't bite her. And that's one of the things he almost always does."

"You just said 'almost,' so why is it odd that he didn't?"

"I should have clarified. The women. And girls. Females. Always bites them if they're female. Doesn't always bite the men. Just two we know of. Zephyr Galka, on the carotid artery and drank from the wound. And, um, Bill Lauterbach. He bit off... Well, so yeah. Rarely the men. But always the women."

Varma was distracted. As they spoke, she continued to sneak glances at the print hanging on the wall beside her desk—the tableau of the three comatose men lying amid piles of food. "You indicated he was in a hurry," she said. "Alarm was blasting. Maybe he felt too rushed to enjoy it, so he didn't bother."

"Yeah. But if that's true, the gloves are even more of a puzzle."

"Agreed."

"And what I really can't figure out is the broom." Jarsdel halted, suddenly uncomfortable. "This is unpleasant stuff. Are you—"

"I really hope you're not about to ask me if I can handle the grisly details. I wouldn't be much use if I couldn't cope with the evil that men do. I'm assuming you're about to tell me the victim was penetrated with a broom?"

"Yes."

"Vaginally? Anally?"

"V—the first one."

"Mmm. And that bothers you. I mean, apart from your aesthetic sensibilities?"

"This doesn't feel like the right time," said Jarsdel.

"As good a time as any to discuss broom rape. What's your concern?"

"My concern is where'd he get it? We go back to the issue of time. He breaks in—which still remains a mystery as to how, because we got no forced entry—and sets off the alarm. Goes right up to her room. Chokes her—and this is a manual air choke, no ligature, thumbs smash her hyoid bone—and then he leaves. But at some point in all of this he has to go out of his way for this broom. And keep in mind it's not heavy enough to use as a weapon, so the only reason he would've picked it up was for the purpose he ended up using it for. So where'd he get it? Because I checked, and it wasn't from anywhere upstairs. No, the broom matched a brush and dustpan set, and the spot it was missing from was a cabinet in the *garage*."

Varma didn't look very impressed. "How do you know the broom was from there?"

"The hardware meant to hold it in place was empty. And I matched a stray bristle on the floor of the cabinet to the broom head."

"So you've proven the broom came from the garage. Sounds like you answered the question as to where he got it. Maybe I'm missing something. What's the big *aha* moment with this?"

Jarsdel was disappointed. Why hadn't she been able to answer that question herself? "Because," he said, taking his time, still hoping she'd jump in with a revelation, "because how did he know it was there? There was no indication he went rifling through the house. There was no disarray, other than in the bedroom, yet he goes right to the one spot in the house he knows there's a broom."

Varma shifted in her chair, glancing again at the print tacked to the wall. "I don't see why the broom couldn't have already been in the bedroom."

"Why? What for?"

"I don't know, Tully. Sweeping, maybe? Isn't that what brooms are for?"

"Sweeping what?"

"You check trash contents?"

"Of course. Nothing. No broken glass, no bread crumbs, not even a dust bunny. In fact, the house had just been cleaned."

Varma raised her hands as if to say, well there you go. "The maid or the housekeeper or whatever left it there. Happens. So hard to find good help these days."

"That's not possible," said Jarsdel.

"Why not? You just said they had the place cleaned."

"They did. The Sponholzes contract with one of those franchised cleaning services. But I checked with them, and they didn't do it."

"You're a very trusting person. Why would they tell you the truth about leaving a broom somewhere?"

"Because they bring all their own equipment."

Jarsdel's words hung out there, unanswered. Varma looked back at him, offering nothing of her own. Finally she shrugged. "No idea, then. I think I'm a little distracted. Sometimes, you know, with what I do, it's complex. There's a lot to balance."

She gestured at her copy of the *Times*. "It still continues. And you know what's really interesting?" she said, speaking quickly now. "I'm amazed no one's yet raised the possibility that this Father Duong was insane, or at least a little bit off, you know, mentally. Not many people are aware of it, but piety is itself a form of narcissism. All that self-flagellating, teetotaling, holier-than-thou crap is designed to make you feel special. To bring you attention and therefore a kind of power. It's a route to power that's critic proof, because it comes across as being so against the ego, when in fact it's just another face of the ego. And could you think of a more spectacular way to immortalize yourself than to pull a stunt like this? It's PR gold."

"But none of this has anything to do with you, does it?" asked Jarsdel.

"Of course not, but I resent how they put it; the implication, however buried or...or cleverly *phrased*, that maybe it's the anti-affordance street furniture that's to blame for this man's death, and not the fact that he set himself on fucking *fire*. And it's astonishing: no one's saying 'Huh, maybe he had some problems?' Anyone else kills themself, and right away it's understood the person was overcome, couldn't function anymore, ran out of answers or coping mechanisms. But *this* guy sets himself on fire on a public bench surrounded by reporters, and no, he's not disturbed. He's making a *statement*."

Jarsdel couldn't think of anything to say to that, and Varma steamed ahead.

"And do you have any idea the damage he caused to that ReliaBench? It's cheaper to replace it than it is to clean it. That's how bad it stinks of smoke. What a selfish, sanctimonious little shit. Ugh."

Jarsdel flinched. He'd never met Father Duong, but accusing him of selfishness felt almost blasphemous. The man had been, by all accounts, a saint.

Varma seemed to sense Jarsdel's unease. She flapped a hand dismissively. "You know what, forget it. Seriously unprofessional, going off like this. I'm just leery of people getting distracted from the real issue here. Have you seen the crime stats from the month since my anti-affordances were put in place? We're talking double-digit reductions across the board. This is *saving lives*. You want to see something else that's going to make a difference?"

From beneath her desk, she pulled out a quart-sized can of paint. The label had a fat green stripe running across it, so Jarsdel assumed that was probably the paint's color.

"You know what this is?" Varma asked.

"Looks like paint."

"It is. It *is* paint. But it's a very special kind of paint. This sample just arrived from a friend of mine in England, where they use it all the time. It's even on the walls surrounding Buckingham Palace."

She worked a car key under the lid and popped it free. The stuff inside was the color of swamp moss. Using a pencil, she scooped up a bit and smeared it on a legal pad. She slid the pad across the table, then tossed the pencil in the trash.

"Go ahead, touch it."

Jarsdel dipped a finger in the paint and drew a sickly looking happy face. "Okay," he said.

"How's it feel?"

"I guess"—he wiped the rest of the paint onto the paper—"a little greasy."

Varma nodded. "Uh-huh. Now that greasiness doesn't go away. It stays like that, even after you paint a surface with it. Never totally dries. See the possibilities?"

"Sounds disastrous. Why would you want a feature like that?"

"Because if you're climbing where you shouldn't be climbing, this stuff'll return you to earth. It also marks the trespasser for later identification. It's called 'anti-climb paint.' And you only put it in strategically designated places. Usually above eight feet, and near anything that someone might try to scale. It's pretty expensive, but so's the damage done by vandals and thieves, right? Anyway, Halberd Systems is working on a more affordable line. You can even send in your paint chips and they'll make a custom batch for you. What do you think?"

Jarsdel found he'd gotten some of the paint on his palm, and rubbed his hands together. Instead of dissipating, the remaining paint seemed to spread. Annoyed, he pulled a tissue from a box nearby and did his best to clean it off.

"I think it's just phenomenal," he said. "Tell me, where can I get some?"

He'd meant it as a joke, but Varma looked wounded. "It's very effective," she said. "You know what someone said? Someone they quoted in here?" She pointed at the newspaper as she spoke, her cadence picking up again. "Some sociologist, he says my innovations reek of fascistic social engineering. I'm thinking, wow, he's a *sociologist*? Does he even understand what fascism *is*? Fascism is a police state. Fascism is about an increased, aggressive, censorious police presence. It's about people living in terror of their own government.

"What I'm doing runs so contrary to that, I mean..." She grunted in frustration. "The whole point, Tully, the whole point is that with my system there's *less* need for police, fewer contacts with law enforcement, fewer crimes because the environment simply doesn't support their commission. Everyone's safer—even the criminals! Because the criminals aren't committing crimes, they're not getting arrested or shot or sent off to prison. It's such a profound misunderstanding. And the *ignorance* of it. The *ignorance*." She held up trembling hands. "It enrages me."

It was tempting to share in her anger. After all, he still couldn't flex the fingers of his left hand, and he supposed that was just fine with sociologists. It was easy to cast down judgments and labels from high above. He'd himself once nurtured such fuzzy-headed notions, back when he didn't know how the world really worked. Back when the most terrifying thing he thought he'd after have to face was a thesis committee. He too would've likely condemned Varma's efforts.

"I understand what you're trying to do," he said. "I think a lot of people do. They're just quick to jump on anything they feel smacks of—I don't know—persuasion. Of getting people to do something without their understanding or consent."

"Oh, *wow*," she said. "That's extraordinary. Have those same people ever wondered how advertising works? Or color selection in restaurants? Or how about the way supermarkets are laid out? The whole *world* is put together to get us to do things without our understanding or consent."

"I know."

She didn't seem to hear him. "What about more basic stuff? What about speed bumps? Are those wrong, too? What about designs meant to improve traffic flow and reduce accidents? How's what I'm doing any different?"

Varma massaged her temples. "I'm sorry. I'm just really frustrated. People are so unbelievably dumb sometimes. They don't understand when you're trying to help them. I'm not even sure why I try so hard. They deserve whatever hell they want to live in. And it *will* be hell—you can free yourself from any doubt about that."

She picked up the copy of the *LA Times* and threw it into her wastebasket. "Utter nonsense. I should sue for libel. But then I'm even more the bad guy. One of the hardest things about being in the public eye is all the shit you have to eat."

"I was thinking," said Jarsdel, hoping to change the subject, "maybe we could go out to dinner tonight?"

"Do what?"

"Dinner, tonight. Take your mind off this stuff." He gestured vaguely at the *Times* jutting from the mouth of the wastebasket. "I could use it, too. A night away from anything Creeper-related."

"You know I can't," said Varma.

"I'll keep things perfectly platonic." He paused, then added, "Unless you feel like doing something else."

"Look, I told you, we can think about that sort of thing in a couple weeks."

Her tone was sharp, and Jarsdel was embarrassed by his overtures. "Yeah, 'course."

Varma rubbed at her bottom lip with her index finger, her gaze going past him, through him. "You know what I used to do? Before I got into security? I was an oral hygienist. Did that job for two years. Two years of that. The money's okay, but you'd never guess how much strength it takes."

Jarsdel wanted to go, felt she didn't really want him there. Yet she continued to speak.

"Not just from holding those awkward positions with your hands—holding your hands that way over a person's face and being so, so careful with every little movement. I mean, most people are already afraid, and you're trying to make it better, or at least trying *not* to make it worse. But that's not the thing that takes the most strength. Any guesses?"

Jarsdel shook his head.

"It's people's tongues. Some'll tell you it's the strongest muscle in the human body. That's not true, but it sure can feel that way. All day long you're battling tongues. They push against you. They want you out of there. The patient can be totally compliant, but the tongue has its own plans. Kinda makes you hate them after a while. Like big slugs. And you've got your scaler instrument—you know, your tartar remover. Sharp little hook." She raised a gently closed fist, as if she held the tool in her hand. "And...by the way, I've talked to many others in the field, and I'm not the only one who's thought about this... You realize it would be so easy to gaff that tongue like a fish. Move it where you want it to go. When you're out of patience, it's an attractive thought. Of course you don't do it. The guy would never come back, and you'd be out of a job."

"Alisha."

Varma looked up at him.

"Call me, okay? You know I'm with you on that city council thing."

"City council," Varma repeated. "Right. Thank you."

"And when all that's over, we can get to know each other."

"Yes." Varma smiled. "Yes, I'm so looking forward to that."

17

Robbery Homicide Division had recently celebrated its fiftieth anniversary. Along the hallways leading to the conference room were tributes to its most celebrated cases; one of the earliest among these was Tate-La Bianca, the mass murders that had drawn the sixties—both the decade and the zeitgeist—to an appropriately grim finale. Jarsdel passed the display each time he went to work, briefly locking eyes with Charles Manson's wild-eyed stare.

He'd been perfectly cast. Haggard, feral, a living raw nerve. Yet under it all beat a certain dark intelligence, along with a showman's knack for generating publicity. His message—impenetrable, almost gleefully incoherent—was in many ways incidental. What mattered was the glimpse of true nihilism he offered an America reeling from war, upheaval, and gnawing disillusionment. He was a boogeyman for everyone, from the Nixon Now crowd to the patchouli-scented masses prowling the Sunset Strip. No matter who you were, Manson was there for you, a gift-wrapped symbol of everything that was wrong with your world. He was chaos and emptiness both at once, given a face.

Jarsdel wondered, as he always did when he passed that photograph, how the Creeper's face would compare. Would he too become an icon of madness? Or would the spotlight neuter him, funnel away his mystique and reveal him to be nothing but a sadistic man-child? One who probably couldn't speak in words of more than a single syllable, and who'd failed at everything he'd ever done, other than murder.

Either way, unmasking the Creeper could only help. Whether he turned out to be a hoofed demon with fangs and bright-yellow cat's eyes, or a drooling, moon-faced imbecile—no matter what flavor of crazy he was, it didn't matter. The public needed to meet him, needed a place to focus its terrors. As long as he remained in the shadows, the Creeper had all the power. He could expand beyond the bounds of his human shape, growing into a legend, a phantom.

Jarsdel entered the conference room and took his seat at the table, noticing that the other detectives—Rall, Mailander, Al-Amuli—all sat with at least two empty chairs between them. None wanted to be there, and none wanted to engage.

Sponholz was on his way. First day back from compassionate leave. His wife's body had been released from the coroner's, cremated following a private, nondenominational ceremony, and the ashes released by helicopter in a small gray puff above Angeles National Forest. And now Sponholz, husband of the murdered deceased, was going to lead the investigation into his wife's homicide.

He shuffled in, shoulders hunched, gripping his doctor's bag in front of him with both hands, the way a shy third-grader might carry a lunch box. Today's tie was a length of dull maroon—no flying saucers or elliptical galaxies. It looked like a cut of liver.

"This is one of those moments," he said, "that isn't really possible to deal with. Socially. I mean, with the tools we have. You're all thinking what a pitiful sight this guy is. You know what happened, and you can't think of what to say. Because you know there's not a single sentence in the English language that can touch what I've gone through."

He stopped at the head of the table and set down his bag. "And then there's me, on the other end of that, wondering what to say to you to put you at ease enough so as we can do our jobs. It's a thorny thing, a very thorny thing."

Al-Amuli was fixated on his own lap. Mailander looked tired—or maybe just bored; it was hard to tell. Rall watched their commanding officer with stony resolve. Jarsdel, meanwhile, could find no comfortable place to rest his gaze. He didn't want to look at Sponholz, but he didn't want to seem as if he were ignoring him, either. His solution was to flit his attention from person to person. He was aware of a tightness in his face, a bunching of the muscles around his mouth that formed pocks and valleys in the otherwise smooth skin. He'd always done it when circumstances weren't merely serious, but gravely so, and to not appear visibly concerned might be read as indifference. Since he was a boy, his dads had called it his "prune chin."

Sponholz brought out a brown paper evidence bag. All of the fields—date of collection, description, location, and so on—had been left blank. "In light of all this awkwardness," he said, "I've decided on a few key things. First, I've decided to continue my compassionate leave. Accordingly, I'll be permanently stepping down from this investigation. It's an obvious conflict of interest, and I think Tricia just hasn't had the heart to tell me yet, so I'm gonna save everyone the trouble and recuse myself."

He gestured at Rall with the evidence bag. "I hope Detective Rall here will be open to my serving as a kind of consultant, but that's going to be the extent of my involvement from here on out. I don't want a micron of this investigation tainted by any accusations whatsoever that my personal feelings muddied the absolutely stellar work of this team. What do you say, Goodwin? You'll be reporting directly to the captain. And I'll help whenever I'm needed."

Rall nodded. "Anything, sir."

"All right. Then I have got something. Don't know if it's legit, but could be a place to start." He set the evidence bag on the table, then produced an iPad. "Got this about an hour ago. It hasn't been to the lab yet, so again I can't vouch for it a hundred percent. And we'll definitely have to collect my own DNA for elimination, because I handled it without knowing what it was."

He pulled up an image on the screen, then held out the iPad for everyone to see. The item, presumably photographed on Sponholz's desk, appeared to be a long strip of lined yellow paper, the kind that made up legal pads. It looked like it had been accordion pleated so it could be handled and transported more easily. Strange writing ran the length of the strip from one end to the other.

Sponholz zoomed in and Jarsdel saw that it wasn't one piece of paper at all, but perhaps a dozen, taped side by side. And what he'd first supposed was writing was in fact a series of holes punched in the shapes of letters. The black wood of Sponholz's desk shone through the holes, making a stark contrast against the yellow paper.

Rall read the words aloud. "'Must kill or die.'"

Al-Amuli looked stunned. "LT, how'd you get this?"

"Must have come in with yesterday's mail. Waiting for me this morning. Nothing exciting, just a plain business envelope addressed to Homicide Special. No return, of course."

"Was it written?" asked Mailander. "The address?"

"Nope. Printed label." Sponholz put the tablet away. "Looks like he was very careful about disguising his handwriting. Pretty clever with the hole punch. Haven't seen that particular approach before. Anyway, I'm getting the note and the envelope over to Cal State for analysis soon's we're done here."

"Wait," said Jarsdel. "If he printed the label, why go through all the trouble of punching out those holes? Why not just print out what he wanted to say? Would've saved a lot of time."

"Hell should I know," said Sponholz, visibly annoyed. "And like I said, could be absolutely nothing. Could be a fake, could be some nut. But we're still gonna treat it as real, see what comes up."

Al-Amuli was whispering something to himself and counting on his fingers. He nearly jumped out of his seat. "LT! *Must kill or die.* Thirteen letters."

Startled, Sponholz looked at the picture again. "I'll be damned. Thirteen letters, thirteen pieces of paper. Well done, Detective." He put away the iPad, then gently pushed the evidence bag in front of Rall. "Wish I had more to give you."

Rall took the bag almost reverently, bowing his head.

"And that's about it," said Sponholz. "I wish all of you the best of luck, of course. It's important we go forward as professionals, and not in a spirit of vendetta. He took my Amy, my sweet Amy, but that mustn't throw us off our game. Which remains, as always, swift, dispassionate justice."

He picked up his valise and, without another word, exited the conference room. Everyone's attention went to the evidence bag now in Rall's custody. "'Must kill or die,'" the big detective said. "Kill so you don't die, huh? Well, you *gonna* die."

"Damn right," said Al-Amuli. "*Damn* right. Direct to Jesus. Fuckin' Q-sign." He stuck his tongue out the corner of his open mouth, approximating the shape of the letter Q.

"Everyone get some sleep," said Rall. "Only got a month before Captain Coryell calls in her marker. Creeper solved, people. Solved by the end of summer."

18

It was an odd little detail, probably insignificant, but it nagged at Jarsdel. It was too obvious to be deliberate—a confusion between two forms of statistical analysis so different that anyone would be able to spot it.

Matter over Mind: Security Concerns from a Psychosocial Perspective. The bible of security solutions, one that tapped into the deepest recesses of our reptile brain. No advancements in technology or methodology would be able to circumvent Varma's analysis, because her data was based on pure anatomy. We couldn't escape our anatomy, couldn't out-think it. We were bound by its limitations, and our limitations told a very predictable story.

That was one reason he liked the book so much. It dispensed with theory and focused on what was actually there—the axons and glial cells shaping our deeply brilliant—and deeply flawed—gray matter.

Twenty-five percent. That was the number she'd quoted. Missouri's Elk River Penitentiary had allowed Varma to implement her program, and at an astonishing bargain of less than fifty thousand dollars. Before she'd arrived, the odds of being involved in a violent altercation were four out of a hundred, or four percent. A year later, that number had dropped to three out of a hundred. Three percent. Or, if you looked at it on an absolute scale, a one percent decrease. Hardly impressive. Statistically insignificant. But instead of a one percent drop, you could phrase it slightly differently.

You could phrase it as a twenty-five percent drop.

Yes, it was true that going from four to three was only a single step, one percentage point. But *relative* to four—well, a step down represented a whopping twenty-five percent difference. An extraordinary feat.

Jarsdel had checked the numbers himself on the Bureau of Justice Statistics website. Elk River Penitentiary—a one percent drop, from four to three. Then *Matter over Mind*—twenty-five percent.

It was too brazen an error to have been done purposely. Too easily uncovered by anyone who cared enough to spend a few minutes double-checking the figures.

Then again, he thought, it was also the kind of statistical flimflam used every day to scare people into buying the latest gizmo or adopting fad diets. Unethical, yes, but technically—*very* technically—not a lie. And in a textbook stuffed with hundreds and hundreds of figures, why would anyone decide to investigate that particular one? The only reason he'd looked into it himself was because she'd asked him to back her up at the upcoming city council hearing, and he'd wanted printouts from the bureau itself as evidence of her successes.

He picked up his phone and brought up Varma's contact info. How would he phrase it? The only other time he'd spoken to her about her work had been with admiration. Maybe he'd lead in with that, something like "Hey, just going through your textbook again—man, it's really something—and I noticed a tiny discrepancy."

Good enough. He touched the green telephone icon and waited.

It was picked up on the third ring. Jarsdel heard several voices, then one—a man's—calling for quiet.

"Hello, who's this?" The voice was familiar to Jarsdel, but he was hearing it out of context and couldn't place it.

"This is Detective Marcus Jarsdel, LAPD. Who's *this*?"

"Tully? Shit. What're you doin'? Why're you calling this number?"

Now the owner of the voice was obvious. Jarsdel was annoyed. "Oscar? Why do you have Dr. Varma's phone?"

"Hey, seriously, why're you calling this number? Why're you calling it right now?"

"Same reason anyone calls a phone number—trying to reach the person it belongs to. Could you put her on, please? And why do you have her phone? Is she even there?"

"Hang on." Morales yelled at someone to be quiet, then came back on the line. "Wait, so Tully, you don't know?"

"Know what?"

"Alisha Varma's dead. Now can you tell me why you were calling?"

Jarsdel took the phone away from his ear and looked at the display. Later he wasn't sure why he'd done that. Perhaps he'd been hoping to see that somehow he'd dialed the wrong number, or that he wasn't on the phone at all and was simply imagining the whole thing.

He read the display, saw Varma's name, and raised the phone again. "Oscar, it's me."

"I know it's you."

"Where is she?"

"Her body was found in the underground garage of her apartment. I'll ask again: why are you calling right now?"

"I'm coming over." Jarsdel hung up before Morales could argue.

Glass and blood were the first things he saw.

How well they complemented each other—the tiny cubes of safety glass and the puddles of coagulating blood. A tableau of trauma. All that was missing was a body, and soon that too came into view.

Alisha Varma's eyes were open wide. Jarsdel read in them surprise, fear, and perhaps some amazement, as though she couldn't believe what had happened to her. A plastic-handled steak knife, its blade smeared with red, lay nearby. He stared at the knife—such a small, cheap-looking thing. A flimsy dollar-store blade that would hardly make it through a lemon before it went dull. But it had done the job well enough here. A wound in her left shoulder and another on the same side near her sternum. That had been the fatal one, soaking her mint-green T-shirt and leaving puddles around the body as she struggled to live.

She'd been found on the bottom floor of her apartment complex's two-level underground parking garage. It was an older building, the kind with one of those ponderously slow swing-up gates. It would've been easy for someone to slip in, especially if a car had been exiting, the driver fixed on the busy street ahead.

Jarsdel did a quick scan of that stretch of parking garage. Brightly lit, yes, but no cameras. Of course.

Dr. Ipgreve, the medical examiner, stood off to the side taking notes. Jarsdel approached him.

"Tell me everything."

Ipgreve glanced up from his work, irritated. "Hello to you, too, Detective. Didn't know you were working this one."

"He isn't."

Both men turned to see Haarmann. It took Jarsdel a second to recognize him out of uniform. The rookie detective filled out a navy-blue suit, his great bull neck straining the collar of his dress shirt. He looked like club security; all he needed was a coiled earpiece. Morales stood by his side, his face unreadable.

"Why're you here, Dad?" said Haarmann. "Things slow on Creeper, so you're poaching?"

Jarsdel looked at Morales. "Who did this?"

"You first," said his ex-partner. "Why were you calling before?"

"Alone."

"Huh?"

"I'll talk to you alone." He pointed at Haarmann. "Without him. Without the Cro-Magnon."

Haarmann looked delighted. Morales glanced at the patrol officer, then back at Jarsdel. He sighed. "Will, give us a few minutes."

"Sure." Haarmann strolled off.

"Okay, we're alone," said Morales. "Explain the phone call."

"I had a question for her."

Morales had his notebook out. "What was it?"

Jarsdel was too drained to go through the whole mess with the Elk River stats. "Just a question. Technical question."

"About?"

"Something from her textbook."

"Yeah, go ahead."

"It was complicated."

Morales looked up. "You wanna go back and forth on this all night? Or is it you think I'm too dumb to process it?"

"It's *nothing*," Jarsdel snapped. "I was curious about some figures she quoted." He saw Morales still wasn't satisfied. Fine. He wanted details? Jarsdel would give him details. "Had to do with the difference between relative and absolute risk."

Morales nodded, scribbling notes. "Like how to look at percentages."

Deflated, Jarsdel didn't comment.

"Why were you asking?"

"I was supposed to attend a presentation she was gonna give to the city council."

"About what?"

"It had to do with outsourcing CCTV camera feeds to a dedicated private security agency."

Morales stopped writing. He regarded Jarsdel with an expression of baffled amusement. "I don't understand—what's that got to do with you?"

"Quite a bit, actually." Jarsdel held up his stitched fingers. "Something like that might've caught the Cro-Mag sticking the blade to my door handle."

"So, what, you were gonna be like her backup at the meeting? The face of human tragedy to beef up her pitch?"

"Her pitch didn't need beefing up. It made good sense. But it's not going to happen now, is it? Maybe you ought to look at people who would've been hurt by Dr. Varma's proposed reallocation of city resources. This could go pretty high up."

Morales didn't seem to hear him. Haarmann had wandered back. "Hey. I'm gonna check out the apartment. You wanna come?"

"Yeah." Morales put away his notebook and began moving off.

"Wait, hang on," said Jarsdel. "Who did this? What's the working theory?"

Morales stopped, shrugged. "Mugging gone wrong, I'd say."

"You *would* say."

"That mean something?"

"Means as usual, you always go with whatever's right in front of you."

Morales crossed his arms.

"She was trying to make a difference," said Jarsdel, "and she was succeeding. Maybe if she'd been around a year ago, we'd have had working cameras outside our own goddamn police station." He locked eyes with Haarmann, who gave the faintest hint of a smile.

"And I have a tough time," Jarsdel went on, "believing this was just a coincidence. Considering who she was."

"Okay," said Morales. "So enlighten us. You think she was—what, assassinated?"

"I think that not to consider such a scenario would be negligent. Willfully negligent."

"Let me give you some perspective, since you're always so generous with yours." Morales crooked a thumb at the body. "This wasn't some civil rights leader, some martyr for a cause. This was basically a DOD lapdog who got a cushy consulting job. In other words, it's not like the man took her out. She *was* the fucking man."

"She had a lot of enemies," said Jarsdel. "Even if you don't think she was worthy of them. I'm not saying it had to be a conspiracy, though. No. It could've been more prosaic. One of the vagrants she'd displaced settling a grudge."

"You're saying one of those poor Skid Row zombies..." Morales began chuckling, actually *chuckling*, with the body just a few feet away. "You're saying one of those skells down there decided to take her out? Like find out where she lived and black-ops her ass?"

Haarmann also grinned at the idea.

Jarsdel considered speaking with Ipgreve alone. Maybe there was a way to persuade him to pass along Varma's autopsy results. But Morales and Haarmann were watching him, so it would have to wait.

"You know," he said to the two men, "this whole thing proves her right. Either way."

Morales and Haarmann just looked at him.

"Because whether she'd spooked the wrong person and that got her targeted and killed—don't make that face, Oscar—or...or she was simply a victim of random street crime, as you suggest. It doesn't matter, because she was right."

"About what?" said Morales. "About crime being a bad thing? That's really super. You oughta do PSAs with McGruff the Crime Dog."

"*No*," said Jarsdel. "She was right that we needed her. That's what I'm saying. That we needed her. That she was going to mold this world, city by city, into something better. Something we could live with." He shook his head, disgusted. "*McGruff*. I love that. I love how you bring up *McGruff*. It fits so well with who you are. You know, you minimize. You minimize and you always try to find a way around everything, because you can't handle having an actual feeling. Gotta keep that cynical shell nice and polished. Emotion beads on it like water and just rolls off."

Haarmann began to laugh. Jarsdel pointed at him. "And it's perfect now, because you've got this empty vessel to back you up on every bit of poison and hopelessness. Your own feedback loop, affirming everything you already believe."

Morales stepped close. "You're making an ass out of yourself."

"It doesn't matter," said Jarsdel. "With Varma gone everything goes back to the way it was. There's no growth, no learning. Back to what's comfortable, even if it's stupid. Even if we're treating the symptom instead of the disease. Which I suppose is great for guys like you and Haarmann. You two are gonna absolutely thrive. Good for you, a shame for the rest of us."

"Professor. Go home."

Jarsdel flinched. Morales's invocation of that first and most hated nickname changed the flavor of the argument. He was dismissing him, dismissing him as if he were a nuisance, an amateur.

"I can offer..." he began, but Morales flicked his hand at him.

"Go home. We'll call if there's anything else we need from you, but don't hold your breath."

19

Ed Sponholz answered the door in a pair of green sweatpants and a sleeveless gray tee with *Donington Park '86* across its breast. When he turned away, Jarsdel saw it was from sort of mega rock concert. The bands listed were Iron Maiden, Dokken, Cinderella, Dangerous Toys, and Pretty Maids. Even if Jarsdel hadn't been a toddler, he very much doubted he would've found himself in Donington Park in 1986.

Sponholz slunk into the house, giving the barest wave to indicate Jarsdel should follow. He led them to the living room and pointed to a black leather couch, the kind that sucked on your thighs if you were wearing shorts. Jarsdel sat while Sponholz moved to the bar and pulled a Calicraft Kolsch from a mini-fridge. He wedged the cap into a wall-mounted opener and, with a practiced turn of the wrist, sent it spinning into a wooden box hanging below. Someone, probably Sponholz, had scrawled on the box in Sharpie, "Don't bother checking your watch—it's five o'clock!"

Jarsdel did check his watch and saw it wasn't quite noon. Sponholz must have caught him doing it, because he said, "If you're gonna be like that, Detective, you might as well take off."

"I'm sorry?"

"You want one?"

"Oh. No thanks. Appreciate it, though."

Sponholz took a swig of the beer, smacked his lips, then fell into a recliner. The footrest deployed automatically, and Sponholz was nearly horizontal. He took another long pull on the bottle.

"Your dime, go ahead. What d'you need?"

Jarsdel cleared his throat. "Just a few questions. About that night. Maybe get your thoughts on a few things."

"Where's Goodwin? And the rest of the team?"

"Everyone's on their own assignments."

Sponholz offered a sad smile. "And you drew the short straw?"

"Not at all, sir," said Jarsdel. "I volunteered."

That gave Sponholz pause. He eyed Jarsdel with curiosity—or perhaps suspicion. "Wow. You volunteered to drive from Downtown LA to Northridge. Must really want to talk."

Jarsdel flipped open his field notebook and turned a few pages, reviewing his notes. It was unnecessary—he knew exactly what he wanted to ask. But it allowed for an easy transition.

"I'm wondering," he began, then corrected himself. "We're all wondering, how did the Creeper know your—uh, Amy, that she was gonna be alone. If you have any ideas."

Sponholz wiped his hand down his face and gave his head a quick little shake. "I can only figure he saw me leave. Or maybe he looked in our garage—there's a little window off the side door where you can see in—and saw my car was gone. Then Amy probably turned on a light or something, so he knew she was there."

"Then I guess my next question would be why'd he wait so long?"

"Don't know what you mean, 'Wait so long.' What's that mean—wait so long for what?"

"If he saw you leave, or if he was watching the place all night, why wait so long to attack? As far as we can tell, he committed the assault maybe ten or fifteen minutes before you arrived. Tempting fate a little, right? I mean, if you'd been any earlier, that would've been it for him."

"I've been asking myself that question over and over. Like he knew my routine, knew around what time I'd be home. The only thing I can figure is that he wanted me to see how close he could get to me, with his planning and his timing."

Jarsdel pursed his lips, considering that. "You said before, back when we talked early that morning at Devonshire Station, that Amy left the back door unlocked a lot of the time."

"Yes."

"How'd he know that, though? That it was unlocked?"

Sponholz shrugged. "I have no idea."

"And what if it hadn't been? What was he going to do then?"

"Again, no idea. I guess we'll never know the answer to that, unfortunately."

"And how did he know she wouldn't be armed? That the wife of a police lieutenant didn't have a spare firearm? Seems like a huge gamble."

"I agree with you," said Sponholz. "Seems pretty nuts. Then again, this guy likes to rape men with their own dicks, so I guess we can't always expect him to behave reasonably."

Sponholz was getting frustrated, so Jarsdel decided to back off a little. He looked again at his notes, counted silently to five, then asked, "Any idea why Amy didn't call the police when the alarm went off?"

"I'm assuming she didn't have time. Pretty easy to make it upstairs from the back door if you're in a hurry."

That was true. Jarsdel had run several trials himself, and it had never taken him more than eight seconds. The Creeper must have moved without hesitation, despite the deafening alarm, to make it upstairs fast enough before Amy could react. All the same...

"All the same," Jarsdel said aloud. "Why didn't she lock the door to the bedroom?"

"What do you mean?"

"She didn't lock the door. No sign of forced entry, and we didn't even find her prints on the knob. That means she didn't so much as touch it since it was cleaned earlier that morning. Now, granted, it probably wouldn't have given her enough time to call the cops and wait to talk to an operator, but when the alarm went off, why didn't she at least lock the door? It was just a little privacy lock on the handle, but it would've slowed him down."

Sponholz looked confused. "It wouldn't have occurred to her."

"It wouldn't have occurred to her to lock the door? With the alarm going off like that? Why not?"

"Because..." Sponholz appeared to realize something, and sighed. "Oh, I see. You guys think..." He took another deep swallow of his Kolsch, then bent his legs sharply. The footrest swung back into the recliner, and Sponholz got to his feet. "Here. Follow me."

The two men left the living room, crossed the foyer, and before long were at the door off the kitchen—the same one the Creeper had come through. Sponholz pointed to an alarm security panel fastened on the wall to the right of the jamb. He approached it and pressed a button marked "STAY." An emotionless male voice announced that the system was "Arming now." A readout on the alarm system began counting down from thirty. Beeping sounded at regular intervals to warn anyone who cared to listen that the house would soon be fully protected.

When the countdown finished, an icon of a closed padlock appeared on the panel's small screen. Sponholz turned to Jarsdel and pointed at the display.

"Okay, I'm with you," said Jarsdel.

Sponholz made his way over to the unlocked back door, turned the handle, and pushed it open. Jarsdel prepared himself for the shrill pealing of the alarm, but it didn't come. Instead, the panel spat out a few indignant beeps, and the readout once again began counting down from thirty.

"That's it," said Sponholz. "It'll make noises like that for thirty seconds, but the actual alarm doesn't go off until the time runs out. This one and the front door both give you a grace period before going full out. Think how annoying that'd be if it didn't do that, right? If you came home and right as you walked in, it started blasting? Nah, you get thirty seconds to turn off the system." He punched in a code, and the countdown ceased.

"I mean yeah, we've got a few windows wired, and those'll go off right away if the alarm's set," he continued. "But in this case, basically he would've had thirty seconds to get upstairs before the alarm actually started howling. So Amy wouldn't have heard a thing, and by then it would've been too late."

"You don't have any panels upstairs?" said Jarsdel.

Sponholz shook his head.

"Nothing that would've been beeping up there?"

"You're welcome to look around if you don't believe me."

"No, 'course I believe you," said Jarsdel. He didn't know why, but he was frustrated. He'd been somehow sure the discrepancy between the tripped alarm and Amy not locking the door would lead to a breakthrough. But Sponholz's solution—banal as it was—made perfect sense. Jarsdel felt silly.

Sponholz offered a sad smile. "I know how you feel. I'm the same way, chasing an idea, then getting to watch it dead-end somewhere. I can tell you it's the sign of a good policeman. Someone who cares deeply for what he does, and for justice as a... as a goddamned law of nature. And he himself as an *agent of that law*." His eyes welled up.

Christ, here we go again, thought Jarsdel. It seemed every time he saw Sponholz, the lieutenant worked himself into tears.

Jarsdel immediately chided himself for judging the man. *He's lost his wife, asshole. Murdered by the dark, twisted thing he's been chasing. And you're going to begrudge him some psychological frailty?*

But some sign of distaste must have nonetheless appeared on Jarsdel's face, because Sponholz's dewy, pleading eyes dulled suddenly. The skin around his mouth, which was on its way from crinkly to craggy, smoothed out. He sniffed and stood up straight.

"Sorry," he said. "Didn't mean to make you uncomfortable."

"Not at all," said Jarsdel. *I'm just a huge dickhead*, he thought. *Your wife is strangled, her body profaned, and I'm here to make you feel awkward for getting a little emotional.* "I can't imagine what you're going through," he added.

"Man. Man oh man oh man," said Sponholz. "There's a part of me—a pretty big part—that can't really imagine it, either. That's telling me this is just some kind of absurd dream, or that I've slipped past the veil into a parallel dimension, and that I just need to—you know—tap my ruby slippers together and I'll end up back where I belong. Back where everything makes sense."

Jarsdel looked over his shoulder at the open door. Beyond was a large yard, the grass long dead. A high cyclone fence separated it from neighboring property. "Do we know how he got into your backyard?" he asked.

"Hmm?" Sponholz turned and followed Jarsdel's gaze. "Oh. I'm assuming he climbed the fence. Isn't too hard to do if you're young and athletic, I presume."

"Such a risk, though," said Jarsdel. "He could've trapped himself. So again I'm just curious how he knew that door was going to be open."

"Maybe he didn't," said Sponholz. "Maybe he had picks on him. Planned on getting in no matter what. We know he's carried other tools in the past. Saws, files, so why not picks?"

"Right, yeah, that makes sense. Still, lucky guy. Always very lucky. Everything always swings his way. Especially how you and he barely missed each other. You were working out, right?"

Sponholz chuckled. "Yeah, I try to stay in shape. If you start putting off workouts just because you're tired, you'll always think of an excuse."

"You were at the gym at PAB?"

"Yup."

"It's open all night?"

"All night, all day."

Jarsdel thought about that, and Sponholz nodded. "Yeah," said the lieutenant. "Believe me, it's only crossed my mind about a million times. If I hadn't gone to the gym, Amy might still be alive."

"I'm sorry. Being the one to dredge all this up."

"Don't be. I'll tell you, this job's easier to do when you don't know the poor souls you gotta interview. You're a professional, though, and I appreciate that. Is there anything else you need from me? Because I'm about through, emotionally."

"No, sir. That's it."

Sponholz clapped him on the shoulder. "Tell the rest of the gang I'm doing okay. As okay as can be. I'll be back when—well, when I'm able."

"There's no hurry."

"Not needed, huh?"

"No, that's not what I meant at—"

"Relax, Detective. Busting your balls. Not really the joking-around type, are you?"

The two men moved through the house toward the foyer. Jarsdel kept getting little whiffs of something unpleasant, like a heavy fish smell. Sponholz must have cooked some recently—a greasy kind, too, like a salmon or maybe a mackerel. Jarsdel could imagine the volatile little molecules wafting throughout the house and burying themselves in the carpet and upholstery and curtains. The house itself was absolutely silent. What a strange thing—a quiet house and a noisy smell. Jarsdel wanted very badly to leave.

Sponholz opened the front door, and to Jarsdel the experience was like clearing your ears after your plane touches down on the runway—the world suddenly alive and rich with all the sounds you didn't even know you'd missed. A wind chime a block away, a playing card snapping through the spokes of some kid's bike, the angry squawk of a crow chasing an intruder from its nest. Ahead of him was life—the sun-swept, humming life of LA in summer. Behind him was death. Heavy, suffocating death. Jarsdel practically leapt outside. He turned and faced Sponholz, who remained in the doorway, a man more of death than of life.

"Sir—" Jarsdel began.

"Ed."

"Ed. Are you sure you want to be staying here? It's none of my business—just seems like it must be really hard."

"You're a good young man," said the lieutenant. "But I want it to hurt. I want every passing day to be a misery. It's not right that Amy's gone, that she suffered the way she did and I got away. So until that monster, that demon from hell is brought in, I don't see why I should get off so easy."

Jarsdel had trouble following the man's logic, but he supposed it made more sense when seen through the lens of grief. Grief was still mostly foreign to him. He thought of how Varma had looked in the parking lot; as bad as it was, she hadn't been his wife. No one Jarsdel loved had ever even been sick, though he suspected—after having last seen his ever-more-skeletal father—that such a reality wasn't too far out of reach.

"I want you to do me a favor, Tully."

"Sure, of course."

"If you do find him, if you do find the Creeper—"

"We *will*. We *will* find him."

"Yeah, I know. Rah-rah and all that. No one's been able to do it so far. But let's say you do find him... I want you to put him down."

Jarsdel wasn't sure what to say to that, and Sponholz went on.

"I know. You're a cop, not an executioner. But spread the word anyway. I do not want to testify. I do not want to get in front of the scum-sucking media and the foul creature itself and bare my heart to the world. Tell everyone what it was like finding my beloved Amy with a *broomstick*..."

He spasmed, shutting his eyes and jamming a fist against his mouth. Jarsdel watched as Sponholz took a series of deep breaths. Ten seconds passed, then twenty, then nearly thirty before Sponholz finally went on. "I want to get a nice phone call from you or Rall or somebody just telling me that it's all over. That our guy got double-tapped into whatever's waiting for him in the great beyond. That's what I'm asking. Think you can do that?"

Jarsdel answered without hesitation. "No."

Sponholz looked at him curiously.

“I can’t imagine”—Jarsdel lifted a hand in the direction of the house—“any of this, but I can’t do what you’re asking. It’s not what our side is supposed to stand for.”

Sponholz smiled. “Exactly. And that’s why I’m so glad I picked you for my team. You’ve got an unshakable moral core, and I admire you so goddamned much.”

He held out his hand, and Jarsdel took it automatically. Sponholz gave it a vigorous squeeze, then let him go.

“I...” Jarsdel began, then reconsidered his words. “So that was some kind of a test?”

“No,” said Sponholz. “I really did want you to gun him down. But the way you put that, how stalwart you are in everything, you’ve reminded me exactly what it is we do. And I’m so very grateful to you.”

Jarsdel studied the lieutenant’s face. There were still shadows. He could see them. Faint shadows of the scratches Sponholz had sustained from falling into the tree. Strange that a tree branch could make those so perfectly. Three scratches, side by side, along his left cheek. Just as a right-handed person would make when trying to defend herself.

“I need to ask you something,” he said.

“Yes. I thought so.”

“You thought so?”

“You had the look. I know that look. A suspicious man.”

“I’m not suspicious,” said Jarsdel.

“Of course you are,” said Sponholz. “It’s what makes you a first-class investigator.”

“It’s something I have to ask. I’m sorry.”

“Don’t be sorry.”

“The night you found your wife’s body. Earlier that day you came into the office with scratches on your face. With scratches on your face and a split lip and, forgive me, an unusual explanation for their occurrence.”

Sponholz considered. "I disagree. I'd say a strange or even a bizarre explanation. One that seems in retrospect a little too neat, a little too convenient. And at the same time a bit far-fetched. Don't you think? All that business with the birds burrowing into the roof? That last one flying out and scaring me off my ladder? Even the way I told it, there in the conference room, making sure I got every detail of the story out to everybody? And my wife getting murdered—no, I should say, her body discovered, so shortly thereafter. My goodness, heck of a coincidence. If I were you, Detective, I wouldn't think that was merely suspicious, I'd say it was well on the way to damning."

Jarsdel was thrown. It was as if Sponholz had listed, in order, everything that had been lining up in his mind. Evidence plus evidence plus evidence, tossed in the machine of deductive reasoning, and the conclusion was right there. Only Sponholz had been the one to point it out, not him.

"It gets worse," said the lieutenant. "Though I'm sure you can already tell me how."

"Life insurance," said Jarsdel. It had been easy to find, emerging in their standard review of the decedent's holdings. The most valuable things Amy Sponholz owned were that life insurance policy, her small ranch in Shadow Hills, and her horse.

"Life insurance," Sponholz agreed. "With a double-indemnity clause. And with me as sole beneficiary. Ever see that movie—*Double Indemnity*?"

"No."

"You should. Excellent film. 'Bout a woman who conspires with an insurance agent to murder her husband. The main guy they have to fool for the plan to work out is the head claims adjustor. So if we were to transpose those roles, I'd be Barbara Stanwyck, you'd be Edward G. Robinson, and some as-yet-named third party would be my lover, the Fred MacMurray character. Found anyone to fill that part yet? The illicit lady love, with whom I conspired to do in my sweet Amy?"

"Sir, we're nowhere near that kind of thinking. Do you have

anything at all you can give us? Anything that could say definitively your wife was alive when you came into the office that morning?"

"You mean other than the time of death set by Dr. Ipgreve? I believe he said it was early the *next* morning that she died. Or do you think I fooled a thirty-year veteran pathologist?"

Jarsdel saw how improbable that was. But it was quite a coincidence—Amy's murder coming so soon on the heels of that ridiculous tree story.

"You're right," said Jarsdel. "Forget it."

"No, I don't wanna forget it. I don't like being looked at that way, and I don't want it to happen again. Let me see what I can come up with."

Jarsdel watched as Sponholz ruminated. The lieutenant's expressions ran the gamut from pained to fearful to wistful.

It's a stall. An act.

Jarsdel chastised himself for thinking that, so he tried to see it differently. Sponholz was a man lost in grief and confusion, and now he'd been accused—however softly—of murdering the very woman he mourned.

"Not every day your life suddenly depends on you being able to come up with an alibi," Sponholz said.

"Lieutenant—"

"No, no. It's fine. Don't beat yourself up. Nature of the work. It is so important to remember that." He exhaled, then raised his head, eyes suddenly alight. "There is something. But if Ipgreve isn't good enough for you, I doubt this will be." A sad, wheezy chuckle. "I guess at least now I know how the guy on the other side of the table feels. A little compassion ain't such a bad thing though, is it?"

Jarsdel didn't comment, didn't want to distract the lieutenant from his point.

"Amy," said Sponholz, "Amy had a, uh—you remember she was in real estate?"

Jarsdel nodded.

"Yeah, so, she had an open house, I think. Or had that been the day before? I don't remember for sure, but it feels right. You could easily find out. She worked at—"

"McWilliams Real Estate Group, yes."

"Oh, of course. You already knew that. Tell me, how long have I been under suspicion?"

"You're not under suspicion. It's just the procedure."

"*Just the procedure*. Oy." When Sponholz spoke again, his manner was indignant. "I know how this *works*, Detective. You can be straight with me. Don't feed me all those lines about procedure. I want to understand, and I'm not angry. I'm *not* angry, but I want to understand why is it that I'm even being asked these questions, put in this position, when the DNA, fingerprints, MO—everything—clearly point to an established perpetrator. Who is it who suspects me?"

"No one, sir, no one at all thinks you had anything to do with this."

"So it's just *you*? What is it exactly you have against me?"

Jarsdel was appalled. "Nothing. I don't have anything against you. I'm not trying to offend you or upset you or anything at all. It's like you pointed out: the injuries, the coincidence of your injuries and her date of death."

"Murder."

"Murder, yes. And you said MO—the Creeper's MO—but it wasn't, sir, not really. He was wearing gloves, and that doesn't track with him. He's never done that before."

"How do you know he was wearing gloves?"

"Traces of leather under her nails, but no human matter."

Sponholz thought about that. "I'm confused. I thought there were prints all over the house."

"There were, which is also a puzzle. It looks like he wore gloves just for the assault, but otherwise wasn't particular about what he touched."

"Who cares?" said Sponholz. "Honestly, Detective, who cares why he did each little thing he did? He's a psychotic, an animal. I'm not interested in psychoanalyzing every crackpot move he makes."

"Because, sir, he still operates within his own sphere of logic. His own eccentricities, his own paraphilia, they make sense to him."

"*Paraphilia*. Sounds so much better than 'perversions.' So much more scientific."

Jarsdel ignored the digression. "And from what we know about him, he'd have no reason to wear gloves. Quite the contrary. It would frustrate his process, make the moment less immediate, less intimate."

"You're speculating."

"And he didn't bite her."

The lieutenant's expression hardened. "That's something I'm grateful for."

"We all are," said Jarsdel. "But it doesn't fit with the Creeper. He always bites the women."

"Remarkable. I'm under suspicion because the murder wasn't as depraved as it could have been."

"You're not under suspicion."

Sponholz grunted. "Punish the victim."

Silence as Jarsdel let the lieutenant's words hang out there. He knew Sponholz was grieving, and he didn't want to engage with him. Maybe if he let him cool down, he'd see he wasn't being reasonable. To encourage a return to good sense, Jarsdel finally said, "If you were in my position, you'd want these issues cleared up as well. Doing so can only help us catch him."

Sponholz closed his eyes, took a slow breath. "You're right. Please accept my apology."

"Isn't needed."

"It is."

"No."

"Please accept it."

"All right, but it's not necessary."

"And Amy," said Sponholz. "Yes, I think so, about what I mentioned before. About the open house. I'm almost positive now that she did have one that day. You'll want to talk to Rich Woolwine. I don't have the number off the top of my head, but it's easy to find. Just google McWilliams Realty Group. It's the office number."

Jarsdel took down the name. "Appreciate that. Thank you, sir. Please let us know if there's anything we can do." He was about to go when something occurred to him. "Who played the husband?"

Sponholz blinked. "The husband?"

"In *Double Indemnity*. You named all the actors who played the wife, the insurance agent, the claims adjustor, but not the husband. Not the actual person who gets murdered."

"Oh." Sponholz looked up, squinting, trying to remember. He shook his head in defeat. "No idea. Old-time character actor. Why do you want to know?"

"No reason, really," said Jarsdel. "It is funny, though, how we always remember the killers, never the victims. Real-life cases too. The killers get to be famous. In ten years, everyone will know who the Eastside Creeper is, but I doubt we'll be able to say the same for Maja Rustad or Joanne Lauterbach."

"Or Amy Sponholz?" The lieutenant's expression was unreadable.

"Dumb thing to say. Thinking out loud. Shouldn't do that."

"No. Maybe not."

Jarsdel backed away. He'd had enough of Sponholz's ever damp, desperate eyes. They reminded him of what he'd heard about drowning victims. How dangerous they could be—how you'd sometimes have to knock them out to rescue them, because the first thing they'd try to do is pull you under. And how their terror and anguish fired their muscle fibers with adrenaline and made them unnaturally strong.

"See you back at work," said Jarsdel.

Sponholz watched him, unblinking, nor did he say anything else as Jarsdel got into his car and drove off.

20

Of the dead, there were three.

Brian Minchew, twenty-nine—and stabbed at least as many times—lay naked on the floor near the bed, half wrapped in a bedsheet. A swollen length of intestine snaked its way out from beneath his body and wound around the man's neck, cinched tightly into the flesh.

Natalie Minchew was on the bed, sprawled diagonally across its length. She'd been nearly decapitated, her throat cut all the way to the spine. The serrated bread knife that'd done the work still protruded from the yawning wound. Either the hand that wielded it had lost its willpower or the blade had lost its edge.

The room stank of putrefaction, of congealing blood and broken bodies. Jarsdel had once read that if you wanted to simulate the stench of death, you should buy the cheapest ground beef you could find, leave it out in the sun a few hours, then take a big whiff of it while you sucked on an old penny. He'd never tried it himself, but figured it wasn't too far off. It had the right ingredients: metal and meat comingling in a unique bouquet that—once it got in—seemed to live in your sinuses far longer than it had a right to. The stench only changed by degree of intensity, but it was always the same, a biological signature writ in the air itself.

At some point, Al-Amuli had wandered over to Jarsdel's side. "Wig snatch."

Jarsdel turned to look at him. "What?"

"Wig snatch." He made a gesture of pulling off a hairpiece.

"What's that mean?"

"It's like, 'holy shit, blown away.' You never heard wig snatch?"

Jarsdel let his gaze hang heavily on Al-Amuli another moment, glanced once more at the Minchews, and made his way out of the master bedroom and across the hall. The smell lingered as he knew it would, a phantom that would cling to him for hours. He'd get whiffs of it until he showered, maybe even after.

He stopped in the doorway and beheld the crumpled form at his feet.

Emma Minchew. Six years old. She wasn't as far into decomp as her parents. Almost would've looked like she was sleeping, if not for the unnatural cant of her limbs.

When first responders had arrived, she'd been covered with a threadbare blanket, rose pink and printed with fat, smiling strawberries. It now lay next to her, tossed aside when EMTs attempted to resuscitate the girl. Chance had arranged the blanket in nearly the same pose as the child, curled in a C-shape, almost fetal. The similarities between them ran deeper. She'd been unplugged from life's great, animating current, and now had more in common with the yard of cloth than she did with any of the investigators drifting in and out of her bedroom.

Jarsdel didn't want to look at the bedroom, and kept his eyes on the body. He would wait to examine the area until after she was taken away. This he had learned to do from painful experience. His first dead child had been about the same age and had taken a bullet fired from across the street during an argument. It was a freak accident, but the child, a boy, was dead all the same. The round pierced his tiny chest while he played with his Legos, planting itself in a lung. He drowned in his own blood, unable to call for help.

Jarsdel remembered seeing the boy's kindergarten graduation

photo—grinning, eyes squinted in the sunlight, a single missing tooth. At the time, Jarsdel had looked away, hoping for something else, something that wouldn't show him the boy in life, and only reaped further horrors. An orange belt in karate, mounted on a wooden display stand, a stuffed polar bear, a novelty trophy for World's Greatest Grandson, a poster of a dozen Pixar characters smiling and waving.

Sleep hadn't come that night for Marcus Tullius Jarsdel, former doctoral candidate in classical antiquity and newly minted patrolman. His closed eyelids became screens on which he played reruns of the crime scene. People died every day, many of them violently. And some of those would, unavoidably, be children. But it was one thing to hear of such things happening, another to stand over the boy and see the bullet hole in his Daniel Tiger pj's, the expression of terror and agony frozen across his features. He'd wept as he lay dying, and his cheeks bore streaks of dried tears.

As bad as the bodies were for Jarsdel, the children's rooms were somehow always worse. Adults scatter their personalities over a wider radius, free to imprint a multitude of spaces with some evidence of their existence. A child's room was his whole world. Each tin of putty and chunk of pyrite and macaroni collage was a story point in the narrative of self. You couldn't be in children's rooms without knowing them at least a little, and Jarsdel didn't want to know them.

"Busy couple months." Ipgreve, the medical examiner, squeezed by Jarsdel and crouched next to the girl's body. With his left hand he thumbed her eyelids open; with his right he trained the beam of a penlight into the fogged irises.

"Subconjunctival hemorrhages in both eyes," said Ipgreve. "No bruising on the neck." He stood and went to the girl's bed. Jarsdel kept his attention on the body.

"Pillow appears to bear residue of mucus and spittle. I see some bloody fingerprints too, but since the girl's not bleeding, I'd say the killer transferred them after he did the parents. Ninety-nine-point-nine-nine out of a hundred the girl was smothered."

"Okay."

"Doesn't seem strange to you, Detective?"

Jarsdel looked at the girl. Her skin had a bluish cast, and even without Ipgreve's penlight, he could see the ruptured capillaries in her cheeks and eyelids.

"Detective?"

"What?"

"I said doesn't that seem strange to you? Her parents are filleted in the bedroom and this girl is quietly suffocated in here?"

"No." Jarsdel turned to go.

"Hey, hey," said Ipgreve. "Hang on. Stop a second."

Jarsdel looked at him. "What is it?"

"I know, okay? I know how it is, but just process something in all your misery and loss of hope for the human race."

"What?"

"This was merciful."

"No. How?"

"It was. Comparatively."

Jarsdel sighed.

"It was," Ipgreve repeated. "Not so much for the girl, true. But for the killer. No blood, for one. And you don't have to see her face as she's breathing her last."

"Fine," said Jarsdel. "Let me know when she's out of here so we can finish up with the room."

"You're welcome anytime. Won't bother me."

Jarsdel spotted Rall heading toward the kitchen. He caught up with him as the detective grabbed a Granny Smith apple from a hanging fruit basket. He dusted it on the sleeve of his coat and took a bite. Seeing Jarsdel, he picked up another apple and held it out to him.

"No. Thanks."

Rall tossed it back into the basket and finished chewing. Jarsdel was about to speak, but Rall took a second, much larger bite, sending a spray of juice into the air. He chewed slowly, leisurely.

"I don't think this is the Creeper," said Jarsdel.

Rall indicated for him to go on.

"It's all off. Single-story apartment, no crawl space or even a walk-in closet. Nowhere to hide and watch the victims."

His superior considered that, shrugged.

"You're going to say that was the same with Amy Sponholz—abandoning the pattern, I mean."

Rall held up a finger, swallowed, then said, "He was on a mission, an objective other than his usual crazy-ass routine. Payback against the LT, hence the straight-up murder without all the drama."

That didn't sit right with Jarsdel. "You're saying that's the case here, too? He was on a mission to kill a random family of three? Wanted them dead so badly he was willing to give up his signature?"

"What you mean, *signature*?"

"His reason for killing. The MO can change, can evolve, but what drives him, what doesn't change, is the signature. In the case of the Creeper it's about the power that comes from living among his victims, watching them, knowing he can take them any time."

Rall looked doubtful, so Jarsdel went on, searching for an analogy. "Like ants under a magnifying glass. From observation to annihilation with a tilt of the lens. That's what excites him, building his own suspense, moving shit around, seeing what he can get away with. And then picking his moment. That's his signature. Serials don't tend to just abandon it, because it's what gets them going in the first place."

"You learn that from Gavin? The signature thing?" asked Rall.

"It's an FBI term," said Jarsdel.

"Ah. An FBI term." Rall rubbed the bridge of his nose. "Well, you and the FBI aren't lookin' too good right now. Creeper's print's on the master bedroom door. So I think he decided to change things up."

"Bullshit. Not possible," said Jarsdel. He couldn't stop the words from tumbling out, but he discovered he wasn't interested in amending them. There was no way this could be the same man.

"I'm just tellin' you the same person who did the Rustads and

Lauterbachs and all the rest, along with Amy Sponholz, put his print on that door."

"All that proves is that he was here, not that he killed anybody."

"On the pillow. Bread knife, too. And we found a tension rod near the front door. From a lockpick set. Which answers our question as to how he got into the LT's house."

"Maybe—"

"Whoa, wait." Rall held up a hand. "You sayin' the Creeper was here, but he didn't hurt nobody. That it was someone else did the actual killing. Am I understanding you correctly?"

Put that way, it sounded ridiculous. But the scene was so different. And as much as it sickened Jarsdel to think about it Ipgreve's way, the ME was right about the child's murder; compared to the rest, it was a mercy. It felt pro forma, something done out of necessity rather than to gratify an impulse. The Creeper wouldn't have been so gentle. *Hadn't* been so gentle. His youngest victim before tonight was ten-year-old Wally Verheugen, and after seeing the crime-scene photos, Jarsdel had gotten blackout drunk, hoping to scrub the images from his memory. It hadn't worked.

"I just..." Jarsdel looked around, hoping for something to jump out at him, to give him an answer.

"Hey." Rall's tone was sympathetic. "Guy's crazy as they come. Not gonna fit into those neat little categories."

"The kid, though. Right? You saw the Verheugen pictures."

Rall shrugged. "Maybe this girl reminded him of his long-lost sister or something. So he decided not to rip her apart like the others. I don't fuckin' know, and I ain't interested in getting inside his brain to figure it out."

Jarsdel shook his head. "I still don't think it's the whole story." An idea occurred to him then, one so fantastical that he immediately decided he shouldn't mention it until he'd thought it through some more. But something on his face must have telegraphed his revelation to Rall, because the detective raised his eyebrows.

"You havin' a Sherlock Holmes moment?"

"No."

"Now I'm curious. What is it?"

"It's probably crazy."

"Probably. Let's do it anyway."

Jarsdel tried to come up with a way of phrasing it that wouldn't sound quite so outlandish, then gave up. "What if someone's using his prints?"

"Come again?"

"I'm not saying the prints aren't his, but what if they've been duplicated? Faked?"

Rall looked mystified. Jarsdel went on.

"I don't know exactly how it would work, but let's say you scanned the exemplars we have on file and fed them into a 3-D printer. Couldn't you make a few rubber fingers with the Creeper's prints? I mean, who better to be a fall guy, right?"

Rall turned his own hand over and examined the lines swirling and looping at the tips of his fingers. He turned what was left of the apple he'd been eating and found a patch of unbroken skin. He pressed his right thumb against the green flesh, then angled the fruit until the light caught it the right way. He looked at the print, then looked at his thumb.

"Nope," he concluded. "Wouldn't work."

"Why not?"

"It'd be backwards." He pointed at the place he'd touched. Jarsdel could only make out a faint smudge, but knew if a crime-scene tech dusted the apple, there'd be a perfect latent of Rall's print.

"Think about it," Rall went on. "You scan that and put it on some dummy hand, you're gonna get the mirror image of your actual thumbprint." He bit off that chunk of apple, cutting through the crisp meat with the sound of a beer can opening.

"Couldn't you just flip the image?" asked Jarsdel. "I don't know much about computers, but I'd think that'd be as easy as clicking on an editing feature."

Rall's paused in his chewing, but only for a moment. He was

about to take another bite, then noticed there was little left of the apple but its core and stem. He ripped a paper towel from the roll by the sink, wrapped up the remains of his apple, and slipped it in his coat pocket.

"But you said a lot of the same 'bout the last scene," said the detective. "LT's wife. How it didn't match and all that. But we got his DNA right outta her mouth. You can't 3-D print someone's DNA, so what's your answer for that one?"

Jarsdel didn't have an answer. "I concede I may have been wrong about that. I can buy that he broke from his pattern to get to the lieutenant."

"Oh, you concede, huh?" Rall shook his head. "You know, I ain't impressed. You spend a lot of time just battin' shit around and tryin' to force it to agree with you. It's like you think you could just come into the police and do it better than everybody else because you're smart at other things. But you got no street degree. You like to think and you like to talk, but when's the last time you tried real police work? The unsexy shit. The shit that actually works. Talk my goddamn ear off with all your pontificatin', but it ain't worth nothin'."

Rall pushed past him and moved back down the short hallway toward the bedrooms. Jarsdel didn't follow. He hadn't been prepared for Rall's fusillade of criticism, perhaps had even—naively—supposed they shared a burgeoning friendship.

Part of him wanted to go back to Hollywood Station and work something else. Then again, Hollywood Station wouldn't solve his problems, either. That was Gavin's domain, and now Haarmann's.

Haarmann, a homicide detective. The inmates were truly running the asylum.

"Hey."

Jarsdel started. It was Mailander. She'd come up beside him during his reverie, and he hadn't noticed. "Oh, hey."

"Didn't mean to scare you."

"No, I'm...I was only woolgathering. What's going on?"

"He's picking up his timeline. Amy Sponholz was less than two weeks ago. And it looks like he's definitely abandoned his routine. No more hiding out. Another blitz attack."

"Yeah." Jarsdel didn't want to talk about it and was hoping she'd go away, but she just stood there. Finally, if only to fill the awkward silence, he said, "Went back to biting, though."

Mailander thought about that a while. "Except for the girl."

Jarsdel grunted. "Ipgreve says it was merciful, the way he killed her."

"Compared to the others, I guess it was."

"He meant for the Creeper. Merciful for himself, so he wouldn't have to see what he was doing."

"Never bothered him before, killing kids."

"No. I don't know. Need some fresh air." He edged past her and found his way outside. Near a dying stand of bougainvillea, he bent over and put his hands on his knees. One deep breath, then another. Could hear his pulse slamming in his ears. Could feel his heart kicking away, like an animal caught in a thorn bush.

Lauterbach, Rustad, Santiago, Verheugen, Galka. Then Amy Sponholz. And now Minchew.

"We're losing," he said into the night.

21

Jarsdel had resolved to at least make an attempt to cull his books. They filled his shelves so tightly that a playing card wouldn't fit between them, and the overflow had spilled onto his bedside tables and dining room chairs.

He'd begun his project an hour earlier and immediately hit a snag in the shape of Walter J. Ong's *Orality and Literacy*. It had been required reading for a sophomore humanities class, and Jarsdel selected it as surely the easiest target for disposal. But in flipping through it to make sure he didn't want it anymore, he'd become ensnared.

His phone rattled on the kitchen countertop. Jarsdel dropped the book to his left, making it the first of his "to keep" pile, and went over to check the display. Morales. Jarsdel hesitated, but curiosity got the better of him. What could his former partner possibly want? Was it something to do with Haarmann?

"Hello?"

"Hey, man, you got a minute?"

"What d'you want?"

"C'mon, Tully. We gotta talk." Morales's use of Jarsdel's actual name—instead of Dad or Prof—was surely calculated. But if nothing else, it signified the importance of the call.

"Okay, what do we need to talk about?"

"In person."

"I'm busy."

"You at home?"

"Yes."

"I'm at the gate. Let me in."

Morales had never been to Jarsdel's apartment before. Now he was showing up just to talk? "What's going on, Oscar?"

"Will you just come out here? There's a guy sleeping under the tree, and he stinks like piss."

Jarsdel hung up and stepped outside the apartment. The fires in Malibu had given a sickly orange glow to the midafternoon light. Millions of years of evolution balked at that light—it was wrong, Jarsdel knew and felt it deeply. It was the light of uncertainty, of an eclipse, as unsettling as a comet smeared across the night sky.

He approached the pedestrian gate at the end of his street, where Morales waited, gripping the bars to take some of the weight off his bad knees.

"Standing behind there, you look like you got locked up," said Jarsdel. "When good detectives go bad, tonight at 11."

Morales didn't answer. He waited for Jarsdel to open the gate, then shuffled in.

"I'm just over here," said Jarsdel. "Not far."

"I'm not an invalid," Morales grumbled.

Once they were inside the apartment, Morales collapsed into Jarsdel's wingback chair. He made a face. "This is uncomfortable as shit. What is this?"

"Danish modern. Worth about seven grand, incidentally."

"What kind of person was this built for? Armrests are digging in. They're like half an inch wide."

"Glad you like it."

Morales shook his head. "White-people furniture. Your people got a guilty conscience, so you find ways of punishing yourselves. Explains opera, tuxedoes, all kinds of stuff." He looked at Jarsdel. "You gonna sit down, too?"

"Should I?"

"It's your house, do what you want."

"If it'll make you more comfortable, I'm happy to." Jarsdel pulled over one of the barstools near his kitchen counter and sat facing Morales. "Okay. I'm here. What's going on?"

Morales seemed unsure how to begin. "You know me and Haarmann are working the Varma thing, right? And, uh, I know you were kinda close to her, so I wanted you to hear this first from me instead of on the news."

Jarsdel leaned forward. "You got the guy."

"Now hang on. Everything we talk about here is between us. Hasn't been released yet."

"Yes, yes, of course, but you got him. That's what you came to tell me?"

From the inside pocket of his sport coat, Morales brought out a thick packet of paper that had been folded into thirds. "Gavin finds out I gave you this, I'm gonna get Bruce-alized, so I need it back before I go."

Jarsdel took the offered pages and unfolded them. He'd been expecting to see a printout of a mug shot, followed by pages of arrest records. Instead, he found a certified copy of Dr. Ipgreve's autopsy report on Alisha Varma.

The heading read, "County of Los Angeles, Department of Medical Examiner-Coroner." Below that were listed Varma's age, sex, race, address, occupation, and a series of boxes to be checked. These included whether the body was clothed, partially clothed, or unclothed, whether the death was the result of a motor vehicle accident, and whether rigor had been present when the body was found. There was another set of boxes dealing specifically with the manner of death, including *violent*, *suddenly when in apparent health*, *casualty*, and *suspicious or unusual*. None of these boxes had been marked.

Instead, Ipgreve had put a slash in the box next to *accident*.

Jarsdel looked up. "What's this?"

"Yeah, I know."

"What do you mean, 'Yeah, I know'? What's he mean it was an accident? Manslaughter?"

"Read the notes."

Jarsdel stared at Morales. "What am I gonna see?"

Morales jutted his chin in the direction of the report.

Jarsdel didn't want to read it, but he forced his gaze downward.

The right side of the form was occupied with the template of a hairless, sexless line drawing of a human body, first front, then back. Upon it, Ipgreve had marked four X's of varying size. One was on the forehead, right between the eyebrows. The next two were located below the left shoulder, one being slightly bigger than the other. The largest X was lower on the same side, between the heart and the sternum.

The notes were handwritten in Ipgreve's crude but dependably legible script.

> Three stab wounds, all ventral. Shallowest located approx. 2 cm left of 2nd rib in pectoralis minor. This was probably first, as didn't fully penetrate epidermis. Very likely a "testing" stab, common in self-inflicted cases to get an idea of pain to be expected, also to work up courage. Next wound 3.5 cm below, diagonally right. Penetrated dermis and subcutaneous tissue. No major blood vessels involved. Fatal injury occurred with third and final wound. Decedent penetrated the intercostal space 1 cm lateral to sternum and lacerated right internal mammary artery. Despite being a small artery, uncontrolled hemorrhage resulted in right hemopneumothorax complicated by hypovolemic shock within 5 minutes and ultimately complete cardiovascular collapse. This occurred prior to

> the contact with the back passenger window and explains the minimal blood loss in the setting of a 6cm scalp laceration with evidence of de-gloving.

Jarsdel looked up. "I don't buy it."

"Buy what?" said Morales.

"Come on—self-inflicted? This was one of the bravest, most outspoken opponents of street crime in Los Angeles. In that capacity she made quite a few enemies. I have a very, *very* tough time believing she did this to herself."

"Thought you liked Ipgreve."

"He's a fine ME, but that doesn't mean he can't be fooled. I mean, if you think about it, really think about it, what would be a better way to tarnish her reputation than to pass her death off as some sort of attention-seeking stunt?"

Morales looked confused. "So you're saying you agree, the scene was staged, but just not by her?"

"It's possible."

"And her killer was so clever he was able to make it look like *she* was the one who staged it."

"I think it would be negligent to dismiss the idea that—"

"It's weird to see you dodging facts." Morales now appeared disappointed, even sad. "When they hooked us up as partners, there wasn't a whole lot I admired or understood about you. But you challenged me every now and then, and as much as that drove me crazy, I saw the value in it."

"Wait, what facts am I dodging?" said Jarsdel. "What about the broken window?"

"It says right there. She fell. She was bleeding to death and passed out, put her head right through it. I'm sure it wasn't part of the plan, but it slowed us down." He considered. "For about two seconds."

"What about—"

"Tully. No defensive wounds. Why not? Why not a single cut on her hand or arm as she fought off her attacker? Explain how come in a brightly lit garage she just stood there while this guy stabbed her three times. Guy just came out of nowhere, delicately poked her in the shoulder, not deep enough to bleed but just leave a little bruise, then again, this time breaking the skin, then a third time, straight in the fucking chest without any tearing around the edges of the wound? Come on, man. Didn't try to get away? Didn't move? Just stood there?"

"She wasn't depressed," said Jarsdel. "She was tough, she was determined. This wasn't some wilting flower. Her anti-affordances were *working*, Oscar. They were—"

Morales laughed. "*Anti-affordances*. All that shit was pure conflict of interest. PuraLux, ReliaBench, that goddamned Sonic Fence that made me want to shoot somebody—those were all her pet projects. She was a silent partner. She wasn't no employee or consultant with that company. She was an *investor*. We checked her bank statements. Regular deposits from Halberd Systems, so we called them up and told them we could either get a warrant to find out what she did for them, or they could just tell us. They decided to play nice. She was making money on every unit the city purchased. You know she even had a reality-show deal? Every week she was gonna go to a different city and solve some social problem. Father Duong's one-man act was gonna cost her the whole thing. Look at it from her point of view. What do you do? You show that crime is everywhere, that no one's safe. You turn the argument around."

"That's all speculation," said Jarsdel.

"No it ain't. Smoking gun: she called 911 twice. First time just to log the number in her phone, so she wouldn't have to type it in while she was bleeding. Save a couple seconds, right? So she dialed 911 and hung up right away before dispatch answered, just to put the number in recent calls. She called again less than two minutes later, this time letting it go through. Obviously she wasn't counting on dying and having her phone looked at. But we got the phone, and that con artist called the number *fucking twice*."

Jarsdel tried to think of another explanation for why she might have done that. Maybe she'd seen something threatening, dialed the number, then for some reason felt safe enough to cancel the call. Perhaps her killer was someone she knew, someone she trusted to get close to her.

"Still not convinced?" said Morales. "Try this one. We got into her laptop and checked out her browser history. Five or six wiki articles on human anatomy. What's your verdict? Sudden fascination with medicine?"

Jarsdel considered that, too. His partner—*ex*-partner—was right; it didn't look good. But if someone were trying to set her up, that would be a great way to dress the scene.

"I know what you're doing," said Morales. "You always make that face when you're trying to work out a puzzle. Only thing, this puzzle's already been solved. You're in denial."

"I'm not in denial," said Jarsdel. "But congratulations on your new job as a psychoanalyst."

"You realize if this were any case but this one, you wouldn't be jumping through so many hoops trying to pitch some half-assed alternate theory. Totality of the circumstances, man. Work it through, just like we used to do over lunch."

Jarsdel handed the papers back to Morales, who put them back into his coat pocket. "Not interested. Got lots to do."

"That's weak sauce, Tully, and you know it."

Jarsdel looked at him, his gaze cold.

"Somethin' you wanna say?" asked Morales.

"I'm fine," said Jarsdel. "Just curious how much Haarmann had to do with your theory."

"Fucking *hell*, dude. It's not a theory. It's overwhelming physical evidence. Along with common sense. Tell you what—define for me exactly what you think. Go ahead, I'm asking you to define it. Explain what's bouncing around in your head, what conclusion you've come to."

"I think that's the point, Oscar. I'm saying I don't see how it benefits anyone to rush to a conclusion. We need to take our time, look at this from every possible angle. And the fact that you're not willing to do that—well, frankly that gives me the creeps a little bit. I'm trying to figure out what you gain from making this go away."

"*Ohhh*," said Morales, drawing out the syllable in a tone of mock epiphany. "So wait a sec, 'cause I just need to run through this to make sure I really got it. This is all a big conspiracy against your girlfriend. Someone killed her and left a double-fake-out staged crime scene, something that would've taken a team of veteran FBI agents to set up convincingly. And we know the truth, but we're gonna sweep it under the rug anyway.

"Oh, and everyone's in on it—Ipgreve, Gavin, Haarmann, and me, too, of course—and we're all doing it why? For what reason? Because we know how much it means to you? Or maybe laziness—just not interested in finding the mastermind who's really behind this? Or, hang on, what if we're part of the murder itself—have you thought about that? It would be negligent *not* to consider it, right?"

Jarsdel took a deep breath, exhaling slowly. "I'm just urging thoroughness."

"No, dude, you're not. You're urging insanity. Spending too much time on the Creeper, you want my opinion."

"If we're expressing opinions," said Jarsdel, "I think you're a fool for trusting Haarmann. He's deeply sick. Dangerous. Guy like that's never gonna have your back. Look what he did to me basically just because I insulted him."

Morales shook his head. "You got no proof about that. Coulda been anyone. Didn't we already have this conversation?"

"I'm sorry, I thought you were a fan of common sense. It's so *obvious* he did it. He *wants* me to know it was him. All those winks and carefully engineered little looks he gives me. So I guess denial's contagious."

Morales looked like he was about to say something, but Jarsdel plowed ahead. "And I know why you like him so much. He's exactly the kind of partner you've always wanted. A backslapping, grunting buffoon who can actually tell you down to the ounce how much he can bench."

Morales laughed. "That what this is about? You jealous? I swear, you can be such a fussy little bitch. You're working a task force in Homicide Special. Most guys would give their left nut to be where you are."

"What about when it's over, Oscar? Gonna have a job waiting for me when I get back? Sturdivant's retiring. They'll need someone experienced to take the reins, and Gavin's got seniority. If HH2 had a reason for being, it's been played out."

"We clear cases," said Morales.

"We clear cases," Jarsdel agreed. "But apparently so do you and Haarmann. So what do they need guys like me for?"

"You're smart. In that Rain Man way you got."

"Overrated. Most of our cases are solved by procedure and persistence. In other words, good police work. They're a classic for a reason, as you'd say. No, I think Gavin wants to fold the squad and move on. He'll probably hang on to you and Haarmann, but Barnhardt and I are gonna get shown the door. Rutenberg's never been one of Gavin's favorites, either, so I'm betting he'll get kicked back to Olympic. Maybe RHD, if Sponholz steps down and they boost Rall to the top spot."

"You're paranoid," said Morales. "They can't demote you for no reason. Even if that's what Gavin wants."

"They don't have to. If the Creeper Task Force is a loser, then so am I by association. I'll keep my badge, but they'll give me freeway therapy to the remotest end of Valley Bureau. Or maybe San Pedro."

Morales shrugged. "What do you want me to say?"

"Nothing. Not your fault. There's something to be said for going through the ranks, putting in your time like everyone else. Your partner was right about that. I don't have my street degree."

"Gotta get out of this dumb-ass chair," Morales said, pushing himself up. As always, his features twisted in pain when his knees took his weight. "I said what I came to say. You can do what you want with it. All this other stuff, I don't know."

"Oscar," said Jarsdel.

Morales paused on his way to the door. "What?"

"What's your gut tell you? Did Varma really do this to herself?"

"I thought I was one of the bad guys. Why you asking me?"

"Please."

Morales sighed. "Yeah, Tully. She did it. The only prints on that knife were hers. Gripping the handle like this." He demonstrated, holding out a fist. "Like an ice cream cone." He turned his hand so that if it had been holding a blade, it would've been pointed at his chest. "Good control, see?" He struck himself one, two, three times.

Jarsdel nodded.

"We think her original plan was to ditch the knife after she called 911. There were lots of places she could've done it. Trash chute, drain. Shit, even her own car, which we never woulda searched if she'd lived. Probably picked the knife up at a 99-cent store, paid cash. It's a piece of shit, and no one would've remembered it. Anonymous as you can get."

Jarsdel thought it over. "Would you have a problem with me going to take a look at her apartment?"

"Jesus, you still don't believe me?"

"It's not that. Guess I just want some closure. See if there's anything she left for me to find."

"You guys were really a thing? I was just giving you shit with that 'girlfriend' stuff."

"I don't know what we were. But I can't leave it like this. I mean, you didn't see her a few days ago. She was excited, ebullient even. She had all these plans for how she was going to transform this city. More than anyone else I've met, she had answers. Real answers."

Morales shrugged. "You wanna go, it's fine. We're releasing the apartment to her dad and brother tomorrow, so if you want to go, go tonight. Have the manager let you in."

"Thanks, Oscar."

"Yeah." He opened the door, then remembered something. "You never came by the house."

"What?"

"Told you I had something for you. 'Case you caught the Creeper." Morales reached into his waistband and brought out a black leather holster. Sticking out of it was the polished wood handle of a revolver. Morales pulled it free and cracked the cylinder.

"Smith & Wesson Bodyguard, 649. Shrouded hammer, so it's double-action only, but you won't get it snagged on your clothes. This one's chambered for .357 rounds—pretty much stop anything. You know me, I like a little extra kick. The loads are all wadcutters."

Jarsdel hadn't used that kind of ammunition since he was in the academy. Wadcutters were perfectly flat at their tips, not tapered like most bullets, and spanned the entire diameter of the cartridge. They were mostly used in target shooting, since they left perfect, clean holes in the paper instead of rips and tears. Beyond about fifty yards, their accuracy dropped off, but at close range they were deadly.

Morales snapped the cylinder closed, replaced the revolver in the holster, and handed it to Jarsdel. "That was reserved for Bell Gardens Butcher, if it came down to it. Work just as well for the Eastside Creeper."

Jarsdel took the weapon. Upon closer inspection, he noticed the holster was an ankle rig.

Morales nodded. "Yeah, can't use that so well anymore. I want the gun back when you close the case. Holster you can keep."

"Thanks, Oscar."

Morales left, closing the door behind him. There was a finality in the sound of it shutting, as of a coffin lid. The silence was oppressive, stifling.

Morales was right, Jarsdel knew. Totality of the circumstances. Varma had tried to set up her own assault. Anything else he found out about her from now on would only confuse things, make it harder to let go.

Still, he needed to see, needed to know.

The remaining afternoon light was stained red from the smoke, deepening the shadows in his apartment and splashing the walls with hues of sickness and rot. He looked at the portrait of Lady Mary, wanting to shake the pall of unease that had settled around him. But the light was wrong, and the portrait didn't take it well. An errant brushstroke, perhaps. Something. But there was a blemish now near her lip, a spot of shading that give the impression of a fold in the skin—a harelip or other deformity. It turned the otherwise sweet, mischievous smile, one born of culture and wit, into a sneer.

Alarmed, Jarsdel approached the painting. The image sharpened as he drew closer, the shadow or blemish or whatever it was tucking itself back into the thousands of other strokes marking the canvas.

But not completely. There was still a hint of it, an odd little pinch or wrinkle in her flesh.

He turned on the hallway light. It was an LED, powerful, bright, and unpleasant. He usually only put it on when he was doing laundry and needed to check for stains.

The mark was still there.

He turned the dimmer all the way up, his eyes watering from the harsh white glare.

Lady Mary's once loving, even sensual features had been corrupted by that single swipe of paint. Jarsdel moved around the painting, trying to see it from different angles, and finally concluded the issue was one of texture. There was a tiny, thin little ridge of paint that hadn't been smoothed. If it caught the light, it cast a shadow that, once seen, was impossible to disregard.

He held up a hand, blocking the offending area from view. That was a little better. The softness returned to her features, her eyes once again filled with a sly humor. He took his hand away and saw a succubus, a resentful, hungry thing that wished him pain and would enjoy delivering it.

Jarsdel hit the switch, and the hall fell back into the muddy light of gloaming. The thing that used to be Lady Mary bored her gaze into him.

A creak. So soft, almost undetectable. Easily dismissed.

But he had heard it. There was no fooling him. The first tentative step, perhaps, of someone descending the stairs.

He turned to look at them. They were just off the hallway, curling up into darkness. There wasn't much on the second floor—a guest room he used as an office, a linen closet, and a bathroom. Some days he never went up there at all. In fact, he couldn't remember the last time he'd checked those rooms. Could he have really been so careless? So stupid?

He listened, staring at the bottom of the stairway. Nothing.

Jarsdel pulled the Bodyguard free, tossing the holster on the kitchen counter. He flicked on the hall light again. Searing, cleansing brightness.

He thought he could feel someone's eyes on him and, when he glanced to his right, found himself face-to-face with Lady Mary again. The blemish was now a canyon, impossible to miss—how could he have not seen it before? Her expression manic, ravenous. Jarsdel set down the gun. For this he needed a knife, and there was one right there in the drying rack. He'd thrust it into the painting, working the blade up and down the canvas until nothing remained but ribbons.

No.

He exhaled, scooped his car keys off the kitchen counter, and stepped outside.

Jarsdel got off at the top floor and followed the apartment numbers to 619. He would've found it anyway—bright-yellow police tape crisscrossed the frame, and a large red sticker had been affixed to both the door and the jamb:

SECURITY SEAL
DO NOT TAMPER

The date had been handwritten on a line beneath, as had the initials of the lead investigator—O.M.—Oscar Morales.

Jarsdel used the key given him by the manager to first slice the seal, then turn the lock. The door swung open.

He didn't know whether or not it was purely his imagination, but Jarsdel had been in enough homes and apartments and trailers belonging to the dead that he'd come to believe there was a palpable difference to them, a unique characteristic that set them apart. They were unnaturally quiet, yes, but it was more than that. The air inside those places felt as dead as their owners, stagnant and beginning to sour.

Varma's apartment was a wreck. Stacks of books and magazines lined the walls of the entryway, and loose papers lay on every flat surface. Several large cardboard boxes were grouped in the center of the living room. The flaps were open, and when Jarsdel approached, he saw that most were nearly full.

Had Varma been moving? If so, to where? Out of LA? Or was this simply how she lived?

Jarsdel surveyed the room, and his skin popped with gooseflesh. An antique carousel horse stood in the corner, the paint so faded that its eyes appeared white. They were so odd and expressionless, particularly compared with the rest of the carved features. The jaw, the open, panting mouth, the great teeth, all told the story of a vigorous animal, full of spirit, pushed to its absolute limit, but the eyes were cold and dead. The juxtaposition bothered him.

To his left, Jarsdel was surprised to see another print of the strange masterwork from Varma's office. The three men—sated, passed-out, or dead, he wasn't sure—along with the running egg and the animated cooked pig and that mysterious figure spooning its way through a cloud of whipped cream or mashed potatoes. A weight-loss ad, circa mid-1500s, perhaps.

Jarsdel stepped around the boxes, then encountered their smaller siblings. One of these, an old Nike shoebox, overflowed with what was probably five solid pounds of Mardi Gras beads. He was about to leave and see what he could find in the bedroom when he noticed

Varma's purse. Her smaller, everyday clutch was the one found at the scene; this was her large business purse—more like a briefcase or a messenger bag, thick black leather and heavy straps. It hung on the back of a dining room chair. The matching table, he saw, was being used as her desk and held mounds of paperwork from one end to the other.

He picked his way across the room, lifted the purse off the chair, and set it down on the floor. He crouched down and began sifting through it. Her day planner was gone, probably still in evidence, and what remained was of little interest. A tube of Varma's cherry-red lipstick, a tin of Altoids, a compact and face powder, a small hairbrush, loose change, some wadded-up tissues.

His phone vibrated. He checked the display and saw it was Rall. Jarsdel wasn't in the mood, but he answered anyway.

"Yeah, it's Jarsdel."

"Where you at?" Rall sounded tired.

"Nowhere."

"I want everyone to come in early tomorrow. Be there by six."

"What? Why?"

"Because this is some bullshit," said Rall. "There's no reason we can't catch him, so we're gonna catch him. And we're gonna make sacrifices so it can be done with."

"Great. That everything?"

No answer. Jarsdel looked down at his phone and saw the detective had already hung up. He touched the icon for his email, and suddenly a bright magenta stain began forming at the top of his display. Startled, he pressed the button for his home screen. It appeared, but the strange smear of color didn't go away.

He picked up the phone, shook it, squinted at the screen. Some of the stain seemed to dissipate, but only a little.

"Piece of absolute *shit*," Jarsdel murmured. He turned the phone over and examined the case, hoping for some explanation of the color show, but there was nothing he could see that appeared suspicious. Puzzled, he set the phone down again, thinking perhaps it had to do with the angle. Maybe there was a leak in the liquid crystal or something—he had no idea how the things worked—and maybe it was made worse when it lay flat.

This time the effect was immediate. At least three-quarters of the screen became an unreadable purple soup. Alarmed, Jarsdel snatched up the phone. He raked his fingers over the carpet, prodding into the soft pile for the culprit, though he wasn't at all sure what it could be.

Nothing.

He went back to his phone, massaging the screen, urging the picture to return. When that didn't work, he tried prying open the case, digging his fingernails into the seam. Maybe it was a moisture issue. Some water had seeped in somehow and was monkeying with the electronics.

The case didn't open, and he was in danger of bending a fingernail. He brought out his car key and wedged the tip between the two halves of the case. The plastic shell popped open, and Jarsdel dropped his key ring onto the carpet to free up his hands.

Instead of falling straight down, however, the keys veered sharply and stuck to the side of Varma's bag. Confused, Jarsdel slipped the phone in his pocket, reached down, and tugged on the key ring. It seemed as if it had been glued to the leather. When he pulled, the entire bag came with the keys. He finally had to push the bag away with one hand while yanking on the keys with the other. Reluctantly, and only after a good twenty pounds of pull, the keys finally let go.

Bizarre. Just holding the keys nearby caused them to fan out, reaching toward the leather like little metal fingers.

Jarsdel reached inside Varma's bag, this time feeling along the lining. There was a large zippered pocket there, probably for holding a wallet or passport, and he could feel something thin and hard beneath the fabric. He opened the zipper and stuck his fingers into the pocket. It was there—a cold metal disk, perhaps the circumference of a rocks glass. He brought it out into the light, careful to hold it at a distance.

Curious, he picked up his keys and slowly brought them closer to the disk. When they were about six inches apart, the keys began to splay again. He closed the distance a little more, and the keys leapt out of his hand and slammed into the disk. The collision pinched the skin on his pinkie, and he dropped everything. Both the disk and the keys hit the carpet with a metallic *thunk*.

Sucking on his finger, Jarsdel tried to figure out why Varma kept an extremely powerful magnet in her purse. She'd have to be very careful not to put her phone in there, or she'd wipe it completely. And what if, in a moment of carelessness, she set her purse near her laptop? Quick way to turn a computer into a two-thousand-dollar paperweight. What a stupid, dangerous thing to carry around.

He stood up and took his phone out of his pocket. The magenta smear was still there, though not quite as pronounced. He had a feeling, however, that if he'd let it stay near the magnet any longer, the damage would've been permanent. Almost the way his previous phone had died with no warning. That had been spectacularly annoying, particularly since his SIM card hadn't survived and he'd lost all his contacts.

Jarsdel thought about that, about how surprised the technician at the store was when the SIM card had come up blank. *Wow*, the guy had said, *did you drop this in the ocean or something?*

No. And it wasn't even that old—no more than two years. Hadn't shown a single sign of trouble until that day.

Until that day.

The same day he'd cut his hand. The same day the cameras had gone out at the station.

When it rains, it pours—that's what he'd thought at the time. Just one of those perfect confluences of shit that crop up every now and then in the infinite Powerball lottery of existence. He'd lost his partner to Haarmann, sliced through his fingers, and had his phone go out on him all in that single day.

Jarsdel yanked his keys from the magnet and held the disk at arm's length, turning it over, not sure what he hoped to find. It took him another moment to realize that he wasn't actually looking for anything at all. He was just buying time, trying to put off acknowledging what he already knew.

Varma's expression, when he'd approached her in I Panini di Ambra. She'd been fidgeting in her purse, he remembered, and the look on her face when she'd recognized him had been more one of guilt than surprise. And that strange question: "Are you okay?" At the time he thought she simply hadn't recognized him—that perhaps his unexpected greeting had caught her off guard, and the question was her way of ducking the fact that she didn't know his name. He'd certainly done similar things himself, so he couldn't fault her for trying to avoid a bit of awkwardness.

But now he decided she'd known exactly who he was, and the question had been no face-saving ploy. Because she'd had very good reason to ask him if he was okay.

After all, she'd just glued a razor blade to his door handle.

Sergeant Curran had been complaining about Varma's visit that morning and how the cameras had chosen that exact moment to crap out on them. Jarsdel could imagine it easily. Varma cooing over the security setup, peppering her observations with selected anecdotes about her work in the defense industry, stopping herself with an apology if she'd skirted a classified subject. The men would've loved her—a woman security geek, someone who specialized in identifying, containing, and eliminating threats. How easy it would've been to sidle up to the right piece of equipment, or maybe even take the purse off and set it down next to it, the magnet silently killing the station's security feed. The same way it had killed Jarsdel's phone when he'd stood too close to her in the restaurant later that same day.

And why disable the cameras? The answer was simple: so she could open up Jarsdel's hand like a ripe fruit without getting caught.

No, that wasn't quite it. She'd had nothing against him. He was a means to an end, part of her grand plan to align the city's interests with her own. She picked him because he'd been the best candidate.

Had even interviewed him for the position, in a way. It had come up in their first meeting, how he'd been featured in two recent true-crime books, and she'd remarked that he was a good face for the modern LAPD. "Someone people can get behind." Those had been her words. He was young with a promising career ahead of him—as far as she knew, a kind of department golden boy. She'd been wrong about that, had grossly overestimated his importance. But that probably wouldn't have mattered too much. Regardless of how much command loved or hated Marcus Jarsdel, his getting maliciously injured during a camera blackout, on city property, could only help her case.

And, of course, she'd known about Haarmann. That had been the cherry on top, Jarsdel concluded. Had made him irresistible to Varma. Everyone at Hollywood Station knew about the arm-wrestling table. Morales had said so. If anything happened to Jarsdel, blame would naturally fall on the beefy patrolman. Haarmann, being the undeniable asshole he was, probably enjoyed the whole thing. He got to see Jarsdel suffer impotently, unable to prove anything, and he hadn't needed to lift a finger. It must have been a phenomenal ego boost. At no risk to himself or his career, he'd established himself as a guy never to cross. There'd certainly never be another Arnold Palmer dumped on his table.

How neatly it had all unfolded in Varma's favor. Jarsdel had been ready to march right into the city council meeting by her side, stalwart and full of righteous anger. Her pet victim, there to offer his tale of woe, to offer his unflinching support for her plans. *If only for Varma*, his motto would have been. If only for Varma, and his hand would be whole. If only for Varma, the city might have a chance at a new, brighter dawn.

The lamb advocating for the wolf. Thinking about it made him feel nauseous.

But in all her plotting, Varma hadn't foreseen Father Ruben Duong. The man traded his life to bring attention to the plight of the city's homeless and had chosen none other than a ReliaBench as the centerpiece of his funeral pyre. His death transformed the concrete log into a symbol of willful neglect, a cynical device thrust upon the least fortunate by a cold, unfeeling bureaucracy. More damaging press would've been difficult to conceive.

Varma had needed a major diversion to keep Duong's ghost from scrapping her project. What could be more effective than casting herself as the target of a senseless, brutal street crime? And if the city council speculated it was part of some broader, albeit totally vague conspiracy to keep her silent, so much the better. Her blood was the currency that would buy her restoration, and it would be spilled on the oil-stained floor of a concrete parking lot. From scrutiny to sympathy in a simple poke of steel.

But it had hurt, even that first exploratory jab. And the second one hadn't bled enough. She'd had to grit her teeth, plant her palm on the hilt, and drive deep.

Shocking pain, no doubt. But there must have been some relief after it was over. She'd suffered through the worst of it and now only had to wait for the EMTs. What would she tell them? One assailant or two? What had they said to her? How hard had she fought? All good questions. The details, the story—that was the fun stuff.

Jarsdel wondered how long it had been before she realized she'd done real damage. What had it felt like? Her blood pressure dropping, watching the world go gray, knowing she'd cut something vital.

He hoped there was some comprehension in that moment, at least a hint that she'd made a mistake, that it was her own toxic ambition that had undone her. But it wasn't likely. She'd probably faded from the world amazed at the gross injustices that forced her to act so drastically.

It hit him for the first time. It was obvious, but he hadn't seen it—or had at least refused to see it—until now. If she'd been willing to maim him to boost her career, that meant all the affection had been a lie. There would've been nothing beyond that kiss at Watts Towers.

She'd set it up perfectly. How they'd have to wait awhile before they could do anything serious, because it would only distract her from her work. Of course. And then once the city council approved her project, she'd have found another reason to put him off. Too busy organizing the CCTV system. Or maybe she'd move and tell him long-distance relationships simply didn't work. "I'll always think of you as a devoted friend. Couldn't have done it without you."

A lie, all of it.

He understood now why victims of con artists hardly ever reported the crimes to the police. It was impossibly difficult, first, to admit to yourself that you'd been duped, that you were the unknowing participant in a piece of cheap theater. That you'd been bested, your vulnerabilities—greed, loneliness, vanity—turned so deftly against you. But then to have to admit it to someone else, to sit across from a stranger in a uniform and explain just how much of a chump you'd been, how credulous and foolish to have believed such a whopping pile of bullshit—well, that was more than most folks cared to do. Why add insult to injury? The money was gone anyway.

Jarsdel put the magnet back in the purse and stood up, absently smoothing out the wrinkles in his trousers. He debated calling Morales, but what would that accomplish? They'd already cleared the case, and nothing he'd discovered in the apartment contradicted Ipgreve's finding of accidental death. All he'd done was prove Varma's deceit was more elaborate and far-reaching than anyone besides him knew. He thought about that discrepancy between her figures and those from Elk River: 25 percent relative versus 1 percent absolute. How he'd agonized over that, tied himself in knots trying to figure out the best way to broach the subject. Because naturally he didn't want her to think he suspected her of having behaved unethically.

He laughed aloud. The sound came out of him and died immediately in the stale air of the apartment. It was as if the atmosphere couldn't support life, and if he stayed there long enough, he'd suffocate. The hairs at the back of his neck prickled at the thought.

He hung the purse back on the chair where he'd found it and was about to leave when something on the dining table caught his attention. It was his name, written in cursive on the back of an envelope. Underneath the card was a gift, wrapped in festive, handmade paper.

Jarsdel opened the envelope and took out the card inside. The artwork on the front was of a beautiful young woman dressed in a sumptuous gown, one hand clutching a decorative fan. He recognized the piece immediately. It was the same one he'd given to the Cal Arts student when he commissioned the portrait of Lady Mary. He opened the card.

Dear Tully,

I'd like to thank you in advance for backing me up at the city council meeting tomorrow. We haven't known each other all that long, and it means a lot to me that you're willing to tell people how my ideas could help. You really get the importance of what I do. I know I said that before but it bears repeating, because as you can see with all the craziness that's been happening lately, not everyone does. I get the sense you'd support me even if that asshole hadn't tried to ruin your hand. (I think I might have a good way to get back at him, by the way. Remind me!)

I hope you like the card. I looked her up after we shared that wonderful moment together in Watts, and I can see why she's such an inspiration to you. And now that I've seen what she looks like, I'm even more flattered that you compared me to her. While I don't think I can compete, I can nevertheless promise you'll find in me a loyal friend and, hopefully, an intellectual equal. I get the sense you don't come across those too often!

You're a special guy, Tully. I could tell that about you right away, and I look forward to getting to know you better...<u>much</u> better.

Yours affectionately (and soon, intimately),
Alisha

A masterstroke. She'd shown just a bit too much of herself that other day in her office. Chilly, impatient, plotting. It wasn't the sort of performance designed to inspire his passionate support. So, in case he'd been waffling on whether or not to follow through at city hall, here was this note. She'd probably planned on leaving it someplace unexpected, like his desk at PAB.

It had all the ingredients for a thorough ego-stroking, along with just the right amount of sexual promise to really set the hook in deep. What an unabashed traitor, what a clumsy saboteur the penis was. Even now, in the depths of his humiliation, his groin buzzed with excitement. The way she'd underlined *much* in *much better*. All the implied promise in that little slash of ink. That simple underline said Varma couldn't wait to have him, that she was as hungry for him as a woman could be for a man. And if that wasn't enough, there was the word *intimately*. She'd known exactly what to say, hadn't she? He could feel the traitor nod in agreement, pressed stupidly against the inside of his pants. For a dead woman who'd mauled his hand, who would've done much worse if it meant a future for her CCTV scheme and PuraLux and any of her other projects. He was lucky *he* hadn't been the one found in a garage, bled out from a stab to the chest.

There was still the gift. A tightly wrapped rectangle—obviously a book. Hardcover, too, he noted as he lifted it. The thick paper showed birds on cherry blossoms. Lovely, the kind of thing you'd try to save and reuse, peeling it apart from the tape so as not to leave bare white patches. But being gentle wasn't high on Jarsdel's list. He tore into it, and the entire thing came off in one ragged piece, parachuting to the floor.

Jarsdel took in a sharp breath.

He couldn't believe what he held, hadn't seen since he'd been a boy. The fuzzy black flocking and silver lettering were as startling and vivid as he remembered them.

We Who Bump in the Night. Below that, *Wherever you lay your head, there's always something under the bed!*

He turned the cover. There, on the flyleaf, Varma had added an inscription: *To the one who hunts boogeymen. Hope you realize now that they're the ones running from you. With admiration, A.V.*

Jarsdel stuck the card in the book and gathered up the wrapping paper. He surveyed the room one last time. A shambles. Boxes, clothes, paperwork. He conjured a memory of Varma and held it up for comparison. Neatly pressed suits, coiffed hair, and that red lipstick that could be at turns sensual or commanding.

A lie, Jarsdel thought again. And after that, *Yes, and she had you cold.* Then Rall's voice, *It's like you think you could just come into the police and do it better than everybody else because you're smart at other things. But you got no street degree.*

Haarmann agreed. *You can't fake that, can't fake a street degree.* Haarmann, goddamned *Haarmann* of all people, being right about something.

Rall again. *Talk my goddamn ear off with all your pontificatin', but it ain't worth nothin'.*

Morales, back when they'd had that first meeting at Fred 62, before the Creeper had been given a name. *Motive, means, and opportunity: it's a classic for a reason*. Morales had been annoyed with him for trying to classify the Creeper, to identify and catalog him like a species of insect. His partner had considered that a useless exercise, a distraction—an intellectual dodge. And as they'd left the restaurant, he'd added, *You know, what's funny is all your lofty, hard-learned bullshit won't do you nearly as much good in this job as watching* Training Day *a few times. Or in this case,* Manhunter. *Because I'm telling you, he's gonna do it again.*

Morales had been right about that. The Creeper had done it again. Right as well about Haarmann not being the razor bandit, and certainly right that Varma's death hadn't been part of a conspiracy to silence her.

And what, Jarsdel reflected, had he himself been right about?

He'd had feelings, formless but still powerful, but that was all. No data, no actual evidence. He'd been bothered by the broom at the Sponholz crime scene. He'd been bothered by Amy Sponholz neglecting to lock the bedroom door, but the LT's explanation on that at least made sense. The lack of matter under the fingernails, even though she'd fought. That made less sense. And no bite marks.

On to the Minchew scene. Brian, Natalie. That time, bite marks on the wife. Okay, that was consistent with all Creeper crime scenes excepting Amy Sponholz. Creeper epithelial matter under the nails. But how had that happened if both adults had been killed in their sleep? When would they have fought their attacker? Then little Emma, smothered to death. A child murderer who'd suddenly found the task perfunctory, perhaps even distasteful. There'd been no reveling in that, no thrill at the total power he had over a small, delicate life.

The tension rod, found just inside the house. Had he really dropped it? That seemed careless. As depraved as he was, he wasn't careless. It was more as if he were trying to fill in gaps for the investigators, trying to retcon the Amy Sponholz scene by getting the Minchew murder "right."

Amy Sponholz: no DNA under the nails, though she'd fought. Natalie Minchew: DNA under the nails, though it was almost impossible she'd fought. Sponholz hadn't been bitten, but Minchew had. Creeper hair follicles at both scenes. Creeper blood at the Sponholz scene, but not at Minchew. That made sense, right? After all, Amy Sponholz had bitten him on the hand. But he'd been wearing gloves, so how had that happened? Had she really torn through both leather and flesh? No, because there would've been traces of the gloves on her teeth. His hand had been bare—bare long enough to be bitten, but not scratched. Gloved when he'd strangled her, bare when he'd left prints all over the bedroom.

Compare with Minchew. No gloves at the Minchew scene. Fingerprints, yes. Was that right? All the ones at Sponholz had been latents, invisible to the naked eye until raised by fingerprint powder. Had there actually been any latents at Minchew? He didn't remember.

Jarsdel left the apartment, stepping out into the open-air hallway and a soft LA night. He could hear the traffic on Franklin, smell burgers grilling at a twenty-four-hour diner across the street. He was suddenly hungry, overcome by a powerful and insistent appetite.

The prints, Tully. First the prints, then food.

No, first food, then the prints. Neither Amy Sponholz nor the Minchews were going anywhere. He didn't know what it was, but he was getting close to something and needed energy.

The fog was finally lifting, and for the first time in months, there was some clarity.

The Creeper had gotten to him. He saw that now—gotten to him more than he'd realized, sent him scurrying for the comfort of his intellect, where he could preen and posture with impunity. It was a sturdy, dependable redoubt, its defensive walls bricked with theories and postulates, its watchtowers stocked with observations, ideas, and clever rebuttals. So hungry had he been for answers that he'd run blindly into the embrace of a sociopath.

"Played me like a fiddle," he said, hurrying down the stairs to the ground floor. He frowned, disappointed with the unoriginality of the simile. And fiddles weren't especially easy to play. Like a what, then? An autoharp? A triangle? A maraca?

Stop. Stop your unceasing, chattering mind.

He reached his car and pulled into traffic, heading east on Franklin. He shook his head, sensing a hard question coming and trying to silence it in utero. But he couldn't stop if from forming.

What was it he actually wanted?

To be among those who renew the world.

Yes, there was that. But did he still believe in the impending birth of a new, enlightened humanity? It seemed harder and harder to recall the true believer who'd abandoned his career, sacrificed his engagement and his parents' affection, all for an inchoate need to *act*.

You don't want to admit it, Tully, but you're no better than your biology. Like everyone else, what you really want is to be in control. It's our species' biggest turn-on. Do something and observe the result. Impose your will and bend your own little corner of the universe. A drive so basic, it can be seen in infants.

Could be, he conceded. Could be he'd engaged in an elaborate self-deception, that his idealism was simply a costume for the primitive human desire to make one's mark.

This is the night we dispense with lies. This is the night we decide what we are.

All right. He'd assume the worst—he didn't have an altruistic bone in his body. Everything he did was borne of selfishness, and he'd left academe because it hadn't sufficiently boosted his esteem, or provided enough opportunities to cause a physical change in the environment and say, "Look, I did that."

He let the idea stay with him, turning it around in his mind like a puzzle piece, seeing if it fit.

He couldn't tell whether or not it was true. Would it make a difference if it were? Varma had said that a fine might be the only reason a company didn't dump its waste in a river. What mattered in the end, however, is that the river stays clean, not what the company's motivations are. Doubtless she'd used a similar rationale to justify doctoring statistics or maiming people to get her projects off the ground.

We're talking about you, not Varma. Tonight you come clean.

He played a scene for himself. Standing in the doorway of Emma Minchew's bedroom. Her small form curled on the carpet. She'd probably heard something—a scream or the sounds of a struggle—and gotten out of bed to investigate. That was when she met up with the killer, her parents' hot blood fresh on his hands, and he'd either led her back into her bedroom or intercepted her before she could come out of her room. Tackled her to the floor so easily—no effort at all, the strength of a grown man against a six-year-old child. And then he sat on her chest, forcing the air from her lungs, pressed the pillow over her face and leaned into it.

The scene changed. A faculty lounge somewhere, and he's trying to avoid another stack of graduate essays on Periclean democracy or the Stoic syllogistic. Someone left the *Los Angeles Times* on the table. He opens it, knowing he's procrastinating, but promises he'll get back to work in five minutes. A headline—*Family Slain in Reseda*, and the subheading, *Police Indicate They May Be Latest Victims of Eastside Creeper.* He reads the article, feels revulsion that the event occurred. Feels sad and depressed that a little girl was murdered. Wonders where he was when the murder took place. Concludes he was probably in bed. Speculates how terrifying it would be to have someone break into your house and kill you. Experiences relief that it hasn't happened to him. Experiences anxiety that it could. Consoles himself with the very long odds of such a scenario unfolding. Revives his anxiety by reminding himself that the odds were long for the girl, too, but she was still dead, wasn't she? Debates keeping a weapon in his bedside drawer. Like what, though? A gun?

Then he'd have to deal with all the rigmarole of buying and storing it. Oh, and learn how to use it, too. And then of course there were the moral implications of such a move. Is it wrong to support a company that makes things that kill people? But what about his right to defend himself? If someone broke in and he didn't have a gun, he'd feel ridiculous for not getting one when he had the chance. Well, he'd feel ridiculous until he died at the hands of the intruder. Then again, he lives in a gated apartment complex.

Back to the odds again—absolutely absurd to be concerned. Much more likely for a kid to come over and pick up the gun and shoot himself. That sort of thing happened all the time. But he doesn't know any kids. Might meet one, though. What if he ends up dating a single mom? What a terrifying thought, her son wandering into his bedroom and finding that gun. And the mom, she'd feel so betrayed. *How could you keep a gun without telling me? Now my son is dead and it's all your fault.*

He now experiences more angst from his inner debate about buying the gun than he had from reading the article. Then he remembers his parents are also potential targets of the Creeper. That worries him. If there's anyone in Los Angeles who'd be an easier mark than he is, it's his dads. He considers telling them to be more vigilant about security. Decides it's probably not a good idea, that it will only frighten them. Reconsiders. Sends them a text to make sure their doors and windows are locked. Finally puts the newspaper aside, peels off the first essay, red pen in hand, and begins to read.

So which is it, Tully? No more hiding. You a murder cop, or not?

22

Back at Homicide Special, the office is dark. The sensors caught Jarsdel coming in and the lights blinked on. He searched for the Minchew murder book at his cubicle, but couldn't find it. Not in Mailander's or Al-Amuli's either, then spotted it in Rall's. He took it back to his desk and opened to Section 6, where the crime lab reports were kept. Combed through the documents—autopsy reports, DNA results from the bite on Natalie Minchew's calf. A left finger and partial palm print in Brian Minchew's blood left on the master bedroom door. Bloody palm print on the handle of the bread knife. But those were patent prints—the kind where the impression was transferred through a foreign substance, like paint or grease, already visible to the naked eye.

Where were the latents? The whole house had been dusted, and not a single latent print raised. Not one contact between the Creeper's natural skin oils and a hard surface, which essentially meant he hadn't touched anything other than the door and the knife. Strange. Why would that be? He hadn't been shy about leaving prints before. The first five scenes, from Lauterbach to Galka—prints everywhere. Not too many at Sponholz, but he hadn't spent much time there. He'd practically lived at those other houses, camping out in basements and attics. But he'd killed Amy Sponholz to torment the lieutenant, or at least that was the theory. That explained the speed at which he carried out her murder. What it didn't explain was why he'd rushed the Minchew scene. He could've taken his time, but he'd torn through there nearly as quickly as he had at Sponholz's house.

Why?

Because it's not the Creeper. Definitely not at Minchew, and probably not at Sponholz, either.

Who, then? DNA a match, fingerprints a match. A forensic odontologist had confirmed that whoever bit Natalie Minchew was the same person who'd savaged Joanne Lauterbach and chewed off her husband's penis. It wasn't in the realm of possibility that two separate killers roamed Los Angeles with identical teeth, DNA, and fingerprints. No two people on the whole planet shared those characteristics, not even identical twins. While their DNA might be the same, their prints were unique.

It *was* the Creeper. Had to be.

And yet, somehow, it isn't.

No forced entry at Sponholz, but then they'd conveniently found a pick at the Minchew scene. A question, then a reply. No tooth marks on Amy Sponholz, then the bite on Minchew's calf. Another question, another reply. No Creeper epithelial tissue under Amy Sponholz's nails, plenty under Natalie Minchew's. A third question, a third reply.

Lieutenant Edwin Darrel Sponholz, blustering into the office that day with a shiner and scratches on his face. Explanation—an atonal symphony of roof repair, birds, and oak trees.

Sponholz, who'd come up with the numerology angle, that the Creeper was some kind of occultist. Then of course he'd been the one to get the hole-punch letter, which further backed up the theory.

Okay, but how? Even if he'd somehow managed to transfer Creeper prints to some sort of surrogate rubber hand, it wouldn't have been able to manufacture the human sweat and oils to make all those latent prints.

It doesn't matter how, not yet. Break the alibi. No one's bothered checking it because they're all so certain the Creeper's their man.

The alibi was twofold, now that he really thought about it. The lieutenant had been at the gym at PAB and had arrived home to find the place already swarming with activity. That was the first alibi. The second had to do with timing. When he showed up at the office covered in scratches, his wife had to have already been dead. But he'd done something to the body that fooled the ME into thinking she was killed much later that night.

Done what? Forensic scientists were famously difficult to fool.

Focus, Tully. One thing at a time.

The gym downstairs. He hadn't been there himself, but had heard the place was usually packed. Keeping in top physical shape was expected of all sworn LAPD personnel. In fact, exercising was considered part of the job. And if you could prove you were injured during your workout—say you'd dropped a barbell on your foot—you were entitled to compensation.

Which is why you were supposed to sign in each time you used the facility.

Lots of officers forgot to do it, so Sponholz's absence from the register on the night in question wouldn't be all that damning. But if every other time he'd remembered to sign in, then his failure to do so on that occasion might provide a toehold, a place for Jarsdel to stand and begin chipping away at the rest of the lieutenant's story.

He picked up the desk phone, realized he had no idea whom he needed to speak to, and replaced the receiver. He'd have to go down there himself.

The gym was on the basement level, and when Jarsdel arrived, there were only a few officers using the facility. He checked his phone—nearly eleven. If Sponholz really had tried squeezing in a workout during the early morning, there would've been hardly anyone who'd have seen him.

There was no desk like there'd be at a normal, membership-based gym. Instead, there was a small table to the right of the door, atop which sat a large, black three-ring binder. It was open, revealing that day's sign-in sheet. Officers were to write their name, badge number, time in, and time out. When he got closer, he saw there were a couple blank spaces left at the bottom. Beside the last four names, only the time-in boxes had been filled in, but not yet the time-out boxes.

Somewhere behind him there was a grunt of exertion, followed by the impact of weights hitting the hard rubber floor. He thought of Will Haarmann, the man who, until just mere hours earlier, had without a doubt sliced his hand open. What was he now, Jarsdel wondered, now that he'd been demoted from mortal enemy? And Varma had actually wanted to fan the fire, keep the hatred going. In probably the last thing she ever wrote, she'd tried to goad him into retaliating. *Remind me!* That's what she'd written. With a cutesy little exclamation point, like a text from a teenager. You could practically hear her tittering.

Jarsdel began turning pages and watched the dates scroll backward. As he did so, he wondered just how often someone came to take the pages away to archives. If that had already happened, it would be a huge headache. First he'd have to find out where they went—probably to some file drawer in Training Division—and then come up with a legitimate reason for asking to see them. And a bureaucracy being what it was, he doubted words alone would get him access. Would he have to get a warrant? Probably.

He was in August now, his fingers speeding up. The 28th, the 27th...

Come on, be there.

The 21st, the 20th...

Be there.

The 19th.

"Excuse me."

Startled, Jarsdel nearly leapt out of the way, but he restrained himself and turned to see who'd spoken. A three-striper—a sergeant—with jowls and a silver flattop, carrying a duffel bag.

"Yes?"

"I need to get in there." The man pointed at the binder.

"Sorry." Jarsdel stepped aside as the sergeant flipped pages in the other direction, looking for the day's sheet. Eventually he found it, glanced up at the wall clock, and scribbled *10:55 p.m.* in the sign-out column. He made sure to give Jarsdel a frown before leaving.

Once he'd gone, Jarsdel was back at the binder, turning the pages fast. He overshot it to August 15, then went back, slowly, until he found it again.

August 19, three densely marked pages. Working backwards, the third beginning with a time at eight o'clock. The second page, a peak between six and seven, tapering off again until midafternoon, a lull, then another spike after five. The first sheet. Jarsdel moved his finger down the page, name by name.

Midnight, one, two...

E. Sponholz—14899—Time In—2:50 a.m.—Time Out—3:35 a.m.

Jarsdel exhaled. He'd been so sure it wouldn't be there. It would've been such an easy thing to forget to do, if murdering your wife was on your mind.

He closed the binder and was almost to the elevator when he revisited that bit of logic. Yes, it would've been such an easy thing to forget to do. Unless it was the basis of your alibi, of course, then you'd be sure to remember.

He nearly ran back to the binder, opened it, began at the very first page, August 5. Names and badge numbers, line by line, tracking them with his finger. August 6, 7, 8. Nothing so far. Encouraged, he kept going, approaching the 19th. Still nothing, and then the 18th...

Yes, nothing.

After the 19th, Sponholz had been on compassionate leave. But in the two weeks between August 5 and the date of the murder, whether he'd worked out at the gym or not, Ed Sponholz never filled out the log. And Jarsdel was willing to bet if he went through the stacks of archives in Training Division, he wouldn't see any sign-ins from the lieutenant there, either. Habits of neglect were very tough to break.

And yet, on the night of Amy's murder, he'd made sure to sign in.

McWilliams Real Estate Group was less than ten minutes away from the Sponholz house, comprising the entire bottom floor of the Huntley Professional Building on Tampa, which shared an outdoor parking lot with Force MMA.

The moment Jarsdel pulled in, he could tell the relationship between the two businesses was frayed. Most of the parking spaces were designated with printed signs, placed at regular intervals. In urgent red on white, they declared, *This ENTIRE ROW reserved for Huntley Professional clients only, 24 hours a day. NO FORCE MMA PARKING. You will be TOWED. We promise!*

If the message was still unclear, the asphalt in front of each spot was stenciled with *HUNTLEY ONLY*. He found one quickly, and noticed several other vacant ones. On the other hand, the meager fraction of the lot serving Force MMA customers was jammed with cars, some triple parked. A group of men with flattened noses and twisted ears were taking a break outside. When they spotted Jarsdel getting out of his car, they stopped chatting and gave him what Morales would've called *a real good mad doggin'*.

Jarsdel looked behind him at the Huntley Building and was happy to see several security cameras trained on the lot. He didn't think he'd be finding any surprises glued to his door handle today. He gave the group in front of the gym a disarming smile, made sure they saw the badge glinting on his belt, and headed for the real estate office.

The Malibu fires had turned the sky an eggshell white and made the air smell like he was always downwind from a barbecue. It had also coated the city in a film of ash. The two easiest ways to tell how bad the air was on any given day was either to run your finger along your windshield or blow your nose. The darker your mucus, the less time you should spend outdoors. Once inside the clean, cool lobby, Jarsdel sneezed, and the contents of his handkerchief worried him. He hadn't smoked a day in his life, and dying of lung cancer would be the height of injustice.

"Hello, can I help you?"

Jarsdel looked up, embarrassed, and stuffed the handkerchief in his pants pocket. A boy in a suit sat behind the reception desk. He looked perhaps fifteen, with pale, lightly freckled cheeks and a haircut that could've been parted with a razor. Jarsdel didn't know what to say. Had he wandered into a comedy sketch?

"Sorry, I'm not sure if I'm..." He glanced at the sleek concrete partition behind the boy, where an inlaid wooden sign read *McWilliams Real Estate Group*. Below that, *A tradition of excellence since 1982.* "I'm looking for Rich Woolwine. He's—"

"Of course. Mr. Woolwine is our executive sales associate and broker of record." He looked meaningfully at Jarsdel's badge and gun. "I don't wish to be intrusive, but is everything all right?"

Jarsdel had been asked that question countless times, but never so eloquently. "Just fine. I have a matter to discuss with him regarding an open investigation."

The boy didn't look happy with that answer. "Do you have an appointment?"

"I do not."

"Okay. Um, please have a seat. I'll see if he's available."

"I'll stand, thanks. Please tell him it's important."

The boy picked up the desk phone and punched a couple numbers. Someone must have answered right away, because the boy began a sotto but still audible conversation. "Dad, I'm sorry, but there's a gentleman here to see you from the police. I said from the *police*. No. No, I really don't think I want to ask him that. Okay, thank you." He replaced the phone in the cradle. "He'll be out momentarily."

"Appreciate it," said Jarsdel. "I don't want to be intrusive, either, but isn't this a school day?"

The boy's cheeks reddened. "It's summer."

"Oh, right. Sorry. You lose track of that sort of thing when you get older."

A man stepped from behind the partition, his hand already extended for a shake. Jarsdel took hold of it, impressed at the resemblance between him and the boy receptionist. The father shared the same lean build, wide brown eyes, small nose, and pale skin. But there was gray at his temples and lines around his mouth and eyes. It was like looking at the boy after he'd gone through cheap old-age makeup.

"I'm Rich Woolwine. Thanks for waiting—could you follow me, please?" He broke away so quickly that Jarsdel almost had to jog to keep up. They passed several desks of politely curious real estate agents until they reached Woolwine's glassed-in office. Once the door was closed behind them, Woolwine was apologetic.

"I'm not gonna close the blinds if that's okay. They're a little skittish out there, and I want them to see us speaking amicably. I know why you're here. Obviously, I know, but...*shit*. Gimme a minute, hang on." He stepped outside again and went all the way back to the reception area, giving reassuring nods to his subordinates as he passed.

Jarsdel sat and noticed the man's name plate: Rich Woolwine, Executive Sales Associate. How much of his own life, Jarsdel wondered, had he spent in office chairs facing someone's desk?

Woolwine returned, shut the door softly, and sat. "I really wish you'd given me a heads-up. Staff's a little freaked out."

"About my visit?"

"Sure. It's something we're all trying to put behind us."

Jarsdel looked at Woolwine, letting silence speak for him.

"It's a tragedy, of course, and we're eager to do everything to help. But you have to consider this is a business, a *people* business, and no one wants a real estate agent who's morose." He returned Jarsdel's gaze with unflappable, steely-eyed confidence.

"I'm assuming," Jarsdel said finally, "we're talking about the same thing. The murder of Amy Sponholz, an employee here at McWilliams Realty."

"No," said Woolwine. "Not an employee. And it's not merely a semantics issue. Our agents are all basically independent contractors. They operate under McWilliams's aegis, and under myself as broker of record. But they're nothing like salaried employees. How often they work and how much they earn is very much up to them. Every desk you passed on your way in here is highly coveted. We associate ourselves with strong, capable agents. They benefit from the company's name, advertising, and office space, and we benefit from their earnings."

"Okay," said Jarsdel, "but one of your employees—"

"Again, not employees. I really can't emphasize that enough."

"Mr. Woolwine. Whatever Amy Sponholz was to this company, she was brutally murdered, and the prevailing theory holds that she was a victim of the Eastside Creeper."

"It's a terrible thing," said Woolwine.

"Were you at all close?"

"No."

"You answered that very quickly."

Woolwine smiled. "Questions with obvious answers may be answered quickly. That's their appeal. Before we continue, may I know your name?"

"Detective Jarsdel."

Woolwine had a pen out. "Spell that please?"

Jarsdel did, and Woolwine copied it down on a notepad. "I'm not being difficult," he said, capping the pen. "But the company's attorney will want to know who I spoke with."

Whom, Jarsdel nearly corrected. "You said you weren't close to Mrs. Sponholz. Any particular reason?"

"You're asking me *why* I wasn't close to one of our many associates? That's an unusual question, I think."

"What was she like? General disposition, I mean. Happy, anxious, thoughtful—how would you've described her?"

Woolwine scratched his elbow. "She was good at what she did. Nowhere near the best, numbers-wise, but she knew the business backwards and forwards. Specialized in commercial properties."

Jarsdel waited for him to go on. “And her personality?”

“Pretty standard. Nothing stood out in particular.”

“Standard personality. Okay. Any change in her behavior around the time of her death?”

“None that I noticed. But I still think your concept of the working relationships in this office is faulty. Interactions between myself and any single associate are minimal and only arise out of necessity. This isn’t a social club.”

“That seems pretty clear,” said Jarsdel. “We’ll move on to her last day, August 19.”

Woolwine nodded. “I remember it well.”

“You do? Why’s that?”

“She bungled the showing of a lot on Nordhoff. Twelve-point-five million.”

Here we go, thought Jarsdel. *This is where he tells me that she didn’t show up that day. Because she was already dead, wasn’t she? And Sponholz somehow fooled the pathologist into miscalculating the time of death. I haven’t figured that out yet, and I still don’t know how he did the Creeper’s prints and the blood in her mouth, but I will. And this is the first step to breaking his story.*

To Woolwine, he said, “How did she bungle the showing?”

“Double-booked one of the slots. Embarrassing. One of the best ways to ensure a first-time client becomes an only-time client.”

He spoke the clunky aphorism with practiced smugness. It was obviously a line he’d used many times before. And he must have misinterpreted the expression on Jarsdel’s face, because he added, “Not to speak ill of the dead.”

“Wait.” Jarsdel leaned forward. “Sorry, back up. You’re saying she came to work that day?”

“Of course.”

“On the 19th of August. You’re saying she was showing a property. You’re absolutely positive about that?”

Woolwine regarded him mildly. “Am I missing the significance of my response? Yes. I’m telling you she came in on the day in question and that she double-booked an appointment to show a valuable property. This was followed by several hours of desk work. I also remember that day because her husband brought her a coffee on his way to work. I mention that because he looked as if he'd been in some kind of altercation. I understand he's in the police as well, so perhaps it happened on the job. We were all relieved when he left."

Jarsdel's mind spun. Woolwine couldn't be right. There had to be an explanation, something he just wasn't seeing yet. The killer had to have been the lieutenant. It was too much of a coincidence—his injuries, the absurd story about the birds, all the little details at the scene that didn't fit with the Creeper's pattern.

He tried one last approach. "Are you sure it was her?"

Woolwine's brow creased. "I don't follow."

"Are you certain the woman you saw that day was actually Amy Sponholz?"

Now it was Woolwine who leaned forward. "Detective, I'm pretty good at recognizing faces, especially those I've encountered daily for almost five years. And Amy Sponholz in particular had very distinctive features. If you've seen her photograph, you probably know what I mean. But if that's not good enough for you, you're welcome to speak with our associates. Any number of them will be able to confirm her presence in the office on August 19th."

Jarsdel stood up. "That won't be necessary. Thank you for your help."

Woolwine rose as well, looking much happier. "Pleasure. Can you see yourself out?"

Jarsdel didn't hear him. He wondered what had made him so certain Sponholz was guilty. He couldn't even be sure at what point he'd come to such a rash conclusion. He felt ridiculous, yes, but that wasn't the worst of it. He'd betrayed his lieutenant, pursued him as he would any other murder suspect, and had done so based on nothing other than a vague sensation of disquiet. No witness statement, no dying declaration, no evidence suggesting he'd been involved. Quite the contrary. Based on the abundant physical evidence, the only conclusion a reasonable person could come to was that, without the faintest doubt, Sponholz *hadn't* done it.

Jarsdel opened the office door, turning his thoughts over, examining them, trying to figure out where he'd gone wrong. Behind him, Woolwine murmured, "Okay, then. Have a wonderful day."

Past the agents at their desks, past the boy receptionist, back outside in the Great LA Cookout. Eyes stinging, nostrils burning in protest with his first breath. Into his car with the AC on full. The air was cooler but otherwise just as bad. He hit the interior air cycle.

It's your reputation you ought to be worried about, not your lungs. When Rall finds out you liked the LT for his own wife's murder, you might as well put in your transfer paperwork. Forget homicide—you're through.

23

The DNA was a match. Whoever the Eastside Creeper was, he'd left his contact DNA on the hole-punch letter to Sponholz. He'd also left his fingerprints, which a Forensic Science Division tech had been able to develop with ninhydrin. The chemical reacted with the amino acids excreted through the skin, and could reveal prints even on porous surfaces like paper, where they emerged as intricate purple stains.

The Creeper was communicating with police. That was good news. Every communication was an opportunity for a slipup, an accidental flashing of a clue. But apparently there was more, something bigger, and Rall had called them in right away.

He stood at the head of the conference table, his normally flat affect replaced by an excitement Jarsdel wouldn't have thought the man capable of. It was unclear, however, if Rall was jubilant or furious or some strange hybrid of the two. He looked from Mailander to Jarsdel, then back to Mailander again.

"Where the hell's—"

Al-Amuli breezed in, sipping from a mug inscribed with the title, "World's Okayest Detective." He took a seat on the other end of the table, as far from the rest as possible.

"You got your coffee?" asked Rall.

"I'm good," said Al-Amuli.

Rall appeared to consider making more out of it, then gave a quick shake of his head. "Okay, we finally got a break. Check it." He swung a briefcase onto the table, popped the latches, and pulled out a manila folder.

"Motherfucker sent us a letter." He waited, probably for the storm of rapid-fire questions he thought would follow. Instead, his three junior detectives simply stared.

Finally, Al-Amuli asked, "You sure it's authentic?"

Rall gave him a contemptuous sneer. "No, man. I thought it'd be cool to waste you all's time. That's where I'm at with you. Burnin' daylight just *'cause.*"

Al-Amuli blinked. Watching him, Jarsdel marveled at how often he looked like he'd just been woken from a nap.

Rall blew out a disgusted breath from between his teeth. "So yeah. Creeper sent us a letter. Came in with yesterday's mail, and we already sent both it and the envelope off to the lab. Got details in it nobody else would know. I'm-a hand it out to you now."

He opened the folder and handed a thin stack of papers to Mailander. "Take one and pass it on. These copies are all accounted for. You lose it and it's your ass. You leak it, and we have a very small suspect pool."

Jarsdel took the sheet Mailander offered him and saw it had been stamped in red with the word COPY, and that beside this Rall had written #2 and signed his name in blue pen. He sailed the remaining page toward Al-Amuli at the end of the table. The detective almost had it, but it went off the side.

"Great. Thank you," he said.

Jarsdel hardly heard him. He couldn't believe what he was holding. Actual words from the demon itself. The letter had been written with heavy black marker in block capitals. The text looked blurry at first, then he realized each letter had been written on top of itself three or four times, the pen probably passed from hand to hand to disguise the penmanship. After that, the document had been photocopied, the resulting generation photocopied again, and so on and so on. What remained was very difficult to trace forensically, either by scientific investigators or a handwriting analyst.

The group read silently.

Dear police detectives and others assisting,

I am the one you know of as the Eastside Creeper, though I am not flattered by the name bestowed upon me. I do not creep rather I hunt and I have not confined these hunts solely to the eastern part of Los Angeles. On the contrary there are victims of my crimes in other parts of the city, even other parts of the state and maybe even beyond. Who knows? I have conscripted many lives for my gallery of dreams.

I understand you may contend with many charlatans claiming to be me for whatever reason, so here is proof that I am who I say. I could provide many, many details obviously, but these give me some pleasure to recount.

At the Lauterbach house, I struck the first (male) officer in the face with a hammer, then hid under the bed until his partner came in, after which I pulled her to the floor. I considered killing her, but left when I heard how close the backup units were. Later I regretted at least not striking her in the face as I had done with her partner.

At the Rustads one of the things I did that was quite fun was when I secured a bike lock cable around the head of the husband. I had already taken a wrench from near the gas shutoff valve in the front yard (which as you know I also used to break Missus Rustad's knees) and this I inserted between the cable and the man's head. Turning the wrench I was able to tighten the cable to an extreme tightness. Since it takes about five hundred pounds of force to crush someone's skull (depending on how much milk they drank in their youth, ha-ha) and the cable was much stronger, the result was that his eyes fairly burst outward. When that happened I stopped out of concern that the man would die and I did not want that to happen as of yet. I let him be and he lived perhaps another hour, though it is difficult to say with certainty as his breathing became more shallow.

I also want you to know that I killed Amy Sponholts (sp?) because she was the wife of the man who pointed at me on TV and said how he'd get me, and I wanted him to know that such threats could go either way.

How I got into the house was like this: I climbed the back-yard fence which was not at all difficult and then I used lockpicks to gain entry. When the alarm began counting down I knew I didn't have much time, so I went upstairs as quickly as I could. She called out asking for hubby and didn't realize the danger until she saw me. I already had my hands around her throat when the alarm began to sound.

I did that thing with the broom because it pleased me to think of the lootenant finding her that way and feeling upset. I was lucky because it was already in the room. I did not bite her as I normally like to do as I did not have time.

The Minchews excited me. I know it's not how I usually do things. Too quick! But I couldn't control myself.

The reason I'm writing is to tell you I'm going to be moving on. Don't bother trying to find me. I promise you will not succeed. In fact, by the time you get this letter I will already be gone. Out of the city not to return. I also plan on changing my methods, so that next time you hear of a crime you will wonder if it is me or not. Maybe it will be, maybe it won't.

It's been fun playing my wits against yours, but alas the time has come to say...

Adieu,
Belphegor

Jarsdel finished reading and looked up. "This is stupid."

The others turned to him, surprised.

"This." Jarsdel tossed the letter onto the table. "It's... I don't know. It's like it's deliberately weird. Forced."

"It's *weird*, Detective," said Rall, "because it was written by some crazy-ass, drooling shitbag."

"Sorry. I don't buy it. I mean, look. Here: 'Bestowed upon me,' 'conscripted many lives,' 'gallery of dreams.' That's awfully arch. Hannibal Lecter meets...I don't know—meets tired, played-out crap. I've read a lot of essays in my life, and if there's anything I'm good at, it's spotting derivative work. This is just dreadful, overly poetic. Grandiose."

Rall glared at him. "You're claiming it's a fake?"

"You tell me," said Jarsdel. "We've all seen the pictures, we've all experienced a taste of what gets this guy's engine going. C'mon, does this really read like the kind of person who makes incisions in people's skin and, um..." He glanced at Mailander, then went on, "copulates with the wounds? And this bit of ridiculousness, the way he spells lieutenant, starting it with *l-o-o*. Why all of a sudden does he regress into phonetic spelling here? His syntax, his diction, both point to someone with an education. 'Playing my wits against yours.' But the *l-o-o* thing seems like a deliberate attempt to dress himself down a couple notches, throw us off, make us think there're gaps in his knowledge. Later he gives himself away, though. He actually closes with 'adieu.' It's pretty amazing." Jarsdel laughed. "Pretty amazing how he misspells 'lieutenant' but gets 'adieu' right, don't you think? Why does he struggle with one Gallicism and not at all with another?"

Mailander looked at him with her usual expression of suspicious dislike, but she appeared to be listening nevertheless. "The details are right. If it's not the Creeper, how'd he know everything?"

Jarsdel had anticipated the question. "Whoever wrote that letter is either in law enforcement or connected to the police in some way. Maybe paid for the information. There're quite a few people familiar with this stuff by now. Any one of them could've given it up."

"Why?" Mailander again.

"What do you mean?"

"Why fuck with the task force? What d'you gain from that?"

The answer was obvious. A double-indemnity life-insurance payoff. One million kicked up to two in case of wrongful or accidental death. Of course, you couldn't collect if you'd been the one who'd killed her. But he'd been wrong about Sponholz, so actually the answer wasn't obvious at all.

To the group, Jarsdel said, "I don't know."

"Don't know what?"

Jarsdel had his back to the door that day, and had to turn in his seat to see who'd entered. When he did, he found himself eye to eye with Lieutenant Sponholz. He wasn't sure if he'd ever seen anyone look so exhausted, so absolutely gutted. His cheeks were hollow, the cleft in his chin now a small crater. Even his hair looked thinner.

"LT," said Rall. "Didn't know you were coming in today."

"Hate being useless, just sitting around at home." Sponholz slunk into the room and found a chair. He eyed Jarsdel. "Shall I repeat the question?"

"I was saying, sir, that I don't know why anyone would try to mislead the task force."

Sponholz appeared dazed. "Sorry, must've missed something. Why're we assuming someone's trying to mislead the task force?"

"We're not assumin', LT," said Rall. "That's only Detective Jarsdel's pet theory."

"Based on?"

Rall gestured at Jarsdel to explain himself. He exchanged looks with Mailander, and thought she might've given him the hint of an encouraging nod. "Well, as I was telling the group before you came in, sir, the note feels pushed. Guy I used to be partners with at Hollywood Station told me I needed to watch more movies, which I did in fact end up doing, and I'm glad because this stuff is painfully overwrought."

Sponholz massaged the space between his eyebrows. "I don't even know what we're looking at. Anyone have a copy for me?"

"Take mine." Al-Amuli handed one of the letters to Sponholz, who read it quickly and without expression. Once he was finished, he grunted and tossed it onto the table. "Who has the original?"

"It's at the lab. Should be almost done."

"Good. Well, far as the letter goes, I don't know. I see the detective's point about the tone, but that's often the way folks like this operate. They're playing out their fantasies, pretending to be Moriarty because it gives them the kind of power and mystique they lack in their humdrum little lives."

Rall's phone buzzed, and he snapped it up to his ear. "Yeah." He held out his hand to indicate he needed it quiet, though no one had said anything. "Yeah. Yeah, okay, thanks." Excited, he hooked the phone back onto his belt and planted his palms onto the conference table. "Okay people, listen up. They got a ninhydrin print off the letter, but it's not the Creeper. Doesn't match any of the exemplars. Somebody new."

Sponholz looked startled. "New?"

Rall nodded. "Big thumb print, clear as can be. Thumb only. FSD tech said it was the prettiest print he ever raised, almost like the guy was tryin' to ID himself. Popped up right away in the database, and they're sending me the full package now."

"But I don't understand," said Sponholz. "If it's not the Creeper, then how would he know all the details in the letter?"

"An accomplice," said Al-Amuli, shaking his head in amazement. "Creeper's not gonna be too happy when he learns his partner blew the whole game."

Mailander regarded him coolly. "Big rush to judgment."

"Whatever. I could say the sky's blue, and you'd find a way of arguing with me."

"Enough," said Rall. His phone gave a single chime, and in a blink it was back in his palm. He scrolled through the information he'd received, his face as still and severe as granite.

"What's it say?" asked Sponholz.

"Hang on, LT."

"Who is it?"

Rall didn't answer. Sponholz searched the faces of his detectives, his eyes oddly desperate. "Do any of *you* know who it is?"

He was behaving strangely, even pitifully. From head of Homicide Special to a doddering old relative, the one who'll quiet down again as long as no one engages with him.

Rall held to the phone to his ear again. "Hey, you got a minute? OFD, my ass—you're gonna want this one." He smiled. "Could be. Come on up and we'll talk." He put the phone on the table and gave it a vigorous spin. It whispered in several brisk circles before slowing down. When it stopped, one end pointed more or less at Al-Amuli. Rall leveled a finger at him. "Don't worry, we ain't gonna kiss. I want you to get an arrest warrant. I'll send you the details while you're in transit. Try to get Judge Monson if you can."

He turned to the others. "Let's go ruin someone's day."

24

Putting a man in custody changed his relationship to the world. A moment earlier, he'd been free to walk or drive or fly as far as he wanted, could speak to anyone for any reason, could eat whatever his wallet or his charm could buy him. Once the cuffs were on, that immediately changed. His life was no longer solely his own; in fact the percentage of it he actively controlled was reduced to somewhere in the single digits.

Some men wept when they were arrested, some panicked, others submitted in a state of stunned, dreamlike silence. The rest raged, cursed, or fought—fought hard, gladly willing to trade a pine box for a steel cage if that's what it took.

Jarsdel never took pleasure in being the one to make an arrest, disliked in particular the span of time after one wrist was secure, but not the other. That was when suspense was at its greatest—the limbo between free and not free, the last possible second a person could decide he really wasn't interested in going to jail that day. A moment like that, short as it was, could seem to go on a long time, especially when you were alone with a suspect.

The arrest of Gaspar Bengochea was unlike any Jarsdel had ever seen. No opportunity to mount a last stand, neither the frantic, flailing kind nor the blaze-of-glory, Butch-and-Sundance variety.

At the Gaspar Bengochea level, the arrest was a perfectly timed piece of flash-mob choreography in which all the participants knew exactly what to do. All except the target, of course. For him, there wasn't even a hint of the ax until well after it had fallen. No sirens, no knock on the door. Radio chatter was coded, with no mention of the target's name or address in case he had a scanner.

Rall and his SWAT buddies had waited until Bengochea pulled into the sharply downward-sloping driveway to his apartment's garage. A maintenance truck from the Department of Water and Power pulled tight in behind him, blocking his escape, and then the action kicked off. Before the gate had even lifted off the ground to admit the car, four officers in full tactical gear charged in, faces wrapped in balaclavas. Two from either side of the building, quick, M4s raised. Rall leaping from the DWP truck, Remington pump angled at the ground. Shouting, loud. Jarsdel, watching in a van across the street, saw the driver's silhouette jump in surprise. Hands raised, shaking. Too slow for Rall. A slap of the shotgun's stock against the window. Safety glass spraying, Bengochea yanked out so fast his legs go sideways.

Now Jarsdel was back home, back at Hollywood Station. It had the closest interview room, and Rall wanted at their suspect before he could come to his senses and decide to lawyer up. Every cop in the station was crowded around the monitors, trying to fathom the man wiping his eyes and rubbing his abused wrists. He was in his early twenties, skinny, wearing khakis and a short-sleeved plaid shirt, buttoned all the way to the neck, Cholo style. Probably to make himself look bigger and tougher than he really was. His head was shaved tight on the sides, the long hair on top slicked back—although most of it hung down in his face.

"Good to see you."

Jarsdel looked to his right and saw Barnhardt. She also was fixated on the interview room's two monitors.

"Me or the guy in there?"

"Both, I suppose." She smiled at him. "Good catch."

"Had nothing to do with it. Wish I could say I did, but I didn't. Put his thumbprint smack on a taunting missive he sent our way."

Barnhardt returned her gaze to the monitor. "He's a little big, isn't he? I thought his shoe size was six-and-a-half."

"Yeah, it's not him, not the Creeper."

"He isn't? What do you mean? I'm confused."

"At this point we're figuring an accomplice of some kind. Friends, or maybe they do burglaries together. Either way, this guy knows stuff that, collectively, would either have to make him an accessory or a police officer. And we checked. He isn't a police officer."

Barnhardt considered the man on the screen, then turned back to Jarsdel. "Priors?"

"Nothing too sexy," Jarsdel confessed. "Stolen credit card, with just enough purchases to knock it up to grand theft. That's what got him printed, I presume, though he does have two juvie charges. One open container and one curfew." He thought about that, then added before Barnhardt could bring it up, "Those were the same night."

"Huh. So he's basically a pretty normal guy—other than the Creeper connection."

Jarsdel looked at her as if she'd gone crazy. "That's a pretty big 'other than,' don't you think?"

"What I mean is he doesn't really fit the profile."

"There *is* no profile. Not for what we're hunting."

"Of course there is," said Barnhardt. "How old's he?"

Jarsdel sighed. "Twenty-two."

"And by the way you said that, I'm guessing you probably know most serials are in their late twenties to early thirties. They also tend to have long and troubled histories with law enforcement. You have anything else? Or even anything sealed back in juvie?"

"No. But I'd like you to consider the case of Dennis Nilsen if you're going to get statistical on me. No contact whatsoever with police until his arrest. And he killed at least twelve men. You also have to remember I'm not saying this is our actual killer, merely some kind of voyeuristic hanger-on."

Barnhardt met his eyes. "You're not thinking objectively."

"Really? What's more objective than physical evidence?"

"Normally I'd agree. But I've been looking at Creeper scenes from the start, and he's never had any help. And the kind of stuff he does is personal to him. It's not to impress anybody. It's not a show. It's his routine, designed to please only himself. We just happen to come along afterward, but he's not trying to shock us. That's just his mind, his fantasies made real. He's not a performer. Those victims, those moments are his, and he certainly wouldn't have a partner."

Jarsdel wasn't interested. "Got a thumbprint the size of Wyoming says you're wrong." If she said anything else, he didn't hear. He pushed through the crowd toward the monitors. "Creeper Task Force, excuse me." Suits and uniforms parted grudgingly until he was up front with Mailander and Al-Amuli.

As they watched the screens, Rall entered the room carrying a medium cardboard box, which he placed on the table between himself and Bengochea. Several cops near Jarsdel hushed their friends. "Shut up, he's in," someone said. All conversations fell silent. Mailander turned up the volume on the interview anyway.

"How's it goin'?" Rall sat, scooting forward in his chair, which made awful squeaking, rasping sounds. Mailander turned the volume down a little.

"Not good," said Bengochea.

"Yeah? Not doin' too good?"

"Don't know why I'm here."

"You don't, huh?" Rall reached into the box and pulled out one of the murder books. "Bill and Joanne Lauterbach, January 31." He dropped it on the table with a smack, then reached back into the box. "Maja and Steffen Rustad, March 2." He dropped the second book on top of the first, then kept going, picking up speed. "Esperanza, Martín, Sebastian, and Juan Carlos Santiago. Sam, Beth, and Wally Verheugen. Benjamin, Margot, Bowie, and Zephyr Galka. Got the dog on that one, too. Natalie, Brian, and Emma

Minchew." He pulled out one last book. "Amy Sponholz." He let it fall onto the stack.

Bengochea gaped at the pile of blue folders, then at the man questioning him. "You're saying I did something to these people?"

Rall didn't answer. He rested his hand atop the books and pushed them in Bengochea's direction. The suspect recoiled. "No, no, no. I never hurt nobody in my life."

"Sure, okay. Hey before we go on, I'm just gonna go over a couple things with you." Rall explained Bengochea his rights, then asked, "So you wanna talk to me?"

"No man, I mean I told you, I don't know anything."

"So you stoppin' the interview?"

"I don't—"

"You can. It's within your rights. But if I were you I'd want to get this cleared up. You don't know what's goin' on, I'm gonna need your help explaining this."

Rall reached back into the box. It reminded Jarsdel of when magicians pulled ever more impressive items from a hat. But Rall's hand came out gripping a glassine envelope, not a rabbit or a goose. He gave it a couple shakes, and the contents slipped out onto the table.

It was a color copy of the latest Creeper letter, Bengochea's own thumbprint pointing back at him in vivid ninhydrin purple.

"What's that?"

"You want me to tell you what this is? Why don't you tell me?"

"Because I've never seen it before."

Rall sat back, crossing his arms. "I love lies, man. People think cops don't like being lied to, but I love 'em, because they're as good as the truth. Either way you're locked in. Now you just locked yourself in with that bullshit. Just denied seeing this letter, but *that*"—he pointed at the print—"is yours. Right thumb."

Bengochea's eyes went wide—the expression of one betrayed by a long-trusted companion. He turned his hand over and examined his thumb. Finding no answers there, he began reading the letter. "No," he said, after only a few seconds. "I didn't write this."

"These ain't your pants, huh?"

"What?"

"When you work patrol, you do a lot of pat-downs. Be surprised how many guys, when you find somethin' on them, tell you those ain't their pants. That's what you just did, basically, only this letter's wearing *you*."

Bengochea opened his mouth to speak, but Rall raised a hand. "Do me a favor. Just stop for a minute. Take a few breaths, collect yourself. Whatever else you feel like saying, I want it to come from you knowing this shit's all over. There's no talking that's gonna take that print off that letter. That part's done, okay?"

He got up and left the room. Jarsdel and the others watched the door close on the monitor, then looked up to see the big detective coming down the hall toward them. "Give him an hour to think about it."

On the screen, Bengochea sagged forward onto the table and began sobbing into the crook of an elbow. His thin body shook under the oversized clothes.

Rall nodded approvingly. He noticed Jarsdel standing next to him. "Then you're up."

By the time Jarsdel entered the interview room, Bengochea had stopped crying. Now he slouched in his chair, staring at the wall across from him. As he sat, Jarsdel positioned his chair directly into Bengochea's line of sight. Even so, the suspect seemed to be looking past him.

"Good evening. I'm Detective Jarsdel. Can I get you something to drink? Or maybe you're hungry?"

No answer.

"You've had quite a day. I don't blame you for feeling a little rattled. But you gotta look at it from our perspective. Most-wanted man in California sends us a letter, and your thumbprint's on it. We gotta get to the bottom of that, of why that is. The quicker you help us figure that out, the quicker we can all get on with our lives."

No answer.

Jarsdel felt himself growing frustrated. "There's another way to see this, and that's basically as your last opportunity to tell us your side of the story. We know you weren't inside any of the houses, okay? We know that. You weren't physically involved. That's a very important thing. That's the difference between a life sentence and a plea bargain. Maybe the situation's even better for you, I don't know. Maybe you didn't even believe him that he was really the Creeper. Maybe you guys are roommates, and you just happen to lean on the worst possible sheet of paper at the worst possible time. But it's a fact that you know who he is. That's nonnegotiable. I think you can agree with that, right? So let's start there. You give us this name now, and I can't even tell you how big that is for you."

Bengochea's head moved from side to side three times. A mechanical gesture. Jarsdel was reminded of a piece of clockwork.

He was denying it? He was actually denying it? "You don't seem to understand." Jarsdel pointed at the ninhydrin print on the letter. "There is literally—and my usage there is correct—*literally* no one else in the universe with that particular pattern on their right thumb. Computer didn't even need to think about it. Just popped right up, there were so many points of comparison. You couldn't have left a nicer print if you'd tried."

No answer.

"You know how prints are formed?" Jarsdel held up his left hand, pointed to the patterns on the pads of his fingers. "Happens when you're an embryo, and the list of factors that influence how the friction ridges are formed is pretty astonishing. Your mom's diet, the density of the amniotic fluid, even the length of the umbilical cord. But what gets me is a lot of it has to do with you, while you're in there, pushing on the interior walls of the uterus. How hard you do that, and how often, that also determines what your prints look like."

The slow head shake again, back and forth three times.

"Okay, what is it exactly you're saying no to?"

No answer.

Jarsdel exhaled through his teeth. "That strategy isn't gonna get you anywhere. You can bury your head in the sand, but here's what's gonna happen. You don't talk to me, I go to the district attorney. She comes back with a charge of first degree murder. Several charges, actually, with special circumstances. And since you won't give up your partner, you get to swing for the whole thing alone. Think you're miserable now? Why, because you got yanked out of your car and some cops yelled at you? Your finite mind cannot begin to grasp what it'll be like to bear the entire weight of this thing. Imagine the collective hatred and repulsion of every civilized human being in Los Angeles. All...directed...at *you*."

He was halfway out of his chair when Bengochea finally spoke. "I didn't do it."

Jarsdel sat back down. "All right. Who did?"

"I don't know."

"Who wrote the letter?"

"I don't know."

"Why's your print on it?"

"I don't know."

Jarsdel crossed his arms. "This isn't much of a step up from your previous approach. The 'I don't know' routine runs pretty thin around here."

"But I really don't!" Animation suddenly poured back into Bengochea. His eyes were pleading, but clear and focused. "Okay? I don't know about any of this stuff. Killing people. That's not me. Nothing like me. I ain't a criminal."

"Well you are, though. You are a criminal. You have a criminal record."

"Hey, that credit card thing was *bullshit*, man. That was... It don't even matter, you won't believe me."

They passed a minute in silence before he spoke again. "Never killed anybody."

"Let's change gears," said Jarsdel. "What do you do? For a living, I mean."

Bengochea looked glad to be talking about something else. He shrugged. "Retail and stuff."

"Yeah? What kind? Clothing?"

"Nah, I wish."

Jarsdel remained quiet, letting Bengochea take over the pace of the conversation. Eventually he said, "Maybe a couple months I'll change it up. My cousin got a job like that at the mall, and he makes pretty good money."

"Where do you work?"

"You know, uh, Send It Packing? On Sunset?"

"No, sorry."

"Near the Arclight. Same side of the street, but a couple blocks east. The mini-mall with that liquor store. Cap'n Cork."

"Okay."

Bengochea grimaced and massaged his wrists. "Man, I think they pinched a nerve or something. Hurts."

"You go to school?"

"Kinda. You know what a notary is?"

"Sure."

"The guys who certify documents and stuff?"

"I know what a notary is."

"My boss wanted me to take the exam on that so I could help out more at the store. Lot of people need that kinda service, and it says it in the window that we do that. When it's just me, though, and people come in lookin' for a notary, I have to say sorry, you gotta come back. So I been studyin', up my value there and everything."

"Makes sense."

"Yeah."

Jarsdel waited, but Bengochea didn't add more. He could tell his own sangfroid wasn't going to last much longer. What did the man hope to gain from all this hemming and hawing?

Bengochea's expression changed. He appeared suddenly hopeful, which was about the last thing Jarsdel would've predicted.

"Hey, wait. You think that's what might've happened here? Someone brought me something and I picked it up?"

Jarsdel shook his head.

"Why not?"

"Because if you'd picked it up, you'd have left prints on the other side of the paper too." To demonstrate, he held the copy of the Creeper letter between his thumb and index finger. "See? Skin on both sides. Would've left amino acids, contact DNA if nothing else. No, looks to me like you put the print on the letter when you mailed it, pushing it into the envelope. Exactly the kind of thing you'd overlook when you're under stress and doing something you shouldn't. Got frazzled, took your gloves off at some point."

The nascent hope refused to leave Bengochea's eyes. "But I didn't."

Jarsdel lined up his own thumb with the print on the letter. "Perpendicular to the short edge. Tip of the thumb pointing down to the words." He placed the letter back into the glassine envelope. "If I wasn't wearing gloves, and this was sticking out a little, I'd push it in the rest of the way with my thumb, but the rest of my fingers would be touching the envelope, which explains why their prints aren't on the back of the letter itself."

"Are my prints on the envelope?" Again, that inexplicable thread of hope.

"I don't have that information right now."

"So you don't know for sure?"

"You have any idea how many people handle an envelope in transit? It'd be covered in prints, most of them overlapping. It's not worth considering from an evidentiary standpoint."

He waited for Bengochea to abandon the straw he was grasping at, but he wasn't ready to give up just yet.

"Can I see it?"

"What, the letter? Sure."

Bengochea took it and studied the words. "This ain't my handwriting."

"It's nobody's handwriting. It's disguised."

"I don't even know what some of these words mean, man."

"Guess I'll have to take your word for that."

"What's a—"

"Hey. Enough." Jarsdel had reached his limit. "I'm—"

"Looks photocopied."

Had Bengochea actually interrupted *him*? He was too amazed to say anything, and the suspect took that as a cue to continue.

"Photocopied a bunch, I mean. No detail, everything's a little fuzzy." He scrutinized the thumbprint, then looked at the offending digit on his own hand. Jarsdel watched him closely. Bengochea did it again, from the print to his thumb, then once more.

Such a simple thing a fingerprint was, and so damning. What he'd told Bengochea wasn't the half of it. The sheer number of ingredients that went into forming them, from genetic to environmental variables, was truly astonishing.

The Creeper hadn't cared about his prints, had left them everywhere. Must have known even in the fog of his madness that they weren't on file. Except at the Sponholz scene, he reminded himself. Only right-hand prints there. And the first letter, the hole-punch letter, only left-hand prints. And then the Minchew scene, those patent prints in blood, also the left hand. On this letter, no Creeper prints. Only Bengochea's.

His subconscious kicked up a reel of stored footage. Ed Sponholz in the RDH conference room that day. Ed Sponholz, the walking apology, his face bruised and scratched.

Only right-hand prints, then only left-hand prints, now none at all.

Jarsdel closed his eyes.

He couldn't help it. So terrific was the fuckup, so unbelievable, that the best thing right then would be another earthquake. Something cataclysmic and final. He willed the ground to open beneath his chair, swallow him, clap shut. Erase him completely.

He opened his eyes and stood. "Excuse me."

"You're leavin'? Wait..."

Jarsdel was outside the interview room, pulling the door shut behind him. He couldn't bear to hear anything else from Bengochea.

It hurt too deeply. And to think how gleeful he'd been when they'd thrown him to the ground and slapped the cuffs on.

Rall saw him coming and put his palms out. "Hey, the hell you doin'?"

"You know the place he's talking about? Send It Packing?"

The detective stared at him, baffled.

"He says it's on Sunset, next to Cap'n Cork."

Rall nodded. "The stop-and-rob, yeah. So?"

"If Send It Packing doesn't have cameras, the liquor store definitely will. Letter was postmarked yesterday, so chances are it'll be yesterday's footage."

"I want you back in there, now. Motherfucker's about to break." Rall's voice was hushed but agitated. The officers around them leaned in, curious.

"No, he isn't. Trust me. Those cameras, that's what counts right now. The cameras in that mini-mall lot."

"Why? What're we looking for?"

"You'll have to see for yourself. I tell you now and you won't believe me." He began to move away.

Rall seized his arm and bent in close. "You are not excused, Detective. Now get back in there and finish the interview."

It was like being gripped by a stone hand. "I can't. I've got to go while there's still time."

"I'm gonna end your career. Disciplinary hearing first thing tomorrow. Gonna have to explain to Captain Coryell why you disobeyed a direct order. Your career, over."

"Maybe," Jarsdel said. "But it won't be because I failed to catch the man who murdered Amy Sponholz."

The certainty with which he made the declaration gave Rall pause. His grip loosened a little. "What do you mean?"

"The footage, sir. I'll be on the road. After you watch it, call me." He pulled away, leaving Rall for a moment with his hand extended, curled around nothing. The detective and the rest of the officers stared after him. He passed Barnhardt, then Haarmann and Gavin, both looking amused. Then Morales, leaning against a domestic violence awareness poster.

His partner gave him a nod, and Jarsdel returned it.

25

The evening rush was over, and the freeways went from being gridlocked to merely slow. He took the 5 off Los Feliz, heading north, passing the LA Zoo and the Gene Autry museum on his left. He stayed on past the 134 interchange, and the traffic began to pick up a little once he hit Burbank.

Beyond the Burbank airport, the road cleared, the speedometer climbing to seventy, then eighty. His phone announced in a clipped British accent that his exit was coming up in one mile.

A tourist driving from Hollywood to Shadow Hills would have trouble believing both neighborhoods were part of the same city. Shadow Hills's population was only a couple thousand, much of the land was given over to horse ranches and olive groves, and the bumper stickers were less NPR than NRA.

He took Sunland and turned right, heading up toward the Verdugo Mountains. There were no streetlights out there, and he flicked on his brights, dousing them whenever a car approached from the opposite direction.

The car climbed awhile, then dipped into black, canopied valleys. The road narrowed, trees hugging close on either side. A series of blind curves. A fawn, eyes wide, then gone, fleeing into the night.

The land swept gently upward again and Jarsdel slowed, glancing from the road to the GPS readout on his phone. A hundred yards from the address. He pulled onto the shoulder, gravel spitting from underneath his tires. Killed the engine.

The farmhouse was set up from the road on a hillock, and stood squat and dark against the clear moonlit sky.

Jarsdel flicked the switch on the dome light—didn't want it coming on when he opened the door.

He stepped out, shoes crunching. Pushed the door closed, softly. Took a few steps. Something got spooked, scurried through the brush. Jarsdel paused. It sounded big—a possum, maybe. Were there snakes out here? Probably. He resumed walking, but each step sounded like someone popping bubble wrap. It was otherwise so quiet, he thought surely anyone would be able to hear him. The road instead. Better, practically no sound.

Closer. A waist-high wooden fence marked the edge of the property, then a driveway came into view. It curved up toward the farmhouse, perhaps twenty yards. To the left was a corral, empty. Behind the corral, further up the hill, a barn. The doors were closed, but light shone around their edges. A flicker of movement, a shadow. Someone inside.

His phone vibrated and he snatched it off his belt. It was Rall. Jarsdel answered, voice low but not whispered. "You watch it yet?"

"Yeah."

"And?"

"Hat and sunglasses. It's not a hundred percent."

"But you recognized him anyway, right?"

Rall blew out a breath. "Yeah. But it don't prove nothin'. Just that the LT was there, not what he did inside."

"Was he holding anything when he went in?"

"A manila envelope. But it's not enough."

"No," Jarsdel agreed.

"Where are you?"

He ignored the question. "You need to get a warrant on his house. The video should be able to do that much."

"Why? What're we gonna find?"

Jarsdel told him, then hung up before Rall could ask more questions. He silenced the ringer and began making his way up the driveway. There was a tube gate blocking the way, but the chain and padlock that would've secured it lay in the dirt nearby. Jarsdel pushed it open, froze at the sound it made, a whine followed by a deep, rattling groan.

Stupid.

Eyes on the barn doors, a slow count to ten. When no one came out, he slipped through and eased the gate closed again, lifting up to take the weight off the hinges.

The lieutenant's car sat at the top of the driveway just a few feet from the farmhouse. The paving stopped there, but a dirt path hooked off toward the barn. Jarsdel drew his weapon, holding it at his side as he crept along.

His foot turned on a stone and he stumbled, hot pain in his ankle. Reflexively, he reached for his Maglite, but stopped himself before he turned it on. He waited, another slow count to ten, making sure he hadn't been detected.

The path steepened as he neared the barn. At first he thought he was going to have to get on his hands and knees to get up there, then noticed a short flight of wide wooden steps jammed into the hillside. He climbed them easily, but made sure to keep his finger on the trigger guard in case he slipped again. Blowing a hole in his foot probably wasn't going to win the day.

You're under arrest—BANG!

Bit his cheek to keep down a manic bray of laughter. Strange how the mind behaved under stress.

Windows too high up, no way to see inside except through the thin space where the two doors met. He switched his gun to a two-handed tactical grip and moved forward toward the sliver of light. Ten feet, body hugging the building. Closer, ready if Sponholz suddenly came bursting out. He paused, straining for any sound. Nothing. Forward again. A faint clatter somewhere inside. Finally at the doors, but the angle was off. He'd have to stand right in front if he wanted to look between them, which would make him a sitting duck if Sponholz saw him and decided to break leather.

Inside, the sound of running water, the impact of heavy spray inside a big, hollow container. Jarsdel decided to risk it. He slipped in front of the doors and looked in.

Harsh fluorescent work lights illuminated the barn. Bales of hay stacked high, a pitchfork with a badly bent tine leaning out of a blue trash can. Tools scattered haphazardly on the dirt floor. An equine first-aid kit, open, contents strewn on a plastic tabletop. Bottles of Betadine and rubbing alcohol, an oral syringe, stethoscope, tweezers, a turkey baster, a book—*Dr. Kellon's Guide to First Aid for Horses*, electrolyte paste, lavender oil. Medications he didn't recognize—AperEze, Vetericyn, ichthammol, nitrofurazone.

A box stall to the right, slatted door ajar and a hose snaking in. A figure popped into view, his back to Jarsdel. More spraying sounds, then the man ducked down.

He gripped the hasp of the left barn door and pulled. It opened on well-greased hinges. The smell of bleach, strong in the air. As he stepped inside, Jarsdel heard scrubbing, then liquid being poured from a container. The scrubbing resumed, and he approached the stall.

It wasn't very big, perhaps ten by twelve feet. Ed Sponholz, unarmed, stood over a large wooden tack box, scrubbing the sides with a dish brush. A bottle of Clorox sat uncapped nearby. Jarsdel lowered the gun to his side, but didn't holster it.

"'Your name points to calamity. It fits you well.'"

Sponholz stopped what he was doing, looked at Jarsdel, smiled, then went back to scrubbing. "What're you doing all the way out here?"

Jarsdel stepped nearer. The tack box was thick and sturdy, the lid fitted with a heavy hasp and staple. "That where you kept him?"

Sponholz gave no sign that he heard. "Might wanna stand back. Could get sprayed." He dropped the brush, picked up the hose, and squeezed the nozzle. A jet of water slapping wood, Sponholz wiggling his wrist back and forth, rinsing away the bleach. He put down the hose, retrieved the brush, and went back to scrubbing.

"Where's the horse?" said Jarsdel.

"Sold. Twenty grand. Guy wanted to put him out to stud, just like Jack Woltz was gonna do with Khartoum."

"How'd you find him?" said Jarsdel.

"Who? Guy who bought the horse?"

"The Creeper."

"The Creeper," said Sponholz. "Pretty crazy question."

"Not really. Not as crazy as kidnapping him and framing him for your wife's murder."

"Tully, I'm starting to get a little annoyed. I don't remember inviting you in here, and I'd really like some alone time right now."

"I'm putting you under arrest, Lieutenant."

Sponholz gave a low chuckle. "No, you're not."

"I am."

"Detective." Sponholz threw the brush into the tack box, hard, then glared at Jarsdel. "Whatever you think you know, you're wrong. Incorrect, understand? If you don't get out of here immediately, like right the hell now, you're finished as a detective. You've got no probable cause to be harassing me."

"I've got you on video going into Send It Packing."

Sponholz laughed. "So what? I go there all the time. They've got a very funny greeting card section."

"They've also got a photocopier. The one you used to make up the latest Creeper letter."

"That's a hell of an accusation. Especially since the only print you've got on it is from some hoodlum somewhere."

Jarsdel reached into his front pants pocket with his left hand, ignoring the sting of his wounds, and took out a folded piece of paper. He handed it to the lieutenant, who opened it. When he saw it was a copy of the Creeper letter from that morning, he looked unimpressed. "I've seen it."

"You didn't know his print was on it. No way you could have, because it would've been invisible until they hit it with the ninhydrin. You thought by photocopying it again and again, you'd make it harder to trace. Ironic—don't you think?—that the final copy you settled on happened to bear the thumbprint of a convicted felon. The most beautiful print the guys over at FSD ever saw, right? I wondered about that, how it got on there that way, with no amino acids on the back of the sheet. I mean, how do you handle a piece of paper without touching both sides? That's why I was so sure it was him at first. I thought he'd gotten sloppy, put his thumb on there when he mailed it. Classic confirmation bias. Decided he was guilty, then tried to make the pieces fit."

Jarsdel shook his head. "Ever load a copy machine, Lieutenant? Something I had to do pretty often when I taught college. It's easy, though. Grab a ream of paper. It's kinda heavy, so you grip it like this..." He demonstrated, shaping his hand as if he were holding a cheeseburger. "Load it in the tray. You do this a couple more times—those big machines can hold several reams. Close the tray. That's it. Of course, you'd leave a nice set of prints on the top and bottom page of each ream. The top one in particular, that'd be the real star, with the angle of the thumb being so straight, and all that downward pressure."

Sponholz looked bored. "You want this back?"

"Five hundred sheets in a ream. Copier probably midsize at a place like that, say five reams max. Means at the most there were ten sheets in that copier that would've sunk you. Ten, out of twenty-five hundred. You should play roulette."

Sponholz let go of the letter. It seesawed downward, landing in the wet dirt. "None of this impresses me, Detective. And it won't impress anybody else."

"Not to file charges, I agree. But it was enough to get the warrant."

The lieutenant cocked his head. He was affecting casual curiosity, but his lips had tightened. A crease appeared on his forehead. "Warrant? You don't need a warrant. You're welcome to look around as much as you like, if it makes you happy. I don't care—bring in a whole FSD team if you think I'm hiding something. I promise you there's nothing to find."

"I'm sure that's true. You had to have known we'd eventually figure out Bengochea didn't do it, and we'd find you on the security footage. Couldn't take the chance we'd come out here and find your prisoner. Had a good head start. And this bleach job looks about as thorough as you can get."

"Like I said," Sponholz shrugged, "feel free to take a tour. You won't find anything to corroborate these fantasies of yours. But if a warrant makes you feel better, I'll call Judge Monson and put it through myself."

"Oh, the warrant's not for here," said Jarsdel.

The lieutenant's eyes narrowed. "Where… I mean, okay, fine. Go execute it, then."

"No need. Detective Rall's on his way there now."

"Goodwin?" Sponholz looked uneasy. "You dragged him into this nonsense?"

Jarsdel examined the lieutenant carefully, paying close attention to his hands, making sure he didn't reach for anything.

"Where's he going? Wait—you know what? Don't tell me. See, I don't care, because it doesn't matter. There's nothing you can find anywhere that's going to implicate me. For the sake of argument, let's say I *wasn't* innocent of these bizarre and very ungentlemanly accusations. You're speaking to one of the most experienced murder cops in the world. A guy like that wouldn't make stupid mistakes."

"Everyone makes mistakes," said Jarsdel. "It was a mistake to alibi yourself at the gym when you normally don't sign in."

Sponholz's mouth twisted in a sneer. "That's your big reveal? Sign-in logs? Forgive me if I don't throw myself at your feet, pleading for mercy. And I gotta be honest with you, I'm not seeing a whole lot of the whiz-bang intellect you're supposed to have."

"Your letters, those were the big slipups," Jarsdel went on. "I understand why you wrote them, though. With the first one you wanted to back up your creaky demonology, numerology angle, get us all sniffing in the wrong direction. You had prints and contact DNA on it, too. With the second letter, you wanted to give a reason why the Creeper murders were about to end. He had to still be out there somewhere for you to get away totally clean. But you also knew he wasn't going to be making any more crime scenes, so you came up with that bit about his moving on and changing up his MO."

"Wow, you've got me," said Sponholz. "Oh, wait. No, you don't."

"No Creeper prints on that second letter. No DNA, either. Didn't have him anymore, did you?"

Sponholz seemed to notice Jarsdel's gun for the first time. "Holster that, Detective."

"Don't run when you're not being chased. Had a professor used to say that. Don't go out of your way to defend points that aren't being attacked. It just calls attention to them. You ran, Lieutenant, and nobody was chasing you."

"Holster your weapon, that's an order."

"You're under arrest. Against the wall."

"You've got no fucking proof!" Sponholz roared. "Not one thing! You're out of your goddamned mind if you think I'm going anywhere with you. Why don't you hand me that Glock and I'll blow your fucking head apart, because you might as well just kill yourself. I can't even tell you how many ways you're done."

He made a move toward him, and Jarsdel raised the gun, pointing it at Sponholz's heart.

Color left the lieutenant's face. "You'll burn for this. My God, what I'm gonna do to you."

"You've already done it," said Jarsdel. "Besides, I have a feeling you'll be pretty well occupied in the foreseeable future. That hole punch is going to be a major problem for your defense."

Sponholz stared at him. Blinked once, twice. "Hole punch?"

"You know, the one you used to make the letters in the first Creeper note."

"Hole punch," the lieutenant repeated. He spoke the words softly, almost lovingly.

"I'm guessing in a desk drawer back at your house." When Sponholz didn't answer, Jarsdel nodded. "Every tool's unique. Wear and tear, dullness, microscopic imperfections in the metal. FSD'll be able to match it to the note. Even if for some reason they couldn't, I bet we'd find the punched-out bits of paper in the little collecting tray."

Sponholz put out a hand, bracing himself against the side of the stall. His knees trembled. Jarsdel kept the gun on him anyway.

The lieutenant mumbled something.

"Again, please?"

"I said I'm very tired."

"Then I guess it's not all bad news," said Jarsdel. "At least you'll have plenty of time to rest. Turn around, hands on the wall."

Sponholz didn't move. "I feel so old now. I'm not that old, not really, but I feel like I am."

"The wall."

"I'm a peaceful person. Before all this, I never even got into a playground scuffle. It's a horrible thing, to be pushed into violence."

Jarsdel dipped his hand to his cuffs. "Hands. That's the last time."

Sponholz sagged, but he did as he was told. Jarsdel stepped forward. Keeping the gun pointed at the lieutenant's spine, Jarsdel snapped the first bracelet around the man's right wrist. The ratchet rasped loud in the empty barn. It was at that moment, just when Jarsdel had finished cuffing the first wrist and was reaching for the second, that it happened.

It didn't matter that Jarsdel had feared such an attack for so long. Even as it occurred, he marveled at the sluggishness of his reaction time. Sponholz went from stooped, dazed victimhood to pure animal frenzy so quickly that Jarsdel hadn't managed to put an ounce of pull on the trigger.

The lieutenant spun, whipping the free handcuff bracelet toward Jarsdel's face. It took him high on the cheek, right on the bone. Sharp, explosive pain, like a brand. Still, he tried bringing the Glock around to fire, but Sponholz was on him, both hands cinched around his forearm, swinging the barrel upward toward the ceiling.

A knee flew into Jarsdel's ribs—once, twice. His gun arm weakened. He tried keeping Sponholz back with the palm of his left hand, planting it on the man's chin and pushing hard.

Sponholz angled out of the way, and Jarsdel's hand went forward into empty space. Before he could recover, Sponholz darted in and seized Jarsdel's fingers between his teeth. Until then, their fight had been mostly silent. But as the lieutenant's teeth found the wounds and sawed through the stitches, Jarsdel screamed. He forgot about the gun—it didn't matter. Nothing mattered but that tremendous, consuming agony. It eclipsed all other thoughts, all other needs. Getting the pain to stop, that was all he wanted.

He let Sponholz have the gun. Sponholz let him have his hand back.

Jarsdel fell to his knees, cradling his mangled fingers. His dressings were sticky with blood. Drops pooled in his nail beds, welled, and fell to the dirt floor. Jarsdel could hear them hit.

"Sorry 'bout that." Sponholz said from somewhere far away. "We don't have a lot of time, though. Can you walk?"

Jarsdel's vision had blurred, even though he could feel his glasses were still on. He blinked, and everything cleared. Tears. He was crying. He couldn't remember the last time he'd cried from pain. He wiped his face with his sleeve.

"C'mon, get up. You gotta get up."

Groggy, Jarsdel lifted his head and found himself staring into the small black eye of his own weapon. A shudder passed through him, and he grew dizzy.

"Uh-uh, stay with me. You pass out and I'm gonna have to shoot you. I don't want to do that unless I absolutely have to."

"Feel sick."

"Throw up if you have to, but stay with me. Seriously, I also need you to get up and get moving. If you don't move, that'll be another reason to shoot you."

Jarsdel gripped the side of the stall and pulled himself to his feet. A new wave of dizziness hit him.

"Take a breath," said Sponholz.

Jarsdel did as he was told. Slowly in and slowly out.

"Hate to rush you, but again you've got about five seconds to get going before I put you out of your misery."

Jarsdel stumbled out of the stall toward the open barn doors. Once outside, he tried to turn and look back at Sponholz.

"Eyes forward," said the lieutenant.

Jarsdel continued on until he reached the steep, sandy slope near the barn. He angled his body sideways and picked his way carefully down the steps to the path below. The crunch of boots against the hard-packed earth told him Sponholz was very close behind.

"Where to now?" Jarsdel asked.

"Well, since I imagine they'll be looking for my car, we'll have to take yours. Give us a bit of a head start. You're parked down the road, I presume?"

Jarsdel nodded.

"Is that a yes? You're stumbling a little and it's pretty dark. You'll have to answer me vocally."

"Yes."

"Then keep doin' what you're doin'. Straight down the path to the gate."

A strange new warmth descended on Jarsdel. A feeling of relaxation totally at odds with his circumstances. He guessed this must be a wave of endorphins dispatched from his brain to help him survive. Part of him understood that if the pain took over, he wouldn't be able to continue, and that would mean the end of his life.

"Can I ask what the plan is?"

Sponholz gave a weary exhale. "I'll be honest with you. I'm kind of winging it here."

"Should I assume I'm not making it out of this alive?"

"I don't know. Please don't put that kind of pressure on me right now."

They were almost to the gate. "You can go ahead and open it," said Sponholz.

Carefully, keeping his left hand pressed protectively against his chest, Jarsdel pushed the gate away from him. It swung out, once again screeching and groaning.

"Awfully loud," said Sponholz. "Never really realized how loud it is. Okay, keep going."

"To where?"

"Oh, sorry. To your car."

The pain and the shot of endorphins acted as a kind of heavy blanket on Jarsdel's cognition. His thoughts were poorly defined, just shapes beneath the fabric, and he struggled to make them out. Soon they were to the main road. Jarsdel turned left, keeping to the shoulder.

"If a car comes, put your hands in your pockets and look casual. Two guys out for a stroll. If whoever's driving stops for whatever reason, I'll have to shoot you and anyone in the car."

"Why'd you kill your wife?" Jarsdel doubted it was a good idea to ask such a question, but he needed to keep his mind moving. If he could do that while keeping Sponholz's thoughts occupied, stalled out on the past, even better. To his surprise, the lieutenant answered.

"That's a very personal question. It's funny—I'm surprised at my own reaction to that. But it's true. Just seems oddly personal. In a way I'm glad you asked—helps to say it aloud. Okay. Number one, it was a loveless situation. I didn't hate her. It was just a cold, cold lifestyle. Never showed any interest in my work. And not in the things that really moved me. You know in all the years we were together, she only went to one play with me? *Miss Saigon*, and that was like two decades ago." He cleared his throat.

"I'm not explaining this very well. It sounds superficial to you, I imagine—*You nuts? Killed your wife over that?* Well, yes. She was a joyless nothing. And she had, as you know, this very lucrative policy in place, and... Well. It wears down on you, being married to someone who doesn't value you, doesn't appreciate you. Murder doesn't have to be about hatred. It can be about freedom. Even when I had my hands around her neck, it was less about doing violence than it was about moving on to something better. It was the least malicious murder in history."

Doing violence. The words echoed in Jarsdel's head, and he realized with a sense of gushing relief that all wasn't yet lost. He still had the Bodyguard Morales had given him. It was there, strapped to his ankle, packed with .357 special wadcutters that would act like mini deer slugs, each capable at this range of putting a hole in Sponholz the size of a quarter on one end and a softball on the other.

How to get to it without Sponholz sending a bullet into his spine?

"When you came to work that day, all beat up," said Jarsdel, "that was the Creeper, I'm assuming. You'd already caught him."

"It was worse than it looked. Fought like an animal. The scratches and bruises you saw, that was nothing. Bit me twice. One on the side and another on my left bicep. Didn't break the skin, but the bruises were hideous."

"And you made sure to bring coffee to Amy's work. Showcase your wounds so everyone could see them, see her alive, too. Roomful of witnesses."

"Pretty good, huh?"

Maybe if he pretended to sprain his ankle, he could reach down and pull the gun from the holster. "You kept him in that tack box? In the barn?"

The lieutenant didn't answer, and Jarsdel stopped moving. "How long?"

"Keep moving."

When Jarsdel resumed his shambling walk, Sponholz said, "Eleven days. Cut a little hole in the side so he'd have fresh air. Fed him. Hosed him down when he got too rank."

"And your wife? What was his role in all that?"

"Generous donor. Donated blood for Amy's mouth and the spatter on the lamp. Few strands of his hair, which I scattered judiciously. And of course he donated his right hand for all the prints I needed."

"Why the broom?"

"Help sell it. Horror and depravity. I see now it wasn't a good idea. You pegged it as bullshit right away. Kudos, et cetera."

The cruiser materialized out of the darkness, no more than a hundred yards away. Jarsdel had to figure out a way to get to the weapon.

"The letters," he began, but Sponholz cut him off.

"Used his left hand, while it was still attached, to deposit prints and contact DNA on letter number one. The right hand by then was highly necrotic, and I was worried there wouldn't have been sufficient oils in the skin, so I threw it out. By the time the Michews came along, the Creeper was dead, hand dried out. That's why I made only patent prints in blood. I also made sure to rake her nails over the skin a few times, get some epithelials in there."

"What about the teeth marks on Natalie Minchew's thigh?"

"Old-fashioned way. With his teeth."

"You removed his teeth?"

"No, that's idiotic. I removed his head. Then it was simply a matter of opening the jaw and clamping it down manually."

Jarsdel felt heat rising in his cheeks. "Why?"

"Why what?"

"Why kill the Minchews? What were they to you?"

"That's the point, Tully. Weren't anything to me. Completely unconnected no matter how many COMPSTAT systems you sicced on 'em. Chosen at random at the Sherman Oaks Galleria."

"I still don't understand."

"You pushed me to it. I didn't have a choice."

"It's my fault?"

"I'm not gonna say it's your fault directly. I'm responsible for the things I do. But I can definitively say that if you hadn't cornered me that day you came over to the house—all your questions and everything... Yeah. They'd still be alive today, least as far as I'd be concerned. Meteors and what not, I can't guarantee."

Fifty yards to the cruiser. An icy fist turned in Jarsdel's stomach. "Clarify this, please."

"Nothing much to it. Needed the Creeper to kill someone else to take suspicion off me. Someone I would've had no motive to harm. Sounds pretty heartless, but until you've been in a situation like that, where you need to keep shoring things up to keep yourself safe, you can't really have an opinion. If you'd asked me a month ago, I would've said I didn't have it in me. You discover things about yourself when the chips are down."

"You suffocated a six-year-old girl."

"Not something I celebrate. But if I'd left her alive, you woulda wondered why. Besides, what kind of life would that've been for her, with both parents gone?"

They were almost at the car. Whatever Sponholz had in store for him would happen soon. Whether he'd gun Jarsdel down and take the cruiser or keep him hostage in case they met up with some cops, it wasn't much of a future. Once Sponholz threw him in the back of the squad car—no door handles, stuck behind a thick plexiglass shield, there was no way it could end well.

"Oh." Jarsdel lurched forward and clutched at his stomach. "Feel sick." He fell to one knee, bracing himself against the night-cooled ground with the palm of his good hand. He immediately realized he'd need that hand to get to the gun, so he pitched sideways, curling his body, bending his knees and scooting the ankle holster within his reach.

He glanced up at Sponholz. The lieutenant looked back at him, his expression oddly vacant. Jarsdel tugged at the leg of his slacks. Night air kissed the skin on his bare calf. His fingers brushed against the warm grip of the pistol.

"Groggy. A little dizzy," he said.

"This the end of the road?" said Sponholz. He made a little figure eight in the air with the Glock.

"I'm almost—"

"This sucks. I'm really sorry."

Jarsdel's hand closed around the grip of the Bodyguard. He tried not to let the victory show on his face. "I'm getting up. Don't shoot." He pulled the gun free and began to roll onto his back.

"Gotta get up quick if you're—hey!" Sponholz leapt forward, slamming his work boot down on Jarsdel's arm, just below the elbow.

Twice more—fast. The twin bones of his forearm snapped—he could hear them go—and the agony followed right behind. He shouted something wild, incoherent—a cry from his soul. It was like no sound he'd made before, and it took a moment to realize it was coming from him. Jarsdel's hand spasmed, releasing the gun. Didn't matter—he wouldn't be able to lift it now anyway.

"Stupid," said Sponholz, nudging the Bodyguard out of reach with the toe of his work boot. "Stupid as the day is long." He raised the Glock, pointing it at Jarsdel's face. "Bet that hurts, huh?"

Jarsdel willed his hand to move, to grab for the gun anyway, and succeeded only in rubbing his fingers against the fabric of his pants. Something in his pocket made a soft *clink*. Curious, he touched it again. Whatever it was separated into several pieces. Small, hard edges, metal. His keys, of course.

His keys.

He worked at them through the cloth, tugging them up toward the lip of his pocket. Terrific, urgent pain as his tendons yanked on his fractured bones. He wouldn't be able to get the keys free.

"Wanna close your eyes?" said Sponholz.

His pants were thin enough that he could make out the shape of each object. It was just one he cared about, small and egg-shaped. And there it was.

"Suit yourself."

Jarsdel's thumb found the raised surface of the button on the SkyTrace key fob. He pressed it twice.

A vibrant green dot appeared on Sponholz's leg. From behind Jarsdel, there came the whir of a motor.

Sponholz squinted at the squad car. "What's the—"

It was all he managed to say. The air cannon gave a short whooshing cough, and the SkyTrace tracker slammed into Sponholz's knee. He yelled in pain and confusion, squeezing the Glock's trigger and firing a shot that went screaming off the asphalt. His hand was unprepared for the recoil, and the gun leapt out of his grip like something alive.

"Wow! Shit—what is it? Tully!"

Sponholz stumbled backward, battling with the strange protrusion, swatting it, yanking at it. Jarsdel swung a leg to intercept the lieutenant's retreating footsteps. He hooked Sponholz's heel, and the man was airborne, eyes bugging in surprise. He landed hard and let out a howl.

"Oh no! Oh my God..."

Jarsdel's right hand was useless, so he had no choice but to use his left. He rolled over his broken arm, straining to reach the Bodyguard. It was too far, at least a foot beyond his fingertips.

"Oh, no, no, no! Wow!"

Jarsdel got to his knees. Neither of his hands could support him, so his knees took the full weight. His progress was slow, the rocks and pebbles of the shoulder pressing into his skin.

"Wow, oh man. Man, oh man." Sponholz groaned. "Right on the tailbone. Could be broken—God! Oh no, no no. What are you doing? What are you gonna do?"

Jarsdel shivered. His skin had broken out in a cool sweat, and the burning in his arm seemed muted somehow.

I'm going into shock.

He reached the Bodyguard and extended his trembling, bloodied left hand.

"Gonna shoot me, Tully?"

Jarsdel sensed movement from Sponholz's direction, heard the slap of hands against asphalt. Another groan as the lieutenant shifted his weight. He was looking for the Glock.

Jarsdel picked up the Bodyguard, astonished at how heavy it seemed. A five-round cylinder, the wadcutters packed inside like little steel fists.

"You shoot me, and you'll never know who the Creeper is."

Jarsdel fell back into a sitting position. He looked over at Sponholz, who was crawling along the shoulder. Moonlight glinted dully off the Glock. Two feet away and closing.

"Be the biggest boogeyman LA's ever had," Sponholz went on. "Tear yourselves to pieces looking for him."

Jarsdel aimed at the lieutenant's ribs, but the macerated fingers of his left hand refused to hold the weapon steady. The barrel sagged. Without thinking, he tried bringing his right hand up to support the gun. His shoulder moved, and the nerves in his forearm shrieked as the fragments of bone ground against each other, but that was all.

Sponholz was almost at the Glock, and there was nothing wrong with his hands.

Jarsdel closed his fingers around the Bodyguard's grip, ignoring the electric pain. He closed his knees, making an impromptu shooting rest, and notched his wrist in the gap.

"You'll tear yours—"

Jarsdel fired three times. Sponholz's body jumped as if pulled by invisible ropes, his jaw vanishing in a spray made black by the moonlight. He spun onto his back—one hand arcing before bouncing lifelessly off the pavement, still clutching the Glock.

Jarsdel watched and listened. He expected a final tremble, an exhale, a slow falling of the chest. Nothing happened, and he thought perhaps Sponholz wasn't really dead, that the best thing to do would be to put the remaining two shots into the sprawled form.

But he realized there would be no change, not while he watched. It had already happened. The teeming bacteria inside the lieutenant's gut would never go to work on another taco plate from Señor Fish. Their next meal would be the host itself.

Jarsdel had killed a man. Had torn Edwin Darrel Sponholz apart with a handful of wadcutters and sent him careening into whatever was next, or whatever wasn't. His mind told him this was the most important moment in his life, the place of starkest divide between before and after. His mind told him he needed to understand the significance of what he'd just done, that he needed to feel it deeply and have it sit with him for days and weeks, and only after an appropriate amount of time had passed could he demote it from his fullest attention. And it had a right to haunt him, because it was a homicide, a taking of a life. Even villains had a right to haunt you if you killed them.

His mind told him these things and a thousand more, but he was too tired to listen. He lay down on the dry grass bordering the gravel shoulder, turning his face to the limitless, twinkling sky.

26

Jarsdel stood in Varma's office. Without her paperwork and laptop, there wasn't much to see. Her two shallow desk drawers were empty except for a dried-out ballpoint and a handful of paper clips. The only thing remaining that hinted at the identity of the late tenant was the poster of the three men, sated to the point of stupefaction, lying beneath the strange, leafless tree. Jarsdel wondered what it meant—the roast pig trotting around with a carving knife shoved in its back, the soft-boiled egg running on those plump little legs, the figure emerging from the thick, creamy cloud, spoon gripped triumphantly ahead.

"Tully? Hey. Didn't know you were back."

Jarsdel turned and saw Kay Barnhardt. "Hey," he said. "Not sure I'm back, actually. Kind of in limbo right now."

"Are you..." She gestured at his right arm. It was visibly thinner than his left, the muscles still awakening from atrophy since the cast was removed.

"Fine," said Jarsdel. "Better every day."

"They gonna put you with Morales again?"

"Gavin hasn't decided yet. So he says."

"He's looking for you, by the way."

"Gavin? Wonderful. Useless mooncalf."

"Might want to tread carefully," said Barnhardt, with an uncharacteristically impish smile. "Hasn't been in the best of moods."

"Yeah?"

"I was in his office the other day about a case, and he started in with his amateur scientist routine again. I was frankly tired of it, so I thought fine, he wants to talk science, we'll talk science."

Jarsdel grinned. "He had trouble keeping up?"

She held her thumb and forefinger an inch apart. "Just a little. I think it really stopped being fun for him when I asked his opinion on the Higgs boson and its relationship to mass generation theory."

"You have the thanks of a grateful department," said Jarsdel.

"My pleasure. So what're you doing in here?"

He glanced at the poster. "Looking for answers, I guess. Don't know exactly what I was hoping for."

"Closure, I'd imagine."

Jarsdel shrugged. "Not really sure what there is to close. Hardly knew each other."

"She was charismatic," said Barnhardt. "It's easy to understand why we believed in her."

Jarsdel was uncomfortable. "What about you? Must bother you. I know you admired her work."

"I did. That's true." Barnhardt stepped into the room, then looked up to study the painting. "Strange choice. Cockaigne. Should've asked her about it."

"What? Cocaine?"

"Cockaigne. Different spelling. The land of plenty, where all your wishes are granted. Medieval peasants used to fantasize about a place where the social order was upended, where food and sex were always available, where you never had to work, and the weather was nice year-round. You know the song 'Big Rock Candy Mountain'?"

"Maybe. Sounds familiar."

"It was in *O Brother, Where Art Thou*? The Coen brothers movie."

Jarsdel shook his head. "Sorry, not a big movie guy. Something I'm working on, though."

"Anyway, it deals with the Cockaigne mythos. Updated for the twentieth century, but the basic ideas are still the same. An Edenic wonderland, a surrogate heaven—maybe even better than the *actual* heaven, since it exists outside the strictures of morality or religion. You don't have to sacrifice anything, don't have to transcend yourself or conquer sin and desire. In other words, no need for the purity of mind and body demanded by God. Come as you are, all your ego intact."

"What's the catch?" said Jarsdel.

"There is no catch. That's the point. You get there and that's the end. That's your destination."

"Where d'you go after? Back to the real world?"

"There is no after. That's the end, that's the reward."

"Reward? These people get to sidestep their final judgment? Seems like the Church wouldn't have liked the concept very much."

"It didn't. But Cockaigne wasn't connected with an opposing theology. I mean, no one actually *believed* in Cockaigne, or thought they'd eventually make it there. There was no pagan deity overseeing the place. It was more like a 'fuck you' to reality. A place to daydream about and escape from the unpleasantries of daily life."

Jarsdel regarded the print on the wall with renewed curiosity. "Doesn't look nearly as much fun as the brochure."

"Well, that's the statement this artist is making. Bruegel the Elder. Didn't think much of gross pleasures, so he envisioned Cockaigne more as a kind of cultural sinkhole." She pointed at the three men lying beneath the craggy tree. "Here're the major archetypes of the time—the knight, the farmer, and the scholar. But they're just deadweight now. Farmer isn't farming. You can see he's sleeping on top of his flail. The scholar isn't reading his book, and the knight has abandoned his lance. Give people everything they want, Bruegel suggests, and they abandon their responsibilities. Society just falls apart."

"But I don't get it," said Jarsdel. "It's not a real place, so it's not as if there was an actual danger of something like this happening. It's like warning people to stay out of Willy Wonka's factory."

Barnhardt considered. "More like he was telling people their fantasies were stupid, shallow, borne of ignorance. That they weren't smart enough to know what was best for them."

"No wonder Varma liked it." Jarsdel looked at the painting again. "Does anyone ever really get closure? I mean in general. Just out of curiosity."

"No."

He turned to face her. "No?"

Barnhardt shook her head. "Closure's not something you can *get* from an external source. It's something you create, something you build within yourself."

"I don't understand her. Why she did the things she did."

"You might never. And that's okay. Not your job to know everything."

"It bothers me for more than just that reason," he said. "She was brilliant. Varma was brilliant. There's no arguing against that. And if here you have a person *that* smart who was pushed to such a desperate act as faking an assault, you have to wonder if maybe the decision was *intelligent*, or that it was at least informed. Maybe her ideas were so obviously correct that she absolutely had to get them into use." He left out the part about her slicing his hand open. He'd somehow been able to quarantine that troublesome fact in his own mind, keeping it separate so it didn't contaminate his new thesis.

Barnhardt looked at him with nearly the identical sad expression Morales had given him in his apartment. "Sounds like special pleading. You really believe that?"

"She was smart."

"Yes."

"She knew better than to fudge her numbers and massage the data to get herself seen."

"Yes."

"Yes—so exactly, right? Doesn't that say something?"

"It does," Barnhardt agreed. "Says she had a personality disorder."

"I was counting on her." The words were out before he could vet them.

"To do what?"

"Don't think I ever really thought it through. Vague stuff, visions of the city coming together, everything made suddenly, effortlessly whole. We'd be model of utopic possibility, and somehow it would just flow outward from there and in a few years we'd be living under the benevolent guidance of philosopher kings."

"A magic bullet?" She didn't make a meal out of it, didn't have to.

"Yeah," said Jarsdel. "I know there's no such thing. Never has been. Except maybe just this once, maybe it was true."

Another meeting in another office. Regardless of what Gavin had to say to him, Jarsdel thought, he was going to take a week off the moment he was out of that chair. He didn't care if the mayor summoned him; it would be a week with no offices or desks. Maybe to Catalina Island. The Pavilion Hotel had wine and cheese on the patio each evening, and he could spend his days walking Avalon and reading—get through two or three books at Café Metropole or the Descanso Beach Club.

Gavin cleared his throat, and Jarsdel reluctantly turned his attention to the present moment.

"I'm putting you and Morales back together."

Jarsdel's surprise was total. He wanted to make sure he'd heard correctly. "Oscar and me?"

"Detective Haarmann's being reassigned."

"Why? To where?"

Gavin regarded Jarsdel with uncharacteristic thoughtfulness. "Anonymous complaint against him through IAG. Unsavory conduct while on duty. It's that easy in today's world, I guess. Anonymous complaint's all it takes, and your life changes."

Jarsdel didn't comment.

"That seem fair to you, Detective?"

"Was it true?"

Gavin hesitated, cleared his throat again. "Looks that way. Man likes his badge bunnies. Not the only one in the department who does, just the one unlucky enough to get caught."

"Then I'm not sure fairness enters into it."

The lieutenant nodded. "Okay. Remember you said that. About fairness not entering into it. Those are the kind of words that have a funny way of coming back around. So remember them. I know I will."

Jarsdel hardly heard him. There was something different about Gavin's office, and it took him a moment to place it. Once he did, he thought of what Barnhardt had said to him about her last meeting in here.

The Max Planck picture was gone, nothing in its place but a bare patch of wall. Jarsdel glanced discreetly around the room. No artfully planted science textbooks, no Newton's cradle, no copies of *A Short History of Nearly Everything* on the bookshelf.

"Anyway, that's it. That's all I wanted to tell you." Gavin leaned back, his attention now on the ceiling.

Jarsdel was apparently dismissed. He stood and reached for the door, then stopped. "Oh, sir?"

"What?"

Jarsdel pointed at the wall behind Gavin's desk. "Where's the picture?"

"Huh?"

"Didn't you have a photo there of Max Planck?"

Gavin sucked on his teeth. It didn't look like he was going to answer, then he said, "Got tired of having to keep explaining who he was."

27

By late October, the summer heat had finally begun to recede, and Angelenos were getting their evenings back. There in Pasadena, it was actually cool.

Jarsdel rang the doorbell. While he waited, he gazed up at the second floor, at a window toward the left-hand corner of the house. His room for eighteen years. He wondered how long it had been since he stood inside and looked out.

There was a rattling sound on the other side of the door. It opened and Baba stood there, clearly surprised to see him. Glad, Jarsdel wasn't sure. But definitely surprised.

"Tully. I didn't know you were coming. Did you call?"

"No."

"You drove all the way over here without calling? What if we hadn't been home?"

"I'd've gone down to Fair Oaks Pharmacy, had an orange cream soda. Then come back later."

Baba regarded him suspiciously. "What's happening?"

"Is Dad home?"

"He's resting."

"Can I come in?"

Baba hesitated, then stood aside. Once Jarsdel had gone past him,

Baba locked the door, set the security chain, and threw a new, shiny dead bolt.

"Creeper's dead, you know," said Jarsdel.

"So they say. Want something to drink?"

"I'm fine."

"Sparkling water? Tea?"

"I'm fine, really."

They went to the living room. A cloud of motes rose in the graying light as Jarsdel sank into the oversoft couch. Baba sat across in his favorite chair—a Louis XIV he insisted was authentic, but Jarsdel had his doubts. No one else ever sat in it. The thing was as rigid and unyielding as its owner.

Baba flicked on a table lamp. "What's going on? Everything all right?"

"I wanted to talk to you about what happened at the Farmers Market."

Baba wagged his finger. "Unnecessary. We got it. It's part of your job. Just made us uncomfortable. But there's no bad feelings."

"I guess I thought—I don't know—like we were close to making some progress, the three of us. And then that guy showed up, and it was just very bad timing."

"Maybe, maybe not. Could be it was very good timing. Certainly gave us a bit of a wake-up call. Your job wasn't so abstract to us after that."

"So now you're even less on board with it?"

"Tully"—Baba sighed—"what do you want from us? We're not your audience for this."

"My audience?"

"Think of it as a literary piece. What's a book you loved that I didn't?"

"Lot to choose from. All the original James Bonds, I guess. Started those when I was nine, and each time you saw me reading one, I thought someone you were close to had died. You honestly looked that stricken."

"I did not. Ridiculous."

Jarsdel nodded. "You absolutely did. Like this." He imitated the sorrowful, agonized expression he remembered so well.

Baba smiled despite himself. "Okay. They're not my favorite. So heteronormative."

Jarsdel rolled his eyes.

"Anyway," Baba went on. "Think of it like that. Like your job is a work of literature that doesn't connect to us, and probably never will. I don't think I'm all of a sudden going to pick up *Thunderfinger* or whatever and say it's great."

"Tully?"

Both men turned to see Dad standing in the doorway. He was even thinner than the last time Jarsdel had seen him, ghostlike in the low light.

"Robert," said Baba, standing. "Did we wake you?"

"I heard my boy," he said. "Scoot over, son."

Jarsdel did, and his father sat next to him, taking his hand. He wore sweatpants and a USC Trojans shirt, which had most certainly been a gift. Jarsdel doubted that in all his father's decades as a tenured professor he'd been to a single game.

Baba returned to his chair, the concern on his face apparent. "Sure you're okay to be up?"

"I feel much better, really." He patted Jarsdel's hand and smiled at him. "Missed you."

"Missed you too, Dad." He noticed deposits of mucus in the corners of his father's mouth, and his breath was terrible. But he didn't move away. Instead he reached for him and they embraced. Jarsdel could feel the man's heart, once so strong, fluttering through the thin cage of his chest.

Dad patted his back and released him. "I didn't know you were coming over. Did you, Dary?"

Baba shook his head.

"Is everything okay? Do you need something?"

"I just wanted to see you. Both of you. I'm having a tough time with something, and I was wondering if I could talk about it with you. I know it's not a subject you enjoy, but I could really use some help right now."

"Of course," Dad said. "Anything."

Jarsdel looked at Baba, who nodded. "Okay. You both saw, probably, about my lieutenant at RHD."

Neither Dad nor Baba replied.

"You heard what I did?"

Baba looked down at his lap, but Dad held Jarsdel's gaze. "We heard. We didn't know what to say to you, or if we should say anything at all."

"Before it happened, he said…he said he killed that family, the one after he killed his wife…he said he killed them because of me. Because I'd forced him into it. Explained that if I hadn't asked him so many questions to try to shoot down his story, he wouldn't've had to do it."

"Oh, Tully." Dad gripped his hand tighter. Baba left the Louis XIV and sat on Jarsdel's right. He had to squeeze in tight between his son and the arm of the sofa, and there was hardly any room. But Jarsdel didn't mind at all. He loved feeling his parents on either side of him, pressing close. Baba kissed the side of his head.

"I don't know why I'm bringing this to you," Jarsdel said. "I know I don't have any right to. It's not your problem to fix. And you warned me. You definitely warned me. How much this job would hurt."

No one spoke for a while, then Baba said, "No. None of that matters. You're our son. You can always come to us. God forgive us if we made you think otherwise."

"Always," Dad agreed. "Always, always, Tully. Our sweet boy."

Jarsdel nodded. "Thank you." He closed his eyes a moment, trying to build enough courage to ask what needed to be asked. It didn't come, so he asked anyway. "You're sick, aren't you?"

"Yes," Dad said. "I am."

"What do we do?"

Baba reached out his arm, drawing in both of them. The three men together, bound tightly.

EPILOGUE: JANUARY

Morales was at already at work, though the sun hadn't yet crested the San Gabriel Mountains.

"Nice of you to join me." His pen flicked down the margins of what looked like an interview transcript.

Jarsdel sat. Their desks faced each other, pressed together to save space in the cramped squad room. He yawned. Morales glanced at him, irritated. "Sorry," said Jarsdel. "Tired."

"Yeah, not having a wife and kids'll do that to you. Maybe you should take some time off."

"What're you working on?"

"The barbershop thing."

The week before, there'd been a shooting outside a barbershop on the corner of Hollywood and Edgemont. The suspect was still at large, but Jarsdel and Morales had a solid description and a partial plate.

"Anything good?" Jarsdel asked.

"Good, not great." Morales circled something on the page and scrawled out a note. He pressed hard into the paper, almost as if he were carving instead of writing. Jarsdel had seen Morales's field notebook, and page after page was pocked with little tears in the paper where the nub of his pen had broken through. "This is from the guy at the car wash down the street. Says he saw someone matching our suspect's description. Arguing, yelling and stuff, right in the doorway with the victim."

"Good," said Jarsdel. "Anything I can help with?"

"How's your Spanish?"

Jarsdel didn't answer.

"All those brains and never thought to learn *español*? In California?"

Jarsdel swung his briefcase into its usual spot underneath his desk, but it struck something heavy and unmoving. He looked to see what the problem was and discovered the box he'd brought back from PAB. This happened every day, sometimes more than once. He'd jam his leg on the box or try to put something under there just to have it bounce off. And each time he'd chastise himself, resolve that would be the day he'd finally deal with those murder books. And each time he'd become distracted and forget—willfully, he supposed—and go through it all over again.

"Oscar."

"What?"

"Need me for anything?"

Morales stopped making notes, the top of his pen hovering above the page. "I said unless—"

"Right, I know. I'm just bringing it up because otherwise I should probably deal with this box I got here."

Morales looked at him, eyes narrowed. "Huh?"

"Mentioning it as a courtesy. It'll take me out of commission for a little bit since I'll have to take these over to archives."

"Who cares? Whatever, go. I'm fine." He went back to the transcript.

Jarsdel glanced at the wall clock. Not quite six thirty. The station was still quiet. Around nine, the first arrests would start trickling in, building steadily throughout the day and eventually hitting their peak at midnight. Then the noise would drop off dramatically, stopping altogether by 5:00 a.m., and for a blissful few hours the station would be quiet again. The five-to-nine ceasefire was so dependable that it seemed like official criminal policy, as if they'd had a union meeting on it.

He was doing it again, he knew. Stalling. "*Fugit inreparabile tempus*," Jarsdel muttered. He reached under the desk, hooked a finger over the side of the box, and dragged it into the light. Of course, the one he least wanted to see was right on top.

```
MURDER          DR 21—0825790
```

The Lauterbachs. Bill and Joanne. A worker's comp attorney and an English teacher, both retired. Bill Lauterbach had been alive when the Creeper cut off his eyelids, though it was doubtful he'd been conscious. He'd already lost so much blood from the bite wound to the groin. Joanne had lived at least another day. The Creeper had used his teeth on her as well, taking her nose, her lips, and the nipples of both breasts. One of which had never been recovered.

Who were you?

He studied the cover of the murder book, running his fingers over the textured letters of the DYMO type.

```
VICTIMS         LAUTERBACH, JOANNE ROSE
                LAUTERBACH, WILLIAM ALAN
                1320 HOLLYRIDGE LOOP
DATE/TIME       1-5-21
DETECTIVES      JARSDEL/MORALES
```

Who were you?

No one would ever know. Sponholz had been right about that. He'd been right as well about Los Angeles tearing itself to pieces. Crime stats had plateaued at a steady high—numbers that hadn't been seen since '81. And since Varma's fall from grace, the city was fighting lawsuits over her anti-affordances. Fourteenth Amendment complaints mostly, though a few were claiming physical damages. Sonic Fence, ReliaBench, PuraLux—their days were numbered.

George E. Waring Park was a hairbreadth away from being handed back over to the Future Felons of America.

The Creeper. It was always back to the Creeper. LA's boogeyman, the true Master of Midnight. Without a name, he wasn't human. Without a face, he'd be immortal.

And yet, Sponholz had found him.

Jarsdel set the Lauterbach book on his desk. Next in the box was the Galka book. He thumbed through the page numbers, careful not to crack it open any more than he had to. The Creeper had given him enough nightmares for a lifetime, and he never wanted to see Margot Galka's mauled genitals or Zephyr's peeled face again. When he found what he was looking for, he laid the book flat.

Six photographs in the spread. Three interior shots—pinecones with feces, blood-smeared family photo, piece of dark-red plastic. Three exterior shots—mailbox, garage, and of course the one Sponholz had claimed to be so crazy about. The Galka's address placard next to a bloody handprint. 10306, five numbers spun into an elaborate, labored misdirection.

Jarsdel had agonized over those photographs. Everyone in RHD had after Sponholz was killed. After they failed to find anything, the FBI had given it a try. Nothing.

What did you see? What did you see on these two pages that led you to him?

Jarsdel set the book on top of the Lauterbachs'.

The Lauterbachs.

Sponholz had asked to see that one, too, hadn't he? Jarsdel tried to remember.

Yes. That day at PAB, the day before he'd shown up with his black eye and bullshit story about falling into a tree, Edwin Darrel Sponholz had asked to borrow the Lauterbach book. It was an impressive performance—overt caginess with just the right amount of Sponholz-brand humility thrown in. How his interest was based on nothing more than a little hunch, something he didn't want to talk about in case he was wrong. "Which I probably am," he'd said.

Jarsdel remembered that. Sponholz, a man who'd throttle the life out of you and apologize the whole time.

First he'd noticed something in the Galka scene; then he'd wanted to see the Lauterbachs'. Why?

Jarsdel took the Lauterbach book from beneath the Galka one and checked the table of contents. Section 17: Crime Scene Photos. He ran his index finger down the tabs until he reached the correct number, then opened to a spread of gore. Jarsdel forced himself to look, and to look carefully.

Joanne's mashed body. Bill's horror-stricken, staring eyes. He turned the pages slowly.

Close-up shots of the claw hammer, of fingerprints, of teeth marks in flesh. More pages. More blood—blood everywhere. Blood on the bed, on the floor, on the walls. Blood on the windows. Blood seeping from a crack in the second-story stucco.

The image called up Porter's haunted voice—

The house is bleeding.

The ground-floor exterior now. The metal watering can Officer Banning had used as a step stool. The Creeper's entry hole, cut right through the wall.

More close-up shots. Strands of hair clinging to plaster, a piece of yellow plastic, footprints preserved in mud.

Jarsdel turned the page, squinted as the merest shadow of an idea passed through his mind, and turned back.

A sliver of yellow plastic. A corner on one side, a nice concave arc on the other. Something cut from a larger piece.

He left the book open at that spot, then turned to the infamous six-picture spread in the Galka book. He put the two side by side.

A sliver of red plastic. Cut the same way—a corner opposite a concave arc.

"Shit."

Jarsdel nearly jumped out of his seat. He looked up to see Morales standing behind him, staring down at the images.

"What are they?"

"Don't know," said Jarsdel, staring at the pieces, willing them to reveal their importance to him.

"They mean anything?"

"I said I don't know."

"Must've meant something to Sponholz though, huh?"

Jarsdel didn't answer. He was thinking about Sponholz, about how the lieutenant had reacted when he'd first been mesmerized by the picture. What had he said? An insult, Jarsdel thought it had been. Asshole? Son of a bitch? No.

"Bastard," said Jarsdel.

"Huh? Who?"

"Sponholz blurted it out when he saw this picture. At the time we all assumed he was talking about the Creeper."

Morales didn't speak, and Jarsdel knew it was because his partner understood how his mind worked—when he needed silence and when he needed to talk. They made a good team.

The house is bleeding.

That again. Why was that important? Yes, the Creeper was a monster, and he'd beaten Joanne Lauterbach so badly that her blood had leaked into the floor and the wall and out the fracture in the stucco. The fracture that wouldn't have been there if not for that earthquake, the one that had released valley fever.

Al-Amuli's voice, of all people, from that night at the Tiki-Ti. Jarsdel had been drunk, but Al-Amuli's soliloquy had come after the reprimand from Sponholz, so it had stuck with him.

Ever since that earthquake. Remember? That earthquake, way back in January. All from there.

Sponholz had even picked up the thread after Al-Amuli had left. He'd talked about the spores, and about how the Creeper seemed to come out of the ground right along with them. The spores that had killed two trees in his yard. He'd called the earthquake the source of all his troubles, even predicted it would cost him his ticket to *Phantom*, which it did.

Jarsdel was aware of Morales standing there, was aware of the pictures in front of him, was aware of the gradually waking station. But his mind was with the past.

My mind's always with the past, Jarsdel thought. *That's my strength. It's where all the answers are.*

What did the Galkas and the Lauterbachs have in common? The plastic—red and yellow, similar size and shape. That, and they'd both been killed after an earthquake. Jarsdel remembered that well. Would always remember those terrible days last summer. The second big earthquake, followed by the death of that poor patrol officer when he'd gone to arrest Degraffenreid. The end-of-watch call. A moment of citywide silence on the police band. Then Jarsdel had woken the next morning to news of the Galkas.

Bastard, Sponholz had said, seeing the sliver of red plastic. Then he'd wanted to see the Lauterbach book, and in that one he'd seen a sliver of yellow plastic. And then he'd caught the Creeper. How had he known to check the Lauterbach book? What did the earthquakes have to do with the plastic?

"Oscar."

"Right here."

Jarsdel gave the cardboard box a shove with his foot. "Check out Santiago, Verheugen, and Rustad. See if you can find any more pictures of plastic looking like these ones here."

"On it." Morales picked up the box and went back to his desk. While Jarsdel waited, he continued to stare at the two pictures.

It's official. LA run of Phantom's *canceled*. Sponholz's words.

Canceled because of the quake. Damage to the theater, to his beloved Pantages.

"No plastic in Verheugen," said Morales. "I mean, I'm going quick, but I don't think it's there."

Jarsdel registered the comment, then put it aside. He was back with Sponholz. Sponholz lamenting that he didn't know when he'd get his refund back. Something else, too.

Right. All those poor actors out of work.

Actors. What had Sponholz said about them? That these days they were spoiled rotten. They didn't have to learn all the crafts of their predecessors. Insurance wouldn't let them. Not like Sponholz, swinging around like Quasimodo, hanging lights from the grid.

Right, thought Jarsdel. *Back then they did it all. Set-building, costumes, everything.*

Sponholz's words came back, louder—

Swinging around like Quasimodo, hanging lights from the grid.

Something about Quasimodo? No. Something about lights?

"No plastic in Santiago," said Morales.

Varma now. Her office the first time they'd met. How she talked about her work with lighting designers.

Jarsdel closed his eyes.

Bastard Red.

The gel in Varma's book of samples. The red plastic on the Galka carpet. Sponholz had known exactly what it was, had nearly blurted out its name.

The plastic slivers were bits of lighting gel.

"You won't find any plastic in Rustad," he said to Morales.

"Why not?"

"Because the Creeper was out of work."

Morales raised his eyes from the Rustad book and stared at Jarsdel.

Swinging around like Quasimodo, hanging lights from the grid. Sponholz's words, and he'd been close. Not Quasimodo, though. It wasn't a great analogy. Quasimodo lived in a cathedral. The Phantom of the Opera, on the other hand, lived in a theater.

"He's a lighting tech," said Jarsdel. "Also explains why he doesn't mind heights. January quake closed the Pantages. Everyone's out of work." He tapped the photograph in the Lauterbach book. "They trim these to cover the stage lights. He still had bits of this on his shoes, maybe his clothes. As the weeks pass, he doesn't come into contact with it again. Kills the Rustads, Santiagos, Verheugens. Then we get that little lull. Why? Because he's back at work. Theater's about to reopen. Then the second earthquake comes along, closes the place for good. He kills the Galkas." Jarsdel pointed to the piece of red plastic on the carpet. "And he leaves this."

Morales stood, putting on his sport coat. "Gotta find out the names of everyone who worked on that show. Cross-reference them with their driver's licenses. Looking for someone small, so we can rule out anyone over five-four. Then we'll just see which of those guys have disappeared."

"Meant to give this back to you," Jarsdel said. He bent over and unstrapped the holstered revolver from his ankle. He offered it to Morales, who shook his head.

"Nah. You keep it, Dragonslayer." He began to move off, then noticed his partner hadn't stood. "What's the matter—you ain't comin'?"

"In a minute."

"Don't go off in your own little world. We got shit to do."

"I know. I'll meet you outside."

Morales left the squad room.

Dragonslayer. He supposed it was an improvement over *Dad* or *Prof*.

"Master of Midnight," he murmured, closing the murder books. "I'll know your name, your face. And you'll be master of nothing."

Tully Jarsdel strapped the Bodyguard back onto his ankle. He'd reloaded it with wadcutters, just like before.

By the time he made it out to the parking lot, a light rain had begun to fall. It had been a cold, dry winter, and the air was suddenly alive and rich with smells. Petrichor, it was called. The peculiar, pleasant bouquet of scents accompanying the first rain after a dry spell.

Your unceasing, chattering mind.

Yes. That was true.

But it also slayed dragons.

READ ON FOR AN EXCERPT FROM THE FIRST TULLY JARSDEL LAPD NOVEL

ONE DAY YOU'LL BURN

1

Hollywood was at its worst in early morning. The gray light hit in all the wrong places, deepening the cracks in the facades and making the black, fossilized stains of chewing gum dotting the sidewalk stand out like leeches. Dawn made Hollywood into an after-hours club at closing time—the party over, the revelers departed or collapsed where they stood, the magic gone.

As the first pale hues spread across the desert sky, a coyote ventured down from Griffith Park. The wildfires that had torn through the hills that summer had scattered the rabbits and scrawny deer she depended on for food, and the coyote had been reduced to competing with raccoons over the contents of trash bins. But she wasn't strong enough to fight them—had already lost an eye—so now she was across Los Feliz and passing Pink Elephant Liquors, suddenly alive to the scent of meat, picking up speed, down Western Avenue and then left onto the boulevard, faster, until her instincts took over fully and sent her streaking along the sidewalk toward her claim.

A block east, Dustin Sparks—whom *Fangoria* magazine had once called the "Godfather of Gore"—stared in amazement at the human-shaped thing lying at his feet. Back in '87, he'd worked on a movie about a gym that had been built over an old prison graveyard. When the local power plant melted down, the radiation cloud woke up the corpses, which broke through the gym's floor and began attacking the members. An aerobics instructor had tried hiding in the sauna, but the murderous dead had jammed the door and cranked the heat up all the way, roasting her in her spandex suit. It was a stupid idea—no way a sauna could get that hot—but he'd been happy to build the dummy of the burned woman. It hadn't been a tough job, technically speaking; he'd begun with a wire frame, wrapped it in foam, then covered the whole thing in strips of latex. Over the barbecue paint job, Sparks had finished with a coat of glossy sealant, which left it all with a wet, organic look.

What lay in front of him now so closely resembled that long-ago prop that, at first, he thought his brain must have finally started to misfire. It was only a matter of time, he knew, considering how many years he'd spent frying it. His arm began throbbing again—invisible, hot bands of iron cinching into his flesh. He gripped the limb, trying to massage the scrambled nerves back into dormancy, and glanced up at the sound of someone approaching.

But it wasn't a person. A coyote—eyes wide, tongue lolling—flashed across the cement and clamped its jaws onto the leg of the Halloween dummy. Sparks stumbled back, but the animal didn't seem to notice him.

At least I know I'm not seeing things, he thought. *Coyotes don't eat hallucinations.*

As Sparks watched, the coyote whipped its head from side to side until it separated a fist-sized chunk from the thigh, then lifted its nose skyward and snapped it down. It lunged forward again, burying its snout into the wound it had made, and repeated the process, trembling with what Sparks could only suppose was primal ecstasy.

The thing on the ground wasn't a dummy. It was too real—the way it lay, the proportions, the viscera, the detail. The smell, which was of roasted meat, not of rubber and paint. Sparks understood these things, but dimly.

Coyotes don't eat hallucinations, he thought again, *but they also don't eat Halloween props.*

The animal licked its chops and looked around. It noticed Sparks, lowered its head, and growled. Sparks backed away, stepping off the sidewalk and turning his ankle in the gutter. The pain was bright and urgent, but there was enough adrenaline kicking into his system to keep his attention on the ragged predator. Holding his palms out in a placating gesture, he shuffled in the direction of his apartment. He realized he was staring into the coyote's eyes and dropped his gaze. *You aren't supposed to look in their eyes, right? Or are you? Do they respect you more if you do?* He couldn't remember, just kept moving.

The coyote waited until Sparks was halfway down the block before returning to its meal. Sparks broke into a limping run, casting anxious glances over his shoulder until he turned onto his street.

The arrival of lights and siren scared off the coyote, and the responding officers, both veterans, had gaped thunderstruck at the remains for a full minute before radioing detectives and blocking off the scene. Paramedics arrived, even though the body was unquestionably that—a body—along with a truck from Fire Station 82, which was just down the street. They were soon joined by more police units and parking enforcement officers, and together, they extended and reinforced the barricade, which now stretched from Western to Harvard. The resulting snarl of traffic pressed against the surge of rush hour commuters filing onto the nearby 101 on-ramp. Like a clog in an artery, the crime scene caused other vital systems to fail. Los Feliz, Sunset, and even Santa Monica Boulevard began to slow. Franklin was at a dead stop in both directions, and Hollywood was a sea of stopped cars from La Brea to Hillhurst.

The corpse lay at the base of a pagoda in Thailand Plaza, a restaurant-market complex west of Little Armenia. The pagoda was tiled in mirrored glass and housed the statue of a deity. The serene, gilded god sat on a throne under an elaborate canopy. It was a local landmark and a sacred site for Thai immigrants, who decorated it daily with garlands of fresh flowers. A rickety table at the foot of the pagoda allowed devotees to leave offerings—mostly food and incense. And at some point in the dark, early morning hours, someone had violently upturned the table and dumped the body of the murdered man.

By the time Tully Jarsdel arrived, he had to navigate between vans from KTLA, FOX, and ABC7. Word of the homicide had reached local anchors, and anyone enjoying the morning news with a cup of coffee would get a rare treat to start their day.

Lieutenant Gavin met him at the perimeter, briefed him on what little they knew, and told him his partner was already on scene. “Been here a half hour already.”

“Sorry,” said Jarsdel. “Traffic from my direction was—”

Gavin waved him away. Jarsdel signed the perimeter log and stepped under the tape. He didn’t need to ask where the body was. Against a backdrop of dingy sidewalk and the sun-faded peach walls of Thailand Plaza, the privacy tent was a stark white anomaly of clean, ordered lines, as conspicuous as an alien craft. Jarsdel headed toward it and the body inside, his heart rate kicking up. It was always that way with him—like those dreams where you’re helplessly drawn toward a door you don’t want to open.

He stopped, distracted by the sound of shouting. An argument had broken out in front of the barricade where Serrano met Hollywood Boulevard. A man with a camera had tried to duck under the tape, and a patrol officer was threatening him with arrest. Jarsdel recognized the cop as Will Haarmann. He’d recently transferred from Valley Bureau, where he’d been picked as the face of a *Los Angeles* magazine article titled “Yes, We Have the Hottest Cops in America.” Jarsdel wouldn’t have known about the piece or about Haarmann, except for some anonymous station comedian who’d cut it out and left it on his desk. It’d been accompanied by a Post-it reading *Tough break—maybe next time!*

Jarsdel watched, fascinated, as the man became more combative. He shouted something to Haarmann about rights of the press, then stepped forward, lifting his camera to take a picture of the officer. Haarmann put his hand out to stop him, and the civilian swatted it aside. The cop went on autopilot then, quickly spinning the man around and bracing him against the squad car. The camera, which looked expensive, sailed a few feet and smashed into the curb with the sound of a champagne glass breaking. Within seconds, the citizen was shoved into the back seat of the car, his loud protests snuffed by the door closing behind him.

Jarsdel thought Haarmann had made a mistake. He hadn't used excessive force, but anyone with a phone could've caught the whole thing, and petty shit like that could antagonize potential witnesses. He made a mental note to avoid working with Haarmann on any sensitive assignments, then reluctantly crossed the last dozen yards to the tent.

The first thing he noticed was the smell. It wasn't the sour-sweet uppercut of putrefaction, nor was it the sickening copper of congealing blood. The smell emanating from the tent was so unusual under the circumstances that Jarsdel thought for a moment his mind was playing tricks on him.

He hadn't yet had breakfast, and the unmistakable odor of cooked meat gave his stomach a twinge. He pushed open the tent flaps and stepped inside.

It didn't look like any body he'd seen before, and in his five years on the force, Jarsdel had lost count of how many times he'd looked upon death.

The corpse was naked. Even its hair was gone, with only a few patches of ash to mark where it had once been. Heat had contorted the body so that it was more or less in a fetal position, what pathologists called the "pugilistic attitude"—elbows flexed, knees bent toward the chest, genitals tucked between the thighs. Patrol had radioed that they'd chased off a coyote, but to Jarsdel, it looked more like a shark had been at work. The right leg was ravaged.

Though the body lay on its side, the head was twisted upward, giving the investigators a clear view of the face, something Jarsdel found at once horrifying yet irresistible to look upon.

The lips had been cooked to nearly nothing, stretching back to expose a set of yellowed teeth, and gave the impression that the man was grinning up at them. The eyes were gone, either having popped in the heat or dried up like raisins and disappeared into the ocular cavities.

Jarsdel wanted to bend down so he could touch it and saw that Ipgreve, the medical examiner, had been smart enough to bring a gardener's pad to cushion his knees.

"Can I borrow that a sec?"

"Sure," said the ME, straightening up.

Jarsdel knelt and ran a gloved hand lightly along the cadaver's thigh. "Still warm. Like a cooked turkey."

"Yup."

"Evenly, though. No charring. Like it was baked slow in an oven."

Jarsdel wiped a sleeve across his forehead. It was getting hot inside the privacy tent, due in no small part to the hundred-fifty-pound slab of cooked human they were sharing the cramped space with. He shook his head as if to clear it. "What are we even looking at here?"

"It gets weirder," Ipgreve said. "Check out his fingers."

Jarsdel did. The hands were curled into fists, but the fingernails he could see were badly damaged—split or melted, others missing entirely. He could tell by their odd cant that a few of the fingers were broken. The victim had tried desperately to claw and beat his way out of whatever had held him prisoner.

The ME squatted beside Jarsdel. "And c'mere. Take a closer look at his face. See?"

Jarsdel had been trying his best not to—thought he might be seeing those gaping black eye sockets and that lipless, grinning mouth in his dreams. Steeling himself, he forced his attention to where Ipgreve was pointing. The burns had turned most of the cadaver's flesh a deep chestnut brown, but the skin on the forehead was splotchy with bruising.

"What do you make of it?" Jarsdel asked. "Knocked unconscious before...before whatever happened to him?"

"No, I don't think so. I'll show you why." Ipgreve lifted the cadaver's head. "If he'd been struck from the front, then we'd also likely have contrecoup bruising on the back or sides of his head, where he fell. But thanks to all the hair being burned off, we can see it's clean. No bruises." Ipgreve gently lowered the head back down. Using a pen, he indicated the discolorations. "We've got several major blows—at least four, probably five. We might even have a skull fracture with this one here. I think these injuries were sustained as he struggled to escape. Either that, or..."

"What?"

The ME made a face. "Might've done it on purpose—tried to knock himself out. Had to've hurt like hell, going out that way."

"Then that's your finding? He was baked alive?"

"You know it's too early for me to say conclusively, but considering the nature and extent of the perimortem trauma, I'd put it at the top of my list." Ipgreve shook his head, marveling at the thing in front of them. "Can't wait to get this guy on my table."

"I admire your enthusiasm."

"You have any idea just how odd this is?" Ipgreve went on. "Yes, it was an oven, but not an ordinary oven. Something big enough to hold a man, but with no element or open flame. The heat was immense but indirect. Not even a rack, else we'd have grill marks on the body. Rules out anything you'd have in a restaurant, even an industrial baking facility. And it's gonna play hell on your timeline. Won't see any of the usual determining factors, like putrefaction or rigor, and obviously, he won't cool like a normal body." As he spoke, Ipgreve inserted a probe below the sternum. He removed it, then fed a thermometer into the hole. The digital readout blinked.

"I'd say our fella here was exposed to temperatures in excess of four hundred fifty degrees. While it won't be any help with time of death, a liver spike'll at least give you an idea of when he got here."

The thermometer beeped, and Jarsdel leaned closer for a better look.

"138.3," said Ipgreve, writing down the temperature. "What'd it get down to last night? Upper fifties? So..." He made some calculations.

Jarsdel knew whatever Ipgreve came up with would be very rough. Time of death using body temperature was usually calculated by an algorithm based on Newton's law of cooling, and ideally incorporated two measurements taken hours apart. The fact that this body was outside, in an unstable temperature, further complicated the estimate.

"What time's it? Almost nine? Then he hasn't been here more than about three hours, give or take." Ipgreve concluded. "If it were much longer, he'd be at more like 120, maybe 110. Air temp has only risen to 66 degrees, which is still on the chilly side, and you also gotta figure the sidewalk would've acted as an effective cooling agent. But the body's still warm. This guy's bigger, of course, but what you said about it being like a turkey wasn't far off. Just imagine taking your bird out of the oven on Thanksgiving and putting it on the patio. Won't stay hot for long."

That wasn't good news. Jarsdel had checked: Thai Pavilion, the restaurant located above the market in Thailand Plaza, closed at midnight, with the last employees leaving around one thirty. That meant that not only would no one at the restaurant have seen anything, but foot traffic would've been practically nonexistent when the body had been dumped that morning.

Ipgreve was right—calculating a timeline would be next to impossible. There was no telling how long the body had been kept in its original location before being moved. They'd have to link it with a name before they'd be able to reconstruct the victim's final hours, and getting an ID was going to be tough. They couldn't exactly put a picture of him on television, and considering the damage to the hands, fingerprints would likely be useless. Forensic dentistry could confirm a victim's identity, but it didn't do any good unless you already had someone in mind. Their best bet was to coordinate with Missing Persons, then arrange for DNA matching once a likely subject emerged.

Jarsdel found his gaze drifting back to the body. He tried to imagine who the man had been and how he'd come to deserve—according to someone's peculiar logic—this particularly gruesome end.

"Gonna go look for my partner." Jarsdel stepped outside. The fresh air felt good. So did being away from that grinning thing in the tent.

He spotted Morales on the other side of the pagoda, conferring with an FSD tech. The man was his partner but also his superior, a fifteen-year veteran with the LAPD—six of those in homicide. He was squat, dark-skinned, with a broad face and almond eyes. His coarse black hair was swept back into a stiff, unmoving helmet with what Jarsdel supposed must have been handfuls of styling gel. When he walked—which he avoided doing as much as possible—he did so stiffly, like a retired athlete who'd amassed a catalogue of injuries.

Morales saw Jarsdel approaching. "Hey, Prof."

Jarsdel smiled without humor. "Morales."

"You know Carl? He's doing our sketch."

Jarsdel shook hands with the FSD tech, who went back to drawing on a tablet with a stylus. The tablet was a recent innovation. Crime scene sketches had always been done by hand, maybe with the aid of a compass to get the scale right. But technicians with the Forensic Science Division used software like ScenePD or Crime Zone, allowing them to create crisp and accurate diagrams of even the most complex scenes in a matter of minutes. And while all officers were trained in sketching a crime scene, the FSD's work was usually more impressive to a jury. Its members were considered impartial specialists, with no particular stake in the direction an investigation went. That made it harder for defense attorneys to cast them as bad guys out to get their clients.

Jarsdel moved closer and looked over Carl's shoulder as he drew. "I know we've got lots of reference pictures, but I want as much detail on the altar as you can get."

Morales looked dubious. "This pagoda thing? You think it's important?"

"I think it's the most startling aspect of the case."

"Startling, huh? Shit, Professor. You oughta take a look at the body, you want startling."

"I already have."

"But this is what gets your attention."

"The body was posed right in front of it. I doubt that was arbitrary."

Morales grunted and studied the pagoda more closely. The head that sprouted from the golden statue's neck featured four faces. "What do you think, Buddha? You an integral part of this investigation?"

Jarsdel glanced up from the tablet. "That's not Buddha. He's Phra Phrom, the Thai representation of Brahma."

"Who cares?"

"It's not a minor distinction. Brahma's a Hindu god, much older than the Buddha. Different cosmology and way of worship. If leaving the body here has any significance, it lies in the killer's understanding of who this god is."

"So what, like, people used to sacrifice to this guy?"

Jarsdel frowned. "No, not at all. That's what's so strange. Brahma's the god of creation, a force of good, of benevolence. He's never associated with harm or destruction."

"So maybe it's just a coincidence the body being here, and your theory's bullshit."

"Possible."

"Besides, I thought your specialty was dead white guys."

"My bachelor's was in political science. Had to take classes in cultural literacy." Morales rolled his eyes, but Jarsdel pretended he didn't notice. "It was a deeply cynical and profane thing to do, dumping the body here."

"Not to mention killing the guy in the first place, though, right?"

Jarsdel looked around. "How are we doing on surveillance cameras?"

Morales pointed to the Thai market, which would normally be open by now. "Just one, but it's trained at an angle on the door.

Wouldn'ta captured anything near the altar. Might be able to get something off a traffic camera, but it's a real long shot. Closest one is three blocks east, so unless the body was strapped to the roof of the car on its way over here, I don't know what we'd be looking for."

Carl, the FSD tech, turned his tablet so Jarsdel could get another look at it. "What do you think?" He rotated the image and zoomed in and out on various points of interest. He'd rendered the image without the privacy tent, of course, and had placed the body exactly as it lay at the foot of the altar.

Jarsdel nodded his approval. "Good. Send it to me."

Another FSD man approached the detectives. "I think we're done. Got a few cigarette butts, a flattened Coke can, some chewing gum. Scene's pretty clean. The pagoda's covered with prints, but it's a public street. Anyone could've left them. I'm ready to release the scene if you are."

Ipgreve emerged from the tent, peeling off his gloves. "We gotta get him indoors," he said. "You almost done?"

Morales turned to Jarsdel. "Well, Prof? We good here?"

"Why are you asking me?"

"Want you to take lead for now."

"Why?"

Morales paused, studying his partner. "Chain of command, rookie. Sounds like you got some specialized knowledge to offer on this case. Put some of that schooling to work." Morales gave him a saccharine smile. "Look on the bright side. When we find the asshole, you can be the one to make the report to the LT. Maybe even get another chevron on your jacket."

Jarsdel knew the inverse of the statement was equally true: that if they didn't find the asshole, he'd be the one having to justify their investigative strategy to Lieutenant Gavin. And Gavin didn't like him any more than Morales did.

A news copter had joined them, beating the air overhead and forcing those on the ground to shout to be heard. Jarsdel looked from his partner to the mass of people pressed against the barricade, then past them, to the crush of traffic struggling up Western. A street vendor was taking advantage of the captive potential customers, moving up and down the rows of cars with bags of cotton candy. Haarmann's prisoner was bucking back and forth in the patrol car. Seeing Jarsdel looking at him, the man stopped, shouted something, and stuck out his tongue. It was a child's gesture and felt strange and ugly coming from a grown man.

"You home, Professor?" asked Morales.

Jarsdel gave a slight nod, looking once more at the statue of Brahma, likely the only witness to the identity of the murderer. He'd sat the night in vigil, in quiet contemplation, tranquil as a frozen lake even while confronted with the astounding savagery visited upon one of his children. Jarsdel felt a sudden sense of shame on behalf of his species, who'd been given so much and repaid it all with blood and steel.

But look, he thought at the statue. *I care. I'm here, and I'll make it right. Just give us a little longer to push back the darkness.*

READING GROUP GUIDE

1. Jarsdel isn't very popular with his coworkers in Hollywood. Do you think this comes from jealousy or something else? Why?

2. One of the reasons Jarsdel tries to classify the killer is to "demystify" him and make him less frightening. Can you think of anything you were afraid of until you learned more about it?

3. Early in the book, reporters call for the Eastside Creeper to be "deleted," saying "we don't need to understand it, and we don't need to reason with it. We just need to get rid of it." Should we classify killers as "inhuman" and refuse to understand their motives? What problems could this type of thinking cause?

4. Jarsdel is asked what one thing he would change to improve the world. How would you answer that question?

5. Did you agree with Jarsdel's decision to avoid filing a report on the car door incident?

6. Varma says that both ugliness and beauty are contagious. How is this demonstrated throughout the book? Can you think of any examples from your own life?

7. Father Ruben Duong protests Varma's crime deterrent measures, such as PuraLux and the ReliaBench, saying, "Treat a man like a criminal and he behaves as criminals do." Do you think Varma's measures would make you feel like a criminal? Would that change your behavior?

8. Jarsdel barely gets to work with Oscar Morales in this book. Do you think his process suffers? How?

9. Jarsdel seriously questions his own motivations for leaving academia. Do you think he was originally looking for an ego boost? Did you think he might leave the police force?

10. What do you make of Ed Sponholz? How does he compare to the Creeper?

A CONVERSATION WITH THE AUTHOR

You discuss weapons in great specificity. How do you research them and choose the ones that make the most sense for the book?

Law enforcement agencies publish lists of firearms their officers are approved to carry, so much of that information is public. You can also search in reverse—looking up the gun manufacturer and seeing which agencies contract with them. If I have a specific scenario I'm unsure about, I'll always ask a technical consultant.

What kinds of resources did you use to learn about behavioral science? Was there anything interesting that you learned but couldn't include in the book?

This is a subject that has always captivated me. In my parallel life as a magician, its understanding is a matter of practical importance, as flashy effects and clever methods carry no substance without some grasp of behavioral science. A few gifted practitioners have dedicated their careers to maximizing the impact of performance through applied psychology, and those whose ideas have influenced me the most have been Juan Tamariz, Derren Brown, Pop Haydn, Eugene Berger, Richard Osterlind, and Kenton Knepper. Their work is so beautiful and mystifying as to practically blur the line between reality and true wizardry, and the world would be a less wondrous place without them.

Many of Alisha Varma's ideas are perversions of principles illustrated by Prof. Don Norman in his extraordinary book, *The Design of Everyday Things*. Also crucial to my understanding of affordances was *The Ecological Approach to Visual Perception*, by Prof. James J. Gibson. One of my academic heroes is professor and polymath Michael D. C. Drout. His lecture, "A Way with Words: Writing, Rhetoric, and the Art of Persuasion," stands as one of the greatest contributions to the relationship between language and behavior.

There was definitely a lot I had to leave out, lest it go from seasoning to becoming the main course. For example, magician John Szeles (aka The Amazing Johnathan) gives a terrific example of a technique we can call "framing." You ask someone what's the proper way to pronounce the capital of Kentucky—is it *LOOEY-ville* or *LEWIS-ville*? If they're like most folks (particularly non-Kentuckians, of course), they'll probably say, "LOOEY-ville." The correct answer, however, is Frankfort. By creating a false dichotomy, the question is framed in such a way as to guide the response.

If you find this sort of thing interesting, or you simply want to be less susceptible to bad logic, cognitive biases, and other neurological glitches, you might enjoy the following: *Your Deceptive Mind: A Scientific Guide to Critical Thinking Skills* by Steven Novella, *The Like Switch* by Jack Schafer and Marvin Karlins, *Thinking Fast & Slow* by Daniel Kahneman, *The Drunkard's Walk: How Randomness Rules Our Lives* by Leonard Mlodinow, *Sleights of Mind* by Stephen Macknik & Susana Martinez-Conde, and *Understanding the Mysteries of Human Behavior* by Mark Leary.

Do you find it difficult to write characters like the Eastside Creeper, who kill with such brutality? How do you work with those characters?

The first house I grew up in was on Waverly Drive, just down the street from where the Manson Family killed Leno and Rosemary La Bianca. It happened a dozen years before I was born, but it made an impression on me when I eventually found out about it—that something so dark and terrible could swoop into your ordinary world, something with motives and desires you could never understand, and that it could destroy you.

I'm not sure to what extent that influenced what I think of as my "terrible fascination," but it's a way of saying that murder has long been a haunting thing for me. I think my readers understand what I mean—that need to see, to try to understand, even in the midst of our fear and dread. And the genre that deals with fear and dread isn't mystery—it's horror.

I've never experienced horror so deeply as when researching material for my books. Some of the crimes you come across don't ever let go of you—so astonishing is their cruelty and depravity, and you can't help but start asking yourself those big questions about life and God and all the rest of it. In *What Waits for You*, I wanted to write a murder mystery that was just as much a horror story, to really explore the fallout of pain and fear and misery following a brutal crime.

In practical terms, the Eastside Creeper is a composite of several killers; some of the more obvious ones—like the Night Stalker, who terrorized LA when I was a little boy—I mention in the book. Others are less well-known. But as to whether or not he was difficult to write? No. And the reason is—apart from that moment Officer Banning sees his silhouette—he isn't actually in the book. You never see his crimes as they're happening, and most of the details I left to the imagination. If you read back, you'll see I was generally unspecific. That wasn't just to avoid sensationalizing the violence; mostly I didn't want to witness those murders in my own head.

That doesn't mean the result is any less easy to read, I imagine, because there's enough in there for readers to do a lot of the work themselves. *Seven* will always be one of my favorite horror films—and murder mysteries—for the same reason. You're given enough images and information to let your mind go wild. There's an elegance to that approach to horror, a restraint that in the end creates a much more devastating work of art.

L.A. remains an important character in this book, especially in response to Varma's anti-affordances. What parts of the city did you want to come across most vividly?

The star location in this book is Watts Towers. I'm embarrassed to admit that even though I grew up in Los Angeles, I didn't visit the site until I conducted my research. I know lots of folks who've similarly spent decades in the city without experiencing Rodia's masterpiece, and I hope some of my readers will take interest in what's certainly one of the great artistic jewels in the US.

Alisha Varma acts as a divisive character. What kind of people inspired you to write a character like her? Where did her belief that "people behave better when they're being observed" come from?

A month or so before I began work on *What Waits for You*, I came across an archived piece on *99% Invisible*, which is this terrific podcast that details the stories behind all the stuff around us that we don't usually bother to notice or think about. The feature story was on something called the Camden Bench, this hulking slab of concrete that Camden Town commissioned to replace its normal bus stop benches. It's designed to discourage undesirable behavior—littering, leafletting, skateboarding, sleeping, graffiti—the list goes on.

I remember being impressed at how many highly intelligent people were behind the design and implementation of this bench, and how just as many highly intelligent people called it out as anathema. Tech writer Frank Swain pointed out that it's "defined far more by what it *is not* than what it *is*," and Selena Savić dubbed it "a masterpiece of unpleasant design"—which remains one of the funniest insults I've ever heard.

The Camden Bench was my introduction to a term I hadn't heard before: "hostile architecture." I'd had no idea that was a thing. I mean, we've all been annoyed when we can't get comfortable in public spaces because of some physical deterrent, but I'd never thought of it conceptually before. When you can't lean against a ledge because of some funny steel protrusions, or you can't lie on a bench because of an armrest installed in the middle, your behavior is being modified. By denying you the opportunity to engage in an "undesirable" act, the designer or civic planner is shaping the social dynamics of the environment.

How interesting, right? I love it as a subject because it's complex, and there aren't easy answers as to where the ethical lines should be drawn. For Alisha Varma, those ethical lines don't exist; an environment should be as engineered as possible. Every aspect of design should be taken into consideration to maximize harmony and flow and to minimize disruption. Don't give people the opportunity to do bad things, she reasons, and bad things won't happen. She's not altogether wrong, which is why I think she makes a good villain, but she wants to remove all human interaction in dealing with a human problem. I don't think this is a compassionate or ultimately effective approach, because you'll have lots of people who feel unwanted and discarded.

Varma's not based on anyone in particular; rather, she's my little dig at bad science. It's remarkable how many brilliant, well-intentioned scientists—the Fritz Habers and Thomas Midgleys—blundered so confidently and disastrously onward, and at the expense of us all.

As far as Varma's hypothesis goes that we behave better when we're being observed, there's actually a lot of solid data indicating that's the case. I think foremost in my mind when I wrote that was the 2006 study by Newcastle University, which demonstrated people were much more likely to contribute to their office's coffee fund when a picture of a pair of human eyes were taped to the wall nearby.

At what point in your writing process do you decide what clues to include? Do you decide the conclusion and add details that support it? How difficult is it to add hints without giving yourself away?

I'm always looking for opportunities to drop in clues; the tricky part is keeping track of them all and making sure they're placed at appropriate intervals. Too often, and the mystery's obvious; too infrequent, and the reader rightly feels cheated. So when I write, I have two documents open side by side: the main manuscript, of course, and a beat sheet listing all the plot points I want to make sure to thread in along the way.

Jarsdel and his colleagues rely on police procedure rather than instinct. What are the challenges of writing characters who work this way? Do you prefer reading procedurals?

Police procedure is the process and science of investigation, whereas instinct is the art. A good detective can make reasonable jumps and connections, and the reading audience won't usually call bullshit if it's established that he or she has good instincts. But I tend to emphasize procedure because detectives are part of our highly codified law enforcement system, and procedure is the vehicle by which they successfully apprehend criminals. The challenge is twofold: to maintain verisimilitude while keeping the story moving. Real life murder investigations are slow and painstaking and would rarely sustain a reader's interest if rendered in real time, so I do my best to indicate the passage of time while maintaining a good pace. And in the end I think an emphasis on procedure helps me write better stories, because I have to really think everything through carefully. No one can suddenly have a revelation as to who did what. It all has to be earned logically.

And yes, I love reading procedurals. One of my all-time favorites is Frederick Forsythe's *The Day of the Jackal*. It's incredibly dense in detail yet absolutely riveting, and every action in the plot turns on a piece of evidence. One of the most beautifully structured thrillers ever written.

What's on your to-read list these days?

Earlier this year I read the late Thomas Thompson's *Serpentine*, which is without a doubt one of the greatest true crime books I've ever read. I was amazed I hadn't read this author before, so now I'm halfway through his masterful *Blood & Money*, for which he won an Edgar.

How has your writing process changed since your first book?

The first book was written over about three years and was full of false starts, dead ends, and lots of cuts. I didn't have that kind of time for the second one, so I worked much more efficiently. I treated it like a movie, writing up a beat sheet and a character manifest. Mostly I did more thinking before I wrote, which saved me time later on (and spared me the grief of major cuts). Using my improved method, I was able to generate a solid first draft in nine months.

ACKNOWLEDGMENTS

As was the case with my last book, I owe an enormous thanks to Det. Rick Jackson, who I'm happy to report—despite his alleged retirement—is busy cracking cold cases in Northern California. Still, he carved out the time to help me construct scenes from an investigator's POV. What are the inconsistencies in a person's routine, and how do they match up with the timeline in question? Sponholz's ultimately damning logbook alibi came straight from one of Rick's stories. If you want to learn more about his work, I recommend Michael Connelly's *Murder Book* podcast, each season of which explores in detail a complex murder investigation in the great detective's career.

I was very lucky to be able to correspond with Special Agent (ret.) Mark Safarik—formerly of the FBI's elite Behavioral Analysis Unit—who shared with me his experience analyzing staged homicides. His extensive work in this area provided me with everything I needed to construct both Sponholz's and Varma's staged scenes. In addition, I received expert guidance from the following professionals: Nina Mannone (real estate), Det. Dan Lynch (police procedure), and Dr. Jonathan Gray (trauma medicine).

At Sourcebooks and Poisoned Pen, I'd like to thank my always extraordinary editor, Anna Michels, whose mastery of story craft helped transform the novel into the thing I'm most proud of having written. My gratitude also goes to the phenomenal production team led by Jessica Thelander, which includes assistant editor Jenna Jankowski and art director Heather VenHuizen. Diane Dannenfeldt was my ace copyeditor, bringing the manuscript up to CMS standards and catching errors I never would've spotted. The very talented Shauneice Robinson was responsible for packaging and marketing.

Eve Attermann of WME New York continues to amaze me with the work and care she puts into my representation. Also at WME are the wonderful Sam Birmingham and Haley Heidemann, who dedicated their time and enthusiasm in helping to bring this book to market.

My deepest thanks to my first readers, Diane Frolov, Andrew Schneider, and Alethea Gard'ner. Further and essential support was provided by Dr. Paul Puri, Dr. Carol Conner, Ellen Evans, and Dr. Bob Royeton. Finally, I'd like to express my appreciation to Laurie Lew and Larry Dilg, two of the finest rhetoric and literature teachers in California.

ABOUT THE AUTHOR

Joseph Schneider lives with his wife and two children in California. His professional affiliations include The Magic Castle and the Imperial Society of Teachers of Dancing. *What Waits for You* is his second novel.